MADAME DE MAUVES
AND OTHER TALES

MADAME DE MAUVES AND OTHER TALES

Henry James

Selected and with a preface by
Frances Wilson

riverrun

This paperback edition first published in Great Britain in 2025 by riverrun

an imprint of Quercus
Part of John Murray Group

1

A CIP catalogue record for this book is available from the British Library

Paperback ISBN 978 1 52943 112 4
eBook ISBN 978 1 52943 113 1

Typeset by Fournier MT Std by Hewer Text UK Ltd, Edinburgh
Printed and bound in Great Britain by Clays Ltd, Elcograf S.p.A.

Papers used by Quercus are from well-managed forests and other responsible sources.

Quercus
Carmelite House
50 Victoria Embankment
London EC4Y 0DZ

John Murray Group
Part of Hodder & Stoughton Limited
An Hachette UK company

The authorised representative in the EEA is Hachette Ireland, 8 Castlecourt
Centre, Dublin 15, D15 XTP3, Ireland (email: info@hbgi.ie)

Contents

Preface

THIS SELECTION OF Henry James's early tales begins with his first, 'A Tragedy of Error', published anonymously when he was twenty-one. The 'error' is that of a boatman employed by Hortense Bernier to drown her husband, returning to France from travels abroad, but who drowns her lover instead. The title, a play on *The Comedy of Errors*, is ironic, but most of James's 112 tales would concern errors of eyesight, judgement, and interpretation, and the fourteen in this volume, which include the first of James's ghost stories, stories of painters and paintings, and those exploring the relations between innocent Americans and experienced Europeans, all describe errors made or narrowly averted.

Error was equally a theme of his novels, the ideas for which were seeded in the stories. 'One is in trouble when one is in error,' Ralph Touchett tells Isabel Archer in *The Portrait of a Lady*. Isabel's marriage to Gilbert Osmond, like Maggie Verver's to Prince Amerigo in *The Golden Bowl*, is an error of catastrophic proportion, while Lambert Strether's error becomes clear in a flash in *The Ambassadors*, when he spies Chad and Mme de Vionnet in a boat one Sunday afternoon, and understands 'the deep deep truth of their intimacy'.

James distinguished in his tales between what he called 'anecdotes', which ran between 7,000 and 14,000 words and were compared by him to 'the hard, shining sonnet', and the 'beautiful and blest *nouvelles*' (such as 'Daisy Miller', 'The Aspern Papers' and 'The Turn of the Screw'), which are between 20,000 and 40,000 words. With the exception of 'Madame de Mauves', which is 31,000 words, the tales in this volume are 'anecdotes', and demonstrate what James called his 'scenic method', whose narration provides the frame. He was drawn from the start to the first-person narrator because he preferred to see his subject, as he reflected in his preface to *The Golden Bowl* (1902), through some 'more or less detached, some not strictly involved, though thoroughly interested and intelligent, witness or reporter' who contributes 'mainly . . . [a] certain amount of criticism and interpretation of it'. 'My story begins with a gentleman coming out of the office and handing her a letter,' we read in the opening paragraph of 'A Tragedy of Error', as though we were sitting around the fire. 'Do you remember how,' begins 'A Landscape-Painter', 'a dozen years ago, a number of our friends were startled by the rupture of young Locksley's engagement with Miss Leary?' 'Conscious as I am,' regrets the narrator of 'My Friend Bingham', 'of a deep aversion to stories of a painful nature . . .'

'The Madonna of the Future' is presented by the anonymous narrator as an after-dinner anecdote told, over port and cigars, by a man known only as 'H—'. James's narrator is often what he called, in the preface to *The Golden Bowl*, an 'unnamed, un-introduced, and (save by right of intrinsic wit) unwarranted participant, the impersonal author's concrete deputy or dele-gate, a convenient substitute or apologant for the creative power otherwise so veiled and qualified'. He might also be seen as a spy, and there is plenty of spying in the tales. In 'A Tragedy of Error', where 'every man's a spy on every other', we watch as the servant, Josephine, plies her eye to the keyhole. This is what she saw: 'Her mistress had gone to the open window, and stood with her back to the door, looking out to sea. She held the bottle by the neck in one hand, which hung listlessly by her side; the other was resting on a glass half filled with water.'

The narrator spies on Josephine spying on her mistress, who refills her glass and swigs down its contents while looking through a lorgnette at the sea in which her husband will, she hopes, soon be drowned, and the reader sees what they see. Forty years later James will construct a similar framing device in *The Ambassadors*: 'This is what Chad sees, and what Mme de Vionnet sees, and what Strether himself sees, and sees what they see, and sees above all what the lady at home sees.'

Henry James, the second son of five children, was born in 1843 in Washington Place, New York City. His older brother was the philosopher and psychologist William James, and his sister was the invalid and diarist Alice James. Their grandfather, who came to New York from County Cavan in 1789, amassed the second largest fortune in the state, which allowed their father, Henry James Senior, to pursue a life of a non-conformist theological study and his children, he hoped, to become 'extraordinary'. To this end, between the ages of ten and fifteen, Henry was given what Percy Lubbock described as an 'extraordinary haphazard and promiscuous' education in the galleries, theatres and bookshops of England, France and Switzerland. The family returned to America in 1860, and one year later, when Henry was eighteen, the Civil War began. His younger brothers enlisted in the Federal Army, and Henry and William continued their education. After a wasted year at Harvard Law School in 1863 – a not to be repeated 'false step' in his forward march – Henry moved with his parents and sister to the red-brick, green-shuttered house on Ashburton Place in Boston where he became a writer.

'A Tragedy of Error', inspired by George Sand's *Léone Léoni*, appeared in *Continental Monthly* in February 1864. Nine months later James published in the *North American Review* an unsigned notice of Nassau W. Senior's *Essays on Fiction*, which took the form of the kind of manifesto a less confident author might wait until the height of his career to produce. Arguing the need for 'precept, canon, codification' and the careful construction of character, James advised Louisa May Alcott to study Balzac for the setting of her scenes and absorb from George Eliot her understanding of realism. Aged twenty-one, James was laying down the credentials for American literary criticism and approaching the art of fiction, as Leon Edel writes, 'more consciously and with greater deliberation than any American novelist before him'.

His voice was that of a worldly observer, but his concerns were those of a young man. The tales he was yet to write return to the idea of the 'passionate pilgrim' poised to begin his journey, looking at what life has to offer. 'The great thing is to *live*, you know,' as Louis Leverett puts it in the last story in this volume, 'A Bundle of Letters', 'to feel, to be conscious of one's possibilities.' ('Live all you can,' says Strether twenty-four years later, sent to France to bring Chad back to America, 'it's a mistake not to.') 'A Bundle of Letters', composed of the letters home from guests in a Parisian pension, none of whom sees the others from the same perspective, was written when James, aged thirty-six, was settled in England, having left America for ever. He now has three novels behind him: *Watch and Ward* (1871), *Roderick Hudson* (1874) and *The American* (1877), as well as his first published collection of stories, *A Passionate Pilgrim and Other Tales* (1874), and his breakthrough success, *Daisy Miller* (1878). His masterpieces, *Washington Square* and *The Portrait of a Lady* (1881), are in larval form.

It is striking how forcefully James reveals, as he sets out the stall of his early fiction, the fear that women will derail his possibilities. Equally striking is how directly he approaches, in 'A Light Man', the theme of homosexuality. Of all the errors to be avoided, the greatest is marriage. In 'A Tragedy of Error', 'De Grey: A Romance', 'The Romance of Certain Old Clothes', 'A Landscape-Painter' and 'Madame de Mauves' marriage is a threat not only to freedom but life itself. The women in his tales are deceptive, unknowable and impossible to interpret. In 'The Story of a Masterpiece', inspired by Robert Browning's dramatic monologue 'My Last Duchess', an artist paints a portrait of his former fiancée for her present fiancé. When the picture – a masterpiece – is complete, the fiancé fears the figure revealed on the canvas, but marries her nonetheless. In 'A Day of Days', Thomas Ludlow has to choose between discovering Europe or staying in America with a woman he has met that afternoon; 'My Friend Bingham' explores the terrifying idea of a man killing a boy while trying to shoot a duck, and then – a graver error still – falling in love with the grieving mother. Marriage as vampirism is the subject of 'De Grey: A Romance': 'she blindly, senselessly, remorselessly drained the life from his being,' the narrator explains. 'As she bloomed and prospered, he drooped and languished. While she was living for him, he was dying of her.'

This selection forms a biography of sorts. Submerged beneath the surface of his melodramas are the unspoken fears that Henry hoped, by living in Europe, to leave behind. Did a husband derive strength or weakness from his spouse? The only marriage he had observed closely was that of his parents, where his father depended entirely on the support of a wife who had no independent existence. 'She *was* he,' James later wrote, '*was* each of us.' James's fear of women was complicated by his identification with his mother and sister: he was also each of them. Before he became known as The Master, he was referred to for forty years as Henry James Junior, a name he loathed. As both father and son were writers, sometimes for the same magazines, they were often confused for one another, but the confusions in the family, who identified so intensely with one another that they lost all sense of themselves, were as extreme as those in *The Comedy of Errors*. Henry, said William, was 'my in many ways twin bro', and like a bifurcated version of a single man they shared their symptoms. The back pain, for example, 'which has long made Henry so interesting', was suffered by William as well: 'It is evidently a family peculiarity.' Investing in his brother's 'moving intestinal drama', William 'blush[ed] to say that detailed bulletins of your bowels, stomach &c., as well as back are of the most enthralling interest to me. A good plan is for you to write such on separate slips of paper marked private.' An idea James had for a tale was a brother and sister 'with the same sensibilities and the same imagination', who 'vibrate with the same nerves, suffer with the same suffering: have, in a word, the same experience of life'. These lines might describe the role of James's unnamed, unintroduced narrators, who similarly immerse themselves entirely into someone else's story, converting into their own experience the experience of others.

One of his lifelong terrors was belatedness, or lateness. 'What is there in the idea of Too Late?' James wondered in his notebooks, plotting another tale. The artist, in 'The Madonna of the Future', 'made his bid for fame, and missed it'. 'Nevertheless', the narrator reveals in 'My Friend Bingham', 'it was not till he was nearly thirty years old that he had begun to live for himself.' James was this same age when he crossed the

Atlantic for good in May 1872. Another of his terrors was lameness. Henry James Senior had lost his left leg as a child, and in the year that the Civil War began, James suffered what he described in *Notes of a Son and Brother* as 'a horrid' and 'obscure hurt'. While it was impossible to tell, he said, whether this 'obscure hurt' came from 'one's own poor organism' or was part of the 'huge comprehensive ache' of the country at war, the effects 'were to draw themselves out incalculably and intolerably'. He never revealed where the hurt was located or what it entailed, but he referred to it as his 'lameness': in 'A Tragedy of Error' the cuckolded husband is also lame. James's stories tend to have devastating endings, but none is more so than the moment Hortense, having paid the boatman to drown her husband, sees 'a figure emerge from below the terrace, and come limping towards her with outstretched arms'.

Frances Wilson

Madame de Mauves
and Other Tales

A Tragedy of Error

I

ALOW ENGLISH PHAETON was drawn up before the door of the post-office of a French seaport town. In it was seated a lady, with her veil down and her parasol held closely over her face. My story begins with a gentleman coming out of the office and handing her a letter.

He stood beside the carriage a moment before getting in. She gave him her parasol to hold, and then lifted her veil, showing a very pretty face. This couple seemed to be full of interest for the passers by, most of whom stared hard and exchanged significant glances. Such persons as were looking on at the moment saw the lady turn very pale as her eyes fell on the direction of the letter. Her companion saw it too, and instantly stepping into the place beside her, took up the reins, and drove rapidly along the main street of the town, past the harbour, to an open road skirting the sea. Here he slackened pace. The lady was leaning back, with her veil down again, and the letter lying open in her lap. Her attitude was almost that of unconsciousness, and he could see that her eyes were closed. Having satisfied himself of this, he hastily possessed himself of the letter, and read as follows:

Southampton, July 16th, 18—

My dear Hortense

You will see by my postmark that I am a thousand leagues nearer home than when I last wrote, but I have hardly time to explain the change. M. P— has given me a most unlooked-for *congé*. After so many months of separation; we shall be able to spend a few weeks together. God be praised! We got in here from New York this morning, and I have had the good luck to find a vessel, the *Armorique*, which sails straight for H—. The mail leaves directly, but we shall probably be detained a few hours by the tide; so this will reach you a day before I arrive: the master calculates we shall get in early Thursday morning. Ah, Hortense! how the time drags! Three whole days! If I did not write from New York, it is because I was unwilling to torment you with an expectancy which, as it is, I venture to hope, you will find long enough. Farewell. To a warmer greeting!

Your devoted

C. B.

When the gentleman replaced the paper on his companion's lap, his face was almost as pale as hers. For a moment he gazed fixedly and vacantly before him, and a half-suppressed curse escaped his lips. Then his eyes reverted to his neighbour. After some hesitation, during which he allowed the reins to hang so loose that the horse lapsed into a walk, he touched her gently on the shoulder.

'Well, Hortense,' said he, in a very pleasant tone, 'what's the matter; have you fallen asleep?'

Hortense slowly opened her eyes, and, seeing that they had left the town behind them, raised her veil. Her features were stiffened with horror.

'Read that,' said she, holding out the open letter.

The gentleman took it, and pretended to read it again.

'Ah! M. Bernier returns. Delightful!' he exclaimed.

'How, delightful?' asked Hortense; 'we mustn't jest at so serious a crisis, my friend.'

'True,' said the other, 'it will be a solemn meeting. Two years of absence is a great deal.'

'O Heaven! I shall never dare to face him,' cried Hortense, bursting into tears.

Covering her face with one hand, she put out the other toward that of her friend. But he was plunged in so deep a reverie, that he did not perceive the movement. Suddenly he came to, aroused by her sobs.

'Come, come,' said he, in the tone of one who wishes to coax another into mistrust of a danger before which he does not himself feel so secure but that the sight of a companion's indifference will give him relief. 'What if he does come? He need learn nothing. He will stay but a short time, and sail away again as unsuspecting as he came.'

'Learn nothing! You surprise me. Every tongue that greets him, if only to say *bon jour*, will wag to the tune of a certain person's misconduct.'

'Bah! People don't think about us quite as much as you fancy. You and I, *n'est-ce-pas?* we have little time to concern ourselves about our neighbours' failings. Very well, other people are in the same box, better or worse. When a ship goes to pieces on those rocks out at sea, the poor devils who are pushing their way to land on a floating spar, don't bestow many glances on those who are battling with the waves beside them. Their eyes are fastened to the shore, and all their care is for their own safety. In life we are all afloat on a tumultuous sea; we are all struggling toward some *terra firma* of wealth or love or leisure. The roaring of the waves we kick up about us and the spray we dash into our eyes deafen and blind us to the sayings and doings of our fellows. Provided we climb high and dry, what do we care for them?'

'Ay, but if we don't? When we've lost hope ourselves, we want to make others sink. We hang weights about their necks, and dive down into the dirtiest pools for stones to cast at them. My friend, you don't feel the shots which are not aimed at you. It isn't of you the town talks, but of me: a poor woman throws herself off the pier yonder, and drowns before a kind hand has time to restrain her, and her corpse floats over the water for all the world to look at. When her husband comes up to see what the crowd means, is there any lack of kind friends to give him the good news of his wife's death?'

'As long as a woman is light enough to float, Hortense, she is not counted drowned. It's only when she sinks out of sight that they give her up.'

Hortense was silent a moment, looking at the sea with swollen eyes.

'Louis,' she said at last, 'we were speaking metaphorically: I have half a mind to drown myself literally.'

'Nonsense!' replied Louis, 'an accused pleads *not guilty*, and hangs himself in prison. What do the papers say? People talk, do they? Can't you talk as well as they? A woman is in the wrong from the moment she holds her tongue and refuses battle. And that you do too often. That pocket-handkerchief is always more or less of a flag of truce.'

'I'm sure I don't know,' said Hortense indifferently; 'perhaps it is.'

There are moments of grief in which certain aspects of the subject of our distress seem as irrelevant as matters entirely foreign to it. Her eyes were still fastened on the sea. There was another silence. 'O my poor Charles!' she murmured, at length, 'to what a hearth do you return!'

'Hortense,' said the gentleman, as if he had not heard her, although, to a third person, it would have appeared that it was because he had done so that he spoke: 'I do not need to tell you that it will never happen to me to betray our secret. But I will answer for it that so long as M. Bernier is at home no mortal shall breathe a syllable of it.'

'What of that?' sighed Hortense. 'He will not be with me ten minutes without guessing it.'

'Oh, as for that,' said her companion, dryly, 'that's your own affair.'

'Monsieur de Meyrau!' cried the lady.

'It seems to me,' continued the other, 'that in making such a guarantee, I have done my part of the business.'

'Your part of the business!' sobbed Hortense.

M. de Meyrau made no reply, but with a great cut of the whip sent the horse bounding along the road. Nothing more was said. Hortense lay back in the carriage with her face buried in her handkerchief, moaning. Her companion sat upright, with contracted brows and firmly set teeth, looking straight before him, and by an occasional heavy lash keeping the horse at a furious pace. A wayfarer might have taken him for a ravisher escaping with a victim worn out with resistance. Travellers to whom they were known would perhaps have seen a deep meaning in this accidental analogy. So, by a *détour*, they returned to the town.

When Hortense reached home, she went straight up to a little boudoir on the second floor, and shut herself in. This room was at the back of the house, and her maid, who was at that moment walking in the long garden which stretched down to the water, where there was a landing place for small boats, saw her draw in the window blind and darken the room, still in her bonnet and cloak. She remained alone for a couple of hours. At five o'clock, some time after the hour at which she was usually summoned to dress her mistress for the evening, the maid knocked at

Hortense's door, and offered her services. Madame called out, from within, that she had a migraine, and would not be dressed.

'Can I get anything for madame?' asked Josephine; 'a *tisane*, a warm drink, something?'

'Nothing, nothing.'

'Will madame dine?'

'No.'

'Madame had better not go wholly without eating.'

'Bring me a bottle of wine – of brandy.'

Josephine obeyed. When she returned, Hortense was standing in the doorway, and as one of the shutters had meanwhile been thrown open, the woman could see that, although her mistress's hat had been tossed upon the sofa, her cloak had not been removed, and that her face was very pale. Josephine felt that she might not offer sympathy nor ask questions.

'Will madame have nothing more?' she ventured to say, as she handed her the tray.

Madame shook her head, and closed and locked the door.

Josephine stood a moment vexed, irresolute, listening. She heard no sound. At last she deliberately stooped down and applied her eye to the keyhole.

This is what she saw:

Her mistress had gone to the open window, and stood with her back to the door, looking out at the sea. She held the bottle by the neck in one hand, which hung listlessly by her side; the other was resting on a glass half filled with water, standing, together with an open letter, on a table beside her. She kept this position until Josephine began to grow tired of waiting. But just as she was about to arise in despair of gratifying her curiosity, madame raised the bottle and glass, and filled the latter full. Josephine looked more eagerly. Hortense held it a moment against the light, and then drained it down.

Josephine could not restrain an involuntary whistle. But her surprise became amazement when she saw her mistress prepare to take a second glass. Hortense put it down, however, before its contents were half gone, as if struck by a sudden thought, and hurried across the room. She stooped down before a cabinet, and took out a small opera glass. With this she returned to the window, put it to her eyes, and again spent some moments in looking seaward. The purpose of this proceeding Josephine could not make out. The only result visible to her was that her mistress suddenly dropped the lorgnette on the table, and sank down on an armchair, covering her face with her hands.

Josephine could contain her wonderment no longer. She hurried down to the kitchen.

'Valentine,' said she to the cook, 'what on earth can be the matter with Madame? She will have no dinner, she is drinking brandy by the glassful, a moment ago she was looking out to sea with a lorgnette, and now she is crying dreadfully with an open letter in her lap.'

The cook looked up from her potato-peeling with a significant wink.

'What can it be,' said she, 'but that monsieur returns?'

II

AT SIX O' CLOCK, Josephine and Valentine were still sitting together, discussing the probable causes and consequences of the event hinted at by the latter. Suddenly Madame Bernier's bell rang. Josephine was only too glad to answer it. She met her mistress descending the stairs, combed, cloaked, and veiled, with no traces of agitation, but a very pale face.

'I am going out,' said Madame Bernier; 'if M. le Vicomte comes, tell him I am at my mother-in-law's, and wish him to wait till I return.'

Josephine opened the door, and let her mistress pass; then stood watching her as she crossed the court.

'Her mother-in-law's,' muttered the maid; 'she has the face!'

When Hortense reached the street, she took her way, not through the town, to the ancient quarter where that ancient lady, her husband's mother, lived, but in a very different direction. She followed the course of the quay, beside the harbour, till she entered a crowded region, chiefly the residence of fishermen and boatmen. Here she raised her veil. Dusk was beginning to fall. She walked as if desirous to attract as little observation as possible, and yet to examine narrowly the population in the midst of which she found herself. Her dress was so plain that there was nothing in her appearance to solicit attention; yet, if for any reason a passer by had happened to notice her, he could not have helped being struck by the contained intensity with which she scrutinized every figure she met. Her manner was that of a person seeking to recognize a long-lost friend, or perhaps, rather, a long-lost enemy, in a crowd. At last she stopped before a flight of steps, at the foot of which was a landing place for half a dozen little boats, employed to carry passengers between the two sides of the port, at times when the drawbridge above was closed for the passage of vessels. While she stood she was witness of the following scene:

A man, in a red woollen fisherman's cap, was sitting on the top of the steps, smoking the short stump of a pipe, with his face to the water. Happening to turn about, his eye fell on a little child, hurrying along the quay toward a dingy tenement close at hand, with a jug in its arms.

'Hullo, youngster!' cried the man; 'what have you got there? Come here.'

The little child looked back, but, instead of obeying, only quickened its walk.

'The devil take you, come here!' repeated the man angrily, 'or I'll wring your beggarly neck. You won't obey your own uncle, eh?'

The child stopped, and ruefully made its way to its relative, looking around several times toward the house, as if to appeal to some counter authority.

'Come, make haste!' pursued the man, 'or I shall go and fetch you. Move!'

The child advanced to within half a dozen paces of the steps, and then stood still, eyeing the man cautiously, and hugging the jug tight.

'Come on, you little beggar, come up close.'

The youngster kept a stolid silence, however, and did not budge. Suddenly its self-styled uncle leaned forward, swept out his arm, clutched hold of its little sunburnt wrist, and dragged it toward him.

'Why didn't you come when you were called?' he asked, running his disengaged hand into the infant's frowsy mop of hair, and shaking its head until it staggered. 'Why didn't you come, you unmannerly little brute, eh? – eh? – eh?' accompanying every interrogation with a renewed shake.

The child made no answer. It simply and vainly endeavoured to twist its neck around under the man's grip, and transmit some call for succour to the house.

'Come, keep your head straight. Look at me, and answer me. What's in that jug? Don't lie.'

'Milk.'

'Who for?'

'Granny.'

'Granny be hanged.'

The man disengaged his hands, lifted the jug from the child's feeble grasp, tilted it toward the light, surveyed its contents, put it to his lips, and exhausted them. The child, although liberated, did not retreat. It stood watching its uncle drink until he lowered the jug. Then, as he met its eyes, it said:

'It was for the baby.'

For a moment the man was irresolute. But the child seemed to have a foresight of the parental resentment, for it had hardly spoken when it darted backward and scampered off, just in time to elude a blow from the jug, which the man sent clattering at its heels. When it was out of sight, he faced about to the water again, and replaced the pipe between his teeth with a heavy scowl and a murmur that sounded to Madame Bernier very like – 'I wish the baby'd choke.'

Hortense was a mute spectator of this little drama. When it was over, she turned around, and retraced her steps twenty yards with her hand to her head. Then she walked straight back, and addressed the man.

'My good man,' she said, in a very pleasant voice, 'are you the master of one of these boats?'

He looked up at her. In a moment the pipe was out of his mouth, and a broad grin in its place. He rose, with his hand to his cap.

'I am, madame, at your service.'

'Will you take me to the other side?'

'You don't need a boat; the bridge is closed,' said one of his comrades at the foot of the steps, looking that way.

'I know it,' said Madame Bernier; 'but I wish to go to the cemetery, and a boat will save me half a mile walking.'

'The cemetery is shut at this hour.'

'*Allons*, leave madame alone,' said the man first spoken to. 'This way, my lady.'

Hortense seated herself in the stern of the boat. The man took the sculls.

'Straight across?' he asked.

Hortense looked around her. 'It's a fine evening,' said she; 'suppose you row me out to the lighthouse, and leave me at the point nearest the cemetery on our way back.'

'Very well,' rejoined the boatman; 'fifteen sous,' and began to pull lustily.

'*Allez*, I'll pay you well,' said Madame.

'Fifteen sous is the fare,' insisted the man.

'Give me a pleasant row, and I'll give you a hundred,' said Hortense.

Her companion said nothing. He evidently wished to appear not to have heard her remark. Silence was probably the most dignified manner of receiving a promise too munificent to be anything but a jest.

For some time this silence was maintained, broken only by the trickling of the oars and the sounds from the neighbouring shores and vessels. Madame Bernier was plunged in a sidelong scrutiny of her ferryman's countenance. He was a man of about thirty-five. His face was dogged, brutal, and sullen. These indications were perhaps exaggerated by the dull monotony of his exercise. The eyes lacked a certain rascally gleam which had appeared in them when he was so *empressé* with the offer of his services. The face was better then – that is, if vice is better than ignorance. We say a countenance is 'lit up' by a smile; and indeed that momentary flicker does the office of a candle in a dark room. It sheds a ray upon the dim upholstery of our souls. The visages of poor men, generally, know few alternations. There is a large class of human beings whom fortune restricts to a single change of expression, or, perhaps, rather to a single expression. Ah me! the faces which wear either nakedness or rags; whose repose is stagnation, whose activity vice; ignorant at their worst, infamous at their best!

'Don't pull too hard,' said Hortense at last. 'Hadn't you better take breath a moment?'

'Madame is very good,' said the man, leaning upon his oars. 'But if you had taken me by the hour,' he added, with a return of the vicious grin, 'you wouldn't catch me loitering.'

'I suppose you work very hard,' said Madame Bernier.

The man gave a little toss of his head, as if to intimate the inadequacy of any supposition to grasp the extent of his labours.

'I've been up since four o'clock this morning, wheeling bales and boxes on the quay, and plying my little boat. Sweating without five minutes' intermission. *C'est comme ça*. Sometimes I tell my mate I think I'll take a plunge in the basin to dry myself. Ha! ha! ha!'

'And of course you gain little,' said Madame Bernier.

'Worse than nothing. Just what will keep me fat enough for starvation to feed on.'

'How? you go without your necessary food?'

'Necessary is a very elastic word, madame. You can narrow it down, so that in the degree above nothing it means luxury. My necessary food is sometimes thin air. If I don't deprive myself of that, it's because I can't.'

'Is it possible to be so unfortunate?'

'Shall I tell you what I have eaten today?'

'Do,' said Madame Bernier.

'A piece of black bread and a salt herring are all that have passed my lips tor twelve hours.'

'Why don't you get some better work?'

'If I should die tonight,' pursued the boatman, heedless of the question, in the manner of a man whose impetus on the track of self-pity drives him past the signal flags of relief, 'what would there be left to bury me? These clothes I have on might buy me a long box. For the cost of this shabby old suit, that hasn't lasted me a twelve-month, I could get one that I wouldn't wear out in a thousand years. *La bonne idée!*'

'Why don't you get some work that pays better?' repeated Hortense.

The man dipped his oars again.

'Work that pays better? I must work for work. I must earn that too. Work is wages. I count the promise of the next week's employment the best part of my Saturday night's pocketings. Fifty casks rolled from the ship to the storehouse mean two things: thirty sous and fifty more to roll the next day. Just so a crushed hand, or a dislocated shoulder, mean twenty francs to the apothecary and *bon jour* to my business.'

'Are you married?' asked Hortense.

'No, I thank you. I'm not cursed with that blessing. But I've an old mother, a sister, and three nephews, who look to me for support. The old woman's too old to work; the lass is too lazy, and the little ones are too young. But they're none of them too old or young to he hungry, *allez*. I'll be hanged if I'm not a father to them all.'

There was a pause. The man had resumed rowing. Madame Bernier sat motionless, still examining her neighbour's physiognomy. The sinking sun, striking full upon his face, covered it with an almost lurid glare. Her own features being darkened against the western sky, the direction of them was quite indistinguishable to her companion.

'Why don't you leave the place?' she said at last.

'Leave it! how?' he replied, looking up with the rough avidity with which people of his class receive proposals touching their interests, extending to the most philanthropic suggestions that mistrustful eagerness with which experience has taught them to defend their own side of a bargain – the only form of proposal that she has made them acquainted with.

'Go somewhere else,' said Hortense.

'Where, for instance!'

'To some new country – America.'

The man burst into a loud laugh. Madame Bernier's face bore more evidence of interest in the play of his features than of that discomfiture which generally accompanies the consciousness of ridicule.

'There's a lady's scheme for you! If you'll write for furnished apartments, *là-bas*, I don't desire anything better. But no leaps in the dark for me. America and Algeria are very fine words to cram into an empty stomach when you're lounging in the sun, out of work, just as you stuff tobacco into your pipe and let the smoke curl around your head. But they fade away before a cutlet and a bottle of wine. When the earth grows so smooth and the air so pure that you can see the American coast from the pier yonder, then I'll make up my bundle. Not before.'

'You're afraid, then, to risk anything?'

'I'm afraid of nothing, *moi*. But I am not a fool either. I don't want to kick away my *sabots* till I am certain of a pair of shoes. I can go barefoot here. I don't want to find water where I counted on land. As for America, I've been there already.'

'Ah! you've been there?'

'I've been to Brazil and Mexico and California and the West Indies.'

'Ah!'

'I've been to Asia, too.'

'Ah!'

'*Pardio*, to China and India. Oh, I've seen the world! I've been three times around the Cape.'

'You've been a seaman then?'

'Yes, ma'am; fourteen years.'

'On what ship?'

'Bless your heart, on fifty ships.'

'French?'

'French and English and Spanish; mostly Spanish.'

'Ah?'

'Yes, and the more fool I was.'

'How so?'

'Oh, it was a dog's life. I'd drown any dog that would play half the mean tricks I used to see.'

'And you never had a hand in any yourself?'

'*Pardon*, I gave what I got. I was as good a Spaniard and as great a devil as any. I carried my knife with the best of them, and drew it as quickly, and plunged it as deep. I've got scars, if you weren't a lady. But I'd warrant to find you their mates on a dozen Spanish hides!'

He seemed to pull with renewed vigour at the recollection. There was a short silence.

'Do you suppose,' said Madame Bernier, in a few moments – 'do you remember – that is, can you form any idea whether you ever killed a man?'

There was a momentary slackening of the boatman's oars. He gave a sharp glance at his passenger's countenance, which was still so shaded by her position, however, as to be indistinguishable. The tone of her interrogation had betrayed a simple, idle curiosity. He hesitated a moment, and then gave one of those conscious, cautious, dubious smiles, which may cover either a criminal assumption of more than the truth or a guilty repudiation of it.

'*Mon Dieu!*' said he, with a great shrug, 'there's a question! . . . I never killed one without a reason.'

'Of course not,' said Hortense.

'Though a reason in South America, *ma foi!*' added the boatman, 'wouldn't be a reason here.'

'I suppose not. What would be a reason there?'

'Well, if I killed a man in Valparaiso – I don't say I did, mind – it's because my knife went in farther than I intended.'

'But why did you use it at all?'

'I didn't. If I had, it would have been because he drew his against me.'

'And why should he have done so?'

'*Ventrebleu!* for as many reasons as there are craft in the harbour.'

'For example?'

'Well, that I should have got a place in a ship's company that he was trying for.'

'Such things as that? is it possible?'

'Oh, for smaller things. That a lass should have given me a dozen oranges she had promised him.'

'How odd!' said Madame Bernier, with a shrill kind of laugh. 'A man who owed you a grudge of this kind would just come up and stab you, I suppose, and think nothing of it?'

'Precisely. Drive a knife up to the hilt into your back, with an oath, and slice open a melon with it, with a song, five minutes afterward.'

'And when a person is afraid, or ashamed, or in some way unable to take revenge himself, does he – or it may be a woman – does she, get someone else to do it for her?'

'*Parbleu!* Poor devils on the look-out for such work are as plentiful all along the South American coast as *commissionaires* on the street corners here.' The ferryman was evidently surprised at the fascination possessed by this infamous topic for so lady-like a person; but having, as you see, a very ready tongue, it is probable that his delight in being able to give her information and hear himself talk were still greater. 'And then down there,' he went on, 'they'll never forget a grudge. If a fellow doesn't serve you one day, he'll do it another. A Spaniard's hatred is like lost sleep – you can put it off for a time, but it will grip you in the end. The rascals always keep their promises to themselves . . . An enemy on shipboard is jolly fun. It's like bulls tethered in the same field. You can't stand still half a minute except against a wall. Even when he makes friends with you, his favours never taste right. Messing with him is like drinking out of a pewter mug. And so it is everywhere. Let your shadow once flit across a Spaniard's path, and he'll always see it there. If you've never lived in any but these damned clockworky European towns, you can't imagine the state of things in a South American seaport – one half the population waiting round the corner for the other half. But I don't see that it's so much better here, where every man's a spy on every other. There you meet an assassin at every turn, here a *sergent de ville* . . . At all events, the life *là-bas* used to remind me, more than anything else, of sailing in a shallow channel, where you don't know what infernal rock you may ground on. Every man has a standing account with his neighbour, just as madame has at her *fournisseur*'s; and, *ma foi*, those are the only accounts they settle. The master of the *Santiago* may pay me one of these days for the pretty names I heaved after him when we parted company, but he'll never pay me my wages.'

A short pause followed this exposition of the virtues of the Spaniard.

'You yourself never put a man out of the world, then?' resumed Hortense.

'Oh, *que si!* . . . Are you horrified?'

'Not at all. I know that the thing is often justifiable.'

The man was silent a moment, perhaps with surprise, for the next thing he said was:

'Madame is Spanish?'

'In that, perhaps, I am,' replied Hortense.

Again her companion was silent. The pause was prolonged. Madame Bernier broke it by a question which showed that she had been following the same train of thought.

'What is sufficient ground in this country for killing a man?'

The boatman sent a loud laugh over the water. Hortense drew her cloak closer about her.

'I'm afraid there is none.'

'Isn't there a right of self-defence?'

'To be sure there is – it's one I ought to know something about. But it's one that *ces messieurs* at the Palais make short work with.'

'In South America and those countries, when a man makes life insupportable to you, what do you do?'

'*Mon Dieu!* I suppose you kill him.'

'And in France?'

'I suppose you kill yourself. Ha! ha! ha!'

By this time they had reached the end of the great breakwater, terminating in a lighthouse, the limit, on one side, of the inner harbour. The sun had set.

'Here we are at the lighthouse,' said the man; 'it's growing dark. Shall we turn?'

Hortense rose in her place a few moments, and stood looking out to sea. 'Yes,' she said at last, 'you may go back – slowly.' When the boat had headed round she resumed her old position, and put one of her hands over the side, drawing it through the water as they moved, and gazing into the long ripples.

At last she looked up at her companion. Now that her face caught some of the lingering light of the west, he could see that it was deathly pale.

'You find it hard to get along in the world,' said she: 'I shall be very glad to help you.'

The man started, and stared a moment. Was it because this remark jarred upon the expression which he was able faintly to discern in her eyes? The next, he put his hand to his cap.

'Madame is very kind. What will you do?'

Madame Bernier returned his gaze.

'I will trust you.'

'Ah!'

'And reward you.'

'Ah? Madame has a piece of work for me?'

'A piece of work,' Hortense nodded.

The man said nothing, waiting apparently for an explanation. His face wore the look of lowering irritation which low natures feel at being puzzled.

'Are you a bold man?'

Light seemed to come in this question. The quick expansion of his features answered it. You cannot touch upon certain subjects with an inferior but by the sacrifice of the barrier which separates you from him. There are thoughts and feelings and glimpses and foreshadowings of thoughts which level all inequalities of station.

'I'm bold enough,' said the boatman, 'for anything you want me to do.'

'Are you bold enough to commit a crime?'

'Not for nothing.'

'If I ask you to endanger your peace of mind, to risk your personal safety for me, it is certainly not as a favour. I will give you ten times the weight in gold of every grain by which your conscience grows heavier in my service.'

The man gave her a long, hard look through the dim light.

'I know what you want me to do,' he said at last.

'Very well,' said Hortense; 'will you do it?'

He continued to gaze. She met his eyes like a woman who has nothing more to conceal.

'State your case.'

'Do you know a vessel named the *Armorique*, a steamer?'

'Yes, it runs from Southampton.'

'It will arrive tomorrow morning early. Will it be able to cross the bar?'

'No; not till noon.'

'I thought so. I expect a person by it – a man.'

Madame Bernier appeared unable to continue, as if her voice had given way.

'Well, well?' said her companion.

'He's the person——' She stopped again.

'The person who——?'

'The person whom I wish to get rid of.'

For some moments nothing was said. The boatman was the first to speak again.

'Have you formed a plan?'

Hortense nodded.

'Let's hear it.'

'The person in question,' said Madame Bernier, 'will be impatient to land before noon. The house to which he returns will be in view of the vessel if, as you say, she lies at anchor. If he can get a boat, he will be sure to come ashore. *Eh bien!* – but you understand me.'

'Aha! you mean my boat – this boat?'

'O God!'

Madame Bernier sprang up in her seat, threw out her arms, and sank down again, burying her face in her knees. Her companion hastily shipped his oars, and laid his hands on her shoulders.

'*Allons donc*, in the devil's name, don't break down,' said he; 'we'll come to an understanding.'

Kneeling in the bottom of the boat, and supporting her by his grasp, he succeeded in making her raise herself, though her head still drooped.

'You want me to finish him in the boat?'

No answer.

'Is he an old man?'

Hortense shook her head faintly.

'My age?'

She nodded.

'*Sapristi!* it isn't so easy.'

'He can't swim,' said Hortense, without looking up; 'he – he is lame.'

'*Nom de Dieu!*' The boatman dropped his hands. Hortense looked up quickly. Do you read the pantomime?'

'Never mind,' added the man at last, 'it will serve as a sign.'

'*Mais oui.* And besides that, he will ask to be taken to the Maison Bernier, the house with its back to the water, on the extension of the great quay. *Tenez*, you can almost see it from here.'

'I know the place,' said the boatman, and was silent, as if asking and answering himself a question.

Hortense was about to interrupt the train of thought which she apprehended he was following, when he forestalled her.

'How am I to be sure of my affair?' asked he.

'Of your reward? I've thought of that. This watch is a pledge of what I shall be able and glad to give you afterward. There are two thousand francs' worth of pearls in the case.'

'*Il faut fixer la somme,*' said the man, leaving the watch untouched.

'That lies with you.'

'Good. You know that I have the right to ask a high price.'

'Certainly. Name it.'

'It's only on the supposition of a large sum that I will so much as consider your proposal. *Songez donc*, that it's a murder you ask of me.'

'The price – the price?'

'*Tenez*,' continued the man, 'poached game is always high. The pearls in that watch are costly because it's worth a man's life to get at them. You want me to be your pearl diver. Be it so. You must guarantee me a safe descent – it's a descent, you know – ha! – you must furnish me the armour of safety; a little gap to breathe through while I'm at my work – the thought of a capful of Napoleons!'

'My good man, I don't wish to talk to you or to listen to your sallies. I wish simply to know your price. I'm not bargaining for a pair of chickens. Propose a sum.'

The boatman had by this time resumed his seat and his oars. He stretched out for a long, slow pull, which brought him closely face to face with his temptress. This position, his body bent forward, his eyes fixed on Madame Bernier's face, he kept for some seconds. It was perhaps fortunate for Hortense's purpose at that moment – it had often aided her purposes before – that she was a pretty woman.* A plain face might have emphasized the utterly repulsive nature of the negotiation. Suddenly, with a quick, convulsive movement, the man completed the stroke.

'*Pas si bête!* propose one yourself.'

---

* I am told that there was no resisting her smile; and that she had at her command, in moments of grief, a certain look of despair which filled even the roughest hearts with sympathy, and won over the kindest to the cruel cause.

'Very well,' said Hortense, 'if you wish it. *Voyons*: I'll give you what I can. I have fifteen thousand francs' worth of jewels. I'll give you them, or, if they will get you into trouble, their value. At home, in a box I have a thousand francs in gold. You shall have those. I'll pay your passage and outfit to America. I have friends in New York. I'll write to them to get you work.'

'And you'll give your washing to my mother and sister *hein?* Ha! ha! Jewels, fifteen thousand francs; one thousand more makes sixteen; passage to America – first class – five hundred francs; outfit – what does Madame understand by that?'

'Everything needful for your success *là-bas*.'

'A written denial that I am an assassin? *Ma foi*, it were better not to remove the impression. It's served me a good turn, on this side of the water at least. Call it twenty-five thousand francs.'

'Very well; but not a sous more.'

'Shall I trust you?'

'Am I not trusting you? It is well for you that I do not allow myself to think of the venture I am making.'

'Perhaps we're even there. We neither of us can afford to make account of certain possibilities. Still, I'll trust you, too … *Tiens!*' added the boatman, 'here we are near the quay.' Then with a mock-solemn touch of his cap, 'Will Madame still visit the cemetery?'

'Come, quick, let me land,' said Madame Bernier, impatiently.

'We *have* been among the dead, after a fashion,' persisted the boatman, as he gave her his hand.

III

IT WAS MORE than eight o'clock when Madame Bernier reached her own house.

'Has M. de Meyrau been here?' she asked of Josephine.

'Yes, ma'am; and on learning that Madame was out, he left a note, *chez monsieur*.'

Hortense found a sealed letter on the table in her husband's old study. It ran as follows:

I was desolated at finding you out. I had a word to tell you. I have accepted an invitation to sup and pass the night at C——, thinking it would look well. For the same reason I have resolved to take the bull by the horns, and go aboard the steamer on my return, to welcome M. Bernier home – the privilege of an old friend. I am told the *Armorique* will anchor off the bar by daybreak. What do you think? But it's too late to let me know. Applaud my *savoir faire* – you will, at all events, in the end. You will see how it will smoothe matters.

'Baffled! baffled!' hissed Madame, when she had read the note; 'God deliver me from my friends!' She paced up and down the room several times, and at last began to mutter to herself, as people often do in moments of strong emotion: 'Bah! but he'll never get up by daybreak. He'll oversleep himself, especially after tonight's supper. The other will be before him . . . Oh, my poor head, you've suffered too much to fail in the end!'

Josephine reappeared to offer to remove her mistress's things. The latter, in her desire to reassure herself, asked the first question that occurred to her.

'Was M. le Vicomte alone?'

'No madame; another gentleman was with him – M. de Saulges, I think. They came in a hack, with two portmanteaus.'

Though I have judged best, hitherto, often from an exaggerated fear of trenching on the ground of fiction, to tell you what this poor lady did and said, rather than what she thought, I may disclose what passed in her mind now:

'Is he a coward? is he going to leave me? or is he simply going to pass these last hours in play and drink? He might have stayed with me. Ah! my friend, you do little for me, who do so much for you; who commit murder, and – Heaven help me! – suicide for you! . . . But I suppose he knows best. At all events, he will make a night of it.'

When the cook came in late that evening, Josephine, who had sat up for her, said:

'You've no idea how Madame is looking. She's ten years older since this morning. Holy mother! what a day this has been for her!'

'Wait till tomorrow,' said the oracular Valentine.

Later, when the women went up to bed in the attic, they saw a light under Hortense's door, and during the night Josephine, whose chamber was above Madame's, and who couldn't sleep (for sympathy, let us say), heard movements beneath her, which told that her mistress was even more wakeful than she.

IV

THERE WAS CONSIDERABLE bustle around the *Armorique* as she anchored outside the harbour of H——, in the early dawn of the following day. A gentleman, with an overcoat, walking stick, and small valise, came alongside in a little fishing-boat, and got leave to go aboard.

'Is M. Bernier here?' he asked of one of the officers, the first man he met.

'I fancy he's gone ashore, sir. There was a boatman inquiring for him a few minutes ago, and I think he carried him off.'

M. de Meyrau reflected a moment. Then he crossed over to the other side of the vessel, looking landward. Leaning over the bulwarks he saw an empty boat moored to the ladder which ran up the vessel's side.

'That's a town boat, isn't it?' he said to one of the hands standing by.

'Yes, sir.'

'Where's the master?'

'I suppose he'll be here in a moment. I saw him speaking to one of the officers just now.'

De Meyrau descended the ladder, and seated himself at the stern of the boat. As the sailor he had just addressed was handing down his bag, a face with a red cap looked over the bulwarks.

'Hullo, my man!' cried De Meyrau, 'is this your boat?'

'Yes, sir, at your service,' answered the red cap, coming to the top of the ladder, and looking hard at the gentleman's stick and portmanteau.

'Can you take me to town, to Madame Bernier's, at the end of the new quay?'

'Certainly, sir,' said the boatman, scuttling down the ladder, 'you're just the gentleman I want.'

An hour later Hortense Bernier came out of the house, and began to walk slowly through the garden toward the terrace which overlooked the water. The servants, when they came down at an early hour, had found her up and dressed, or rather, apparently, not undressed, for she wore the same clothes as the evening before.

'*Tiens!*' exclaimed Josephine, after seeing her, 'Madame gained ten years yesterday; she has gained ten more during the night.'

When Madame Bernier reached the middle of the garden she halted, and stood for a moment motionless, listening. The next, she uttered a great cry. For she saw a figure emerge from below the terrace, and come limping toward her with outstretched arms.

A Landscape-Painter

D O YOU REMEMBER how, a dozen years ago, a number of our friends were startled by the report of the rupture of young Locksley's engagement with Miss Leary? This event made some noise in its day. Both parties possessed certain claims to distinction: Locksley in his wealth, which was believed to be enormous, and the young lady in her beauty, which was in truth very great. I used to hear that her lover was fond of comparing her to the Venus of Milo; and, indeed, if you can imagine the mutilated goddess with her full complement of limbs, dressed out by Madame de Crinoline, and engaged in small-talk beneath the drawing-room chandelier, you may obtain a vague notion of Miss Josephine Leary. Locksley, you remember, was rather a short man, dark, and not particularly good-looking; and when he walked about with his betrothed it was half a matter of surprise that he should have ventured to propose to a young lady of such heroic proportions. Miss Leary had the grey eyes and auburn hair which I have always attributed to the famous statue. The one defect in her face, in spite of an expression of great candour and sweetness, was a certain lack of animation. What it was besides her beauty that attracted Locksley I never discovered; perhaps, since his attachment was so short-lived, it was her beauty alone. I say that his attachment was of brief duration, because the break was understood to have come from him. Both he and Miss Leary very wisely held their tongues on the matter; but among their friends and enemies it of course received a hundred explanations. That most popular with Locksley's well-wishers was, that he had backed out (these events are discussed, you know, in fashionable circles very much as an expected prize-fight which has miscarried is canvassed in reunions of another kind) only on flagrant evidence of the lady's – what, faithlessness? – on overwhelming proof of the most *mercenary* spirit on the part of Miss Leary. You see, our friend was held capable of doing battle for an 'idea'. It must be owned that this was a novel charge; but, for myself, having long known Mrs Leary, the mother, who was a widow with four daughters, to be an inveterate old screw, it was not impossible for me to believe that her first-born had also shown the cloven foot. I suppose that the young lady's family had, on their own side, a very plausible version of their disappointment. It was, however, soon made up to them by Josephine's marriage with a gentleman of expectations very nearly as brilliant as those of her old suitor. And what was *his* compensation? That is precisely my story.

Locksley disappeared, as you will remember, from public view. The events above alluded to happened in March. On calling at his lodgings in April I was told he had gone to the country. But toward the last of May I met him. He told me that he was on the look-out for a quiet, unfrequented place at the seaside, where he might rusticate and sketch. He was looking very poorly. I suggested Newport, and I remember he hardly had the energy to smile at the simple joke. We parted without my having been able to satisfy him, and for a very long time I quite lost sight of him. He died seven years ago, at the age of thirty-five. For five years, accordingly, he managed to shield his life from the eyes of men. Through circumstances which I need not go into, a good many of his personal belongings have become mine. You will remember that he was a man of what are called cultivated tastes; that is, he was fond of reading, wrote a little, and painted a good deal. He wrote some rather amateurish verse, but he produced a number of remarkable paintings. He left a mass of papers, on many subjects, few of which are calculated to be generally interesting. A few of them, however, I highly prize – that portion which constitutes his private diary. It extends from his twenty-fifth to his thirtieth year, at which period it breaks off suddenly. If you will come to my house I will show you such of his pictures and sketches as I possess, and, I trust, convert you to my opinion that he had in him the stuff of a charming artist. Meanwhile I will place before you the last hundred pages of his diary, as an answer to your inquiry regarding the ultimate view taken by the great Nemesis of his treatment of Miss Leary – his scorn of the magnificent Venus Victrix. The recent passing away of the one person who had a voice paramount to mine in the disposal of Locksley's effects enables me to act without reserve.

Chowderville, June 9th. – I have been sitting some minutes, pen in hand, wondering whether on this new earth, beneath this new sky, I had better resume this occasional history of nothing at all. I think I will at all events make the experiment. If we fail, as Lady Macbeth remarks, we fail. I find my entries have been longest when I have had least to say. I doubt not, therefore, that, once I have had a sufficient dose of dullness, I shall sit scribbling from morning till night. If nothing happens – But my prophetic soul tells me that something *will* happen. I am determined that something shall – if it be nothing else than that I paint a picture.

When I came up to bed half an hour ago I was deadly sleepy. Now, after looking out of the window a little, my brain is immensely refreshed, and I feel as if I could write till morning. But, unfortunately, I have nothing to write about. And then, if I expect to rise early, I must turn in betimes. The whole village is asleep, godless metropolitan that I am! The lamps on the square, outside, flicker in the wind; there is nothing abroad but the blue darkness and the smell of the rising tide. I have spent the whole day on my legs, trudging from one side of the peninsula to the other. What a trump is old Mrs Monkhouse, to have thought of this place! I must write her a letter of passionate thanks. Never before have I seen such a pretty little coast – never before have I been so taken with wave and rock and cloud. I am filled with ecstasy at the life, light, and transparency of the air. I am enamoured of all the moods and tenses of the ocean; and as yet, I suppose, I have not seen half of them. I came in to supper hungry, weary, footsore, sunburnt, dirty – happier, in short, than I have been for a twelvemonth. And now, if you please, for the prodigies of the brush!

June 11th. – Another day afoot, and also afloat. I resolved this morning to leave this abominable little tavern; I can't stand my feather-bed another night. I determined to find some other prospect than the town-pump and the 'drug-store'. I questioned my host, after breakfast, as to the possibility of getting lodgings in any of the outlying farms and cottages. But my host either did not or would not know anything about the matter. So I resolved to wander forth and seek my fortune – to roam inquisitive through the neighbourhood and appeal to the indigenous sentiment of hospitality. But never have I seen a folk so devoid of this amiable quality. By dinner-time I had given up in despair. After dinner I strolled down to the harbour, which is close at hand. The brightness and breeziness of the water tempted me to hire a boat and resume my explorations. I procured an old tub, with a short stump of a mast, which, being planted quite in the centre, gave the craft much the appearance of an inverted mushroom. I made for what I took to be, and what is, an island, lying long and low, some four or five miles over against the town. I sailed for half an hour directly before the wind, and at last found myself a ground on the shelving beach of a quiet little cove. Such a dear little cove – so bright, so still, so warm, so remote from Chowderville, which lay in the distance, white and semi-circular! I leaped ashore, and dropped my anchor. Before me rose a steep cliff, crowned with an old ruined fort or tower. I made my way up, and round to the landward entrance. The fort is a hollow old shell; looking upwards, from the beach, you see the harmless blue sky through the gaping loopholes. Its interior is choked with rocks and brambles and masses of fallen masonry. I scrambled up to the parapet, and obtained a noble sea-view. Beyond the broad bay I saw the miniature town and country mapped out before me; and on the other hand, I saw the infinite Atlantic – over which, by the by, all the pretty things are brought from Paris. I spent the whole afternoon in wandering hither and thither on the hills that encircle the little cove in which I had landed, heedless of the minutes and the miles, watching the sailing clouds and the flitting, gleaming sails, listening to the musical attrition of the tidal pebbles, passing the time anyhow. The only particular sensation I remember was that of being ten years old again, together with a general impression of Saturday afternoon, of the liberty to go in wading or even swimming, and of the prospect of limping home in the dusk with a wondrous story of having almost caught a turtle. When I returned I found – but I know very well what I found, and I need hardly repeat it here for my mortification. Heaven knows I never was a practical character. What thought I about the tide? There lay the old tub, high and dry, with the rusty anchor protruding from the flat green stones and the shallow puddles left by the receding wave. Moving the boat an inch, much more a dozen yards, was quite beyond my strength. I slowly reascended the cliff, to see if from its summit any help was discernible. None was within sight, and I was about to go down again, in profound dejection, when I saw a trim little sail-boat shoot out from behind a neighbouring bluff, and advance along the shore. I quickened pace. On reaching the beach I found the newcomer standing out about a hundred yards. The man at the helm appeared to regard me with some interest. With a mute prayer that his disposition might not be hostile – he didn't look like a wild islander – I invited him by voice and gesture to make for a little point of rocks a short distance above us, where I proceeded to join him. I told him my story, and he readily took me aboard. He was a civil old gentleman, of the seafaring sort, who appeared to be cruising about in the evening-breeze for his pleasure. On landing I visited the proprietor of my old tub, related my misadventure, and offered to pay damages if the boat shall turn out in the morning to have sustained any. Meanwhile, I suppose, it is held secure against the next tidal revolution, however violent.

But for my old gentleman. I have decidedly picked up an acquaintance, if not made a friend. I gave him a very good cigar, and before we reached home we had become thoroughly intimate. In exchange for my cigar he gave me his name; and there was that in his tone which seemed to imply that I had by no means the worst of the exchange. His name is Richard Quarterman, 'though most people,' he added, 'call me Cap'n, for respect.' He then proceeded to inquire my own titles and pretensions. I told him no lies, but I told him only half the truth;

and if he chooses to indulge mentally in any romantic under-
statements, why, he is welcome, and bless his simple heart! The
fact is, I have simply broken with the past. I have decided, coolly
and calmly, as I believe, that it is necessary to my success, or, at
any rate, to my happiness, to abjure for a while my conventional
self, and to assume a simple, natural character. How can a man
be simple and natural who is known to have a large income?
That is the supreme curse. It's bad enough to have it; to be
known to have it, to be known only because you have it, is most
damnable. I suppose I am too proud to be successfully rich. Let
me see how poverty will serve my turn. I have taken a fresh start
– I have determined to stand upon my merits. If they fail me I
shall fall back upon my dollars, but with God's help I will test
them, and see what kind of stuff I am made of. To be young,
strong and poor – such in this blessed nineteenth century, is the
great basis of solid success. I have resolved to take at least one
brief draught from the founts of inspiration of my time. I replied
to Captain Quarterman with such reservations as a brief survey
of these principles dictated. What a luxury to pass in a poor
man's mind for his brother! I begin to respect myself. Thus
much the Captain knows: that I am an educated man, with a
taste for painting; that I have come hither for the purpose of
studying and sketching coast-scenery; toning myself up with
the sea air. I have reason to believe, moreover, that he suspects
me of limited means and of being of a very frugal mind. Amen!
Vogue la galère! But the point of my story is in his very hospita-
ble offer of lodgings – I had been telling him of my want of

success in the morning in the pursuit of the same. He is a queer mixture of the gentleman of the old school and the hot-headed merchant-captain.

'Young man,' said he, after taking several meditative puffs of his cigar, 'I don't see the point of your living in a tavern when there are folks about you with more house-room than they know what to do with. A tavern is only half a house, just as one of these new-fashioned screw-propellers is only half a ship. Suppose you walk round and take a look at my place. I own quite a respectable tenement over yonder to the left of the town. Do you see that old wharf with the tumble-down warehouses, and the long row of elms behind it? I live right in the midst of the elms. We have the sweetest little garden in the world, stretching down to the water's edge. It's all as quiet as anything can be, short of a churchyard. The back windows, you know, overlook the harbour; and you can see twenty miles up the bay, and fifty miles out to sea. You can paint to yourself there the livelong day, with no more fear of intrusion than if you were out yonder at the light-ship. There's no one but myself and my daughter, who's a perfect lady, sir. She teaches music in a young ladies' school. You see, money's an object, as they say. We have never taken boarders yet, because none ever came in our track; but I guess we can learn the ways. I suppose you've boarded before; you can put us up to a thing or two.'

There was something so kindly and honest in the old man's weather-beaten face, something so friendly in his address, that I forthwith struck a bargain with him, subject to his daughter's approval. I am to have her answer tomorrow. This same daughter strikes me as rather a dark spot in the picture. Teacher in a young ladies' school – probably the establishment of which Mrs Monkhouse spoke to me. I suppose she's over thirty. I think I know the species.

June 12th, a.m. – I have really nothing to do but to scribble, 'Barkis is willing.' Captain Quarterman brought me word this morning that his daughter makes no objection. I am to report this evening; but I shall send my slender baggage in an hour or two.

p.m. – Here I am, domiciled, almost domesticated. The house is less than a mile from the inn, and reached by a very pleasant road, which skirts the harbour. At about six o'clock I presented myself; Captain Quarterman had described the place. A very civil old negress admitted me, and ushered me into the garden, where I found my friends watering their flowers. The old man was in his house-coat and slippers – he gave me a cordial welcome. There is something delightfully easy in his manners – and in Miss Quarterman's, too for that matter. She received me very nicely. The late Mrs Quarterman was probably a superior being. As for the young lady's being thirty, she is about twenty-four. She wore a fresh white dress, with a blue ribbon on her neck, and a rosebud in her button-hole – or whatever corresponds to the button-hole on the feminine bosom. I thought I discerned in this costume, a vague intention of courtesy, of gaiety, of celebrating my arrival. I don't believe Miss Quarterman wears white muslin every day. She shook hands with me, and made me a pleasing little speech about their taking me in. 'We have never had any inmates before,' said she; 'and we are consequently new to the business. I don't know what you expect. I hope you don't expect a great deal. You must ask for anything you want. If we can give it, we shall be very glad to do so; if we can't, I give you warning that we shall simply tell you so.' Brava, Miss Quarterman! The best of it is, that she is decidedly beautiful — and in the grand manner; tall, and with roundness in her lines. What is the orthodox description of a pretty girl? — white and red? Miss Quarterman is not a pretty girl, she is a handsome woman. She leaves an impression of black and red; that is, she is a brunette with colour. She has a great deal of wavy black hair, which encircles her head like a dusky glory, a smoky halo. Her eyebrows, too, are black, but her eyes themselves are of a rich blue grey, the colour of those slate-cliffs which I saw yesterday, weltering under the tide. She has perfect teeth, and her smile is almost unnaturally brilliant. Her chin is surpassingly round. She has a capital movement, too, and looked uncommonly well as she strolled in the garden-path with a big spray of geranium lifted to her nose. She has very little to say, apparently; but when she speaks, it is to the point, and if the point suggests it, she doesn't hesitate to laugh very musically. Indeed, if she is not talkative, it is not from timidity. Is it from indifference? Time will elucidate this, as well as other mysteries. I cling to the hypothesis that she is amiable. She is, moreover, intelligent; she is probably fond of keeping herself to herself, as the phrase is, and is even, possibly, very proud. She is, in short, a woman of character. There you are, Miss Quarterman, at as full length as I can paint you. After tea she gave us some music in the parlour. I confess that I was more taken with the picture of the dusky little room, lighted by the single candle on the piano, and by her stately way of sitting at the instrument, than by the quality of her playing, though that is evidently high.

June 18th. – I have now been here almost a week. I occupy two very pleasant rooms. My painting-room is a large and rather bare apartment, with a very good north-light. I have decked it out with a few old prints and sketches, and have already grown very fond of it. When I had disposed my artistic odds and ends so as to make it look as much like a studio as possible, I called in my hosts. The Captain snuffed about, silently, for some moments, and then inquired hopefully if I had ever tried my hand at a ship. On learning that I had not yet got to ships, he relapsed into a prudent reserve. His daughter smiled and questioned, very graciously, and called everything beautiful and delightful; which rather disappointed me, as I had taken her to be a woman of some originality. She is rather a puzzle. Or is she, indeed, a very commonplace person, and the fault in me, who am forever taking women to mean a great deal more than their Maker intended? Regarding Miss Quarterman I have collected a few facts. She is not twenty-four, but twenty-seven years old.

She has taught music ever since she was twenty, in a large boarding-school just out of the town, where she originally obtained her education. Her salary in this establishment, which is, I believe, a tolerably flourishing one, and the proceeds of a few additional lessons, constitute the chief revenues of the household. But the Captain fortunately owns his house, and his needs and habits are of the simplest kind. What does he or his daughter know of the great worldly theory of necessities, the great worldly scale of pleasures? The young lady's only luxuries are a subscription to the circulating library, and an occasional walk on the beach, which, like one of Miss Brontë's heroines, she paces in company with an old Newfoundland dog. I am afraid she is sadly ignorant. She reads nothing but novels. I am bound to believe, however, that she has derived from the perusal of these works a certain second-hand acquaintance with life. 'I read all the novels I can get,' she said yesterday; 'but I only like the good ones. I do so like *The Missing Bride*, which I have just finished.' I must set her to work at some of the masters. I should like some of those fretful daughters of gold, in New York, to see how this woman lives. I wish, too, that half a dozen of *ces messieurs* of the clubs might take a peep at the present way of life of their humble servant. We breakfast at eight o'clock. Immediately afterwards Miss Quarterman, in a shabby old bonnet and shawl, starts off to school. If the weather is fine the Captain goes a-fishing, and I am left quite to my own devices. Twice I have accompanied the old man. The second time I was lucky enough to catch a big blue-fish, which we had for dinner.

The Captain is an excellent specimen of the pure navigator, with his loose blue clothes, his ultra-divergent legs, his crisp white hair, his jolly thick-skinned visage. He comes of a sea-faring English race. There is more or less of the ship's cabin in the general aspect of this antiquated house. I have heard the wind whistle about its walls, on two or three occasions, in true mid-ocean style. And then the illusion is heightened, somehow or other, by the extraordinary intensity of the light. My painting-room is a grand observatory of the clouds. I sit by the half-hour watching them sail past my high uncurtained windows. At the back part of the room something tells you that they belong to an ocean-sky; and there, in truth, as you draw nearer, you behold the vast grey complement of sea. This quarter of the town is perfectly quiet. Human activity seems to have passed over it, never again to return, and to have left a deposit of melancholy resignation. The streets are clean, bright and airy; but this fact only deepens the impression of vanished uses. It seems to say that the protecting heavens look down on their decline and can't help them. There is something ghostly in the perpetual stillness. We frequently hear the rattling of the yards and the issuing of orders on the barks and schooners anchored out in the harbour.

June 28th. – My experiment works far better than I had hoped. I am thoroughly at my ease; my peace of mind quite passeth understanding. I work diligently; I have none but pleasant thoughts. The past has almost lost its bitterness. For a week, now, I have been out sketching daily. The Captain carries me to a certain point on the shore of the bay, I disembark and strike across the uplands to a spot where I have taken a kind of tryst with a particular effect of rock and shadow, which has been tolerably faithful to its appointment. Here I set up my easel, and paint till sunset. Then I retrace my steps and meet the boat. I am in every way much encouraged; the horizon of my work grows perceptibly wider. And then I am inexpressibly happy in the conviction that I am not wholly unfit for a life of (moderate) industry and (comparative) privation. I am quite in love with my poverty, if I may call it so. And why should I not? At this rate I don't spend eight hundred a year.

July 12th. – We have been having a week of bad weather: constant rain, night and day. This is certainly at once the brightest and the blackest spot in New England. The skies can smile, assuredly, but they have also lachrymal moods. I have been painting rather languidly, and at a great disadvantage, at my window . . . Through all this pouring and pattering Miss Miriam – her name is Miriam, and it exactly fits her – sallies forth to her pupils. She envelops her beautiful head in a great woollen hood, her beautiful figure in a kind of feminine mackintosh; her feet she puts into heavy clogs, and over the whole she balances a cotton umbrella. When she comes home, with the rain-drops glistening on her rich cheeks and her dark lashes, her cloak bespattered with mud and her hands red with the cool damp, she is a very honourable figure. I never fail to make her a very low bow, for which she repays me with a familiar, but not a vulgar, nod. The working-day side of her character is what especially pleases me in Miss Quarterman. This holy working-dress sits upon her with the fine effect of an antique drapery. Little use has she for whale-bones and furbelows. What a poetry there is, after all, in red hands! I kiss yours, Mademoiselle. I do so because you are self-helpful; because you earn your living; because you are honest, simple, and ignorant (for a sensible woman, that is); because you speak and act to the point; because, in short, you are so unlike – certain of your sisters.

July 16th. – On Monday it cleared up generously. When I went to my window, on rising, I found sky and sea looking, for their brightness and freshness, like a clever English water-colour. The ocean is of a deep purple blue; above it, the pure, bright sky looks pale, though it hangs over the island horizon a canopy of denser tissue. Here and there on the dark, breezy water gleams the white cap of a wave, or flaps the white cloak of a fishing-boat. I have been sketching sedulously; I have discovered, within a couple of miles' walk, a large, lonely pond, set in a really grand landscape of barren rocks and grassy slopes. At one extremity is a broad outlook on the open sea; at the other, buried in the foliage of an apple-orchard, stands an old haunted-looking farm-house. To the west of the pond is a wide expanse of rock and grass, of sand and marsh. The sheep browse over it – poorly – as they might upon a Highland moor. Except a few stunted firs and cedars, there is not a tree in sight. When I want shade I have to look for it in the shelter of one of the large stones which hold up to the sun a shoulder coated with delicate grey, figured over with fine, pale, sea-green moss, or else in one of the long, shallow dells where a tangle of blackberry-bushes hedges about a pool that reflects the sky. I am giving my best attention to a plain brown hillside, and trying to make it look like something in nature; and as we have now had the same clear sky for several days, I have almost finished quite a satisfactory little study. I go forth immediately after breakfast. Miss Quarterman supplies me with a little parcel of bread and cold meat, which at the noonday hour, in my sunny solitude, within sight of the slumbering ocean, I voraciously convey to my lips with my discoloured fingers. At seven o'clock I return to tea, at which repast we each tell the story of our day's work. For poor Miss Quarterman it is always the same story: a wearisome round of visits to the school, and to the houses of the mayor, the parson, the butcher, the baker, whose young ladies, of course, all receive instruction on the piano. But she doesn't complain, nor, indeed, does she look very weary. When she has put on a fresh light dress for tea, and arranged her hair anew, and with these improvements flits about with the quiet hither and thither of her gentle footstep, preparing our evening meal, peeping into the teapot, cutting the solid loaf – or when, sitting down on the low door-step, she reads out select scraps from the evening-paper – or else, when tea being over, she folds her arms (an attitude which becomes her mightily) and, still sitting on the door-step, gossips away the evening in comfortable idleness, while her father and I indulge in the fragrant pipe and watch the lights shining out, one by one, in different quarters of the darkening bay: at these moments she is as pretty, as cheerful, as careless as it becomes a sensible woman to be. What a pride the Captain takes in his daughter, and she, in return, how perfect is her devotion to the old man! He is proud of her grace, of her tact, of her good sense, of her wit, such as it is. He believes her to be the most accomplished of women. He waits upon her as if, instead of his old familiar Miriam, she were some new arrival – say a daughter-in-law lately brought home. And *à propos* of daughters-in-law, if I were his own son he could not be kinder to me. They are certainly – nay, why should I not say it? – *we* are certainly a very happy little household. Will it last for ever? I say *we*, because both father and daughter have given me a hundred assurances – he direct, and she, if I don't flatter myself, after the manner of her sex, indirect – that I am already a valued friend. It is natural enough that they should like me, because I have tried to please them. The way to the old man's heart is through a studied consideration of his daughter. He knows, I imagine, that I admire Miss Quarterman, but if I should at any time fall below the mark of ceremony, I should have an account to settle with him. All this is as it should be. When people have to economize with the dollars and cents, they have a right to be splendid in their feelings. I have done my best to be nice to the stately Miriam without making love to her. That I haven't done *that*, however, is a fact which I do not, in any degree, set down here to my credit; for I would defy the most impertinent of men (whoever he is) to forget himself with this young lady. Those animated eyes have a power to keep people in their place. I mention the circumstance simply because in future years, when my charming friend shall have become a distant shadow, it will be pleasant, in turning over these pages, to find written testimony to a number of points which I shall be apt to charge solely upon my imagination. I wonder whether Miss Quarterman, in days to come, referring to the tables of her memory for some trivial matter-of-fact, some prosaic date or half-buried landmark, will also encounter this little secret of ours, as I may call it – will decipher an old faint note to this effect, overlaid with the memoranda of intervening years. Of course she will. Sentiment aside, she is a woman of a retentive faculty. Whether she forgives or not I know not; but she certainly doesn't forget. Doubtless, virtue is its own reward; but there is a double satisfaction in being polite to a person on whom it tells!

Another reason for my pleasant relations with the Captain is, that I afford him a chance to rub up his rusty worldly lore and trot out his little scraps of old-fashioned reading, some of which are very curious. It is a great treat for him to spin his threadbare yarns over again to a submissive listener. These warm July evenings, in the sweet-smelling garden, are just the proper setting for his traveller's tales. An odd enough understanding subsists between us on this point. Like many gentlemen of his calling, the Captain is harassed by an irresistible desire to romance, even on the least promising themes; and it is vastly amusing to observe how he will auscultate, as it were, his auditor's inmost mood, to ascertain whether it is in condition to be practised upon. Sometimes his artless fables don't 'take' at all: they are very pretty, I conceive, in the deep and briny well of the Captain's fancy, but they won't bear being transplanted into the dry climate of my land-bred mind. At other times, the auditor being in a dreamy, sentimental, and altogether unprincipled mood, he will drink the old man's salt-water by the bucketful and feel none the worse for it. Which is the worse, wilfully to tell, or wilfully to believe, a pretty little falsehood which will not hurt anyone? I suppose you can't believe wilfully; you only pretend to believe. My part of the game, therefore, is certainly as bad as the Captain's. Perhaps I take kindly to his beautiful perversions of fact because I am myself engaged in one, because I am sailing under false colours of the deepest dye. I wonder whether my friends have any suspicion of the real state of the case. How should they? I take for granted that I play my little part pretty well. I am delighted to find it comes so easy. I do not mean that I find little difficulty in forgoing my old luxuries and pleasures – for to these, thank Heaven, I was not so indissolubly wedded that one wholesome shock could not loosen my bonds – but that I manage more cleverly than I expected to stifle those innumerable tacit allusions which might serve effectually to belie my character.

Sunday, July 20th. – This has been a very pleasant day for me; although in it, of course, I have done no manner of work. I had this morning a delightful *tête-à-tête* with my hostess. She had sprained her ankle coming downstairs, and so, instead of going forth to Sunday-school and to meeting, she was obliged to remain at home on the sofa. The Captain, who is of a very punctilious piety, went off alone. When I came into the parlour, as the church-bells were ringing, Miss Quarterman asked me if I never went to a place of worship.

'Never when there is anything better to do at home,' said I.

'What is better than going to church?' she asked, with charming simplicity.

She was reclining on the sofa, with her foot on a pillow and her Bible in her lap. She looked by no means afflicted at having to be absent from divine service; and, instead of answering her question, I took the liberty of telling her so.

'I *am* sorry to be absent,' said she. 'You know it's my only festival in the week.'

'So you look upon it as a festival.'

'Isn't it a pleasure to meet one's acquaintance? I confess I am never deeply interested in the sermon, and I very much dislike teaching the children; but I like wearing my best bonnet, and singing in the choir, and walking part of the way home with—'

'With whom?'

'With anyone who offers to walk with me.'

'With Mr Prendergast, for instance,' said I.

Mr Prendergast is a young lawyer in the village, who calls here once a week, and whose attentions to Miss Quarterman have been remarked.

'Yes,' she answered, 'Mr Prendergast will do as an instance.'

'How he will miss you!'

'I suppose he will. We sing off the same book. What are you laughing at? He kindly permits me to hold the book, while he stands with his hands in his pockets. Last Sunday I quite lost patience. "Mr Prendergast," said I, "do hold the book! Where are your manners?" He burst out laughing in the midst of the reading. He will certainly have to hold the book today.'

'What a masterful soul he is! I suppose he will call after meeting.'

'Perhaps he will. I hope so.'

'I hope he won't,' said I, frankly. 'I am going to sit down here and talk to you, and I wish our conversation not to be interrupted.'

'Have you anything particular to say?'

'Nothing so particular as Mr Prendergast, perhaps.'

Miss Quarterman has a very pretty affectation of being more matter-of-fact than she really is.

'His rights, then,' she remarked, 'are paramount to yours.'

'Ah, you admit that he has rights?'

'Not at all. I simply assert that you have none.'

'I beg your pardon. I have claims which I mean to enforce. I have a claim upon your undivided attention when I pay you a morning-call.'

'You have had all the attention I am capable of. Have I been so very rude?'

'Not so very rude, perhaps, but rather inconsiderate. You have been sighing for the company of a third person, whom you can't expect me to care much about.'

'Why not, pray? If I, a lady, can put up with Mr Prendergast's society, why shouldn't you, one of his own sex?'

'Because he is so outrageously conceited. You, as a lady, or at any rate as a woman, like conceited men.'

'Ah, yes; I have no doubt that I, as a woman, have all kinds of weak tastes. That's a very old story.'

'Admit, at any rate, that our friend is conceited.'

'Admit it! Why, I have said so a hundred times. I have told him so.'

'Indeed, it has come to that, then?'

'To what, pray?'

'To that critical point in the friendship of a lady and gentleman when they bring against each other all kinds of delightful accusations and rebukes. Take care, Miss Quarterman! A couple of intelligent New Englanders, of opposite sexes, young, unmarried, are pretty far gone, when they begin to scan each other's faults. So you told Mr Prendergast that he is conceited? And I suppose you added that he was also dreadfully satirical and sceptical? What was his rejoinder? Let me see. Did he ever tell you that you were a wee bit affected?'

'No; he left that for you to say, in this very ingenious manner. Thank you, sir.'

'He left it for me to deny, which is a great deal prettier. Do you think the manner ingenious?'

'I think the matter, considering the day and hour, very profane, Mr Locksley. Suppose you go away and let me peruse my Bible.'

'Meanwhile what shall I do?'

'Go and read yours, if you have one.'

'My Bible,' I said, 'is the female mind.'

I was nevertheless compelled to retire, with the promise of a second audience in half an hour. Poor Miss Quarterman owes it to her conscience to read a certain number of chapters. In what a terrible tradition she has been reared, and what an edifying spectacle is the piety of women! Women find a place for everything in their commodious little minds, just as they do in their wonderfully sub-divided trunks when they go on a journey. I have no doubt that this young lady stows away her religion in a corner, just as she does her Sunday-bonnet – and, when the proper moment comes, draws it forth, and reflects, while she puts it on before the glass and blows away the strictly imaginary dust (for what worldly impurity can penetrate through half a dozen layers of cambric and tissue-paper?): 'Dear me, what a comfort it is to have a nice, fresh holiday-creed!' When I returned to the parlour Miriam was still sitting with her Bible in her lap. Somehow or other I no longer felt in the mood for jesting; so I asked her, without chaffing, what she had been reading, and she answered me in the same tone. She inquired how I had spent my half-hour.

'In thinking good Sabbath thoughts,' I said. 'I have been walking in the garden.' And then I spoke my mind. 'I have been thanking Heaven that it has led me, a poor friendless wanderer, into so peaceful an anchorage.'

'Are you so very poor and friendless?'

'Did you ever hear of an art-student who was not poor? Upon my word, I have yet to sell my first picture. Then, as for being friendless, there are not five people in the world who really care for me.'

'*Really* care? I am afraid you look too close. And then I think five good friends is a very large number. I think myself very well-off with half-a-one. But if you are friendless, it's probably your own fault.'

'Perhaps it is,' said I, sitting down in the rocking-chair; 'and also, perhaps it isn't. Have you found me so very difficult to live with? Haven't you, on the contrary, found me rather sociable?'

She folded her arms, and quietly looked at me for a moment, before answering. I shouldn't wonder if I blushed a little.

'You want a lump of sugar, Mr Locksley; that's the long and short of it. I haven't given you one since you have been here. How you must have suffered! But it's a pity you couldn't have waited a little longer, instead of beginning to put out your paws and bark. For an artist, you are very slap-dash. Men never know how to wait. "Have I found you very difficult to live with? haven't I found you sociable?" Perhaps, after all, considering what I have in my mind, it is as well that you asked for your lump of sugar. I have found you very indulgent. You let us off easily, but you wouldn't like us a bit if you didn't pity us. Don't I go deep? Sociable? ah, well, no – decidedly not! You are entirely too particular. You are considerate of me, because you know that I know that you are so. There's the rub, you see: I know that you know that I know it! Don't interrupt me; I am going to be striking. I want you to understand why I don't consider you sociable. You call poor Mr Prendergast conceited; but, really, I believe he has more humility than you. He envies my father and me – thinks us so cultivated. You don't envy anyone, and yet I don't think you're a saint. You treat us kindly because you think virtue in a lowly station ought to be encouraged. Would you take the same amount of pains for a person you thought your equal, a person equally averse with yourself to being under an obligation? There are differences. Of course it's very delightful to fascinate people. Who wouldn't? There is no harm in it, as long as the fascinator doesn't set up for a public benefactor. If I were a man, a clever man like yourself, who had seen the world, who was not to be dazzled and encouraged, but to be listened to, counted with, would you be equally amiable? It will perhaps seem absurd to you, and it will certainly seem egotistical, but I consider myself sociable, for all that I have only a couple of friends – my father and Miss Blankenberg. That is, I mingle with people without any *arrière-pensée*. Of course the people I see are mainly women. Not that I wish you to do so: on the contrary, if the contrary is agreeable to you. But I don't believe you mingle in the same way with men. You may ask me what I know about it! Of course I know nothing; I simply guess. When I have done, indeed, I mean to beg your pardon for all I have said; but until then, give me a chance. You are incapable of exposing yourself to be bored, whereas I take it as my waterproof takes the rain. You have no idea what heroism I show in the exercise of my profession! Every day I have occasion to pocket my pride and to stifle my sense of the ridiculous – of which of course you think I haven't a bit. It is for instance a constant vexation to me to be poor. It makes me frequently hate rich women; it makes me despise poor ones. I don't know whether you suffer acutely from the smallness of your own means; but if you do, I daresay you shun rich men. I don't, I like to bleed; to go into rich people's houses, and to be very polite to the ladies, especially if they are very much dressed, very ignorant and vulgar. All women are like me in this respect, and all men more or less like you. That is, after all, the text of my sermon. Compared with us it has always seemed to me that you are arrant cowards – that we alone are brave. To be sociable you must have a great deal of patience. You are too fine a gentleman. Go and teach school, or open a corner-grocery, or sit in a law-office all day, waiting for clients: then you will be sociable. As yet you are only selfish. It *is* your own fault if people don't care for you; you don't care for them. That you should be indifferent to their good opinion is all very well; but you don't care for their indifference. You are amiable, you are very kind, and you are also very lazy. You consider that you are working now, don't you? Many persons would not call it work.'

It was now certainly my turn to fold my arms.

'And now,' added my companion, as I did so, 'be so good as to excuse me.'

'This was certainly worth waiting for,' said I. 'I don't know what answer to make. My head swims. Sugar, did you say? I don't know whether you have been giving me sugar or vitriol. So you advise me to open a corner-grocery, do you?'

'I advise you to do something that will make you a little less satirical. You had better marry, for instance.'

'*Je ne demande pas mieux*. Will you have me? I can't afford it.'

'Marry a rich woman.'

I shook my head.

'Why not?' asked Miss Quarterman. 'Because people would accuse you of being mercenary? What of that? I mean to marry the first rich man who offers. Do you know that I am tired of living alone in this weary old way, teaching little girls their scales, and turning and patching my dresses? I mean to marry the first man who offers.'

'Even if he is poor?'

'Even if he is poor and has a hump.'

'I am your man, then. Would you take me if I were to offer?'

'Try and see.'

'Must I get upon my knees?'

'No, you needn't even do that. Am I not on mine? It would be too fine an irony. Remain as you are, lounging back in your chair, with your thumbs in your waistcoat.'

If I were writing a romance now, instead of transcribing facts, I would say that I knew not what might have happened at this juncture had not the door opened and admitted the Captain and Mr Prendergast. The latter was in the highest spirits.

'How are you, Miss Miriam? So you have been breaking your

leg, eh? How are you, Mr Locksley? I wish I were a doctor now. Which is it, right or left?'

In this simple fashion he made himself agreeable to Miss Miriam. He stopped to dinner and talked without ceasing. Whether our hostess had talked herself out in her very animated address to myself an hour before, or whether she preferred to oppose no obstacle to Mr Prendergast's fluency, or whether she was indifferent to him, I know not; but she held her tongue with that easy grace, that charming tacit intimation of 'We could if we would', of which she is so perfect a mistress. This very interesting woman has a number of pretty traits in common with her town-bred sisters; only, whereas in these they are laboriously acquired, in her they are richly natural. I am sure that, if I were to plant her in Madison Square tomorrow, she would, after one quick, all-compassing glance, assume the *nil admirari* in a manner to drive the finest lady of them all to despair. Prendergast is a man of excellent intentions but no taste. Two or three times I looked at Miss Quarterman to see what impression his sallies were making upon her. They seemed to produce none whatever. But I know better, *moi*. Not one of them escaped her. But I suppose she said to herself that her impressions on this point were no business of mine. Perhaps she was right. It is a disagreeable word to use of a woman you admire; but I can't help fancying that she has been a little soured. By what? Who shall say? By some old love-affair, perhaps.

*   *   *

July 24th. – This evening the Captain and I took a half-hour's turn about the port. I asked him frankly, as a friend, whether Prendergast wants to marry his daughter.

'I guess he does,' said the old man, 'and yet I hope he don't. You know what he is: he's smart, promising, and already sufficiently well-off. But somehow he isn't for a man what my Miriam is for a female.'

'That he isn't!' said I; 'and honestly, Captain Quarterman, I don't know who is—'

'Unless it be yourself,' said the Captain.

'Thank you. I know a great many ways in which Mr Prendergast is more worthy of her than I.'

'And I know one in which you are more worthy of her than he – that is in being what we used to call one of the old sort.'

'Miss Quarterman made him sufficiently welcome in her quiet way on Sunday,' I rejoined.

'Oh, she respects him,' said Quarterman. 'As she's situated, she might marry him on that. You see, she's weary of hearing little girls drum on the piano. With her ear for music,' added the Captain, 'I wonder she has borne it so long.'

'She is certainly meant for better things,' said I.

'Well,' answered the Captain, who has an honest habit of deprecating your agreement when it occurs to him that he has obtained it for sentiments which fall somewhat short of the stoical – 'well,' said he, with a very dry, edifying expression, 'she's born to do her duty. We are all of us born for that.'

'Sometimes our duty is rather dismal,' said I.

'So it be; but what's the help for it? I don't want to die without seeing my daughter provided for. What she makes by teaching is a pretty slim subsistence. There was a time when I thought she was going to be fixed for life, but it all blew over. There was a young fellow here, from down Boston way, who came about as near to it as you can come when you actually don't. He and Miriam were excellent friends. One day Miriam came up to me, and looked me in the face, and told me she had passed her word.

'"Who to?" says I, though of course I knew, and Miriam told me as much. "When do you expect to marry?" I asked.

'"When Alfred" – his name was Alfred – "grows rich enough," says she.

'"When will that be?"

'"It may not be for years," said poor Miriam.

'A whole year passed, and, so far as I could see, the young man hadn't accumulated very much. He was forever running to and fro between this place and Boston. I asked no questions, because I knew that my poor girl wished it so. But at last, one day, I began to think it was time to take an observation, and see whereabouts we stood.

'"Has Alfred made his little pile yet?" I asked.

'"I don't know, father," said Miriam.

'"When are you to be married?"

'"Never!" said my poor little girl, and burst into tears. "Please ask me no questions," said she. "Our engagement is over. Ask me no questions."

'"Tell me one thing," said I: "Where is that d——d scoundrel who has broken my daughter's heart?"

'You should have seen the look she gave me.

'"Broken my heart, sir? You are very much mistaken. I don't know who you mean."

'"I mean Alfred Bannister," said I. That was his name.

'"I believe Mr Bannister is in China," says Miriam, as grand as the Queen of Sheba. And there was an end of it. I never learned the ins and outs of it. I have been told that Bannister is amassing considerable wealth in the China-trade.'

August 7th. – I have made no entry for more than a fortnight. They tell me I have been very ill; and I find no difficulty in believing them. I suppose I took cold, sitting out so late, sketching. At all events, I have had a mild intermittent fever. I have slept so much, however, that the time has seemed rather short. I have been tenderly nursed by this kind old mariner, his daughter, and his black domestic. God bless them, one and all! I say his daughter, because old Cynthia informs me that for half an hour one morning, at dawn, after a night during which I had been very feeble, Miss Quarterman relieved guard at my bedside, while I lay sleeping like a log. It is very jolly to see sky and ocean once again. I have got myself into my easy-chair, by the best window, with my shutters closed and the lattice open; and here I sit with my book on my knee, scratching away feebly enough. Now and then I peep from my cool, dark sick-chamber out into the world of light. High noon at midsummer – what a spectacle! There are no clouds in the sky, no waves on the ocean, the sun has it all to himself. To look long at the garden makes the eyes water. And we – 'Hobbs, Nobbs, Stokes and Nokes' – propose to paint that luminosity. *Allons donc!*

The handsomest of women has just tapped, and come in with a plate of early peaches. The peaches are of a gorgeous colour and plumpness; but Miss Quarterman looks pale and thin. The hot weather doesn't agree with her, and besides she is over-worked. Damn her drudgery! Of course I thanked her warmly for her attentions during my illness. She disclaims all gratitude, and refers me to her father and the dusky Cynthia.

'I allude more especially,' I said, 'to that little hour at the end of a weary night when you stole in, like a kind of moral Aurora, and drove away the shadows from my brain. That morning, you know, I began to get better.'

'It was indeed a very little hour,' said Miss Quarterman, colouring. 'It was about ten minutes.' And then she began to scold me for presuming to touch a pen during my convalescence. She laughs at me, indeed, for keeping a diary at all. 'Of all things, a sentimental man is the most despicable!' she exclaimed.

I confess I was somewhat nettled – the thrust seemed gratuitous.

'Of all things a woman without sentiment is the most want-ing in sweetness.'

'Sentiment and sweetness are all very well when you have time for them,' said Miss Quarterman. 'I haven't. I am not rich enough. Good morning!'

Speaking of another woman, I would say that she flounced out of the room. But such was the gait of Juno when she moved stiffly over the grass from where Paris stood with Venus holding the apple, gathering up her divine vestment and leaving the others to guess at her face.

Juno has just come back to say that she forgot what she came for half an hour ago. What will I be pleased to like for dinner?

'I have just been writing in my diary that you flounced out of the room,' said I.

'Have you, indeed? Now you can write that I have bounced in. There's a nice cold chicken downstairs,' etc. etc.

August 14th. – This afternoon I sent for a light vehicle, and treated Miss Quarterman to a drive. We went successively over the three beaches. What a spin we had coming home! I shall never forget that breezy trot over Weston's Beach. The tide was very low, and we had the whole glittering, weltering strand to ourselves. There was a heavy blow last night, which has not yet subsided, and the waves have been lashed into a magnificent fury. Trot, trot, trot, trot, we trundled over the hard sand. The sound of the horse's hoofs rang out sharp against the monotone of the thunderous surf, as we drew nearer and nearer to the long line of the cliffs. At our left, almost from the zenith of the pale evening-sky to the high western horizon of the tumultuous dark-green sea, was suspended, so to speak, one of those gorgeous vertical sunsets that Turner sometimes painted. It was a splendid confusion of purple and green and gold – the clouds flying and floating in the wind like the folds of a mighty banner borne by some triumphal fleet which had rounded the curve of the globe. As we reached the point where the cliffs begin I pulled up, and we remained for some time looking at their long, diminishing, crooked perspective, blue and dun as it receded, with the white surge playing at their feet.

August 17th. — This evening, as I lighted my bedroom-candle, I saw that the Captain had something to say to me. So I waited below until my host and his daughter had performed their usual osculation, and the latter had given me that confiding handshake which I never fail to extract.

'Prendergast has got his discharge,' said the old man, when he heard his daughter's door close.

'What do you mean?'

He pointed with his thumb to the room above, where we heard, through the thin partition, the movement of Miss Quarterman's light step.

'You mean that he has proposed to Miss Miriam?'

The Captain nodded.

'And has been refused?'

'Flat.'

'Poor fellow!' said I, very honestly. 'Did he tell you himself?'

'Yes, with tears in his eyes. He wanted me to speak for him. I told him it was no use. Then he began to say hard things of my poor girl.'

'What kind of things?'

'A pack of falsehoods. He says she has no heart. She has promised always to regard him as a friend; it's more than I will, hang him!'

'Poor fellow!' said I; and now, as I write, I can only repeat, considering what a hope was here disappointed, Poor fellow!

August 23rd. – I have been lounging about all day, thinking of it, dreaming of it, spooning over it, as they say. This is a decided waste of time. I think, accordingly, the best thing for me to do is to sit down and lay the ghost by writing out my little story.

On Thursday evening, Miss Quarterman happened to intimate that she had a holiday on the morrow, it being the birthday of the lady in whose establishment she teaches.

'There is to be a tea-party at four o'clock in the afternoon for the resident pupils and teachers,' Miriam said. 'Tea at four! what do you think of that? And then there is to be a speech-making by the smartest young lady. As my services are not required I propose to be absent. Suppose, father, you take us out in your boat. Will you come, Mr Locksley? We shall have a neat little picnic. Let us go over to old Fort Plunkett, across the bay. We will take our dinner with us, and send Cynthia to spend the day with her sister, and put the house-key in our pocket, and not come home till we please.'

I entered into the project with passion, and it was accordingly carried into execution the next morning, when – about ten o'clock – we pushed off from our little wharf at the garden-foot. It was a perfect summer's day; I can say no more for it; and we made a quiet run over to the point of our destination. I shall never forget the wondrous stillness which brooded over earth and water as we weighed anchor in the lee of my old friend – or old enemy – the ruined fort. The deep, translucent water reposed at the base of the warm sunlit cliff like a great basin of glass, which I half expected to hear shiver and crack as our keel ploughed through it. And how colour and sound stood out in the transparent air! How audibly the little ripples on the beach whispered to the open sky. How our irreverent voices seemed to jar upon the privacy of the little cove! The delicate rocks doubled themselves without a flaw in the clear, dark water. The gleaming white beach lay fringed with its deep deposits of odorous sea-weed, which looked like masses of black lace. The steep, straggling sides of the cliffs lifted their rugged angles against the burning blue of the sky. I remember, when Miss Quarterman stepped ashore and stood upon the beach, relieved against the cool darkness of a recess in the cliff, while her father and I busied ourselves with gathering up our baskets and fastening the anchor – I remember, I say, what a picture she made. There is a certain purity in the air of this place which I have never seen surpassed – a lightness, a brilliancy, a *crudity*, which allows perfect liberty of self-assertion to each individual object in the landscape. The prospect is ever more or less like a picture which lacks its final process, its reduction to unity. Miss Quarterman's figure, as she stood there on the beach, was almost *criarde*; but how it animated the whole scene! Her light muslin dress, gathered up over her white petticoat, her little black mantilla, the blue veil which she had knotted about her neck, the little silken dome which she poised over her head in one gloved hand, while the other retained her crisp draperies, and which cast down upon her face a sharp circle of shade, where her cheerful eyes shone darkly and her parted lips said things I lost – these are some of the points I hastily noted.

'Young woman,' I cried out, over the water, 'I do wish you might know how pretty you look!'

'How do you know I don't?' she answered. 'I should think I might. You don't look so badly yourself. But it's not I; it's the aerial perspective.'

'Hang it – I am going to become profane!' I called out again.

'Swear ahead,' said the Captain.

'I am going to say you are infernally handsome.'

'Dear me! is that all?' cried Miss Quarterman, with a little light laugh which must have made the tutelar sirens of the cove ready to die with jealousy down in their submarine bowers.

By the time the Captain and I had landed our effects our companion had tripped lightly up the forehead of the cliff – in one place it is very retreating – and disappeared over its crown. She soon returned, with an intensely white pocket-handkerchief added to her other provocations, which she waved to us, as we trudged upward, carrying our baskets. When we stopped to take breath on the summit and wipe our foreheads, we of course rebuked her for roaming about idly with her parasol and gloves.

'Do you think I am going to take any trouble or do any work?' cried Miss Miriam, in the greatest good-humour. 'Is not this my holiday? I am not going to raise a finger, nor soil these beautiful gloves, for which I paid so much at Mr Dawson's at Chowderville. After you have found a shady place for your provisions, I should like you to look for a spring. I am very thirsty.'

'Find the spring yourself, miss,' said her father. 'Mr Locksley and I have a spring in this basket. Take a pull, sir.'

And the Captain drew forth a stout black bottle.

'Give me a cup, and I will look for some water,' said Miriam. 'Only I'm so afraid of the snakes! If you hear a scream you may know it's a snake.'

'Screaming snakes!' said I; 'that's a new species.'

What cheap fun it all sounds now! As we looked about us shade seemed scarce, as it generally is in this region. But Miss Quarterman, like the very adroit and practical young person she is, for all that she would have me believe the contrary, immediately discovered flowing water in the shelter of a pleasant little dell, beneath a clump of firs. Hither, as one of the young gentlemen who imitate Tennyson would say, we brought our basket, he and I; while Miriam dipped the cup, and held it dripping to our thirsty lips, and laid the cloth, and on the grass disposed the platters round. I should have to be a poet, indeed, to describe half the happiness and the silly sweetness and artless revelry of this interminable summer's day. We ate and drank and talked; we ate occasionally with our fingers, we drank out of the necks of our bottles, and we talked with our mouths full, as befits (and excuses) those who talk perfect nonsense. We told stories without the least point. The Captain and I made atrocious puns. I believe, indeed, that Miss Quarterman herself made one little punkin, as I called it. If there had been any superfluous representative of humanity present to notice the fact, I should say that we made fools of ourselves. But as there was no one to criticize us we were brilliant enough. I am conscious myself of having said several witty things, which Miss Quarterman understood: *in vino veritas*. The dear old Captain twanged the long bow indefatigably. The bright high sun dawdled above us, in the same place, and drowned the prospect with light and warmth. One of these days I mean to paint a picture which, in future ages, when my dear native land shall boast a national school of art, will hang in the Salon Carré of the great central museum (located, let us say, in Chicago) and recall to folks – or rather make them forget – Giorgione, Bordone, and Veronese: *A Rural Festival*; three persons feasting under some trees; scene, nowhere in particular; time and hour, problematical. Female figure, a rich *brune*; young man reclining on his elbow; old man drinking. An empty sky, with no end of expression. The whole stupendous in colour, drawing, feeling. Artist uncertain; supposed to be Robinson, 1900.

After dinner the Captain began to look out across the bay, and, noticing the uprising of a little breeze, expressed a wish to cruise about for an hour or two. He proposed to us to walk along the shore to a point a couple of miles northward, and there meet the boat. His daughter having agreed to this proposition, he set off with the lightened hamper, and in less than half an hour we saw him standing out from shore. Miss Quarterman and I did not begin our walk for a long, long time. We sat and talked beneath the trees. At our feet a wide cleft in the hills – almost a glen – stretched down to the silent beach; beyond lay the familiar ocean-line. But, as many philosophers have observed, there is an end to all things. At last we got up. My companion remarked that, as the air was freshening, she supposed she ought to put on her shawl. I helped her to fold it into the proper shape, and then I placed it on her shoulders; it being an old shawl of faded red (Canton crape, I believe they call it), which I have seen very often. And then she tied her veil once more about her neck, and gave me her hat to hold, while she effected a partial redistribution of her hair-pins. By way of being humorous, I spun her hat round on my stick; at which she was kind enough to smile, as with downcast face and uplifted elbows she fumbled among her braids. And then she shook out the creases of her dress and drew on her gloves; and finally she said 'Well!' – that inevitable tribute to time and morality which follows upon even the mildest forms of dissipation. Very slowly it was that we wandered down the little glen. Slowly, too, we followed the course of the narrow and sinuous beach, as it keeps to the foot of the low cliffs. We encountered no sign of human life. Our conversation I need hardly repeat. I think I may trust it to the keeping of my memory; it was the sort of thing that comes back to one – after. If something ever happens which I think *may*, that apparently idle hour will seem, as one looks back, very symptomatic, and what we didn't say be perceived to have been more significant than what we did. There was something between us – there *is* something between us – and we listened to its impalpable presence – I liken it to the hum (very faint) of an unseen insect – in the golden stillness of the afternoon. I must add that if she expects, foresees, if she waits, she does so with a supreme serenity. If she is my fate (and she has the air of it), she is conscious that it's *her* fate to be so.

September 1st. – I have been working steadily for a week. This is the first day of autumn. Read aloud to Miss Quarterman a little Wordsworth.

September 10th. Midnight. – Worked without interruption – until yesterday, inclusive, that is. But with the day now closing – or opening – begins a new era. My poor vapid old diary, at last you shall hold a *fact*.

For three days past we have been having damp, autumnal weather; dusk has gathered early. This evening, after tea, the Captain went into town – on business, as he said: I believe, to attend some Poorhouse or Hospital Board. Miriam and I went into the parlour. The place seemed cold; she brought in the lamp from the dining-room, and proposed we should have a little fire. I went into the kitchen, procured half a dozen logs, and, while she drew the curtains and wheeled up the table, I kindled a lively, crackling blaze. A fortnight ago she would not have allowed me to do this without a protest. She would not have offered to do it herself – not she! – but she would have said that I was not here to serve, but to be served, and would at least have made a show of calling the negress. I should have had my own way, but we have changed all that. Miriam went to her piano, and I sat down to a book. I read not a word, but sat considering my fate and watching it come nearer and nearer. For the first time since I have known her (my fate) she had put on a dark, warm dress; I think it was of the material called alpaca. The first time I saw her (I remember such things) she wore a white dress with a blue neck-ribbon; now she wore a black dress with the same ribbon. That is, I remember wondering, as I sat there eyeing her, whether it *was* the same ribbon, or merely another like it. My heart was in my throat; and yet I thought of a number of trivialities of the same kind. At last I spoke.

'Miss Quarterman,' I said, 'do you remember the first evening I passed beneath your roof, last June?'

'Perfectly,' she replied, without stopping.

'You played that same piece.'

'Yes; I played it very badly, too. I only half knew it. But it is a showy piece, and I wished to produce an effect. I didn't know then how indifferent you are to music.'

'I paid no particular attention to the piece. I was intent upon the performer.'

'So the performer supposed.'

'What reason had you to suppose so?'

'I am sure I don't know. Did you ever know a woman to be able to give a reason when she has guessed aright?'

'I think they generally contrive to make up a reason afterwards. Come, what was yours?'

'Well, you stared so hard.'

'Fie! I don't believe it. That's unkind.'

'You said you wished me to invent a reason. If I really had one, I don't remember it.'

'You told me you remembered the occasion in question perfectly.'

'I meant the circumstances. I remember what we had for tea; I remember what dress I wore. But I don't remember my feelings. They were naturally not very memorable.'

'What did you say when your father proposed that I should come here?'

'I asked how much you would be willing to pay.'

'And then?'

'And then, if you looked respectable.'

'And then?'

'That was all. I told my father to do as he pleased.'

She continued to play, and leaning back in my chair I continued to look at her. There was a considerable pause.

'Miss Quarterman,' said I, at last.

'Well, sir?'

'Excuse me for interrupting you so often. But –' and I got up and went to the piano – 'but, you know, I thank Heaven that it has brought you and me together.'

She looked up at me and bowed her head with a little smile, as her hands still wandered over the keys.

'Heaven has certainly been very good to us,' said she.

'How much longer are you going to play?' I asked.

'I'm sure I don't know. As long as you like.'

'If you want to do as I like, you will stop immediately.'

She let her hands rest on the keys a moment, and gave me a rapid, questioning look. Whether she found a sufficient answer in my face I know not; but she slowly rose, and, with a very pretty affectation of obedience, began to close the instrument. I helped her to do so.

'Perhaps you would like to be quite alone,' she said. 'I suppose your own room is too cold.'

'Yes,' I answered, 'you have hit it exactly. I wish to be alone. I wish to monopolize this cheerful blaze. Hadn't you better go into the kitchen and sit with the cook? It takes you women to make such cruel speeches.'

'When we women are cruel, Mr Locksley, it is the merest accident. We are not wilfully so. When we learn that we have been unkind we very humbly ask pardon, without even knowing what our crime has been.' And she made me a very low curtsy.

'I will tell you what your crime has been,' said I. 'Come and sit by the fire. It's rather a long story.'

'A long story? Then let me get my work.'

'Confound your work! Excuse me, but you exasperate me. I want you to listen to me. Believe me, you will need all your attention.'

She looked at me steadily a moment, and I returned her glance. During that moment I was reflecting whether I might put my arm round her waist and kiss her; but I decided that I might do nothing of the sort. She walked over and quietly seated herself in a low chair by the fire. Here she patiently folded her arms. I sat down before her.

'With you, Miss Quarterman,' said I, 'one must be very explicit. You are not in the habit of taking things for granted. You have a great deal of imagination, but you rarely exercise it on behalf of other people.'

'Is that my crime?' asked my companion.

'It's not so much a crime as a vice, and perhaps not so much a vice as a virtue. Your crime is, that you are so stone-cold to a poor devil who loves you.'

She burst into a rather shrill laugh. I wonder whether she thought I meant Prendergast.

'Who are you speaking for, Mr Locksley?' she asked.

'Are there so many? For myself.'

'Honestly?'

'Do you think me capable of deceiving you?'

'What is that French phrase that you are forever using? I think I may say "*Allons donc!*"'

'Let us speak plain English, Miss Quarterman.'

'"Stone-cold" is certainly very plain English. I don't see the relative importance of the two branches of your proposition. Which is the principal, and which the subordinate clause – that I am stone-cold, as you call it, or that you love me, as you call it?'

'As I call it? What would you have me call it? For pity's sake, Miss Quarterman, be serious, or I shall call it something else. Yes, I love you. Don't you believe it?'

'How can I help believing what you tell me?'

'Dearest, bravest of women,' said I.

And I attempted to take her hand.

'No, no, Mr Locksley,' said she – 'not just yet, if you please.'

'Actions speak louder than words,' said I.

'There is no need of speaking loud. I hear you perfectly.'

'I certainly shall not whisper,' said I; 'although it is the custom, I believe, for lovers to do so. Will you be my wife?'

I don't know whether *she* whispered or not, but before I left her she consented.

September 12th. – We are to be married in about three weeks.

September 19th. – I have been in New York a week, transacting business. I got back yesterday. I find everyone here talking about our engagement. Miriam tells me that it was talked about a month ago, and that there is a very general feeling of disappointment that I am so very poor.

'Really, if you don't mind it,' I remarked, 'I don't see why others should.'

'I don't know whether you are poor or not,' says Miriam, 'but I know that I am rich.'

'Indeed! I was not aware that you had a private fortune,' etc. etc.

This little farce is repeated in some shape every day. I am very idle. I smoke a great deal, and lounge about all day, with my hands in my pockets. I am free from that ineffable weariness of ceaseless *buying* which I suffered from six months ago. That intercourse was conducted by means of little parcels, and I have resolved that this engagement, at all events, shall have no connection with the shops. I was cheated of my poetry once; I shan't be a second time. Fortunately there is not much danger of this, for my mistress is positively lyrical. She takes an enthusiastic interest in her simple outfit – showing me triumphantly certain of her purchases, and making a great mystery about others, which she is pleased to denominate table-cloths and napkins. Last evening I found her sewing buttons on a table-cloth. I had heard a great deal of a certain pink silk dress, and this morning, accordingly, she marched up to me, arrayed in this garment, upon which all the art and taste and eyesight, and all the velvet and lace, of Chowderville have been lavished.

'There is only one objection to it,' said Miriam, parading before the glass in my painting-room: 'I am afraid it is above our station.'

'By Jove! I will paint your portrait in it and make our fortune,' said I. 'All the other men who have handsome wives will bring them to be painted.'

'You mean all the women who have handsome dresses,' Miriam replied, with great humility.

Our wedding is fixed for next Thursday. I tell Miriam that it will be as little of a wedding, and as much of a marriage, as possible. Her father and her good friend Miss Blankenberg (the schoolmistress) alone are to be present. My secret oppresses me considerably; but I have resolved to keep it for the honeymoon, when it may leak out as occasion helps it. I am harassed with a dismal apprehension that if Miriam were to discover it now, the whole thing would have to be done over again. I have taken rooms at a romantic little watering-place called Cragthorpe, ten miles off. The hotel is already quite purged of cockneys, and we shall be almost alone.

September 28th. — We have been here two days. The little transaction in the church went off smoothly. I am truly sorry for the Captain. We drove directly over here, and reached the place at dusk. It was a raw, black day. We have a couple of good rooms, close to the savage sea. I am nevertheless afraid I have made a mistake. It would perhaps have been wiser to go to New York. These things are not immaterial; we make our own heaven, but we scarcely make our own earth. I am writing at a little table by the window, looking out on the rocks, the gathering dusk, the rising fog. My wife has wandered down to the rocky platform in front of the house. I can see her from here, bareheaded, in that old crimson shawl, talking to one of the landlord's little boys. She has just given the infant a kiss, bless her tender heart! I remember her telling me once that she was very fond of little boys; and, indeed, I have noticed that they are seldom too dirty for her to take on her knee. I have been reading over these pages for the first time in — I don't know when. They are filled with *her* — even more in thought than in word. I believe I will show them to her when she comes in. I will give her the book to read, and sit by her, watching her face – watching the great secret dawn upon her.

Later. – Somehow or other, I can write this quietly enough; but I hardly think I shall ever write any more. When Miriam came in I handed her this book.

'I want you to read it,' said I.

She turned very pale and laid it on the table, shaking her head.

'I know it,' she said.

'What do you know?'

'That you have ever so much money. But believe me, Mr Locksley, I am none the worse for the knowledge. You intimated in one place in your book that I am born for wealth and splendour. I verily believe I am. You pretend to hate your money; but you would not have had me without it. If you really love me – and I think you do – you will not let this make any difference. I am not such a fool as to attempt to talk now about what passed through me when you asked me to – to do *this*. But I remember what I said.'

'What do you expect me to do?' I asked. 'Shall I call you some horrible name and cast you off?'

'I expect you to show the same courage that I am showing. I never said I loved you. I never deceived you in that. I said I would be your wife. So I will, faithfully. I haven't so much heart as you think; and yet, too, I have a great deal more. I am incapable of more than one deception. – Mercy! didn't you see it?

didn't you know it? see that I saw it? know that I knew it? It was diamond cut diamond. You cheated me and I mystified you. Now that you tell me your secret I can tell you mine. *Now* we are free, with the fortune that you know. Excuse me, but it sometimes comes over me! *Now* we can be good and honest and true. It was all a make-believe virtue before.'

'So you read that thing?' I asked: actually – strange as it may seem – for something to say.

'Yes, while you were ill. It was lying with your pen in it, on the table. I read it because I suspected. Otherwise I wouldn't have done so.'

'It was the act of a false woman,' said I.

'A false woman? No, it was the act of any woman – placed as I was placed. You don't believe it?' And she began to smile. 'Come, you may abuse me in your diary if you like – I shall never peep into it again!'

A Day of Days

M R HERBERT MOORE, a gentleman of the highest note in the scientific world, and a childless widower, finding himself at last unable to reconcile his sedentary habits with the management of a household, had invited his only sister to come and superintend his domestic affairs. Miss Adela Moore had assented the more willingly to his proposal as by her mother's death she had recently been left without a formal protector. She was twenty-five years of age, and was a very active member of what she and her friends called society. She was almost equally at home in the best company of three great cities, and she had encountered most of the adventures which await a young girl on the threshold of life. She had become rather hastily and imprudently engaged, but she had eventually succeeded in disengaging herself. She had spent a summer or two in Europe, and she had made a voyage to Cuba with a dear friend in the last stage of consumption, who had died at the hotel in Havana. Although by no means perfectly beautiful in person she was yet thoroughly pleasing, rejoicing in what young ladies are fond of calling an *air*;

that is, she was tall and slender, with a long neck, a low forehead, and a handsome nose. Even after six years of the best company, too, she still had excellent manners. She was, moreover, mistress of a very pretty little fortune, and was accounted clever without detriment to her amiability and amiable without detriment to her wit. These facts, as the reader will allow, might have ensured her the very best prospects; but he has seen that she had found herself willing to forfeit her prospects and bury herself in the country. It seemed to her that she had seen enough of the world and of human nature, and that a period of seclusion might yield a fine refreshment. She had begun to suspect that for a girl of her age she was unduly old and wise – and, what is more, to suspect that others suspected as much. A great observer of life and manners, so far as her opportunities went, she conceived that it behoved her to organize the results of her observation into principles of conduct and belief. She was becoming – so she argued – too impersonal, too critical, too intelligent, too contemplative, too just. A woman had no business to be so just. The society of nature, of the great expansive skies and the primeval woods, would check the morbid development of her brain-power. She would spend her time in the fields and merely vegetate; walk and ride, and read the old-fashioned books in Herbert's library.

She found her brother established in a very pretty house, at about a mile's distance from the nearest town, and at about six miles' distance from another town, the seat of a small but ancient college, before which he delivered a weekly lecture. She had seen so little of him of late years that his acquaintance was almost to make; but there were no barriers to break down. Herbert Moore was one of the simplest and least aggressive of men, and one of the most patient and conscientious of students. He had had a vague notion that Adela was a young woman of extravagant pleasures, and that, somehow, on her arrival, his house would be overrun with the train of her attendant revellers. It was not until after they had been six months together that he became aware that his sister had led almost an ascetic life. By the time six months more had passed Adela had recovered a delightful sense of youth and *naïveté*. She learned, under her brother's tuition, to walk – nay, to climb, for there were great hills in the neighbourhood – to ride and to botanize. At the end of a year, in the month of August, she received a visit from an old friend, a girl of her own age, who had been spending July at a watering-place, and who was now about to be married. Adela had begun to fear that she had declined into an almost irreclaimable rusticity and had rubbed off the social facility, the 'knowledge of the world' for which she was formerly distinguished; but a week spent in intimate conversation with her friend convinced her not only that she had not forgotten much that she had feared, but had also not forgotten much that she had hoped. For this, and other reasons, her friend's departure left her slightly depressed. She felt lonely and even a little elderly – she had lost another illusion. Laura Benton, for whom a year ago she had entertained a serious regard, now impressed her as a very flimsy little person, who talked about her lover with almost indecent flippancy.

Meanwhile, September was slowly running its course. One morning Mr Moore took a hasty breakfast and started to catch the train for Slowfield, whither a scientific conference called him, which might, he said, release him that afternoon in time for dinner at home, or might, on the other hand, detain him until the night. It was almost the first time during the term of Adela's rustication that she had been left alone for several hours. Her brother's quiet presence was inappreciable enough; yet now that he was at a distance she felt a singular sense of freedom: a return of that condition of early childhood when, through some domestic catastrophe, she had for an infinite morning been left to her own devices. What should she do? she asked herself, with the smile that she reserved for her maidenly monologues. It was a good day for work, but it was a still better one for play. Should she drive into town and call on a lot of tiresome local people? Should she go into the kitchen and try her hand at a pudding for dinner? She felt a delectable longing to do something illicit, to play with fire, to discover some Bluebeard's closet. But poor Herbert was no Bluebeard; if she were to burn down his house he would exact no amends. Adela went out to the verandah, and, sitting down on the steps, gazed across the country. It was apparently the last day of summer. The sky was faintly blue; the woody hills were putting on the morbid colours of autumn; the great pine-grove behind the house seemed to have caught and imprisoned the protesting breezes. Looking down the road toward the village, it occurred to Adela that she might have a visit, and so human was her mood that if any of the local people were to come to her she felt it was in her to humour them. As the sun rose higher she went in and established herself with a piece of embroidery in a deep bow-window, in the second storey, which, betwixt its muslin curtains and its external frame-work of high-creeping plants, commanded most insidiously the principal approach to the house. While she drew her threads she surveyed the road with a deepening conviction that she was destined to have a caller. The air was warm, yet not hot; the dust had been laid during the night by a gentle rain. It had been from the first a source of complaint among Adela's new friends that she was equally gracious to all men, and, what was more remarkable, to all women. Not only had she dedicated herself to no friendships, but she had committed herself to no preferences. Nevertheless, it was with an imagination by no means severely impartial that she sat communing with her open casement. She had very soon made up her mind that, to answer the requirements of the hour, her visitor must be of a sex as different as possible from her own; and as, thanks to the few differences in favour of any individual she had been able to discover among the young males of the country-side, her roll-call in this her hour of need was limited to a single name, so her thoughts were now centred upon the bearer of that name, Mr Weatherby Pynsent, the Unitarian minister. If instead of being Miss Moore's story this were Mr Pynsent's, it might easily be condensed into the simple statement that he was very far gone indeed. Although affiliated to a richer ceremonial that his own she had been so well pleased with one of his sermons, to which she had allowed herself to lend a tolerant ear, that, meeting him some time afterward, she had received him with what she considered a rather knotty doctrinal question; whereupon, gracefully waiving the question, he had asked permission to call upon her and talk over her 'difficulties'. This short interview had enshrined her in the young minister's heart; and the half a dozen occasions on which he had subsequently contrived to see her had each contributed another candle to her altar. It is but fair to add, however, that, although a captive, Mr Pynsent was as yet no captor. He was simply an honourable young parson, who happened at this moment to be the most sympathetic companion within reach. Adela, at twenty-five years of age, had both a past and a future. Mr Pynsent reminded her of the one and gave her a foretaste of the other.

So, at last, when, as the morning waned toward noon, Adela descried in the distance a man's figure treading the grassy margin of the road, and swinging his stick as he came, she smiled to herself with some complacency. But even while she smiled she became conscious that her heart was beating quite idiotically. She rose, and, resenting her gratuitous emotion, stood for a moment half resolved to see no one at all. As she did so she glanced along the road again. Her friend had drawn nearer, and as the distance lessened she began to perceive that he was not her friend. Before many moments her doubts were removed; the gentleman was a stranger. In front of the house three roads went their different ways, and a spreading elm, tall and slim, like the feathery sheaf of a gleaner, with an ancient bench beneath it, made an informal *rond-point*. The stranger came along the opposite side of the highway, and when he reached the elm stopped and looked about him, as if to verify some direction that had been given him. Then he deliberately crossed over. Adela had time to see, unseen, that he was a robust young man, with a bearded chin and a soft white hat. After the due interval Becky the maid came up with a card somewhat rudely superscribed in pencil:

THOMAS LUDLOW,
New York.

Turning it over in her fingers, Adela saw the gentleman had made use of the reverse of a pasteboard abstracted from the basket on her own drawing-room table. The printed name on the other side was dashed out; it ran: *Mr Weatherby Pynsent*.

'He asked me to give you this, ma'am,' said Becky. 'He helped himself to it out of the tray.'

'Did he ask for me by name?'

'No, ma'am; he asked for Mr Moore. When I told him Mr Moore was away, he asked for some of the family. I told him you was all the family, ma'am.'

'Very well,' said Adela, 'I will go down.' But, begging her pardon, we will precede her by a few steps.

Tom Ludlow, as his friends called him, was a young man of twenty-eight, concerning whom you might have heard the most various opinions; for, as far as he was known (which, indeed, was not very far), he was at once one of the best liked and one of the best hated of men. Born in one of the lower walks of New York life, he still seemed always to move in his native element. A certain crudity of manner and aspect proved him to belong to the great vulgar, muscular, popular majority. On this basis, however, he was a sufficiently good-looking fellow: a middle-sized, agile figure, a head so well shaped as to be handsome, a pair of inquisitive, responsive eyes, and a large, manly mouth, constituting the most expressive part of his equipment. Turned upon the world at an early age, he had, in the pursuit of a subsistence, tried his head at everything in succession, and had generally found it to be quite as hard as the opposing substance; and his person may have been thought to reflect this experience in an air of taking success too much for granted. He was a man of strong faculties and a strong will, but it is doubtful whether his feelings were stronger than he. People liked him for his directness, his good-humour, his general soundness and serviceableness, and disliked him for the same qualities under different names; that is, for his impudence, his offensive optimism, his inhuman avidity for facts. When his friends insisted upon his noble disinterestedness, his enemies were wont to reply it was all very well to ignore, to suppress, one's own sensibilities in the pursuit of knowledge, but to trample the rest of mankind at the same time betrayed an excess of zeal. Fortunately for Ludlow, on the whole, he was no great listener, and even if he had been, a certain plebeian thick-skinnedness would always have saved his tenderer parts;

although it must be added that, if, like a genuine democrat, he was very insensitive, like a genuine democrat, too, he was unexpectedly proud. His tastes, which had always been for the natural sciences, had recently led him to the study of fossil remains, the branch cultivated by Herbert Moore; and it was upon business connected with this pursuit that, after a short correspondence, he had now come to see him.

As Adela went to him he came out from the window, where he had been looking at the lawn. She acknowledged the friendly nod which he apparently intended for a greeting.

'Miss Moore, I believe,' said Ludlow.

'Miss Moore,' said Adela.

'I beg your pardon for this intrusion, but as I have come from a distance to see Mr Moore, on business, I thought I might venture either to ask at headquarters how he may most easily be reached, or even to give you a message for him.' These words were accompanied with a smile under the influence of which it had been written on the scroll of Adela's fate that she was to descend from her pedestal.

'Pray make no apologies,' she said. 'We hardly recognize such a thing as intrusion in this simple little place. Won't you sit down? My brother went away only this morning, and I expect him back this afternoon.'

'This afternoon? indeed. In that case I believe I'll wait. It was very stupid of me not to have dropped a word beforehand. But I have been in the city all summer long, and I shall not be sorry to squeeze a little vacation out of this business. I'm tremendously fond of the country, and I have been working for many months in a musty museum.'

'It's possible that my brother may not come home until the evening,' Adela said. 'He was uncertain. You might go to him at Slowfield.'

Ludlow reflected a moment, with his eyes on his hostess. 'If he does return in the afternoon, at what hour will he arrive?'

'Well, about three.'

'And my own train leaves at four. Allow him a quarter of an hour to come from town and myself a quarter of an hour to get there (if he would give me his vehicle back). In that case I should have about half an hour to see him. We couldn't do much talk, but I could ask him the essential questions. I wish chiefly to ask him for some letters – letters of recommendation to some foreign scientists. He is the only man in this country who knows how much I know. It seems a pity to take two superfluous – that is, possibly superfluous – railway-journeys, of an hour apiece; for I should probably come back with him. Don't you think so?' he asked, very frankly.

'You know best,' said Adela. 'I am not particularly fond of the journey to Slowfield, even when it's absolutely necessary.'

'Yes; and then this is such a lovely day for a good long ramble in the fields. That's a thing I haven't had since I don't know when. I guess I'll remain.' And he placed his hat on the floor beside him.

'I am afraid, now that I think of it,' said Adela, 'that there is no train until so late an hour that you would have very little time left on your arrival to talk with my brother, before the hour at which he himself might have determined to start for home. It's true that you might induce him to stop over till the evening.'

'Dear me! I shouldn't want to do that. It might be very inconvenient for Mr Moore, don't you see? Besides, I shouldn't have time. And then I always like to see a man in his home – or at some place of my own; a man, that is, whom I have any regard for – and I have a very great regard for your brother, Miss Moore. When men meet at a half-way house neither feels at his ease. And then this is such an attractive country residence of yours,' pursued Ludlow, looking about him.

'Yes, it's a very pretty place,' said Adela.

Ludlow got up and walked to the window. 'I want to look at your view,' he remarked. 'A lovely little spot. You are a happy woman, Miss Moore, to have the beauties of nature always before your eyes.'

'Yes, if pretty scenery can make one happy, I ought to be happy.' And Adela was glad to regain her feet and stand on the other side of the table, before the window.

'Don't you think it can?' asked Ludlow, turning around. 'I don't know, though; perhaps it can't. Ugly sights can't make you unhappy, necessarily. I have been working for a year in one of the narrowest, darkest, dirtiest, busiest streets in New York, with rusty bricks and muddy gutters for scenery. But I think I can hardly set up to be miserable. I wish I could! It might be a claim on your benevolence.' As he said these words he stood leaning against the window-shutter, outside the curtain, with folded arms. The morning light covered his face, and, mingled with that of his radiant laugh, showed Adela that his was a nature very much alive.

'Whatever else he may be,' she said to herself, as she stood within the shade of the other curtain, playing with the paper-knife, which she had plucked from the table, 'I think he is honest. I am afraid he isn't a gentleman – but he isn't a bore.' She met his eye, freely, for a moment. 'What do you want of my benevolence?' she asked, with an abruptness of which she was perfectly conscious. 'Does he wish to make friends,' she pursued, tacitly, 'or does he merely wish to pay me a vulgar compliment? There is bad taste, perhaps, in either case, but especially in the latter.' Meanwhile her visitor had already answered her.

'What do I want of your benevolence? Why, what does one want of any pleasant thing in life?'

'Dear me, if you never have anything pleasanter than that!' our heroine exclaimed.

'It will do very well for the present occasion,' said the young man, blushing, in a large masculine way, at his own quickness of repartee.

Adela glanced toward the clock on the chimney-piece. She was curious to measure the duration of her acquaintance with this breezy invader of her privacy, with whom she so suddenly found herself bandying jokes so personal. She had known him some eight minutes.

Ludlow observed her movement. 'I am interrupting you and detaining you from your own affairs,' he said; and he moved toward his hat. 'I suppose I must bid you good-morning.' And he picked it up.

Adela stood at the table and watched him cross the room. To express a very delicate feeling in terms comparatively crude, she was loath to see him depart. She divined, too, that he was very sorry to go. The knowledge of this feeling on his side, however, affected her composure but slightly. The truth is – we say it with all respect – Adela was an old hand. She was modest, honest and wise; but, as we have said, she had a past – a past of which importunate swains in the guise of morning-callers had been no inconsiderable part; and a great dexterity in what may be called outflanking these gentlemen was one of her registered accomplishments. Her liveliest emotion at present, therefore, was less one of annoyance at her companion than of surprise at her own mansuetude, which was yet undeniable. 'Am I dreaming?' she asked herself. She looked out of the window, and then back at Ludlow, who stood grasping his hat and stick, contemplating her face. Should she give him leave to remain? 'He is honest,' she repeated; 'why should not I be honest for once?' 'I am sorry you are in a hurry,' she said, aloud.

'I am in no hurry,' he answered.

Adela turned her face to the window again, and toward the opposite hills. There was a moment's pause.

'I thought *you* were in a hurry,' said Ludlow.

Adela shifted her eyes back to where they could see him. 'My brother would be very glad that you should stay as long as you

97

like. He would expect me to offer you what little hospitality is in my power.'

'Pray, offer it then.'

'That is very easily done. This is the parlour, and there, beyond the hall, is my brother's study. Perhaps you would like to look at his books and his collections. I know nothing about them, and I should be a very poor guide. But you are welcome to go in and use your discretion in examining what may interest you.'

'This, I take it, would be but another way of separating from you.'

'For the present, yes.'

'But I hesitate to take such liberties with your brother's things as you recommend.'

'Recommend? I recommend nothing.'

'But if I decline to penetrate into Mr Moore's sanctum, what alternative remains?'

'Really – you must make your own alternative.'

'I think you mentioned the parlour. Suppose I choose that.'

'Just as you please. Here are some books, and if you like I will bring you some periodicals. There are ever so many scientific papers. Can I serve you in any other way? Are you tired by your walk? Would you like a glass of wine?'

'Tired by my walk? – not exactly. You are very kind, but I feel no immediate desire for a glass of wine. I think you needn't trouble yourself about the scientific periodicals either. I am not exactly in the mood to read.' And Ludlow pulled out his watch and compared it with the clock. 'I am afraid your clock is fast.'

'Yes,' said Adela; 'very likely.'

'Some ten minutes. Well, I suppose I had better be walking.' And, coming toward Adela, he extended his hand.

She gave him hers. 'It is a day of days for a long, slow ramble,' she said.

Ludlow's only rejoinder was his hand-shake. He moved slowly toward the door, half accompanied by Adela. 'Poor fellow!' she said to herself. There was a summer-door, composed of lattices painted green, like a shutter; it admitted into the hall a cool, dusky light, in which Adela looked pale. Ludlow pushed its wings apart with his stick, and disclosed a landscape, long, deep, and bright, framed by the pillars of the porch. He stopped on the threshold, swinging his cane. 'I hope I shall not lose my way,' he said.

'I hope not. My brother will not forgive me if you do.'

Ludlow's brows were slightly contracted by a frown, but he contrived to smile with his lips. 'When shall I come back?' he asked, abruptly.

Adela found but a low tone – almost a whisper – at her command to answer – 'Whenever you please.'

The young man turned about, with his back to the bright doorway, and looked into Adela's face, which was now covered with light. 'Miss Moore,' said he, 'it's very much against my will that I leave you at all!'

Adela stood debating within herself. After all, what if her companion should stay with her? It would, under the circumstances, be an adventure; but was an adventure necessarily a criminal thing? It lay wholly with herself to decide. She was her own mistress, and she had hitherto been a just mistress. Might she not for once be a generous one? The reader will observe in Adela's meditation the recurrence of this saving clause 'for once'. It was produced by the simple fact that she had begun the day in a romantic mood. She was prepared to be interested; and now that an interesting phenomenon had presented itself, that it stood before her in vivid human — nay, manly — shape, instinct with reciprocity, was she to close her hand to the liberality of fate? To do so would be only to expose herself the more, for it would imply a gratuitous insult to human nature. Was not the man before her redolent of good intentions, and was that not enough? He was not what Adela had been used to call a gentleman; at this conviction she had arrived by a rapid diagonal, and now it served as a fresh starting-point. 'I have seen all the gentlemen can show me' (this was her syllogism): 'let us try something new!' 'I see no reason why you should run away so fast, Mr Ludlow,' she said, aloud.

'I think it would be the greatest piece of folly I ever committed!' cried the young man.

'I think it would be rather a pity,' Adela remarked.

'And you invite me into your parlour again? I come as *your* visitor, you know. I was your brother's before. It's a simple enough matter. We are old friends. We have a solid common ground in your brother. Isn't that about it?'

'You may adopt whatever theory you please. To my mind it is indeed a very simple matter.'

'Oh, but I wouldn't have it too simple,' said Ludlow, with a genial smile.

'Have it as you please!'

Ludlow leaned back against the doorway. 'Look here, Miss Moore; your kindness makes me as gentle as a little child. I am passive; I am in your hands; do with me what you please. I can't help contrasting my fate with what it might have been but for you. A quarter of an hour ago I was ignorant of your existence; you were not in my programme. I had no idea your brother had a sister. When your servant spoke of "Miss Moore", upon my word I expected something rather elderly – something venerable – some rigid old lady, who would say "exactly", and "very well, sir", and leave me to spend the rest of the morning tilting back in a chair on the piazza of the hotel. It shows what fools we are to attempt to forecast the future.'

'We must not let our imagination run away with us in any direction,' said Adela, sententiously.

'Imagination? I don't believe I have any. No, madam –' and Ludlow straightened himself up – 'I live in the present. I write my programme from hour to hour – or, at any rate, I will in the future.'

'I think you are very wise,' said Adela. 'Suppose you write a programme for the present hour. What shall we do? It seems to me a pity to spend so lovely a morning in-doors. There is something in the air – I can't imagine what – which seems to say it is the last day of summer. We ought to commemorate it. How should you like to take a walk?' Adela had decided that, to reconcile her aforesaid benevolence with the proper maintenance of her dignity, her only course was to be the perfect hostess. This decision made, very naturally and gracefully she played her part. It was the one possible part; and yet it did not preclude those delicate sensations with which so rare an episode seemed charged: it simply legitimated them. A romantic adventure on so conventional a basis would assuredly hurt no one.

'I should like a walk very much,' said Ludlow; 'a walk with a halt at the end of it.'

'Well, if you will consent to a short halt at the beginning of it,' Adela rejoined, 'I will be with you in a very few minutes.' When she returned, in her little hat and jacket, she found her friend seated on the steps of the verandah. He arose and gave her a card.

'I have been requested, in your absence, to hand you this.'

Adela read with some compunction the name of Mr Weatherby Pynsent.

'Has he been here?' she asked. 'Why didn't he come in?'

'I told him you were not at home. If it wasn't true then, it was going to be true so soon that the interval was hardly worth taking account of. He addressed himself to me, as I seemed from my position to be quite in possession; that is, I put myself in his way, as it were, so that he had to speak to me: but I confess he looked at me as if he doubted my word. He hesitated as to whether he should confide his name to me, or whether he should ring for the servant. I think he wished to show me that he suspected my veracity, for he was making rather grimly for the door-bell when I, fearing that once inside the house he might encounter the living truth, informed him in the most good-humoured tone possible that I would take charge of his little tribute, if he would trust me with it.'

'It seems to me, Mr Ludlow, that you are a strangely unscrupulous man. How did you know that Mr Pynsent's business was not urgent?'

I didn't know it! But I knew it could be no more urgent than mine. Depend upon it, Miss Moore, you have no case against me. I only pretend to be a man; to have admitted that sweet little cleric – isn't he a cleric, eh? – would have been the act of an angel.'

Adela was familiar with a sequestered spot, in the very heart of the fields, as it seemed to her, to which she now proposed to conduct her friend. The point was to select a goal neither too distant nor too near, and to adopt a pace neither too rapid nor too slow. But, although Adela's happy valley was at least two miles away, and they had dawdled immensely over the interval, yet their arrival at a certain little rustic gate, beyond which the country grew vague and gently wild, struck Adela as sudden. Once on the road she felt a precipitate conviction that there could be no evil in an excursion so purely pastoral and no guile in a spirit so deeply sensitive to the influences of nature, and to the melancholy aspect of incipient autumn, as that of her companion. A man with an unaffected relish for small children is a man to inspire young women with a confidence; and so, in a less degree, a man with a genuine feeling for the unsophisticated

beauties of a casual New England landscape may not unreason-
ably be regarded by the daughters of the scene as a person whose
motives are pure. Adela was a great observer of the clouds, the
trees and the streams, the sounds and colours, the transparent
airs and blue horizons of her adopted home; and she was reassured by Ludlow's appreciation of these modest phenomena.
His enjoyment of them, deep as it was, however, had to struggle
against the sensuous depression natural to a man who has spent
the summer looking over dry specimens in a laboratory, and
against an impediment of a less material order – the feeling that
Adela was a remarkably attractive woman. Still, naturally a
great talker, he uttered his various satisfactions with abundant
humour and point. Adela felt that he was decidedly a companion for the open air – he was a man to make use, even to abuse,
of the wide horizon and the high ceiling of nature. The freedom
of his gestures, the sonority of his voice, the keenness of his
vision, the general vivacity of his manners, seemed to necessi-
tate and to justify a universal absence of resisting surfaces. They
passed through the little gate and wandered over empty pastures,
until the ground began to rise, and stony surfaces to crop
through the turf, when, after a short ascent, they reached a
broad plateau, covered with boulders and shrubs, which lost
itself on one side in a short, steep cliff, whence fields and marshes
stretched down to the opposite river, and on the other, in scattered clumps of cedar and maple, which gradually thickened
and multiplied, until the horizon in that quarter was purple with
mild masses of forest. Here was both sun and shade – the

unobstructed sky, or the whispering dome of a circle of trees which had always reminded Adela of the stone-pines of the Villa Borghese. Adela led the way to a sunny seat among the rocks which commanded the course of the river, where the murmuring cedars would give them a kind of human company.

'It has always seemed to me that the wind in the trees is always the voice of coming changes,' Ludlow said.

'Perhaps it is,' Adela replied. 'The trees are forever talking in this melancholy way, and men are forever changing.'

'Yes, but they can only be said to express the foreboding of coming events – that is what I mean – when there is someone there to hear them; and more especially someone in whose life a change is, to his knowledge, about to take place. Then they are quite prophetic. Don't you know Longfellow says so?'

'Yes, I know Longfellow says so. But you seem to speak from your own inspiration.'

'Well, I rather think I do.'

'Is there some great change hanging over you?'

'Yes, rather an important one.'

'I believe that's what men say when they are going to be married,' said Adela.

'I am going to be divorced, rather. I am going to Europe.'

'Indeed! soon?'

'Tomorrow,' said Ludlow, after an instant's pause.

'Oh!' exclaimed Adela. 'How I envy you!'

Ludlow, who sat looking over the cliff and tossing stones down into the plain, observed a certain inequality in the tone of his companion's two exclamations. The first was nature, the second art. He turned his eyes upon her, but she had directed hers away into the distance. Then, for a moment, he retreated within himself and thought. He rapidly surveyed his position. Here was he, Tom Ludlow, a hard-headed son of toil; without fortune, without credit, without antecedents, whose lot was cast exclusively with vulgar males, and who had never had a mother, a sister, nor a well-bred sweetheart, to pitch his voice for the feminine tympanum, who had seldom come nearer an indubitable lady than, in a favouring crowd, to receive a mechanical 'thank you' (as if he were a policeman) for some accidental assistance: here he found himself up to his neck in a sudden pastoral with a young woman who was evidently altogether superior. That it was in him to enjoy the society of such a person (provided, of course, she were not a chit) he very well knew; but he had never happened to suppose that he should find it open to him. Was he now to infer that this brilliant gift was his – the gift of what is called in the relation between the sexes success? The inference was at least logical. He had made a good impression. Why else should an eminently discriminating girl have fraternized with him at such a rate? It was with a little thrill of satisfaction that Ludlow reflected upon the directness of his course. 'It all comes back to my old theory that a process can't be too simple. I used no arts. In such an enterprise I shouldn't have known where to begin. It was my ignorance of the regular way that saved me. Women like a gentleman, of course; but they like a man better.' It was the little touch of nature he had detected in Adela's tone that set him thinking; but as compared with the frankness of his own attitude it betrayed after all no undue emotion. Ludlow had accepted the fact of his adaptability to the idle mood of a cultivated woman in a thoroughly rational spirit, and he was not now tempted to exaggerate its bearings. He was not the man to be intoxicated by a triumph after all possibly superficial. 'If Miss Moore is so wise – or so foolish – as to like me half an hour for what I am, she is welcome,' he said to himself. 'Assuredly,' he added, as he glanced at her intelligent profile, 'she will not like me for what I am not.' It needs a woman, however, far more intelligent than (thank Heaven!) most women are – more intelligent, certainly, than Adela was – to guard her happiness against a clever man's consistent assumption of her intelligence; and doubtless it was from a sense of this general truth that, as Ludlow continued to observe his companion, he felt an emotion of manly tenderness. 'I wouldn't offend her for the world,' he thought. Just then Adela, conscious of his contemplation, looked about; and before he knew it, Ludlow had repeated aloud, 'Miss Moore, I wouldn't offend you for the world.'

Adela eyed him for a moment with a little flush that subsided into a smile. 'To what dreadful impertinence is that the prelude?' she inquired.

'It's the prelude to nothing. It refers to the past – to any possible displeasure I may have caused you.'

'Your scruples are unnecessary, Mr Ludlow. If you had given me offence, I should not have left you to apologize for it. I should not have left the matter to occur to you as you sat dreaming charitably in the sun.'

'What would you have done?'

'Done? nothing. You don't imagine I would have scolded you – or snubbed you – or answered you back, I take it. I would have left undone – what, I can't tell you. Ask yourself what I *have* done. I am sure I hardly know myself,' said Adela, with some intensity. 'At all events, here I am sitting with you in the fields, as if you were a friend of many years. Why do you speak of offence?' And Adela (an uncommon accident with her) lost command of her voice, which trembled ever so slightly. 'What an odd thought! why should you offend me? Do I seem so open to that sort of thing?' Her colour had deepened again, and her eyes had brightened. She had forgotten herself, and before speaking had not, as was her wont, sought counsel of that staunch conservative, her taste. She had spoken from a full heart – a heart which had been filling rapidly, since the outset of their walk, with a feeling almost passionate in its quality, and which that little puff of the actual conveyed in Mr Ludlow's announcement of his departure had caused to overflow. The reader may give this feeling whatever name he chooses. We will content ourselves with saying that Adela had played with fire so effectually that she had been scorched. The slight violence of the speech just quoted may represent her sensation of pain.

'You pull one up rather short, Miss Moore,' said Ludlow. 'A man says the best he can.'

Adela made no reply – for a moment she hung her head. Was she to cry out because she was hurt? Was she to thrust her injured heart into a company in which there was, as yet at least, no question of hearts? No! here our reserved and contemplative heroine is herself again. Her part was still to be the youthful woman of the world, the perfect young lady. For our own part, we can imagine no figure more engaging than this civilized and disciplined personage under such circumstances; and if Adela had been the most accomplished of coquettes she could not have assumed a more becoming expression than the air of judicious consideration which now covered her features. But having paid this generous homage to propriety, she felt free to suffer in secret. Raising her eyes from the ground, she abruptly addressed her companion.

'By the way, Mr Ludlow, tell me something about yourself.'

Ludlow burst into a laugh. 'What shall I tell you?'

'Everything.'

'Everything? Excuse me, I'm not such a fool. But do you know that's a very tempting request you make? I suppose I ought to blush and hesitate; but I never yet blushed or hesitated in the right place.'

'Very good. There is one fact. Continue. Begin at the beginning.'

'Well, let me see. My name you know. I am twenty-eight years old.'

'That's the end,' said Adela.

'But you don't want the history of my babyhood, I take it. I imagine that I was a very big, noisy, ugly baby – what's called a "splendid infant". My parents were poor, and, of course, honest. They belonged to a very different set – or "sphere", I suppose you call it – from any you probably know. They were working people. My father was a chemist, in a small way of business, and I suspect my mother was not above using her hands to turn a penny. But although I don't remember her, I am sure she was a good, sound woman; I feel her occasionally in my own sinews. I myself have been at work all my life, and a very good worker I am, let me tell you. I am not patient, as I imagine your brother to be – although I have more patience than you might suppose – but I don't let go easily. If I strike you as very egotistical, remember 'twas you began it. I don't know whether I am clever, and I don't much care; that's a kind of metaphysical, sentimental, vapid word. But I know what I want to know, and I generally manage to find it out. I don't know much about my moral nature; I have no doubt I am beastly selfish. Still, I don't like to hurt people's feelings, and I am rather fond of poetry and flowers. I don't believe I am very "high-toned", all the same. I should not be at all surprised to discover I was prodigiously conceited; but I am afraid the discovery wouldn't cut me down much. I am remarkably hard to keep down, I know. Oh, you would think me a great brute if you knew me. I shouldn't recommend anyone to count too much on my being of an amiable disposition. I am often very much bored with people who are fond of me – because some of them are, really; so I am afraid I am ungrateful. Of course, as a man speaking to a woman, there's nothing for it but to say I am very low; but I hate to talk about things you can't prove. I have got very little "general culture", you know, but first and last I have read a great many books – and, thank Heaven, I remember things. And I have some tastes, too. I am very fond of music. I have a good young voice of my own: *that* I can't help knowing; and I am not one to be bullied about pictures. I know how to sit on a horse, and how to row a boat. Is that enough? I am conscious of a great inability to say anything to the point. To put myself in a nutshell, I am a greedy specialist – and not a bad fellow. Still, I am only what I am – a very common creature.'

'Do you call yourself a very common creature because you really believe yourself to be one, or because you are weakly tempted to disfigure your rather flattering catalogue with a great final blot?'

'I am sure I don't know. You show more subtlety in that one question than I have shown in a whole string of affirmations. You women are strong on asking embarrassing questions. Seriously, I believe I *am* second-rate. I wouldn't make such an admission to everyone though. But to you, Miss Moore, who sit there under your parasol as impartial as the muse of history, to you I owe the truth. I am no man of genius. There is something I miss; some final distinction I lack; you may call it what you please. Perhaps it's humility. Perhaps you can find it in Ruskin, somewhere. Perhaps it's delicacy – perhaps it's imagination. I am very vulgar, Miss Moore. I am the vulgar son of vulgar people. I use the word, of course, in its literal sense. So much I grant you at the outset, but it's my last concession!'

'Your concessions are smaller than they sound. Have you any sisters?'

'Not a sister; and no brothers, nor cousins, nor uncles, nor aunts.'

'And you sail for Europe tomorrow?'

'Tomorrow, at ten o'clock.'

'To be away how long?'

'As long as I can. Five years, if possible.'

'What do you expect to do in those five years?'

'Well, study.'

'Nothing but study?'

'It will all come back to that, I guess. I hope to enjoy myself considerably, and to look at the world as I go. But I must not waste time; I am growing old.'

'Where are you going?'

'To Berlin. I wanted to get some letters of introduction from your brother.'

'Have you money? Are you well-off?'

'Well-off? Not I, Heaven forgive me! I am very poor. I have in hand a little money that has just come to me from an unexpected quarter: an old debt owing my father. It will take me to Germany and keep me for six months. After that I shall work my way.'

'Are you happy? Are you contented?'

'Just now I am pretty comfortable, thank you.'

'But shall you be so when you get to Berlin?'

'I don't promise to be contented; but I am pretty sure to be happy.'

'Well,' said Adela, 'I sincerely hope you will succeed in everything.'

'Thank you, awfully,' said Ludlow.

Of what more was said at this moment no record may be given here. The reader has been put into possession of the key of our friends' conversation; it is only needful to say that in this key it was prolonged for half an hour more. As the minutes elapsed Adela found herself drifting further and further away from her anchorage. When at last she compelled herself to consult her watch and remind her companion that there remained but just time enough for them to reach home in anticipation of her brother's arrival, she knew that she was rapidly floating seaward. As she descended the hill at her companion's side she felt herself suddenly thrilled by an acute temptation. Her first instinct was to close her eyes upon it, in the trust that when she should open them again it would have vanished; but she found that it was not to be so uncompromisingly dismissed. It pressed her so hard that before she walked a mile homeward she had succumbed to it, or had at least given it the pledge of that quickening of the heart which accompanies a bold resolution. This little sacrifice allowed her no breath for idle words, and she accordingly advanced with a bent and listening head. Ludlow marched along, with no apparent diminution of his habitual buoyancy of mien, talking as fast and as loud as at the outset. He risked a prophecy that Mr Moore would not have returned, and charged Adela with a comical message of regrets. Adela had begun by wondering whether the approach of their separation had wrought within him any sentimental depression at all commensurate with her own, with that which sealed her lips and weighed upon her heart; and now she was debating as to whether his express declaration that he felt 'awfully blue' ought necessarily to remove her doubts. Ludlow followed up this declaration with a very pretty review of the morning, and a leave-taking speech which, whether intensely sincere or not, struck Adela as at least in very good taste. He might be a common creature – but he was certainly a very uncommon one. When they reached the garden-gate it was with a fluttering heart that Adela scanned the premises for some accidental sign of her brother's presence. She felt that there would be an especial fitness in his not having returned. She led the way in. The hall table was bare of his usual hat and overcoat, his silver-headed stick was not in the corner. The only object that struck her was Mr Pynsent's card, which she had deposited there on her exit. All that was represented by that little white ticket seemed a thousand miles away. She looked for Mr Moore in his study, but it was empty.

As Adela went back from her quest into the drawing-room she simply shook her head at Ludlow, who was standing before the fireplace; and as she did so she caught her reflection in the mantel-glass. 'Verily,' she said to herself, 'I have travelled far.' She had pretty well unlearned her old dignities and forms, but she was to break with them still more completely. It was with a singular hardihood that she prepared to redeem the little pledge which had been extorted from her on her way home. She felt that there was no trial to which her generosity might now be called which she would not hail with enthusiasm. Unfortunately, her generosity was not likely to be challenged; although she nevertheless had the satisfaction of assuring herself at this moment that, like the mercy of the Lord, it was infinite. Should she satisfy herself of her friend's? or should she leave it delightfully uncertain? These had been the terms of what has been called her temptation, at the foot of the hill.

'Well, I have very little time,' said Ludlow; 'I must get my dinner and pay my bill and drive to the train.' And he put out his hand.

Adela gave him her own, without meeting his eyes. 'You are in a a great hurry,' said she, rather casually.

'It's not I who am in a hurry. It's my confounded destiny. It's the train and the steamer.'

'If you really wished to stay you wouldn't be bullied by the train and the steamer.'

'Very true – very true. But *do* I really wish to stay?'

'That's the question. That's exactly what I want to know.'

'You ask difficult questions, Miss Moore.'

'Difficult for me – yes.'

'Then, of course, you are prepared to answer easy ones.'

'Let me hear what you call easy.'

'Well, then, do you wish me to stay? All I have to do is to throw down my hat, sit down, and fold my arms for twenty minutes. I lose my train and my ship. I remain in America, instead of going to Europe.'

'I have thought of all that.'

'I don't mean to say it's a great deal. There are attractions on both sides.'

'Yes, and especially on one. It *is* a great deal.'

'And you request me to give it up – to renounce Berlin?'

'No; I ought not to do that. What I ask of you is whether, if I *should* so request you, you would say "yes".'

'That *does* make the matter easy for you, Miss Moore. What attractions do you hold out?'

'I hold out nothing whatever, sir.'

'I suppose that means a great deal.'

'A great deal of absurdity.'

'Well, you are certainly a most interesting woman, Miss Moore – a charming woman.'

'Why don't you call me irresistible at once, and bid me good-morning?'

'I don't know but that I shall have to come to that. But I will give you no answer that leaves you at an advantage. Ask me to stay – order me to stay, if that suits you better – and I will see how it sounds. Come, you must not trifle with a man.' He still held Adela's hand, and now they were looking watchfully into each other's eyes. He paused, waiting for an answer.

'Good-bye, Mr Ludlow,' said Adela. 'God bless you!' And she was about to withdraw her hand; but he held it.

'Are we friends?' said he.

Adela gave a little shrug of her shoulders. 'Friends of three hours!'

Ludlow looked at her with some sternness. 'Our parting could at best hardly have been sweet,' said he; 'but why should you make it bitter, Miss Moore?'

'If it's bitter, why should you try to change it?'

'Because I don't like bitter things.'

Ludlow had caught a glimpse of the truth – that truth of which the reader has had a glimpse – and he stood there at once thrilled and annoyed. He had both a heart and a conscience. 'It's not my fault,' he murmured to the latter; but he was unable to add, in all consistency, that it was his misfortune. It would be very heroic, very poetic, very chivalric, to lose his steamer, and he felt that he could do so for sufficient cause – at the suggestion of a fact. But the motive here was less than a fact – an idea; less than an idea – a mere guess. 'It's a very pretty little romance as it is,' he said to himself. 'Why spoil it? She's a different sort from any I have met, and just to have seen her like this – that is enough for me!' He raised her hand to his lips, pressed them to it, dropped it, reached the door, and bounded out of the garden-gate.

My Friend Bingham

CONSCIOUS AS I am of a deep aversion to stories of a painful nature, I have often asked myself whether, in the events here set forth, the element of pain is stronger than that of joy. An affirmative answer to this question would have stood as a veto upon the publication of my story, for it is my opinion that the literature of horrors needs no extension. Such an answer, however, I am unwilling to pronounce; while, on the other hand, I hesitate to assume the responsibility of a decided negative. I have therefore determined to leave the solution to the reader. I may add, that I am very sensible of the superficial manner in which I have handled my facts, I bore no other part in the accomplishment of these facts than that of a cordial observer; and it was impossible that, even with the best will in the world, I should fathom the emotions of the actors. Yet, as the very faintest reflection of human passions, under the pressure of fate, possesses an immortal interest, I am content to appeal to the reader's sympathy, and to assure him of my own fidelity.

Towards the close of summer, in my twenty-eighth year, I went down to the seaside to rest from a long term of work, and to enjoy, after several years of separation, a *tête-à-tête* with an intimate friend. My friend had just arrived from Europe, and we had agreed to spend my vacation together by the side of the sounding sea, and within easy reach of the city. On taking possession of our lodgings, we found that we should have no fellow-idlers, and we hailed joyously the prospect of the great marine solitudes which each of us declared that he found so abundantly peopled by the other. I hasten to impart to the reader the following facts in regard to the man whom I found so good a companion.

George Bingham had been born and bred among people for whom, as he grew to manhood, he learned to entertain a most generous contempt – people in whom the hereditary possession of a large property – for he assured me that the facts stood in the relation of cause and effect – had extinguished all intelligent purpose and principle. I trust that I do not speak rhetorically when I describe in these terms the combined ignorance and vanity of my friend's progenitors. It was their fortune to make a splendid figure while they lived, and I feel little compunction in hinting at their poverty in certain human essentials. Bingham was no declaimer, and indeed no great talker; and it was only now and then, in an allusion to the past as the field of a wasted youth, that he expressed his profound resentment. I read this for the most part in the severe humility with which he regarded the future, and under cover of which he seemed to salute it as void at least (whatever other ills it might contain) of those domestic embarrassments which had been the bane of his first manhood. I have no doubt that much may be said, within limits, for the graces of that society against which my friend embodied so violent a reaction, and especially for its good-humour – that home-keeping benevolence which accompanies a sense of material repletion. It is equally probable that to persons of a simple constitution these graces may wear a look of delightful and enduring mystery; but poor Bingham was no simpleton. He was a man of opinions numerous, delicate, and profound. When, with the lapse of his youth, he awoke to a presentiment of these opinions, and cast his first interrogative glance upon the world, he found that in his own little section of it he and his opinions were a piece of melancholy impertinence. Left, at twenty-three years of age, by his father's death, in possession of a handsome property, and absolute master of his actions, he had thrown himself blindly into the world. But, as he afterwards assured me, so superficial was his knowledge of the real world – the world of labour and inquiry – that he had found himself quite incapable of intelligent action. In this manner he had wasted a great deal of time. He had travelled much, however; and, being a keen observer of men and women, he had acquired a certain practical knowledge of human nature. Nevertheless, it was not till he was nearly thirty years old that he had begun to live for himself. 'By myself,' he explained, 'I mean something else than this monstrous hereditary faculty for doing nothing and thinking of nothing.' And he led me to believe, or I should rather say he allowed me to believe, that at this moment he had made a serious attempt to study. But upon this point he was not very explicit; for if he blushed for the manner in which he had slighted his opportunities, he blushed equally for the manner in which he had used them. It is my belief that he had but a limited capacity for study, and I am certain that to the end of his days there subsisted in his mind a very friendly relation between fancies and facts.

Bingham was *par excellence* a moralist, a man of sentiment. I know – he knew himself – that, in this busy Western world, this character represents no recognized avocation; but in the absence of such avocation, its exercise was nevertheless very dear to him. I protest that it was very dear to me, and that, at the end of a long morning devoted to my office-desk, I have often felt as if I had contributed less to the common cause than I have felt after moralizing – or, if you please, sentimentalizing – half an hour with my friend. He was an idler, assuredly; but his candour, his sagacity, his good taste, and, above all, a certain diffident enthusiasm which followed its objects with the exquisite trepidation of an unconfessed and despairing lover – these things, and a hundred more, redeemed him from vulgarity. For three years before we came together, as I have intimated, my impressions of my friend had rested on his letters; and yet, from the first hour which we spent together, I felt that they had done him no wrong. We were genuine friends. I don't know that I can offer better proof of this than by saying that, as our old personal relations resumed their force, and the time-shrunken outlines of character filled themselves out, I greeted the reappearance of each familiar foible on

Bingham's part quite as warmly as I did that of the less punctual virtue. Compared, indeed, with the comrade of earlier years, my actual companion was a well-seasoned man of the world; but with all his acquired humility and his disciplined *bonhomie*, he had failed to divest himself of a certain fastidiousness of mind, a certain formalism of manner, which are the token and the prerogative of one who has not been obliged to address himself to practical questions. The charm bestowed by these facts upon Bingham's conversation – a charm often vainly invoked in their absence – is explained by his honest indifference to their action, and his indisposition to turn them to account in the interest of the picturesque – an advantage but too easy of conquest for a young man, rich, accomplished, and endowed with good looks and a good name. I may say, perhaps, that to a critical mind my friend's prime distinction would have been his very positive refusal to drape himself, after the current taste, with those brilliant stuffs which fortune had strewn at his feet.

Of course, a great deal of our talk bore upon Bingham's recent travels, adventures, and sensations. One of these last he handled very frankly, and treated me to a bit of genuine romance. He had been in love, and had been cruelly jilted, but had now grown able to view the matter with much of the impartial spirit of those French critics whose works were his favourite reading. His account of the young lady's character and motives would indeed have done credit to many a clever *feuilleton*. I was the less surprised, however, at his severely dispassionate tone, when, in retracing the process of his opinions, I discerned the traces – the ravages, I may almost say – of a solemn act of renunciation. Bingham had forsworn marriage. I made haste to assure him that I considered him quite too young for so austere a resolve.

'I can't help it,' said he; 'I feel a foreboding that I shall live and die alone.'

'A foreboding?' said I. 'What's a foreboding worth?'

'Well, then, rationally considered, my marriage is improbable.'

'But it's not to be rationally considered,' I objected. 'It belongs to the province of sentiment.'

'But you deny me sentiment. I fall back upon my foreboding.'

'That's not sentiment – it's superstition,' I answered. 'Your marrying will depend upon your falling in love; and your falling in love will certainly not depend upon yourself.'

'Upon whom, then?'

'Upon some unknown fair one – Miss A, B, or C.'

'Well,' said Bingham, submissively, 'I wish she would make haste and reveal herself.'

These remarks had been exchanged in the hollow of a cliff which sloped seaward, and where we had lazily stretched ourselves at length on the grass. The grass had grown very long and brown; and as we lay with our heads quite on a level with it, the view of the immediate beach and the gentle breakers was so completely obstructed by the rank, coarse herbage, that our prospect was reduced to a long, narrow band of deep blue ocean traversing its black fibres, and to the great vault of the sky. We had strolled out a couple of hours before, bearing each a borrowed shot-gun and accompanied by a friendly water-dog, somewhat languidly disposed towards the slaughter of wild ducks. We were neither of us genuine sportsmen, and it is certain that, on the whole, we meant very kindly to the ducks. It was at all events fated that on that day they should suffer but lightly at our hands. For the half-hour previous to the exchange of the remarks just cited, we had quite forgotten our real business; and, with our pieces lost in the grass beside us, and our dog, weary of inaction, wandering far beyond call, we looked like any straw-picking truants. At last Bingham rose to his feet, with the asseveration that it would never do for us to return empty-handed. 'But, behold,' he exclaimed, as he looked down across the breadth of the beach, 'there is our friend of the cottage, with the sick little boy.'

I brought myself into a sitting posture, and glanced over the cliff. Down near the edge of the water sat a young woman, tossing stones into it for the amusement of a child, who stood lustily crowing and clapping his hands. Her title to be called our friend lay in the fact, that on our way to the beach we had observed her issuing from a cottage hard by the hotel, leading by the hand a pale-faced little boy, muffled like an invalid. The hotel, as I have said, was all but deserted, and this young woman had been the first person to engage our idle observation. We had seen that, although plainly dressed, she was young, pretty, and modest; and, in the absence of heavier cares, these facts had sufficed to make her interesting. The question had arisen between us, whether she was a native of the shore, or a visitor like ourselves.

Bingham inclined to the former view of the case, and I to the latter. There was, indeed, a certain lowliness in her aspect; but I had contended that it was by no means a rustic lowliness. Her dress was simple, but it was well made and well worn; and I noticed that, as she strolled along, leading her little boy, she cast upon sky and sea the lingering glance of one to whom, in their integrity, these were unfamiliar objects. She was the wife of some small tradesman, I argued, who had brought her child to the seaside by the physician's decree. But Bingham declared that it was utterly illogical to suppose her to be a mother of five years' motherhood; and that, for his part, he saw nothing in her appearance inconsistent with rural influences. The child was her nephew, the son of a married sister, and she a sentimental maiden aunt. Obviously the volume she had in her hand was Tennyson. In the absence on both sides of authentic data, of course the debate was not prolonged; and the subject of it had passed from our memories some time before we again met her on the beach. She soon became aware of our presence, however; and, with a natural sense of intrusion, we immediately resumed our walk. The last that I saw of her, as we rounded a turn in the cliff which concealed the backward prospect, was a sudden grasp of the child's arm, as if to withdraw him from the reach of a hastily advancing wave.

Half an hour's further walk led us to a point which we were not tempted to exceed. We shot between us some half a dozen birds; but as our dog, whose talents had been sadly misrepresented, proved very shy of the deep water, and succeeded in bringing no more than a couple of our victims to shore, we resolved to abstain from further destruction, and to return home quietly along the beach, upon which we had now descended.

'If we meet our young lady,' said Bingham, 'we can gallantly offer her our booty.'

Some five minutes after he had uttered these words, a couple of great sea-gulls came flying landward over our heads, and, after a long gyration in mid-air, boldly settled themselves on the slope of the cliff at some three hundred yards in front of us, a point at which it projected almost into the waves. After a momentary halt, one of them rose again on his long pinions and soared away seaward; the other remained. He sat perched on a jutting boulder some fifteen feet high, sunning his fishy breast.

'I wonder if I could put a shot into him,' said Bingham.

'Try,' I answered; and, as he rapidly charged and levelled his piece, I remember idly repeating, while I looked at the great bird,

> '*God save thee, ancient mariner,*
> *From the fiends that plague thee thus!*
> *Why look'st thou so? "With my cross-bow*
> *I shot the albatross."*'

'He's going to rise,' I added.

But Bingham had fired. The creature rose, indeed, half sluggishly, and yet with too hideous celerity. His movement drew from us a cry which was almost simultaneous with the report of Bingham's gun. I cannot express our relation to what followed it better than by saying that it exposed to our sight, beyond the space suddenly left vacant, the happy figure of the child from whom we had parted but an hour before. He stood with his little hands extended, and his face raised toward the retreating bird. Of the sickening sensation which assailed our common vision as we saw him throw back his hands to his head, and reel downwards out of sight, I can give no verbal account, nor of the rapidity with which we crossed the smooth interval of sand, and rounded the bluff.

The child's companion had scrambled up the rocky bank towards the low ledge from which he had fallen, and to which access was of course all too easy. She had sunk down upon the stones, and was wildly clasping the boy's body. I turned from this spectacle to my friend, as to an image of equal woe. Bingham, pale as death, bounded over the stones, and fell on his knees. The woman let him take the child out of her arms, and bent over, with her forehead on a rock, moaning. I have never seen helplessness so vividly embodied as in this momentary group.

'Did it strike his head?' cried Bingham. 'What the devil was he doing up there?'

'I told him he'd get hurt,' said the young woman, with harrowing simplicity. 'To shoot straight at him! – He's killed!'

'Great Heavens! Do you mean to say that I saw him?' roared Bingham. 'How did I know he was there? Did you see us?'

The young woman shook her head. 'Of course I didn't see you. I saw you with your guns before. Oh, he's killed!'

'He's not killed. It was mere duck shot. Don't talk such stuff. — My own poor little man!' cried George. 'Charles, where *were* our eyes?'

'He wanted to catch the bird,' moaned our companion. 'Baby, my boy! open your eyes. Speak to your mother. For God's sake, get some help!'

She had put out her hands to take the child from Bingham, who had half angrily lifted him out of her reach. The senseless movement with which, as she disengaged him from Bingham's grasp, he sank into her arms, was clearly the senselessness of death. She burst into sobs. I went and examined the child.

'He may not be killed,' I said, turning to Bingham; 'keep your senses. It's not your fault. We couldn't see each other.'

Bingham rose stupidly to his feet.

'She must be got home,' I said.

'We must get a carriage. Will you go or stay?'

I saw that he had seen the truth. He looked about him with an expression of miserable impotence. 'Poor little devil!' he said, hoarsely.

'Will you go for a carriage?' I repeated, taking his hand, 'or will you stay?'

Our companion's sobs redoubled their violence.

'I'll stay,' said he. 'Bring some woman.'

I started at a hard run. I left the beach behind me, passed the white cottage at whose garden-gate two women were gossiping, and reached the hotel stable, where I had the good fortune to find a vehicle at my disposal. I drove straight back to the white cottage. One of the women had disappeared, and the other was lingering among her flowers – a middle-aged, keen-eyed person. As I descended and hastily addressed her, I read in her rapid glance an anticipation of evil tidings.

'The young woman who stays with you—' I began.

'Yes,' she said, 'my second-cousin. Well?'

'She's in trouble. She wants you to come to her. Her little boy has hurt himself.' I had time to see that I need fear no hysterics.

'Where did you leave her?' asked my companion.

'On the beach.'

'What's the matter with the child?'

'He fell from a rock. There's no time to be lost.' There was a certain antique rigidity about the woman which was at once irritating and reassuring. I was impelled both to quicken her apprehensions and to confide in her self-control. 'For all I know, ma'am,' said I, 'the child is killed.'

She gave me an angry stare. 'For all you know!' she exclaimed. 'Where were your wits? Were you afraid to look at him?'

'Yes, half afraid.'

She glanced over the paling at my vehicle. 'Am I to get into that?' she asked.

'If you will be so good.'

She turned short about, and re-entered the house, where, as I stood out among the dahlias and the pinks, I heard a rapid opening and shutting of drawers. She shortly reappeared, equipped for driving; and, having locked the house-door, and pocketed the key, came and faced me, where I stood ready to help her into the wagon.

'We'll stop for the doctor,' she began.

'The doctor,' said I, 'is of no use.'

A few moments of hard driving brought us to my starting-point. The tide had fallen perceptibly in my absence; and I remember receiving a strange impression of the irretrievable nature of the recent event from the sight of poor Bingham, standing down at the low-water-mark, and looking seaward with his hands in his pockets. The mother of his little victim still sat on the heap of stones where she had fallen, pressing her child to her breast. I helped my companion to descend, which she did with great deliberation. It is my belief that, as we drove along the beach, she derived from the expression of Bingham's figure, and from the patient aversion of his face, a suspicion of his relation to the opposite group. It was not till the elder woman had come within a few steps of her, that the younger became aware of her approach. I merely had time to catch the agonized appeal of her upward glance, and the broad compassion of the other's stooping movement, before I turned my back upon their encounter, and walked down towards my friend. The monotonous murmur of the waves had covered the sound of our wagon-wheels, and Bingham stood all unconscious of the coming of relief – distilling I know not what divine relief from the simple beauty of sea and sky. I had laid my hand on his shoulder before he turned about. He looked towards the base of the cliff. I knew that a great effusion of feeling would occur in its natural order; but how should I help him across the interval?

'That's her cousin,' I said at random. 'She seems a very capable woman.'

'The child is quite dead,' said Bingham, for all answer. I was struck by the plainness of his statement. In the comparative freedom of my own thoughts I had failed to make allowance for the embarrassed movement of my friend's. It was not, therefore, until afterwards that I acknowledged he had thought to better purpose than I; inasmuch as the very simplicity of his tone implied a positive acceptance (for the moment) of the dreadful fact which he uttered.

'The sooner they get home, the better,' I said. It was evident that the elder of our companions had already embraced this conviction. She had lifted the child and placed him in the carriage, and she was now turning towards his mother and inviting her to ascend. Even at the distance at which I stood, the mingled firmness and tenderness of her gestures were clearly apparent. They seemed, moreover, to express a certain indifference to our movements, an independence of our further interference, which – fanciful as the assertion may look – was not untinged with irony. It was plain that, by whatever rapid process she had obtained it, she was already in possession of our story. 'Thank God for strong-minded women!' I exclaimed; – and yet I could not repress a feeling that it behooved me, on behalf of my friend, to treat as an equal with the vulgar movement of antipathy which he was destined to encounter, and of which, in the irresistible sequence of events, the attitude of this good woman was an index.

We walked towards the carriage together. 'I shall not come home directly,' said Bingham; 'but don't be alarmed about me.'

I looked at my watch. 'I give you two hours,' I said, with all the authority of my affection. The new-comer had placed herself on the back seat of the vehicle beside the sufferer, who on entering had again, possessed herself of her child. As I went about to mount in front, Bingham came and stood by the wheel. I read his purpose in his face – the desire to obtain from the woman he had wronged some recognition of his human character, some confession that she dimly distinguished him from a wild beast or a thunderbolt. One of her hands lay exposed, pressing together on her knee the lifeless little hands of her boy. Bingham removed his hat, and placed his right hand on that of the young woman. I saw that she started at his touch, and that he vehemently tightened his grasp.

'It's too soon to talk of forgiveness,' said he, 'for it's too soon for me to think intelligently of the wrong I have done you. God has brought us together in a very strange fashion.'

The young woman raised her bowed head, and gave my friend, if not just the look he coveted, at least the most liberal glance at her command – a look which, I fancy, helped him to face the immediate future. But these are matters too delicate to be put into words. I spent the hours that elapsed before Bingham's return to the inn in gathering information about the occupants of the cottage. Impelled by that lively intuition of calamity which is natural to women, the housekeeper of the hotel, a person of evident kindliness and discretion, lost no time in winning my confidence. I was not unwilling that the tragic incident which had thus arrested our idleness should derive its earliest publicity from my own lips; and I was forcibly struck with the exquisite impartiality with which this homely creature bestowed her pity. Miss Horner, I learned, the mistress of the cottage, was the last representative of a most respectable family, native to the neighbouring town. It had been for some years her practice to let lodgings during the summer. At the close of the present season she had invited her kinswoman, Mrs Hicks, to spend the autumn with her. That this lady was the widow of a Baptist minister; that her husband had died some three years before; that she was very poor; that her child had been sickly, and that the care of his health had so impeded her exertions for a livelihood, that she had been intending to leave him with Miss Horner for the winter, and obtain a 'situation' in town; – these facts were the salient points of the housekeeper's somewhat prolix recital.

The early autumn dusk had fallen when Bingham returned. He looked very tired. He had been walking for several hours, and, as I fancied, had grown in some degree familiar with his new responsibilities. He was very hungry, and made a vigorous attack upon his supper. I had been indisposed to eat, but the sight of his healthy appetite restored my own. I had grown weary of my thoughts, and I found something salutary in the apparent simplicity and rectitude of Bingham's state of mind.

'I find myself taking it very quietly,' he said, in the course of his repast. 'There is something so absolute in the nature of the calamity, that one is compelled to accept it. I don't see how I could endure to have mutilated the poor little mortal. To kill a human being is, after all, the least injury you can do him.' He spoke these words deliberately, with his eyes on mine, and with an expression of perfect candour. But as he paused, and in spite of my perfect assent to their meaning, I could not help mentally reverting to the really tragic phase of the affair; and I suppose my features revealed to Bingham's scrutiny the process of my thoughts. His pale face flushed a burning crimson, his lips trembled. 'Yes, my boy!' he cried; 'that's where it's damnable.' He buried his head in his hands, and burst into tears.

We had a long talk. At the end of it, we lit our cigars, and came out upon the deserted piazza. There was a lovely starlight, and, after a few turns in silence, Bingham left my side and strolled off towards a bend in the road, in the direction of the sea. I saw him stand motionless for a long time, and then I heard him call me. When I reached his side, I saw that he had been watching a light in the window of the white cottage. We heard the village bell in the distance striking nine.

'Charles,' said Bingham, 'suppose you go down there and make some offer of your services. God knows whom the poor creatures have to look to. She has had a couple of men thrust into her life. She must take the good with the bad.'

I lingered a moment. 'It's a difficult task,' I said. 'What shall I say?'

Bingham silently puffed his cigar. He stood with his arms folded, and his head thrown back, slowly measuring the starry sky. 'I wish she could come out here and look at that sky,' he said at last. 'It's a sight for bereaved mothers. Somehow, my dear boy,' he pursued, 'I never felt less depressed in my life. It's none of my doing.'

'It would hardly do for me to tell her that,' said I.

'I don't know,' said Bingham. 'This isn't an occasion for the exchange of compliments. I'll tell you what you may tell her. I suppose they will have some funeral services within a day or two. Tell her that I should like very much to be present.'

I set off for the cottage. Its mistress in person introduced me into the little parlour.

'Well, sir?' she said, in hard, dry accents.

'I've come,' I answered, 'to ask whether I can be of any assistance to Mrs Hicks.'

Miss Horner shook her head in a manner which deprived her negation of half its dignity.

'What assistance is possible?' she asked.

'A man,' said I, 'may relieve a woman of certain cares—'

'O, men are a blessed set! You had better leave Mrs Hicks to me.'

'But will you at least tell me how she is — if she has in any degree recovered herself?'

At this moment the door of the adjoining room was opened, and Mrs Hicks stood on the threshold, bearing a lamp — a graceful and pathetic figure. I now had occasion to observe that she was a woman of decided beauty. Her fair hair was drawn back into a single knot behind her head, and the lamplight deepened the pallor of her face and the darkness of her eyes. She wore a calico dressing-gown and a shawl.

'What do you wish?' she asked, in a voice clarified, if I may so express it, by long weeping.

'He wants to know whether he can be of any assistance,' said the elder lady.

Mrs Hicks glanced over her shoulder into the room she had left. 'Would you like to look at the child?' she asked, in a whisper.

'Lucy!' cried Miss Horner.

I walked straight over to Mrs Hicks, who turned and led the way to a little bed. My conductress raised her lamp aloft, and let the light fall gently on the little white-draped figure. Even the bandage about the child's head had not dispelled his short-lived prettiness. Heaven knows that to remain silent was easy enough; but Heaven knows, too, that to break the silence – and to break it as I broke it – was equally easy. 'He must have been a very pretty child,' I said.

'Yes, he was very pretty. He had black eyes. I don't know whether you noticed.'

'No, I didn't notice,' said I. 'When is he to be buried?'

'The day after tomorrow. I am told that I shall be able to avoid an inquest.'

'Mr Bingham has attended to that,' I said. And then I paused, revolving his petition.

But Mrs Hicks anticipated it. 'If you would like to be present at the funeral,' she said, 'you are welcome to come. – And so is your friend.'

'Mr Bingham bade me ask leave. There is a great deal that I should like to say to you for him,' I added, 'but I won't spoil it by trying. It's his own business.'

The young woman looked at me with her deep, dark eyes. 'I pity him from my heart,' she said, pressing her hands to her breast. 'I had rather have my sorrow than his.'

'They are pretty much one sorrow,' I answered. 'I don't see that you can divide it. You are two to bear it. Bingham is a wise, good fellow,' I went on. 'I have shared a great many joys with him. In Heaven's name,' I cried, 'don't bear hard on him!'

'How can I bear hard?' she asked, opening her arms and letting them drop. The movement was so deeply expressive of weakness and loneliness, that, feeling all power to reply stifled in a rush of compassion, I silently made my exit.

On the following day, Bingham and I went up to town, and on the third day returned in time for the funeral. Besides the two ladies, there was no one present but ourselves and the village minister, who of course spoke as briefly as decency allowed. He had accompanied the ladies in a carriage to the graveyard, while Bingham and I had come on foot. As we turned away from the grave, I saw my friend approach Mrs Hicks. They stood talking beside the freshly turned earth, while the minister and I attended Miss Horner to the carriage. After she had seated herself, I lingered at the door, exchanging sober commonplaces with the reverend gentleman. At last Mrs Hicks followed us, leaning on Bingham's arm.

'Margaret,' she said, 'Mr Bingham and I are going to stay here awhile. Mr Bingham will walk home with me. I'm very much obliged to you, Mr Bland,' she added, turning to the minister and extending her hand.

I bestowed upon my friend a glance which I felt to be half interrogative and half sympathetic. He gave me his hand, and answered the benediction by its pressure, while he answered the inquiry by his words. 'If you are still disposed to go back to town this afternoon,' he said, 'you had better not wait for me. I may not have time to catch the boat.' I of course made no scruple of returning immediately to the city.

Some ten days elapsed before I again saw Bingham; but I found my attention so deeply engrossed with work, that I scarcely measured the interval. At last, one morning, he came into my office.

'I take for granted,' I said, 'that you have not been all this time at B——.'

'No; I've been on my travels. I came to town the day after you came. I found at my rooms a letter from a lawyer in Baltimore, proposing the sale of some of my property there, and I seized upon it as an excuse for making a journey to that city. I felt the need of movement, of action of some kind. But when I reached Baltimore, I didn't even go to see my correspondent. I pushed on to Washington, walked about for thirty-six hours, and came home.'

He had placed his arm on my desk, and stood supporting his head on his hand, with a look of great physical exhaustion.

'You look very tired,' said I.

'I haven't slept,' said he. 'I had such a talk with that woman!'

'I'm sorry that you should have felt the worse for it.'

'I feel both the worse and the better. She talked about the child.'

'It's well for her,' said I, 'that she was able to do it.'

'She wasn't able, strictly speaking. She began calmly enough, but she very soon broke down.'

'Did you see her again?'

'I called upon her the next day, to tell her that I was going to town, and to ask if I could be useful to her. But she seems to stand in perfect isolation. She assured me that she was in want of nothing.'

'What sort of a woman does she seem to be, taking her in herself?'

'Bless your soul! I can't take her in herself,' cried Bingham, with some vehemence. 'And yet, stay,' he added; 'she's a very pleasing woman.'

'She's very pretty.'

'Yes; she's very pretty. In years, she's little more than a young girl. In her ideas, she's one of "the people".'

'It seems to me,' said I, 'that the frankness of her conduct toward you is very much to her credit.

'It doesn't offend you, then?'

'Offend me? It gratifies me beyond measure.'

'I think that, if you had seen her as I have seen her, it would interest you deeply. I'm at a loss to determine whether it's the result of great simplicity or great sagacity. Of course, it's absurd to suppose that, ten days ago, it could have been the result of anything but a beautiful impulse. I think that tomorrow I shall again go down to B——.'

I allowed Bingham time to have made his visit and to have brought me an account of his further impressions; but as three days went by without his reappearance, I called at his lodgings. He was still out of town, The fifth day, however, brought him again to my office.

'I've been at B—— constantly,' he said, 'and I've had several interviews with our friend.'

'Well; how fares it?'

'It fares well. I'm forcibly struck with her good sense. In matters of mind – in matters of soul, I may say – she has the touch of an angel, or rather the touch of a woman. That's quite sufficient.'

'Does she keep her composure?'

'Perfectly. You can imagine nothing simpler and less sentimental than her manner. She makes me forget myself most divinely. The child's death colours our talk; but it doesn't confine or obstruct it. You see she has her religion: she can afford to be natural.'

Weary as my friend looked, and shaken by his sudden subjection to care, it yet seemed to me, as he pronounced these words, that his eye had borrowed a purer light and his voice a fresher tone. In short, where I discerned it, how I detected it, I know not; but I felt that he carried a secret. He sat poking with his walking-stick at a nail in the carpet, with his eyes dropped. I saw about his mouth the faint promise of a distant smile – a smile which six months would bring to maturity.

'George,' said I, 'I have a fancy.'

He looked up. 'What is it?'

'You've lost your heart.'

He stared a moment, with a sudden frown. 'To whom?' he asked.

'To Mrs Hicks.'

With a frown, I say, but a frown that was as a smile to the effect of my rejoinder. He rose to his feet; all his colour deserted his face and rushed to his eyes.

'I beg your pardon if I'm wrong,' I said.

Bingham had turned again from pale to crimson. 'Don't beg *my* pardon,' he cried. 'You may say what you please. Beg *hers*!' he added, bitterly.

I resented the charge of injustice. 'I've done *her* no wrong!' I answered. 'I haven't said,' I went on with a certain gleeful sense that I was dealing with massive truths – 'I haven't said that she had lost her heart to you!'

'Good God, Charles!' cried Bingham, 'what a horrid imagination you have!'

'I am not responsible for my imagination.'

'Upon my soul, I hope *I*'m not!' cried Bingham, passionately. 'I have enough without that.'

'George,' I said, after a moment's reflection, 'if I thought I had insulted you, I would make amends. But I have said nothing to be ashamed of. I believe that I have hit the truth. Your emotion proves it. I spoke hastily; but you must admit that, having caught a glimpse of the truth, I couldn't stand indifferent to it.'

'The truth! the truth! What truth?'

'Aren't you in love with Mrs Hicks? Admit it like a man.'

'Like a man! Like a brute. Haven't I done the woman wrong enough?'

'Quite enough, I hope.'

'Haven't I turned her simple joys to bitterness?'

'I grant it.'

'And now you want me to insult her by telling her that I love her?'

'I want you to tell her nothing. What you tell her is your own affair. Remember that, George. It's as little mine as it is the rest of the world's.'

Bingham stood listening, with a contracted brow and his hand grasping his stick. He walked to the dusty office-window and halted a moment, watching the great human throng in the street. Then he turned and came towards me. Suddenly he stopped short. 'God forgive me!' he cried; 'I believe I do love her.'

The fountains of my soul were stirred. 'Combining my own hasty impressions of Mrs Hicks with yours, George,' I said, 'the consummation seems to me exquisitely natural.'

It was in these simple words that we celebrated the sacred fact. It seemed as if, by tacit agreement, the evolution of this fact was result enough for a single interview.

A few days after this interview, in the evening, I called at Bingham's lodgings. His servant informed me that my friend was out of town, although he was unable to indicate his whereabouts. But as I turned away from the door a hack drew up, and the object of my quest descended, equipped with a travelling-bag. I went down and greeted him under the gas-lamp.

'Shall I go in with you?' I asked; 'or shall I go my way?'

'You had better come in,' said Bingham. 'I have something to say. – I have been down to B——,' he resumed, when the servant had left us alone in his sitting-room. His tone bore the least possible tinge of a confession; but of course it was not as a confessor that I listened.

'Well,' said I, 'how is our friend?'

'Our friend——' answered Bingham. 'Will you have a cigar?'

'No, I thank you.'

'Our friend—— Ah, Charles, it's a long story.'

'I shan't mind that, if it's an interesting one.'

'To a certain extent it's a painful one. It's painful to come into collision with incurable vulgarity of feeling.'

I was puzzled. 'Has that been your fortune?' I asked.

'It has been my fortune to bring Mrs Hicks into a great deal of trouble. The case, in three words, is this. Miss Horner has seen fit to resent, in no moderate terms, what she calls the "extraordinary intimacy" existing between Mrs Hicks and myself. Mrs Hicks, as was perfectly natural, has resented her cousin's pretension to regulate her conduct. Her expression of this feeling has led to her expulsion from Miss Horner's house.'

'Has she any other friend to turn to?'

'No one, except some relatives of her husband, who are very poor people, and of whom she wishes to ask no favours.'

'Where has she placed herself?'

'She is in town. We came up together this afternoon. I went with her to some lodgings which she had formerly occupied, and which were fortunately vacant.'

'I suppose it's not to be regretted that she has left B——. She breaks with sad associations.'

'Yes; but she renews them too, on coming to town.'

'How so?'

'Why, damn it,' said Bingham, with a tremor in his voice, 'the woman is utterly poor.'

'Has she no resources whatever?'

'A hundred dollars a year, I believe – worse than nothing.'

'Has she any marketable talents or accomplishments?'

'I believe she is up to some pitiful needle-work or other. Such a woman! O horrible world!'

'Does *she* say so?' I asked.

'She? No indeed. She thinks it's all for the best. I suppose it is. But it seems but a bad best.'

'I wonder,' said I, after a pause, 'whether I might see Mrs Hicks. Do you think she would receive me?'

Bingham looked at me an instant keenly. 'I suppose so,' said he. 'You can try.'

'I shall go, not out of curiosity,' I resumed, 'but out of—'

'Out of what?'

'Well, in fine, I should like to see her again.'

Bingham gave me Mrs Hicks's address, and in the course of a few evenings I called upon her. I had abstained from bestowing a fine name upon the impulse which dictated this act; but I am nevertheless free to declare that kindliness and courtesy had a large part in it. Mrs Hicks had taken up her residence in a plain, small house, in a decent by-street, where, upon presenting myself, I was ushered into a homely sitting-room (apparently her own), and left to await her coming. Her greeting was simple and cordial, and not untinged with a certain implication of gratitude. She had taken for granted, on my part, all possible sympathy and good-will; but as she had regarded me besides as a man of many cares, she had thought it improbable that we should meet again. It was no long time before I became conscious of that generous charm which Bingham had rigorously denominated her good-sense. Good-sense assuredly was there, but good-sense mated and prolific. Never had I seen, it seemed to me, as the moments elapsed, so exquisitely modest a use of such charming faculties – an intelligence so sensible of its obligations and so indifferent to its privileges. It was obvious that she had been a woman of plain associations: her allusions were to homely facts, and her manner direct and unstudied; and yet, in spite of these limitations, it was equally obvious that she was a person to be neither patronized, dazzled, nor deluded. O the satisfaction which, in the course of that quiet dialogue, I took in this sweet infallibility! How it effaced her loneliness and poverty, and added dignity to her youth and beauty! It made her, potentially at least, a woman of the world. It was an anticipation of the self-possession, the wisdom, and perhaps even in some degree of the wit, which comes through the experience of society – the result, on Mrs Hicks's part, of I know not what hours of suffering, despondency, and self-dependence. With whatever intentions, therefore, I might have come before her, I should have found it impossible to address her as any other than an equal, and to regard her affliction as anything less than an absolute mystery. In fact, we hardly touched upon it; and it was only covertly that we alluded to Bingham's melancholy position. I will not deny that in a certain sense I regretted Mrs Hicks's reserve. It is true that I had a very informal claim upon her confidence; but I had gone to her with a half-defined hope that this claim would be liberally interpreted. It was not even recognized; my vague intentions of counsel and assistance had lain undivined; and I departed with the impression that my social horizon had been considerably enlarged, but that my charity had by no means secured a pensioner.

Mrs Hicks had given me permission to repeat my visit, and after the lapse of a fortnight I determined to do so. I had seen Bingham several times in the interval. He was of course much interested in my impressions of our friend; and I fancied that my admiration gave him even more pleasure than he allowed himself to express. On entering Mrs Hicks's parlour a second time, I found him in person standing before the fireplace, and talking apparently with some vehemence to Mrs Hicks, who sat listening on the sofa. Bingham turned impatiently to the door as I crossed the threshold, and Mrs Hicks rose to welcome me with all due composure. I was nevertheless sensible that my entrance was ill-timed; yet a retreat was impossible. Bingham kept his place on the hearth-rug, and mechanically gave me his hand – standing irresolute, as I thought, between annoyance and elation. The fact that I had interrupted a somewhat passionate interview was somehow so obvious, that, at the prompting of a very delicate feeling, Mrs Hicks hastened to anticipate my apologies.

'Mr Bingham was giving me a lecture,' she said; and there was perhaps in her accent a faint suspicion of bitterness. 'He will doubtless be glad of another auditor.'

'*No*,' said Bingham, 'Charles is a better talker than listener. You shall have two lectures instead of one.' He uttered this sally without even an attempt to smile.

'What is your subject?' said I. 'Until I know that, I shall promise neither to talk nor to listen.'

Bingham laid his hand on my arm. 'He represents the world,' he said, addressing our hostess. 'You're afraid of the world. There, make your appeal.'

Mrs Hicks stood silent a moment, with a contracted brow and a look of pain on her face.

Then she turned to me with a half-smile. 'I don't believe you represent the world,' she said; 'you are too good.'

'She flatters you,' said Bingham. 'You wish to corrupt him, Mrs Hicks.'

Mrs Hicks glanced for an instant from my friend to myself. There burned in her eyes a far-searching light, which consecrated the faint irony of the smile which played about her lips. 'O you men!' she said – 'you are so wise, so deep!' It was on Bingham that her eyes rested last; but after a pause, extending her hand, she transferred them to me. 'Mr Bingham,' she pursued, 'seems to wish you to be admitted to our counsels. There is every reason why his friends should be my friends. You will be interested to know that he has asked me to be his wife.'

'Have you given him an answer?' I asked.

'He was pressing me for an answer when you came in. He conceives me to have a great fear of the judgements of men, and he was saying very hard things about them. But they have very little, after all, to do with the matter. The world may heed it, that Mr Bingham should marry Mrs Hicks, but it will care very little whether or no Mrs Hicks marries Mr Bingham. You are the world, for me,' she cried with beautiful inconsequence, turning to her suitor; 'I know no other.' She put out her hands, and he took them.

I am at a loss to express the condensed force of these rapid words – the amount of passion, of reflection, of experience, which they seemed to embody. They were the simple utterance of a solemn and intelligent choice; and, as such, the whole phalanx of the Best Society assembled in judgement could not have done less than salute them. What honest George Bingham said, what I said, is of little account. The proper conclusion of my story lies in the highly dramatic fact that out of the depths of her bereavement – out of her loneliness and her pity – this richly gifted woman had emerged, responsive to the passion of him who had wronged her all but as deeply as he loved her. The reader will decide, I think, that this catastrophe offers as little occasion for smiles as for tears. My narrative is a piece of genuine prose.

It was not until six months had elapsed that Bingham's marriage took place. It has been a truly happy one. Mrs Bingham is now, in the fullness of her bloom, with a single exception, the most charming woman I know. I have often assured her – once too often, possibly – that, thanks to that invaluable good-sense of hers, she is also the happiest. She has made a devoted wife; but – and in occasional moments of insight it has seemed to me that this portion of her fate is a delicate tribute to a fantastic principle of equity – she has never again become a mother. In saying that she has made a devoted wife, it may seem that I have written Bingham's own later history. Yet as the friend of his younger days, the comrade of his *belle jeunesse*, the partaker of his dreams, I would fain give him a sentence apart. What shall it be? He is a truly incorruptible soul; he is a confirmed philosopher; he has grown quite stout.

The Story of a Masterpiece

I

N O LONGER AGO than last Summer, during a six weeks' stay at Newport, John Lennox became engaged to Miss Marian Everett of New York. Mr Lennox was a widower, of large estate, and without children. He was thirty-five years old, of a sufficiently distinguished appearance, of excellent manners, of an unusual share of sound information, of irreproachable habits, and of a temper which was understood to have suffered a trying and salutary probation during the short term of his wedded life. Miss Everett was, therefore, all things considered, believed to be making a very good match and to be having by no means the worst of the bargain.

And yet Miss Everett, too, was a very marriageable young lady – *the pretty Miss Everett*, as she was called, to distinguish her from certain plain cousins, with whom, owing to her having no mother and no sisters, she was constrained, for decency's sake, to spend a great deal of her time – rather to her own satisfaction, it may be conjectured, than to that of these excellent young women.

Marian Everett was penniless, indeed; but she was richly endowed with all the gifts which make a woman charming. She was, without dispute, the most charming girl in the circle in which she lived and moved. Even certain of her elders, women of a larger experience, of a heavier calibre, as it were, and, thanks to their being married ladies, of greater freedom of action, were practically not so charming as she. And yet, in her emulation of the social graces of these, her more fully licensed sisters, Miss Everett was quite guiltless of any aberration from the strict line of maidenly dignity. She professed an almost religious devotion to good taste, and she looked with horror upon the boisterous graces of many of her companions. Beside being the most entertaining girl in New York, she was, therefore, also the most irreproachable. Her beauty was, perhaps, contestable, but it was certainly uncontested. She was the least bit below the middle height, and her person was marked by a great fullness and roundness of outline; and yet, in spite of this comely ponderosity, her movements were perfectly light and elastic. In complexion, she was a genuine blonde – a warm blonde; with a midsummer bloom upon her cheek, and the light of a midsummer sun wrought into her auburn hair. Her features were not cast upon a classical model, but their expression was in the highest degree pleasing. Her forehead was low and broad, her nose small, and her mouth – well, by the envious her mouth was called *enormous*. It is certain that it had an immense capacity for smiles, and that when she opened it to sing (which she did with infinite sweetness) it emitted a copious flood of sound. Her face was, perhaps, a trifle too circular, and her shoulders a trifle too high; but, as I say, the general effect left nothing to be desired. I might point out a dozen discords in the character of her face and figure, and yet utterly fail to invalidate the impression they produced. There is something essentially uncivil, and, indeed, unphilosophical, in the attempt to verify or to disprove a woman's beauty in detail, and a man gets no more than he deserves when he finds that, in strictness, the aggregation of the different features fails to make up the total. Stand off, gentlemen, and let *her* make the addition. Beside her beauty, Miss Everett shone by her good nature and her lively perceptions. She neither made harsh speeches nor resented them; and, on the other hand, she keenly enjoyed intellectual cleverness, and even cultivated it. Her great merit was that she made no claims or pretensions. Just as there was nothing artificial in her beauty, so there was nothing pedantic in her acuteness and nothing sentimental in her amiability. The one was all freshness and the others all *bonhommie*.

John Lennox saw her, then loved her and offered her his hand. In accepting it Miss Everett acquired, in the world's eye, the one advantage which she lacked – a complete stability and regularity of position. Her friends took no small satisfaction in contrasting her brilliant and comfortable future with her somewhat precarious past. Lennox, nevertheless, was congratulated on the right hand and on the left; but none too often for his faith. That of Miss Everett was not put to so severe a test, although she was frequently reminded by acquaintances of a moralizing turn that she had reason to be very thankful for Mr Lennox's choice. To these assurances Marian listened with a look of patient humility, which was extremely becoming. It was as if for *his* sake she could consent even to be bored.

Within a fortnight after their engagement had been made known, both parties returned to New York. Lennox lived in a house of his own, which he now busied himself with repairing and refurnishing; for the wedding had been fixed for the end of October. Miss Everett lived in lodgings with her father, a decayed old gentleman, who rubbed his idle hands from morning till night over the prospect of his daughter's marriage.

John Lennox, habitually a man of numerous resources, fond of reading, fond of music, fond of society and not averse to politics, passed the first weeks of the Autumn in a restless, fidgety manner. When a man approaches middle age he finds it difficult to wear gracefully the distinction of being engaged. He finds it difficult to discharge with becoming alacrity the various *petits soins* incidental to the position. There was a certain pathetic gravity, to those who knew him well, in Lennox's attentions. One-third of his time he spent in foraging in Broadway, whence he returned half a dozen times a week, laden with trinkets and gimcracks, which he always finished by thinking it puerile and brutal to offer his mistress. Another third he passed in Mr Everett's drawing-room, during which period Marian was denied to visitors. The rest of the time he spent, as he told a friend, God knows how. This was stronger language than his friend expected to hear, for Lennox was neither a man of precipitate utterance, nor, in his friend's belief, of a strongly passionate nature. But it was evident that he was very much in love; or at least very much off his balance.

'When I'm with her it's all very well,' he pursued, 'but when I'm away from her I feel as if I were thrust out of the ranks of the living.'

'Well, you must be patient,' said his friend; 'you're destined to live hard, yet.'

Lennox was silent, and his face remained rather more sombre than the other liked to see it.

'I hope there's no particular difficulty,' the latter resumed; hoping to induce him to relieve himself of whatever weighed upon his consciousness.

'I'm afraid sometimes I – afraid sometimes she doesn't really love me.'

'Well, a little doubt does no harm. It's better than to be too sure of it, and to sink into fatuity. Only be sure you love her.'

'Yes,' said Lennox, solemnly, 'that's the great point.'

One morning, unable to fix his attention on books and papers, he bethought himself of an expedient for passing an hour.

He had made, at Newport, the acquaintance of a young artist named Gilbert, for whose talent and conversation he had conceived a strong relish. The painter, on leaving Newport, was to go to the Adirondacks, and to be back in New York on the first of October, after which time he begged his friend to come and see him.

It occurred to Lennox on the morning I speak of that Gilbert must already have returned to town, and would be looking for his visit. So he forthwith repaired to his studio.

Gilbert's card was on the door, but, on entering the room, Lennox found it occupied by a stranger – a young man in painter's garb, at work before a large panel. He learned from this gentleman that he was a temporary sharer of Mr Gilbert's studio, and, that the latter had stepped out for a few moments. Lennox accordingly prepared to await his return. He entered into conversation with the young man, and, finding him very intelligent, as well as, apparently, a great friend of Gilbert, he looked at him with some interest. He was of something less than thirty, tall and robust, with a strong, joyous, sensitive face, and a thick auburn beard. Lennox was struck with his face, which seemed both to express a great deal of human sagacity and to indicate the essential temperament of a painter.

'A man with that face,' he said to himself, 'does work at least worth looking at.'

He accordingly asked his companion if he might come and look at his picture. The latter readily assented, and Lennox placed himself before the canvas.

It bore a representation of a half-length female figure, in a costume and with an expression so ambiguous that Lennox remained uncertain whether it was a portrait or a work of fancy: a fair-haired young woman, clad in a rich mediaeval dress, and looking like a countess of the Renaissance. Her figure was relieved against a sombre tapestry, her arms loosely folded, her head erect and her eyes on the spectator, toward whom she seemed to move – '*Dans un flot de velours traînant ses petits pieds*'.

As Lennox inspected her face it seemed to reveal a hidden likeness to a face he well knew – the face of Marian Everett. He was of course anxious to know whether the likeness was accidental or designed.

'I take this to be a portrait,' he said to the artist, 'a portrait "in character".'

'No,' said the latter, 'it's a mere composition: a little from here and a little from there. The picture has been hanging about me for the last two or three years, as a sort of receptacle of waste ideas. It has been the victim of innumerable theories and experiments. But it seems to have survived them all. I suppose it possesses a certain amount of vitality.'

'Do you call it anything?'

'I called it originally after something I'd read – Browning's poem, "My Last Duchess". Do you know it?'

'Perfectly.'

'I am ignorant of whether it's an attempt to embody the poet's impression of a portrait actually existing. But why should I care? This is simply an attempt to embody my own private impression of the poem, which has always had a strong hold on my fancy. I don't know whether it agrees with your own impression and that of most readers. But I don't insist upon the name. The possessor of the picture is free to baptize it afresh.'

The longer Lennox looked at the picture the more he liked it, and the deeper seemed to be the correspondence between the lady's expression and that with which he had invested the heroine of Browning's lines. The less accidental, too, seemed that element which Marian's face and the face on the canvas possessed in common. He thought of the great poet's noble lyric and of its exquisite significance, and of the physiognomy of the woman he loved having been choson as the fittest exponent of that significance.

He turned away his head; his eyes filled with tears. 'If I were possessor of the picture,' he said, finally, answering the artist's last words, 'I should feel tempted to call it by the name of a person of whom it very much reminds me.'

'Ah?' said Baxter; and then, after a pause – 'a person in New York?'

It had happened, a week before, that, at her lover's request, Miss Everett had gone in his company to a photographer's and had been photographed in a dozen different attitudes. The proofs of these photographs had been sent home for Marian to choose from. She had made a choice of half a dozen – or rather Lennox had made it – and the latter had put them in his pocket, with the intention of stopping at the establishment and giving his orders. He now took out his pocket-book and showed the painter one of the cards.

'I find a great resemblance,' said he, 'between your Duchess and that young lady.'

The artist looked at the photograph. 'If I am not mistaken,' he said, after a pause, 'the young lady is Miss Everett.'

Lennox nodded assent.

His companion remained silent a few moments, examining the photograph with considerable interest; but, as Lennox observed, without comparing it with his picture.

'My Duchess very probably bears a certain resemblance to Miss Everett, but a not exactly intentional one,' he said, at last. 'The picture was begun before I ever saw Miss Everett. Miss Everett, as you see – or as you know – has a very charming face, and, during the few weeks in which I saw her, I continued to work upon it. You know how a painter works – how artists of all kinds work: they claim their property wherever they find it. What I found to my purpose in Miss Everett's appearance I didn't hesitate to adopt; especially as I had been feeling about in the dark for a type of countenance which her face effectually realized. The Duchess was an Italian, I take it; and I had made up my mind that she was to be a blonde. Now, there is a decidedly southern depth and warmth of tone in Miss Everett's complexion, as well as that breadth and thickness of feature which is common in Italian women. You see the resemblance is much more a matter of type than of expression. Nevertheless, I'm sorry if the copy betrays the original.'

'I doubt,' said Lennox, 'whether it would betray it to any other perception than mine. I have the honour,' he added, after a pause, 'to be engaged to Miss Everett. You will, therefore, excuse me if I ask whether you mean to sell your picture?'

'It's already sold – to a lady,' rejoined the artist, with a smile; 'a maiden lady, who is a great admirer of Browning.'

At this moment Gilbert returned. The two friends exchanged greetings, and their companion withdrew to a neighbouring studio. After they had talked awhile of what had happened to each since they parted, Lennox spoke of the painter of the Duchess and of his remarkable talent, expressing surprise that he shouldn't have heard of him before, and that Gilbert should never have spoken of him.

'His name is Baxter – Stephen Baxter,' said Gilbert, 'and until his return from Europe, a fortnight ago, I knew little more about him than you. He's a case of improvement. I met him in Paris in '62; at that time he was doing absolutely nothing. He has learned what you see in the interval. On arriving in New York he found it impossible to get a studio big enough to hold him. As, with my little sketches, I need only occupy one corner of mine, I offered him the use of the other three, until he should be able to bestow himself to his satisfaction. When he began to unpack his canvases I found I had been entertaining an angel unawares.'

Gilbert then proceeded to uncover, for Lennox's inspection, several of Baxter's portraits, both of men and women. Each of these works confirmed Lennox's impression of the painter's power. He returned to the picture on the easel. Marian Everett reappeared at his silent call, and looked out of the eyes with a most penetrating tenderness and melancholy.

'He may say what he pleases,' thought Lennox, 'the resemblance is, in some degree, also a matter of expression. Gilbert,' he added, wishing to measure the force of the likeness, 'whom does it remind you of?'

'I know,' said Gilbert, 'of whom it reminds you.'

'And do you see it yourself?'

'They are both handsome, and both have auburn hair. That's all I can see.'

Lennox was somewhat relieved. It was not without a feeling of discomfort – a feeling by no means inconsistent with his first moment of pride and satisfaction – that he thought of Marian's peculiar and individual charms having been subjected to the keen appreciation of another than himself. He was glad to be able to conclude that the painter had merely been struck with what was most superficial in her appearance, and that his own imagination supplied the rest. It occurred to him, as he walked home, that it would be a not unbecoming tribute to the young girl's loveliness on his own part, to cause her portrait to be painted by this clever young man. Their engagement had as yet been an affair of pure sentiment, and he had taken an almost fastidious care not to give himself the vulgar appearance of a mere purveyor of luxuries and pleasures. Practically, he had been as yet for his future wife a poor man – or rather a man, pure and simple, and not a million-aire. He had ridden with her, he had sent her flowers, and he had gone with her to the opera. But he had neither sent her sugar-plums, nor made bets with her, nor made her presents of jewel-lery. Miss Everett's female friends had remarked that he hadn't as yet given her the least little betrothal ring, either of pearls or of diamonds. Marian, however, was quite content. She was, by nature, a great artist in the *mise-en-scène* of emotions, and she felt instinctively that this classical moderation was but the converse presentment of an immense matrimonial abundance. In his attempt to make it impossible that his relations with Miss Everett should be tinged in any degree with the accidental condition of the fortunes of either party, Lennox had thoroughly understood his own instinct. He knew that he should some day feel a strong and irresistible impulse to offer his mistress some visible and artistic token of his affection, and that his gift would convey a greater satisfaction from being sole of its kind. It seemed to him now that his chance had come. What gift could be more delicate than the gift of an opportunity to contribute by her patience and good-will to her husband's possession of a perfect likeness of her face?

On that same evening Lennox dined with his future father-in-law, as it was his habit to do once a week.

'Marian,' he said, in the course of the dinner, 'I saw, this morning, an old friend of yours.'

'Ah,' said Marian, 'who was that?'

'Mr Baxter, the painter.'

Marian changed colour – ever so little; no more, indeed, than was natural to an honest surprise.

Her surprise, however, could not have been great, inasmuch as she now said that she had seen his return to America mentioned in a newspaper, and as she knew that Lennox frequented the society of artists. 'He was well, I hope,' she added, 'and prosperous.'

'Where did you know this gentleman, my dear?' asked Mr Everett.

'I knew him in Europe two years ago – first in the Summer in Switzerland, and afterward in Paris. He is a sort of cousin of Mrs Denbigh.' Mrs Denbigh was a lady in whose company Marian had recently spent a year in Europe – a widow, rich, childless, an invalid, and an old friend of her mother. 'Is he always painting?'

'Apparently, and extremely well. He has two or three as good portraits there as one may reasonably expect to see. And he has, moreover, a certain picture which reminded me of you.'

'His "Last Duchess"?' asked Marian, with some curiosity. 'I should like to see it. If you think it's like me, John, you ought to buy it up.'

'I wanted to buy it, but it's sold. You know it then?'

'Yes, through Mr Baxter himself I saw it in its rudimentary state, when it looked like nothing that I should care to look like. I shocked Mrs Denbigh very much by telling him I was glad it was his "last". The picture, indeed, led to our acquaintance.'

'And not *vice versa*,' said Mr Everett, facetiously.

'How *vice versa*?' asked Marian, innocently. 'I met Mr Baxter for the first time at a party in Rome.'

'I thought you said you met him in Switzerland,' said Lennox.

'No, in Rome. It was only two days before we left. He was introduced to me without knowing I was with Mrs Denbigh, and indeed without knowing that she had been in the city. He was very shy of Americans. The first thing he said to me was that I looked very much like a picture he had been painting.'

'That you realized his ideal, etc.'

'Exactly, but not at all in that sentimental tone. I took him to Mrs Denbigh; they found they were sixth cousins by marriage; he came to see us the next day, and insisted upon our going to his studio. It was a miserable place. I believe he was very poor. At least Mrs Denbigh offered him some money, and he frankly accepted it. She attempted to spare his sensibilities by telling him that, if he liked, he could paint her a picture in return. He said he would if he had time. Later, he came up into Switzerland, and the following Winter we met him in Paris.'

If Lennox had had any mistrust of Miss Everett's relations with the painter, the manner in which she told her little story would have effectually blighted it. He forthwith proposed that, in consideration not only of the young man's great talent, but of his actual knowledge of her face, he should be invited to paint her portrait.

Marian assented without reluctance and without alacrity, and Lennox laid his proposition before the artist. The latter requested a day or two to consider, and then replied (by note) that he would be happy to undertake the task.

Miss Everett expected that, in view of the projected renewal of their old acquaintance, Stephen Baxter would call upon her, under the auspices of her lover. He called in effect, alone, but Marian was not at home, and he failed to repeat the visit. The day for the first sitting was therefore appointed through Lennox. The artist had not as yet obtained a studio of his own, and the latter cordially offered him the momentary use of a spacious and well-lighted apartment in his house, which had been intended as a billiard-room, but was not yet fitted up. Lennox expressed no wishes with regard to the portrait, being content to leave the choice of position and costume to the parties immediately interested. He found the painter perfectly well acquainted with Marian's 'points', and he had an implicit confidence in her own good taste.

Miss Everett arrived on the morning appointed, under her father's escort, Mr Everett, who prided himself largely upon doing things in proper form, having caused himself to be introduced beforehand to the painter. Between the latter and Marian there was a brief exchange of civilities, after which they addressed themselves to business. Miss Everett professed the most cheerful deference to Baxter's wishes and fancies, at the same time that she made no secret of possessing a number of strong convictions as to what should be attempted and what should be avoided.

It was no surprise to the young man to find her convictions sound and her wishes thoroughly sympathetic. He found himself called upon to make no compromise with stubborn and unnatural prejudices, nor to sacrifice his best intentions to a short-sighted vanity. Whether Miss Everett was vain or not need not here be declared. She had at least the wit to perceive that the interests of an enlightened sagacity would best be served by a painting which should be good from the painter's point of view, inasmuch as these are the painting's chief end. I may add, moreover, to her very great credit, that she thoroughly understood how great an artistic merit should properly attach to a picture executed at the behest of a passion, in order that it should be anything more than a mockery – a parody – of the duration of that passion; and that she knew instinctively that there is nothing so chilling to an artist's heat as the interference of illogical self-interest, either on his own behalf or that of another.

Baxter worked firmly and rapidly, and at the end of a couple of hours he felt that he had begun his picture. Mr Everett, as he sat by, threatened to be a bore; labouring apparently under the impression that it was his duty to beguile the session with cheap aesthetic small talk. But Marian good-humouredly took the painter's share of the dialogue, and he was not diverted from his work.

The next sitting was fixed for the morrow. Marian wore the dress which she had agreed upon with the painter, and in which, as in her position, the 'picturesque' element had been religiously suppressed. She read in Baxter's eyes that she looked supremely beautiful, and she saw that his fingers tingled to attack his subject. But she caused Lennox to be sent for, under the pretense of obtaining his adhesion to her dress. It was black, and he might object to black. He came, and she read in his kindly eyes an augmented edition of the assurance conveyed in Baxter's. He was enthusiastic for the black dress, which, in truth, seemed only to confirm and enrich, like a grave maternal protest, the young girl's look of undiminished youth.

'I expect you,' he said to Baxter, 'to make a masterpiece.'

'Never fear,' said the painter, tapping his forehead. 'It's made.'

On this second occasion, Mr Everett, exhausted by the intellectual strain of the preceding day, and encouraged by his luxurious chair, sank into a tranquil sleep. His companions remained for some time, listening to his regular breathing; Marian with her eyes patiently fixed on the opposite wall, and the young man with his glance mechanically travelling between his figure and the canvas. At last he fell back several paces to survey his work. Marian moved her eyes, and they met his own.

'Well, Miss Everett,' said the painter, in accents which might have been tremulous if he had not exerted a strong effort to make them firm.

'Well, Mr Baxter,' said the young girl.

And the two exchanged a long, firm glance, which at last ended in a smile – a smile which belonged decidedly to the family of the famous laugh of the two angels behind the altar in the temple.

'Well, Miss Everett,' said Baxter, going back to his work; 'such is life!'

'So it appears,' rejoined Marian. And then, after a pause of some moments: 'Why didn't you come and see me?' she added.

'I came and you weren't at home.'

'Why didn't you come again?'

'What was the use, Miss Everett?'

'It would simply have been more decent. We might have become reconciled.'

'We seem to have done that as it is.'

'I mean "in form".'

'That would have been absurd. Don't you see how true an instinct I had? What could have been easier than our meeting? I assure you that I should have found any talk about the past, and mutual assurances or apologies extremely disagreeable.'

Miss Everett raised her eyes from the floor and fixed them on her companion with a deep, half-reproachful glance. 'Is the past, then,' she asked, 'so utterly disagreeable?'

Baxter stared, half amazed. 'Good Heavens!' he cried, 'of course it is.'

Miss Everett dropped her eyes and remained silent.

I may as well take advantage of the moment, rapidly to make plain to the reader the events to which the above conversation refers.

Miss Everett had found it expedient, all things considered, not to tell her intended husband the whole story of her acquaintance with Stephen Baxter; and when I have repaired her omissions, the reader will probably justify her discretion.

She had, as she said, met this young man for the first time at Rome, and there in the course of two interviews had made a deep impression upon his heart. He had felt that he would give a great deal to meet Miss Everett again. Their reunion in Switzerland was therefore not entirely fortuitous; and it had been the more easy for Baxter to make it possible, for the reason that he was able to claim a kind of roundabout relationship with Mrs Denbigh, Marian's companion. With this lady's permission he had attached himself to their party. He had made their route of travel his own, he had stopped when they stopped and been prodigal of attentions and civilities. Before a week was over, Mrs Denbigh, who was the soul of confiding good nature, exulted in the discovery of an invaluable kinsman. Thanks not only to her naturally unexacting disposition, but to the apathetic and inactive habits induced by constant physical suffering, she proved a very insignificant third in her companions' spending of the hours. How delightfully these hours were spent, it requires no great effort to imagine. A suit conducted in the midst of the most romantic scenery in Europe is already half won. Marian's social graces were largely enhanced by the satisfaction which her innate intelligence of natural beauty enabled her to take in the magnificent scenery of the Alps. She had never appeared to such advantage; she had never known such perfect freedom and frankness and gaiety. For the first time in her life she had made a captive without suspecting it. She had surrendered her heart to the mountains and the lakes, the eternal snows and the pastoral valleys, and Baxter, standing by, had intercepted it. He felt his long-projected Swiss tour vastly magnified and beautified by Miss Everett's part in it – by the constant feminine sympathy which gushed within earshot, with the coolness and clearness of a mountain spring. Oh! if only it too had not been fed by the eternal snows! And then her beauty – her indefatigable beauty – was a continual enchantment. Miss Everett looked so thoroughly in her place in a drawing-room that it was almost logical to suppose that she looked well nowhere else. But in fact, as Baxter learned, she looked quite well enough in the character of what ladies call a 'fright' – that is, sunburnt, travel-stained, overheated, exhilarated and hungry – to elude all invidious comparisons.

At the end of three weeks, one morning as they stood together on the edge of a falling torrent, high above the green concavities of the hills, Baxter felt himself irresistibly urged to make a declaration. The thunderous noise of the cataract covered all vocal utterance; so, taking out his sketch-book, he wrote three short words on a blank leaf. He handed her the book. She read his message with a beautiful change of colour and a single rapid glance at his face. She then tore out the leaf.

'Don't tear it up!' cried the young man.

She understood him by the movement of his lips and shook her head with a smile. But she stooped, picked up a little stone, and wrapping it in the bit of paper, prepared to toss it into the torrent.

Baxter, uncertain, put out his hand to take it from her. She passed it into the other hand and gave him the one he had attempted to take.

She threw away the paper, but she let him keep her hand.

Baxter had still a week at his disposal, and Marian made it a very happy one. Mrs Denbigh was tired; they had come to a halt, and there was no interruption to their being together. They talked a great deal of the long future, which, on getting beyond the sound of the cataract, they had expeditiously agreed to pursue in common.

It was their misfortune both to be poor. They determined, in view of this circumstance, to say nothing of their engagement until Baxter, by dint of hard work, should have at least quadrupled his income. This was cruel, but it was imperative, and Marian made no complaint. Her residence in Europe had enlarged her conception of the material needs of a pretty woman, and it was quite natural that she should not, close upon the heels of this experience, desire to rush into marriage with a poor artist. At the end of some days Baxter started for Germany and Holland, portions of which he wished to visit for purposes of study. Mrs Denbigh and her young friend repaired to Paris for the Winter. Here, in the middle of February, they were rejoined by Baxter, who had achieved his German tour. He had received, while absent, five little letters from Marian, full of affection. The number was small but the young man detected in the very temperance of his mistress a certain delicious flavour of implicit constancy. She received him with all the frankness and sweetness that he had a right to expect, and listened with great interest to his account of the improvement in his prospects. He had sold three of his Italian pictures and had made an invaluable collection of sketches. He was on the high road to wealth and fame, and there was no reason their engagement should not be announced. But to this latter proposition Marian demurred – demurred so strongly, and yet on grounds so arbitrary, that a somewhat painful scene ensued. Stephen left her, irritated and perplexed. The next day, when he called, she was unwell and unable to see him; and the next – and the next. On the evening of the day that he had made his third fruitless call at Mrs Denbigh's, he overheard

Marian's name mentioned at a large party. The interlocutors were two elderly women. On giving his attention to their talk, which they were taking no pains to keep private, he found that his mistress was under accusal of having trifled with the affections of an unhappy young man, the only son of one of the ladies. There was apparently no lack of evidence or of facts which might be construed as evidence. Baxter went home, *la mort dans l'âme*, and on the following day called again on Mrs Denbigh. Marian was still in her room, but the former lady received him. Stephen was in great trouble, but his mind was lucid, and he addressed himself to the task of interrogating his hostess. Mrs Denbigh, with her habitual indolence, had remained unsuspicious of the terms on which the young people stood.

'I'm sorry to say,' Baxter began, 'that I heard Miss Everett accused last evening of very sad conduct.'

'Ah, for heaven's sake, Stephen,' returned his kinswoman, 'don't go back to that. I've done nothing all Winter but defend and palliate her conduct. It's hard work. Don't make me do it for you. You know her as well as I do. She was indiscreet, but I know she is penitent, and for that matter she's well out of it. He was by no means a desirable young man.'

'The lady whom I heard talking about the matter,' said Stephen, 'spoke of him in the highest terms. To be sure, as it turned out, she was his mother.'

'His mother? You're mistaken. His mother died ten years ago.'

Baxter folded his arms with a feeling that he needed to sit firm, '*Allons*,' said he, 'of whom do you speak?'

'Of young Mr King.'

'Good Heavens,' cried Stephen. 'So there are two of them?'

'Pray, of whom do *you* speak?'

'Of a certain Mr Young. The mother is a handsome old woman with white curls.'

'You don't mean to say there has been anything between Marian and Frederic Young?'

'*Voilà!* I only repeat what I hear. It seems to me, my dear Mrs Denbigh, that you ought to know.'

Mrs Denbigh shook her head with a melancholy movement. 'I'm sure I don't,' she said. 'I give it up. I don't pretend to judge. The manners of young people to each other are very different from what they were in my day. One doesn't know whether they mean nothing or everything.'

'You know, at least, whether Mr Young has been in your drawing-room?'

'Oh, yes, frequently. I'm very sorry that Marian is talked about. It's very unpleasant for me. But what can a sick woman do?'

'Well,' said Stephen, 'so much for Mr Young. And now for Mr King.'

'Mr King is gone home. It's a pity he ever came away.'

'In what sense?'

'Oh, he's a silly fellow. He doesn't understand young girls.'

'Upon my word,' said Stephen, *with expression*, as the music sheets say, 'he might be very wise and not do that.'

'Not but that Marian was injudicious. She meant only to be amiable, but she went too far. She became adorable. The first thing she knew he was holding her to an account.'

'Is he good-looking?'

'Well enough.'

'And rich?'

'Very rich, I believe.'

'And the other?'

'What other – Marian?'

'No, no; your friend Young.'

'Yes, he's quite handsome.'

'And rich, too?'

'Yes, I believe he's also rich.'

Baxter was silent a moment. 'And there's no doubt,' he resumed, 'that they were both far gone?'

'I can only answer for Mr King.'

'Well, I'll answer for Mr Young. His mother wouldn't have talked as she did unless she'd seen her son suffer. After all, then, it's perhaps not so much to Marian's discredit. Here are two handsome young millionaires, madly smitten. She refuses them both. She doesn't care for good looks and money.'

'I don't say that,' said Mrs Denbigh, sagaciously. 'She doesn't care for those things alone. She wants talent, and all the rest of it. Now, if you were only rich, Stephen—' added the good lady, innocently.

Baxter took up his hat. 'When you wish to marry Miss Everett,' he said, 'you must take good care not to say too much about Mr King and Mr Young.'

Two days after this interview, he had a conversation with the young girl in person. The reader may like him the less for his easily shaken confidence, but it is a fact that he had been unable to make light of these lightly made revelations. For him his love had been a passion; for her, he was compelled to believe, it had been a vulgar pastime. He was a man of a violent temper; he went straight to the point.

'Marian,' he said, 'you've been deceiving me.'

Marian knew very well what he meant; she knew very well that she had grown weary of her engagement and that, however little of a fault her conduct had been to Messrs Young and King, it had been an act of grave disloyalty to Baxter. She felt that the blow was struck and that their engagement was clean broken. She knew that Stephen would be satisfied with no half-excuses or half-denials; and she had none others to give. A hundred such would not make a perfect confession. Making no attempt, therefore, to save her 'prospects', for which she had ceased to care, she merely attempted to save her dignity. Her dignity for the moment was well enough secured by her natural half-cynical coolness of temper. But this same vulgar placidity left in Stephen's memory an impression of heartlessness and shallowness, which in that particular quarter, at least, was destined to be forever fatal to her claims to real weight and worth. She denied the young man's right to call her to account and to interfere with her conduct; and she almost anticipated his proposal that they should consider their engagement at an end. She even declined the use of the simple logic of tears. Under these circumstances, of course, the interview was not of long duration.

'I regard you,' said Baxter, as he stood on the threshold, 'as the most superficial, most heartless of women.'

He immediately left Paris and went down into Spain, where he remained till the opening of the Summer. In the month of May Mrs Denbigh and her *protégée* went to England, where the former, through her husband, possessed a number of connections, and where Marian's thoroughly un-English beauty was vastly admired. In September they sailed for America. About a year and a half, therefore, had elapsed between Baxter's separation from Miss Everett and their meeting in New York.

During this interval the young man's wounds had had time to heal. His sorrow, although violent, had been short-lived, and when he finally recovered his habitual equanimity, he was very glad to have purchased exemption at the price of a simple heartache. Reviewing his impressions of Miss Everett in a calmer mood, he made up his mind that she was very far from being the woman of his desire, and that she had not really been the woman of his choice. 'Thank God,' he said to himself, 'it's over. She's irreclaimably light. She's hollow, trivial, vulgar.' There had been in his addresses something hasty and feverish, something factitious and unreal in his fancied passion. Half of it had been the work of the scenery, of the weather, of mere juxtaposition, and, above all, of the young girl's picturesque beauty; to say nothing of the almost suggestive tolerance and indolence of poor Mrs Denbigh. And finding himself very much interested in Velázquez, at Madrid, he dismissed Miss Everett from his thoughts. I do not mean to offer his judgement of Miss Everett as final; but it was at least conscientious. The ample justice, moreover, which, under the illusion of sentiment, he had rendered to her charms and graces, gave him a right, when free from that illusion, to register his estimate of the arid spaces of her nature. Miss Everett might easily have accused him of injustice and brutality; but this fact would still stand to plead in his favour, that he cared with all his strength for truth. Marian, on the contrary, was quite indifferent to it. Stephen's angry sentence on her conduct had awakened no echo in her contracted soul.

The reader has now an adequate conception of the feelings with which these two old friends found themselves face to face. It is needful to add, however, that the lapse of time had very much diminished the force of those feelings. A woman, it seems to me, ought to desire no easier company, none less embarrassed or embarrassing, than a disenchanted lover; premising, of course, that the process of disenchantment is thoroughly complete, and that some time has elapsed since its completion.

Marian herself was perfectly at her ease. She had not retained her equanimity – her philosophy, one might almost call it – during that painful last interview, to go and lose it now. She had no ill feeling toward her old lover. His last words had been – like all words in Marian's estimation – a mere *façon de parler*. Miss Everett was in so perfect a good humour during these last days of her maidenhood that there was nothing in the past that she could not have forgiven.

She blushed a little at the emphasis of her companion's remark; but she was not discountenanced. She summoned up her good humour. 'The truth is, Mr Baxter,' she said, 'I feel at the present moment on perfect good terms with the world; I see everything *en rose*; the past as well as the future.'

'I, too, am on very good terms with the world,' said Baxter, 'and my heart is quite reconciled to what you call the past. But, nevertheless, it's very disagreeable to me to think about it.'

'Ah then,' said Miss Everett, with great sweetness, 'I'm afraid you're not reconciled.'

Baxter laughed – so loud that Miss Everett looked about at her father. But Mr Everett still slept the sleep of gentility. 'I've no doubt,' said the painter, 'that I'm far from being so good a Christian as you. But I assure you I'm very glad to see you again.'

'You've but to say the word and we're friends,' said Marian.

'We were very foolish to have attempted to be anything else.'

'"Foolish", yes. But it was a pretty folly.'

'Ah no, Miss Everett. I'm an artist, and I claim a right of property in the word "pretty". You mustn't stick it in there. Nothing could be pretty which had such an ugly termination. It was all false.'

'Well – as you will. What have you been doing since we parted?'

'Travelling and working. I've made great progress in my trade. Shortly before I came home I became engaged.'

'Engaged? – *à la bonne heure*. Is she good? – is she pretty?'

'She's not nearly so pretty as you.'

'In other words, she's infinitely more good. I'm sure I hope she is. But why did you leave her behind you?'

'She's with a sister, a sad invalid, who is drinking mineral waters on the Rhine. They wished to remain there to the cold weather. They're to be home in a couple of weeks, and we are straightway to be married.'

'I congratulate you, with all my heart,' said Marian.

'Allow me to do as much, sir,' said Mr Everett, waking up; which he did by instinct whenever the conversation took a ceremonious turn.

Miss Everett gave her companion but three more sittings, a large part of his work being executed with the assistance of photographs. At these interviews also, Mr Everett was present, and still delicately sensitive to the soporific influences of his position. But both parties had the good taste to abstain from further reference to their old relations, and to confine their talk to less personal themes.

II

ONE AFTERNOON, WHEN the picture was nearly finished, John Lennox went into the empty painting-room to ascertain the degree of its progress. Both Baxter and Marian had expressed a wish that he should not see it in its early stages, and this, accordingly, was his first view. Half an hour after he had entered the room, Baxter came in, unannounced, and found him sitting before the canvas, deep in thought. Baxter had been furnished with a house-key, so that he might have immediate and easy access to his work whenever the humour came upon him.

'I was passing,' he said, 'and I couldn't resist the impulse to come in and correct an error which I made this morning, now that a sense of its enormity is fresh in my mind.' He sat down to work, and the other stood watching him.

'Well,' said the painter, finally, 'how does it satisfy you?'

'Not altogether.'

'Pray develop your objections. It's in your power materially to assist me.'

'I hardly know how to formulate my objections. Let me, at all events, in the first place, say that I admire your work immensely. I'm sure it's the best picture you've painted.'

'I honestly believe it is. Some parts of it,' said Baxter, frankly, 'are excellent.'

'It's obvious. But either those very parts or others are singularly disagreeable. That word isn't criticism, I know; but I pay you for the right to be arbitrary. They are too hard, too strong, of too frank a reality. In a word, your picture frightens me, and if I were Marian I should feel as if you'd done me a certain violence.'

'I'm sorry for what's disagreeable; but I meant it all to be real. I go in for reality; you must have seen that.'

'I approve you; I can't too much admire the broad and firm methods you've taken for reaching this same reality. But you can be real without being brutal – without attempting, as one may say, to be *actual*.'

'I deny that I'm brutal. I'm afraid, Mr Lennox, I haven't taken quite the right road to please you. I've taken the picture too much *au sérieux*. I've striven too much for completeness. But if it doesn't please you it will please others.'

'I've no doubt of it. But that isn't the question. The picture is good enough to be a thousand times better.'

'That the picture leaves room for infinite improvement, I, of course, don't deny; and, in several particulars, I see my way to make it better. But, substantially, the portrait is there. I'll tell you what you miss. My work isn't "classical"; in fine, I'm not a man of genius.'

'No; I rather suspect you are. But, as you say, your work isn't classical. I adhere to my term *brutal*. Shall I tell you? It's too much of a study. You've given poor Miss Everett the look of a professional model.'

'If that's the case I've done very wrong. There never was an easier, a less conscious sitter. It's delightful to look at her.'

'Confound it, you've given all her ease, too. Well, I don't know what's the matter. I give up.'

'I think,' said Baxter, 'you had better hold your verdict in abeyance until the picture is finished. The classical element is there, I'm sure; but I've not brought it out. Wait a few days, and it will rise to the surface.'

Lennox left the artist alone; and the latter took up his brushes and painted hard till nightfall. He laid them down only when it was too dark to see. As he was going out, Lennox met him in the hall.

'*Exegi monumentum*,' said Baxter; 'it's finished. Go and look at your ease. I'll come tomorrow and hear your impressions.'

The master of the house, when the other had gone, lit half a dozen lights and returned to the study of the picture. It had grown prodigiously under the painter's recent handling, and whether it was that, as Baxter had said, the classical element had disengaged itself, or that Lennox was in a more sympathetic mood, it now impressed him as an original and powerful work, a genuine portrait, the deliberate image of a human face and figure. It was Marian, in very truth, and Marian most patiently measured and observed. Her beauty was there, her sweetness, and her young loveliness and her aerial grace, imprisoned for ever, made inviolable and perpetual. Nothing could be more simple than the conception and composition of the picture. The figure sat peacefully, looking slightly to the right, with the head erect and the hands – the virginal hands, without rings or brace-lets – lying idle on its knees. The blonde hair was gathered into a little knot of braids on the top of the head (in the fashion of the moment), and left free the almost childish contour of the ears and cheeks. The eyes were full of colour, contentment and light; the lips were faintly parted. Of colour in the picture, there was, in strictness, very little; but the dark draperies told of reflected sunshine, and the flesh-spaces of human blushes and pallors, of throbbing life and health. The work was strong and simple, the figure was thoroughly void of affectation and stiffness, and yet supremely elegant.

'That's what it is to be an artist,' thought Lennox. 'All this has been done in the past two hours.'

It was his Marian, assuredly, with all that had charmed him – with all that still charmed him when he saw her: her appealing confidence, her exquisite lightness, her feminine enchantments. And yet, as he looked, an expression of pain came into his eyes, and lingered there, and grew into a mortal heaviness.

Lennox had been as truly a lover as a man may be; but he loved with the discretion of fifteen years' experience of human affairs. He had a penetrating glance, and he liked to use it. Many a time when Marian, with eloquent lips and eyes, had poured out the treasures of her nature into his bosom, and he had taken them in his hands and covered them with kisses and passionate vows; he had dropped them all with a sudden shudder and cried out in silence, 'But ah! where is the heart?' One day he had said to her (irrelevantly enough, doubtless), 'Marian, where is your heart?'

'*Where* – what do you mean?' Miss Everett had said.

'I think of you from morning till night. I put you together and take you apart, as people do in that game where they make words out of a parcel of given letters. But there's always one letter wanting. I can't put my hand on your heart.'

'My heart, John,' said Marian, ingeniously, 'is the whole world. My heart's everywhere.'

This may have been true enough. Miss Everett had distributed her heart impartially throughout her whole organism, so that, as a natural consequence, its native seat was somewhat scantily occupied. As Lennox sat and looked at Baxter's consummate handiwork, the same question rose again to his lips; and if Marian's portrait suggested it, Marian's portrait failed to answer it. It took Marian to do that. It seemed to Lennox that some strangely potent agency had won from his mistress the confession of her inmost soul, and had written it there upon the canvas in firm yet passionate lines. Marian's person was lightness – her charm was lightness; could it be that her soul was levity too? Was she a creature without faith and without conscience? What else was the meaning of that horrible blankness and deadness that quenched the light in her eyes and stole away the smile from her lips? These things were the less to be eluded because in so many respects the painter had been profoundly just. He had been as loyal and sympathetic as he had been intelligent. Not a point in the young girl's appearance had been slighted; not a feature but had been forcibly and delicately rendered. Had Baxter been a man of marvellous insight – an unparalleled observer; or had he been a mere patient and unflinching painter, building infinitely better than he knew? Would not a mere painter have been content to paint Miss Everett in the strong, rich, objective manner of which the work was so good an example, and to do nothing more? For it was evident that Baxter had done more. He had painted with something more than knowledge – with imagination, with feeling. He had almost composed;

and his composition had embraced the truth. Lennox was unable to satisfy his doubts. He would have been glad to believe that there was no imagination in the picture but what his own mind supplied; and that the unsubstantial sweetness on the eyes and lips of the image was but the smile of youth and innocence. He was in a muddle – he was absurdly suspicious and capricious; he put out the lights and left the portrait in kindly darkness. Then, half as a reparation to his mistress, and half as a satisfaction to himself, he went up to spend an hour with Marian. She, at least, as he found, had no scruples. She thought the portrait altogether a success, and she was very willing to be handed down in that form to posterity. Nevertheless, when Lennox came in, he went back into the painting-room to take another glance. This time he lit but a single light. Faugh! it was worse than with a dozen. He hastily turned out the gas.

Baxter came the next day, as he had promised. Meanwhile poor Lennox had had twelve hours of uninterrupted reflection, and the expression of distress in his eyes had acquired an intensity which, the painter saw, proved it to be of far other import than a mere tribute to his power.

'Can the man be jealous?' thought Baxter. Stephen had been so innocent of any other design than that of painting a good portrait, that his conscience failed to reveal to him the source of his companion's trouble. Nevertheless he began to pity him. He had felt tempted, indeed, to pity him from the first. He had liked him and esteemed him; he had taken him for a man of sense and of feeling, and he had thought it a matter of regret that such a man – a creature of strong spiritual needs – should link his destiny with that of Marian Everett. But he had very soon made up his mind that Lennox knew very well what he was about, and that he needed no enlightenment. He was marrying with his eyes open, and had weighed the risks against the profits. Everyone had his particular taste, and at thirty-five years of age John Lennox had no need to be told that Miss Everett was not quite all that she might be. Baxter had thus taken for granted that his friend had designedly selected as his second wife a mere pretty woman – a woman with a genius for receiving company, and who would make a picturesque use of his money. He knew nothing of the serious character of the poor man's passion, nor of the extent to which his happiness was bound up in what the painter would have called his delusion. His only concern had been to do his work well; and he had done it the better because of his old interest in Marian's bewitching face. It is very certain that he had actually infused into his picture that force of characterization and that depth of reality which had arrested his friend's attention; but he had done so wholly without effort and without malice. The artistic half of Baxter's nature exerted a lusty dominion over the human half – fed upon its disappointments and grew fat upon its joys and tribulations. This, indeed, is simply saying that the young man was a true artist. Deep, then, in the unfathomed recesses of his strong and sensitive nature, his genius had held communion with his heart and had transferred to canvas the burden of its disenchantment and its resignation. Since his little affair with Marian, Baxter had made the acquaintance of a young girl whom he felt that he could love and trust for ever; and, sobered and strengthened by this new emotion, he had been able to resume with more distinctness the shortcomings of his earlier love. He had, therefore, painted with feeling. Miss Everett could not have expected him to do otherwise. He had done his honest best, and conviction had come in unbidden and made it better.

Lennox had begun to feel very curious about the history of his companion's acquaintance with his destined bride; but he was far from feeling jealous. Somehow he felt that he could never again be jealous. But in ascertaining the terms of their former intercourse, it was of importance that he should not allow the young man to suspect that he discovered in the portrait any radical defect.

'Your old acquaintance with Miss Everett,' he said, frankly, 'has evidently been of great use to you.'

'I suppose it has,' said Baxter. 'Indeed, as soon as I began to paint, I found her face coming back to me like a half-remembered tune. She was wonderfully pretty at that time.'

'She was two years younger.'

'Yes, and I was two years younger. Decidedly, you are right. I have made use of my old impressions.'

Baxter was willing to confess to so much; but he was resolved not to betray anything that Marian had herself kept secret. He was not surprised that she had not told her lover of her former engagement; he expected as much. But he would have held it inexcusable to attempt to repair her omission.

Lennox's faculties were acutely sharpened by pain and suspicion, and he could not help detecting in his companion's eyes an intention of reticence. He resolved to baffle it.

'I am curious to know,' he said, 'whether you were ever in love with Miss Everett?'

'I have no hesitation in saying Yes,' rejoined Baxter; fancying that a general confession would help him more than a particular denial. 'I'm one of a thousand, I fancy. Or one, perhaps, of only a hundred. For you see I've got over it. I'm engaged to be married.'

Lennox's countenance brightened. 'That's it,' said he. 'Now I know what I didn't like in your picture – the point of view. I'm not jealous,' he added. 'I should like the picture better if I were. You evidently care nothing for the poor girl. You have got over your love rather too well. You loved her, she was indifferent to you, and now you take your revenge.' Distracted with grief, Lennox was taking refuge in irrational anger.

Baxter was puzzled. 'You'll admit,' said he, with a smile, 'that it's a very handsome revenge.' And all his professional self-esteem rose to his assistance. 'I've painted for Miss Everett the best portrait that has yet been painted in America. She herself is quite satisfied.'

'Ah!' said Lennox, with magnificent dissimulation; 'Marian is generous.'

'Come, then,' said Baxter; 'what do you complain of? You accuse me of scandalous conduct, and I'm bound to hold you to an account.' Baxter's own temper was rising, and with it his sense of his picture's merits. 'How have I perverted Miss Everett's expression? How have I misrepresented her? What does the portrait lack? Is it ill-drawn? Is it vulgar? Is it ambiguous? Is it immodest?' Baxter's patience gave out as he recited these various charges. 'Fiddlesticks!' he cried; 'you know as well as I do that the picture is excellent.'

'I don't pretend to deny it. Only I wonder that Marian was willing to come to you.'

It is very much to Baxter's credit that he still adhered to his resolution not to betray the young girl, and that rather than do so he was willing to let Lennox suppose that he had been a rejected adorer.

'Ah, as you say,' he exclaimed, 'Miss Everett is so generous!'

Lennox was foolish enough to take this as an admission. 'When I say, Mr Baxter,' he said, 'that you have taken your revenge, I don't mean that you've done so wantonly or consciously. My dear fellow, how could you help it? The disappointment was proportionate to the loss and the reaction to the disappointment.'

'Yes, that's all very well; but, meanwhile, I wait in vain to learn wherein I've done wrong.'

Lennox looked from Baxter to the picture, and from the picture back to Baxter.

'I defy you to tell me,' said Baxter. 'I've simply kept Miss Everett as charming as she is in life.'

'Oh, damn her charms!' cried Lennox.

'If you were not the gentleman, Mr Lennox,' continued the young man, 'which, in spite of your high temper, I believe you to be, I should believe you—'

'Well, you should believe me?'

'I should believe you simply bent on cheapening the portrait.'

Lennox made a gesture of vehement impatience. The other burst out laughing and the discussion closed. Baxter instinctively took up his brushes and approached his canvas with a vague desire to detect latent errors, while Lennox prepared to take his departure.

'Stay!' said the painter, as he was leaving the room; 'if the picture really offends you, I'll rub it out. Say the word,' and he took up a heavy brush, covered with black paint.

But Lennox shook his head with decision and went out. The next moment, however, he reappeared. 'You *may* rub it out,' he said. 'The picture is, of course, already mine.'

But now Baxter shook his head. 'Ah! now it's too late,' he answered. 'Your chance is gone.'

Lennox repaired directly to Mr Everett's apartments. Marian was in the drawing-room with some morning-callers, and her lover sat by until she had got rid of them. When they were alone together, Marian began to laugh at her visitors and to parody certain of their affectations, which she did with infinite grace and spirit. But Lennox cut her short and returned to the portrait. He had thought better of his objections of the preceding evening; he liked it.

'But I wonder, Marian,' he said, 'that you were willing to go to Mr Baxter.'

'Why so?' asked Marian, on her guard. She saw that her lover knew something, and she intended not to commit herself until she knew how much he knew.

'An old lover is always dangerous.'

'An old lover?' and Marian blushed a good honest blush. But she rapidly recovered herself. 'Pray where did you get that charming news?'

'Oh, it slipped out,' said Lennox.

Marian hesitated a moment. Then with a smile: 'Well, I was brave,' she said. 'I went.'

'How came it,' pursued Lennox, 'that you didn't tell me?'

'Tell you what, my dear John?'

'Why, about Baxter's little passion. Come, don't be modest.'

Modest! Marian breathed freely. 'What do you mean, my dear, by telling your wife not to be modest? Pray don't ask me about Mr Baxter's passions. What do I know about them?'

'Did you know nothing of this one?'

'Ah, my dear, I know a great deal too much for my comfort. But he's got bravely over it. He's engaged.'

'Engaged, but not quite disengaged. He's an honest fellow, but he remembers his penchant. It was as much as he could do to keep his picture from turning to the sentimental. He saw you as he fancied you – as he wished you; and he has given you a little look of what he imagines moral loveliness, which comes within an ace of spoiling the picture. Baxter's imagination isn't very strong, and this same look expresses, in point of fact, nothing but inanity. Fortunately he's a man of extraordinary talent, and a real painter, and he has made a good portrait in spite of himself.'

To such arguments as these was John Lennox reduced, to stifle the evidence of his senses. But when once a lover begins to doubt, he cannot cease at will. In spite of his earnest efforts to believe in Marian as before, to accept her without scruple and without second thought, he was quite unable to repress an impulse of constant mistrust and aversion. The charm was broken, and there is no mending a charm. Lennox stood half-aloof, watching the poor girl's countenance, weighing her words, analysing her thoughts, guessing at her motives.

Marian's conduct under this trying ordeal was truly heroic. She felt that some subtle change had taken place in her future husband's feelings, a change which, although she was powerless to discover its cause, yet obviously imperilled her prospects. Something had snapped between them; she had lost half of her power. She was horribly distressed, and the more so because that superior depth of character which she had all along gladly conceded to Lennox, might now, as she conjectured, cover some bold and portentous design. Could he meditate a direct rupture? Could it be his intention to dash from her lips the sweet, the spiced and odorous cup of being the wife of a good-natured millionaire? Marian turned a tremulous glance upon her past, and wondered if he had discovered any dark spot. Indeed, for that matter, might she not defy him to do so? She had done nothing really amiss. There was no visible blot in her history. It was faintly discoloured, indeed, by a certain vague moral dinginess; but it compared well enough with that of other girls. She had cared for nothing but pleasure; but to what else were girls brought up? On the whole, might she not feel at ease? She assured herself that she might; but she nevertheless felt that if John wished to break off his engagement, he would do it on high abstract grounds, and not because she had committed a naughtiness the more or the less. It would be simply because he had ceased to love her. It would avail her but little to assure him that she would kindly overlook this circumstance and remit the obligations of the heart. But, in spite of her hideous apprehensions, she continued to smile and smile.

The days passed by, and John consented to be still engaged. Their marriage was only a week off – six days, five days, four. Miss Everett's smile became less mechanical. John had apparently been passing through a crisis – a moral and intellectual crisis, inevitable in a man of his constitution, and with which she had nothing to do. On the eve of marriage he had questioned his heart; he had found that it was no longer young and capable of the vagaries of passion, and he had made up his mind to call things by their proper names, and to admit to himself that he was marrying not for love, but for friendship, and a little, perhaps, for prudence. It was only out of regard for what he supposed Marian's own more exalted theory of the matter, that he abstained from revealing to her this common-sense view of it. Such was Marian's hypothesis.

Lennox had fixed his wedding-day for the last Thursday in October. On the preceding Friday, as he was passing up

Broadway, he stopped at Goupil's to see if his order for the framing of the portrait had been fulfilled. The picture had been transferred to the shop, and, when duly framed, had been, at Baxter's request and with Lennox's consent, placed for a few days in the exhibition room. Lennox went up to look at it.

The portrait stood on an easel at the end of the hall, with three spectators before it – a gentleman and two ladies. The room was otherwise empty. As Lennox went toward the picture, the gentleman turned out to be Baxter. He proceeded to introduce his friend to his two companions, the younger of whom Lennox recognized as the artist's betrothed. The other, her sister, was a plain, pale woman, with the look of ill health, who had been provided with a seat and made no attempt to talk. Baxter explained that these ladies had arrived from Europe but the day before, and that his first care had been to show them his masterpiece.

'Sarah,' said he, 'has been praising the model very much to the prejudice of the copy.'

Sarah was a tall, black-haired girl of twenty, with irregular features, a pair of luminous dark eyes, and a smile radiant of white teeth – evidently an excellent person. She turned to Lennox with a look of frank sympathy, and said in a deep, rich voice:

'She must be very beautiful.'

'Yes, she's very beautiful,' said Lennox, with his eyes lingering on her own pleasant face. 'You must know her – she must know you.'

'I'm sure I should like very much to see her,' said Sarah.

'This is very nearly as good,' said Lennox. 'Mr Baxter is a great genius.'

'I know Mr Baxter is a genius. But what is a picture, at the best? I've seen nothing but pictures for the last two years, and I haven't seen a single pretty girl.'

The young girl stood looking at the portrait in very evident admiration, and, while Baxter talked to the elder lady, Lennox bestowed a long, covert glance upon his *fiancée*. She had brought her head into almost immediate juxtaposition with that of Marian's image, and, for a moment, the freshness and the strong animation which bloomed upon her features seemed to obliterate the lines and colours on the canvas. But the next moment, as Lennox looked, the roseate circle of Marian's face blazed into remorseless distinctness, and her careless blue eyes looked with cynical familiarity into his own.

He bade an abrupt good-morning to his companions, and went toward the door. But beside it he stopped. Suspended on the wall was Baxter's picture, *My Last Duchess*. He stood amazed. Was *this* the face and figure that, a month ago, had reminded him of his mistress? Where was the likeness now? It was as utterly absent as if it had never existed. The picture, moreover, was a very inferior work to the new portrait. He looked back at Baxter, half tempted to demand an explanation, or at least to express his perplexity. But Baxter and his sweetheart had stooped down to examine a minute sketch near the floor, with their heads in delicious contiguity.

How the week elapsed, it were hard to say. There were moments when Lennox felt as if death were preferable to the heartless union which now stared him in the face, and as if the only possible course was to transfer his property to Marian and to put an end to his existence. There were others, again, when he was fairly reconciled to his fate. He had but to gather his old dreams and fancies into a faggot and break them across his knee, and the thing were done. Could he not collect in their stead a comely cluster of moderate and rational expectations, and bind them about with a wedding favour? His love was dead, his youth was dead; that was alt There was no need of making a tragedy of it. His love's vitality had been but small, and since it was to be short-lived it was better that it should expire before marriage than after. As for marriage, that should stand, for that was not of necessity a matter of love. He lacked the brutal consistency necessary for taking away Marian's future. If he had mistaken her and overrated her, the fault was his own, and it was a hard thing that she should pay the penalty. Whatever were her failings, they were profoundly involuntary, and it was plain that with regard to himself her intentions were good. She would be no companion, but she would be at least a faithful wife.

With the help of this grim logic, Lennox reached the eve of his wedding day. His manner toward Miss Everett during the preceding week had been inveterately tender and kind. He felt that in losing his love she had lost a heavy treasure, and he offered her instead the most unfailing devotion. Marian had questioned him about his lassitude and his preoccupied air, and he had replied that he was not very well. On the Wednesday afternoon, he mounted his horse and took a long ride. He came home toward sunset, and was met in the hall by his old housekeeper.

'Miss Everett's portrait, sir,' she said, 'has just been sent home, in the most beautiful frame. You gave no directions, and I took the liberty of having it carried into the library. I thought,' and the old woman smiled deferentially, 'you'd like best to have it in your own room.'

Lennox went into the library. The picture was standing on the floor, back to back with a high arm-chair, and catching, through the window, the last horizontal rays of the sun. He stood before it a moment, gazing at it with a haggard face.

'Come!' said he, at last, 'Marian may be what God has made her; but this detestable creature I can neither love nor respect!'

He looked about him with an angry despair, and his eye fell on a long, keen poinard, given him by a friend who had bought it in the East, and which lay as an ornament on his mantel-shelf. He seized it and thrust it, with barbarous glee, straight into the lovely face of the image. He dragged it downward, and made a long fissure in the living canvas. Then, with half a dozen strokes, he wantonly hacked it across. The act afforded him an immense relief.

I need hardly add that on the following day Lennox was married. He had locked the library door on coming out the evening before, and he had the key in his waistcoat pocket as he stood at

the altar. As he left town, therefore, immediately after the ceremony, it was not until his return, a fortnight later, that the fate
of the picture became known. It is not necessary to relate how
he explained his exploit to Marian and how he disclosed it to
Baxter. He at least put on a brave face. There is a rumour current
of his having paid the painter an enormous sum of money. The
amount is probably exaggerated, but there can be no doubt that
the sum was very large. How he has fared – how he is destined
to fare – in matrimony, it is rather too early to determine. He
has been married scarcely three months.

De Grey: A Romance

I T WAS THE year 1820, and Mrs De Grey, by the same token,
as they say in Ireland (and, for that matter, out of it), had
reached her sixty-seventh spring. She was, nevertheless, still a
handsome woman, and, what is better yet, still an amiable
woman. The untroubled, unruffled course of her life had left
as few wrinkles on her temper as on her face. She was tall and
full of person, with dark eyes and abundant white hair, which
she rolled back from her forehead over a cushion, or some
such artifice. The freshness of youth and health had by no
means faded out of her cheeks, nor had the smile of her imperturbable courtesy expired on her lips. She dressed, as became
a woman of her age and a widow, in black garments, but
relieved with a great deal of white, with a number of handsome rings on her fair hands. Frequently, in the spring, she
wore a little flower or a sprig of green leaves in the bosom of
her gown. She had been accused of receiving these little floral
ornaments from the hands of Mr Herbert (of whom I shall
have more to say); but the charge is unfounded, inasmuch as

they were very carefully selected from a handful cut in the garden by her maid.

That Mrs De Grey should have been just the placid and elegant old lady that she was, remained, in the eyes of the world at large, in spite of an abundance of a certain sort of evidence in favour of such a result, more or less of a puzzle and a problem. It is true, that everyone who knew anything about her knew that she had enjoyed great material prosperity, and had suffered no misfortunes. She was mistress in her own right of a handsome property and a handsome house; she had lost her husband, indeed, within a year after marriage; but, as the late George De Grey had been of a sullen and brooding humour – to that degree, indeed, as to incur the suspicion of insanity – her loss, leaving her well provided for, might in strictness have been accounted a gain. Her son, moreover, had never given her a moment's trouble; he had grown up a charming young man, handsome, witty, and wise; he was a model of filial devotion. The lady's health was good; she had half a dozen perfect servants; she had the perpetual company of the incomparable Mr Herbert; she was as fine a figure of an elderly woman as any in town; she might, therefore, very well have been happy and have looked so. On the other hand, a dozen sensible women had been known to declare with emphasis, that not for all her treasures and her felicity would they have consented to be Mrs De Grey. These ladies were, of course, unable to give a logical reason for so strong an aversion. But it is certain that there hung over Mrs De Grey's history and circumstances a film, as it were, a shadow of mystery, which struck a chill upon imaginations which might easily have been kindled into envy of her good fortune. 'She lives in the dark,' someone had said of her. Close observers did her the honour to believe that there was a secret in her life, but of a wholly undefined character. Was she the victim of some lurking sorrow, or the mistress of some clandestine joy? These imputations, we may easily believe, are partially explained by the circumstance that she was a Catholic, and kept a priest in her house. The unexplained portion might very well, moreover, have been discredited by Mrs De Grey's perfectly candid and complacent demeanour. It was certainly hard to conceive, in talking with her, to what part of her person one might pin a mystery – whether on her dear, round eyes or her handsome, benevolent lips. Let us say, then, in defiance of the voice of society, that she was no tragedy queen. She was a fine woman, a dull woman, a perfect gentlewoman. She had taken life, as she liked a cup of tea – weak, with an exquisite aroma and plenty of cream and sugar. She had never lost her temper, for the excellent reason that she had none to lose. She was troubled with no fears, no doubts, no scruples, and blessed with no sacred certainties. She was fond of her son, of the church, of her garden, and of her toilet. She had the very best taste; but, morally, one may say that she had had no history.

Mrs De Grey had always lived in seclusion; for a couple of years previous to the time of which I speak she had lived in solitude. Her son, on reaching his twenty-third year, had gone to Europe for a long visit, in pursuance of a plan discussed at intervals between his mother and Mr Herbert during the whole course of his boyhood. They had made no attempt to forecast his future career, or to prepare him for a profession. Strictly, indeed, he was at liberty, like his late father, to dispense with a profession. Not that it was to be wished that he should take his father's life as an example. It was understood by the world at large, and, of course, by Mrs De Grey and her companion in particular, that this gentleman's existence had been blighted, at an early period, by an unhappy love-affair; and it was notorious that, in consequence, he had spent the few years of his maturity in gloomy idleness and dissipation. Mrs De Grey, whose own father was an Englishman, reduced to poverty, but with claims to high gentility, professed herself unable to understand why Paul should not live decently on his means. Mr Herbert declared that in America, in any walk of life, idleness was indecent; and that he hoped the young man would – nominally at least – select a career. It was agreed on both sides, however, that there was no need for haste; and that it was proper, in the first place, he should see the world. The world, to Mrs De Grey, was little more than a name; but to Mr Herbert, priest as he was, it was a vivid reality. Yet he felt that the generous and intelligent youth upon whose education he had lavished all the treasures of his tenderness and sagacity, was not unfitted, either by nature or culture, to measure his sinews against its trials and temptations; and that he should love him the better for coming home at twenty-five an accomplished gentleman and a good Catholic, sobered and seasoned by experience, sceptical in small matters, confident in great, and richly replete with good stories. When he came of age, Paul received his walking-ticket, as they say, in the shape of a letter of credit for a handsome sum on certain London bankers. But the young man pocketed the letter, and remained at home, poring over books, lounging in the garden, and scribbling heroic verses. At the end of a year, he plucked up a little ambition, and took a turn through the country, travelling much of the way on horseback. He came back an ardent American, and felt that he might go abroad without danger. During his absence in Europe he had written home innumerable long letters – compositions so elaborate (in the taste of that day, recent as it is) and so delightful, that, between their pride in his epistolary talent, and their longing to see his face, his mother and his ex-tutor would have been at a loss to determine whether he gave them more satisfaction at home or abroad.

With his departure the household was plunged in unbroken repose. Mrs De Grey neither went out nor entertained company. An occasional morning-call was the only claim made upon her hospitality. Mr Herbert, who was a great scholar, spent all his hours in study; and his patroness sat for the most part alone, arrayed with a perfection of neatness which there was no one to admire (unless it be her waiting-maid, to whom it remained a constant matter of awe), reading a pious book or knitting undergarments for the orthodox needy. At times, indeed, she wrote long letters to her son – the contents of which Mr Herbert found it hard to divine. This was accounted a dull life forty years ago; now, doubtless, it would be considered no life at all. It is no matter of wonder, therefore, that finally, one April morning, in her sixty-seventh year, as I have said, Mrs De Grey suddenly began to suspect that she was lonely. Another long year, at least, was to come and go before Paul's return. After meditating for a while in silence, Mrs De Grey resolved to take counsel with Father Herbert.

This gentleman, an Englishman by birth, had been an intimate friend of George De Grey, who had made his acquaintance during a visit to Europe, before his marriage. Mr Herbert was a younger son of an excellent Catholic family, and was at that time beginning, on small resources, the practice of the law. De Grey met him in London, and the two conceived a strong mutual sympathy. Herbert had neither taste for his profession nor apparent ambition of any sort. He was, moreover, in weak health; and his friend found no difficulty in persuading him to accept the place of travelling companion through France and Italy. De Grey carried a very long purse, and was a most liberal friend and patron; and the two young men accomplished their progress as far as Venice in the best spirits and on the best terms. But in Venice, for reasons best known to themselves, they bitterly and irretrievably quarrelled. Some persons said it was over a card-table, and some said it was about a woman. At all events, in consequence, De Grey returned to America, and Herbert repaired to Rome. He obtained admission into a monastery, studied theology, and finally was invested with priestly orders. In America, in his thirty-third year, De Grey married the lady whom I have described. A few weeks after his marriage he wrote to Herbert, expressing a vehement desire to be reconciled. Herbert felt that the letter was that of a most unhappy man; he had already forgiven him; he pitied him, and after a short delay succeeded in obtaining an ecclesiastical mission to the United States. He reached New York and presented himself at his friend's house, which from this moment became his home. Mrs De Grey had recently given birth to a son; her husband was confined to his room by illness, reduced to a shadow of his former self by repeated sensual excesses. He survived Herbert's arrival but a couple of months; and after his death the rumour went abroad that he had by his last will settled a handsome income upon the priest, on condition that he would continue to reside with his widow, and take the entire charge of his boy's education.

This rumour was confirmed by the event. For twenty-five years, at the time of which I write, Herbert had lived under Mrs De Grey's roof as her friend and companion and counsellor, and as her son's tutor. Once reconciled to his friend, he had gradually dropped his priestly character. He was of an essentially devout temperament, but he craved neither parish nor pulpit. On the other hand, he had become an indefatigable student. His late friend had bequeathed to him a valuable library, which he gradually enlarged. His passion for study, however, appeared singularly disinterested, inasmuch as, for many years, his little friend Paul was the sole witness and receptacle of his learning. It is true that he composed a large portion of a History of the Catholic Church in America, which, although the manuscript exists, has never seen, and, I suppose, is never destined to see, the light. It is in the very best keeping, for it contains an immense array of facts. The work is written, not from a sympathetic, but from a strictly respectful point of view; but it has a fatal defect – it lacks unction.

The same complaint might have been made of Father Herbert's personal character. He was the soul of politeness, but it was a cold and formal courtesy. When he smiled, it was, as the French say, with the end of his lips, and when he took your hand, with the end of his fingers. He had had a charming face in his younger days, and, when gentlemen dressed their hair with powder, his fine black eyes must have produced the very best effect. But he had lost his hair, and he wore on his naked crown a little black silk cap. Round his neck he had a black cravat of many folds, without any collar. He was short and slight, with a stoop in his shoulders, and a handsome pair of hands.

'If it were not for a sad sign to the contrary,' said Mrs De Grey, in pursuance of her resolve to take counsel of her friend, 'I should believe I am growing younger.'

'What is the sign to the contrary?' asked Herbert.

'I'm losing my eyes. I can't see to read. Suppose I should become blind.'

'And what makes you suspect that you are growing young again?'

'I feel lonely. I lack company. I miss Paul.'

'You will have Paul back in a year.'

'Yes; but in the meanwhile I shall be miserable. I wish I knew some nice person whom I might ask to stay with me.'

'Why don't you take a companion – some poor gentlewoman in search of a home? She would read to you, and talk to you.'

'No; that would be dreadful. She would be sure to be old and ugly. I should like someone to take Paul's place – someone young and fresh like him. We're all so terribly old, in the house. You're at least seventy; I'm sixty-five' (Mrs De Grey was pleased to say); 'Deborah is sixty, the cook and coachman are fifty-five apiece.'

'You want a young girl then?'

'Yes, some nice, fresh young girl, who would laugh once in a while, and make a little music – a little sound in the house.'

'Well,' said Herbert, after reflecting a moment, 'you had better suit yourself before Paul comes home. You have only a year.'

'Dear me,' said Mrs De Grey; 'I shouldn't feel myself obliged to turn her out on Paul's account.'

Father Herbert looked at his companion with a penetrating glance. 'Nevertheless, my dear lady,' he said, 'you know what I mean.'

'O yes, I know what you mean – and you, Father Herbert, know what I think.'

'Yes, madam, and, allow me to add, that I don't greatly care. Why should I? I hope with all my heart that you'll never find yourself compelled to think otherwise.'

'It is certain,' said Mrs De Grey, 'that Paul has had time to play out his little tragedy a dozen times over.'

'His father,' rejoined Herbert, gravely, 'was twenty-six years old.'

At these words Mrs De Grey looked at the priest with a slight frown and a flushed cheek. But he took no pains to meet her eyes, and in a few moments she had recovered, in silence, her habitual calmness.

Within a week after this conversation Mrs De Grey observed at church two persons who appeared to be strangers in the congregation: an elderly woman, meanly clad, and evidently in ill health, but with a great refinement of person and manner; and a young girl whom Mrs De Grey took for her daughter. On the following Sunday she again found them at their devotions, and was forcibly struck by a look of sadness and trouble in their faces and attitude. On the third Sunday they were absent; but it happened that during the walk, going to confession, she met the young girl, pale, alone, and dressed in mourning, apparently just leaving the confessional. Something in her gait and aspect assured Mrs De Grey that she was alone in the world, friendless and helpless; and the good lady, who at times was acutely sensible of her own isolation in society, felt a strong and sympathetic prompting to speak to the stranger, and ask the secret of her sorrow. She stopped her before she left the church, and, addressing her with the utmost kindness, succeeded so speedily in winning her confidence that in half an hour she was in possession of the young girl's entire history. She had just lost her mother, and she found herself in the great city penniless, and all but houseless. They were from the South; her father had been an officer in the navy, and had perished at sea, two years before. Her mother's health had failed, and they had come to New

York, ill-advisedly enough, to consult an eminent physician. He had been very kind, he had taken no fees, but his skill had been applied in vain. Their money had melted away in other directions – for food and lodging and clothing. There had been enough left to give the poor lady a decent burial; but no means of support save her own exertions remained for the young girl. She had no relatives to look to, but she professed herself abundantly willing to work. 'I look weak,' she said, 'and pale, but I'm really strong. It's only that I'm tired – and sad. I'm ready to do anything. But I don't know where to look.' She had lost her colour and the roundness and elasticity of youth; she was thin and ill-dressed; but Mrs De Grey saw that at her best she must be properly a very pretty creature, and that she was evidently, by rights, a charming girl. She looked at the elder lady with lustrous, appealing blue eyes from under the hideous black bonnet in which her masses of soft light hair were tucked away. She assured her that she had received a very good education, and that she played on the piano-forte. Mrs De Grey fancied her divested of her rusty weeds, and dressed in a white frock and a blue ribbon, reading aloud at an open window, or touching the keys of her old not unmelodious spinet; for if she took her (as she mentally phrased it) Mrs De Grey was resolved that she would not be harassed with the sight of her black garments. It was plain that, frightened and faint and nervous as she was, the poor child would take any service unconditionally. She kissed her then tenderly within the sacred precinct, and led her away to her carriage, quite forgetting her business with her confessor.

On the following day Margaret Aldis (such was the young girl's name) was transferred in the same vehicle to Mrs De Grey's own residence.

This edifice was demolished some years ago, and the place where it stood forms at the present moment the very centre of a turbulent thoroughfare. But at the period of which I speak it stood on the outskirts of the town, with as vast a prospect of open country in one direction as in the other of close-built streets. It was an excellent old mansion, moreover, in the best taste of the time, with large square rooms and broad halls and deep windows, and, above all, a delightful great garden, hedged off from the road by walls of dense verdure. Here, steeped in repose and physical comfort, rescued from the turbid stream of common life, and placed apart in the glow of tempered sunshine, valued, esteemed, caressed, and yet feeling that she was not a mere passive object of charity, but that she was doing her simple utmost to requite her protectress, poor Miss Aldis bloomed and flowered afresh. With rest and luxury and leisure, her natural gaiety and beauty came back to her. Her beauty was not dazzling, indeed, nor her gaiety obtrusive; but, united, they were the flower of girlish grace. She still retained a certain tenuity and fragility of aspect, a lightness of tread, a softness of voice, a faintness of colouring, which suggested an intimate acquaintance with suffering. But there seemed to burn, nevertheless, in her deep blue eyes the light of an almost passionate vitality; and there sat on her firm, pale lips the utterance of a determined, devoted will. It seemed at times as if she gave herself up with a

sensuous, reckless, half-thankless freedom to the mere consciousness of security. It was evident that she had an innate love of
luxury. She would sometimes sit, motionless, for hours, with her
head thrown back, and her eyes slowly wandering, in a silent
ecstasy of content. At these times Father Herbert, who had
observed her attentively from the moment of her arrival (for,
scholar and recluse as he was, he had not lost the faculty of
appreciating feminine grace) – at these times the old priest would
watch her covertly and marvel at the fantastic, soulless creature
whom Mrs De Grey had taken to her side. One evening, after a
prolonged stupor of this sort, in which the young girl had neither
moved nor spoken, sitting like one whose soul had detached
itself and was wandering through space, she rose, on Mrs De
Grey's at last giving her an order, and moved forward as if in
compliance; and then, suddenly rushing toward the old woman,
she fell on her knees, and buried her head in her lap and burst
into a paroxysm of sobs. Herbert, who had been standing by,
went and laid one hand on her head, and with the other made
over it the sign of the cross, in the manner of a benediction – a
consecration of the passionate gratitude which had finally broken
out into utterance. From this moment he loved her.

Margaret read aloud to Mrs De Grey, and on Sunday evenings
sang in a clear, sweet voice the chants of their Church, and
occupied herself constantly with fine needle-work, in which she
possessed great skill. They spent the long summer mornings
together, in reading and work and talk. Margaret told her
companion the simple, sad details of the history of which she

had already given her the outline; and Mrs De Grey, who found it natural to look upon them as a kind of practical romance organized for her entertainment, made her repeat them over a dozen times. Mrs De Grey, too, honoured the young girl with a recital of her own biography, which, in its vast vacuity, produced upon Margaret's mind a vague impression of grandeur. The vacuity, indeed, was relieved by the figure of Paul, whom Mrs De Grey never grew weary of describing, and of whom, finally, Margaret grew very fond of thinking. She listened most attentively to Mrs De Grey's eulogies of her son, and thought it a great pity he was not at home. And then she began to long for his return, and then, suddenly, she began to fear it. Perhaps he would dislike her being in the house, and turn her out of doors. It was evident that his mother was not prepared to contradict him. Perhaps – worse still – he would marry some foreign woman, and bring her home, and she would turn wickedly jealous of Margaret (in the manner of foreign women). De Grey, roaming through Europe, took for granted, piously enough, that he was never absent from his good mother's thoughts; but he remained superbly unconscious of the dignity which he had usurped in the meditations of her humble companion. Truly, we know where our lives begin, but who shall say where they end? Here was a careless young gentleman whose existence enjoyed a perpetual echo in the soul of a poor girl utterly unknown to him. Mrs De Grey had two portraits of her son, which, of course, she lost no time in exhibiting to Margaret – one taken in his boyhood, with brilliant red hair and cheeks, the lad's body encased in a bright blue jacket, and his neck encircled in a frill, open very low; the other, executed just before his departure, a handsome young man in a buff waistcoat, clean-shaven, with an animated countenance, dark, close-curling auburn hair, and very fine eyes. The former of these designs Margaret thought a very pretty child; but to the other the poor girl straightway lost her heart – the more easily that Mrs De Grey assured her, that, although the picture was handsome enough, it conveyed but the faintest idea of her boy's adorable flesh and blood. In a couple of months arrived a long-expected letter from Paul, and with it another portrait – a miniature, painted in Paris by a famous artist. Here Paul appeared a far more elegant figure than in the work of the American painter. In what the change consisted it was hard to tell; but his mother declared that it was easy to see that he had spent two years in the best company in Europe.

'O, the best company!' said Father Herbert, who knew the force of this term. And, smiling a moment with inoffensive scorn, he relapsed into his wonted gravity.

'I think he looks very sad,' said Margaret, timidly.

'Fiddlesticks!' cried Herbert, impatiently. 'He looks like a coxcomb. Of course, it's the Frenchman's fault,' he added, more gently. 'Why on earth does he send us his picture at all? It's a great piece of impertinence. Does he think we've forgotten him? When I want to remember my boy, I have something better to look to than that flaunting bit of ivory.'

At these words the two ladies went off, carrying the portrait with them, to read Paul's letter in private. It was in eight pages, and Margaret read it aloud. Then, when she had finished, she read it again; and in the evening she read it once more. The next day, Mrs De Grey, taking the young girl quite into her confidence, brought out a large packet containing his earlier letters, and Margaret spent the whole morning in reading them over aloud. That evening she took a stroll in the garden alone – the garden in which he had played as a boy, and lounged and dreamed as a young man. She found his name – his beautiful name – rudely cut on a wooden bench. Introduced, as it seemed to her that she had been by his letters, into the precincts of his personality, the mystery of his being, the magic circle of his feelings and opinions and fancies; wandering by his side, unseen, over Europe, and treading, unheard, the sounding pavements of famous churches and palaces, she felt that she tasted for the first time of the substance and sweetness of life. Margaret walked about for an hour in the starlight, among the dusky, perfumed alleys. Mrs De Grey, feeling unwell, had gone to her room. The young girl heard the far-off hum of the city slowly decrease and expire, and then, when the stillness of the night was unbroken, she came back into the parlour across the long window, and lit one of the great silver candlesticks that decorated the ends of the mantel. She carried it to the wall where Mrs De Grey had suspended her son's miniature, having first inserted it in an immense gold frame, from which she had expelled a less valued picture. Margaret felt that she must see the portrait before she went to bed. There was a certain charm and ravishment in beholding it privately by candlelight. The wind had risen – a warm west wind – and the long white curtains of the open windows swayed and bulged in the gloom in a spectral fashion. Margaret guarded the flame of the candle with her hand, and gazed at the polished surface of the portrait, warm in the light, beneath its glittering plate of glass. What an immensity of life and passion was concentrated into those few square inches of artificial colour! The young man's eyes seemed to gaze at her with a look of profound recognition. They held her fascinated; she lingered on the spot, unable to move. Suddenly the clock on the chimney-piece rang out a single clear stroke. Margaret started and turned about, at the thought that it was already half-past ten. She raised her candle aloft to look at the dial-plate; and perceived three things: that it was one o'clock in the morning, that her candle was half burnt out, and that someone was watching her from the other side of the room. Setting down her light, she recognized Father Herbert.

'Well, Miss Aldis,' he said, coming into the light, 'what do you think of it?'

Margaret was startled and confused, but not abashed. 'How long have I been here?' she asked, simply.

'I have no idea. I myself have been here half an hour.'

'It was very kind of you not to disturb me,' said Margaret, less simply.

'It was a very pretty picture,' said Herbert.

'O, it's beautiful!' cried the young girl, casting another glance at the portrait over her shoulder.

The old man smiled sadly, and turned away, and then, coming back, 'How do you like our young man, Miss Aldis?' he asked, apparently with a painful effort.

'I think he's very handsome,' said Margaret, frankly.

'He's not so handsome as that,' said Herbert.

'His mother says he's handsomer.'

'A mother's testimony in such cases is worth very little. Paul is well enough, but he's no miracle.'

'I think he looks sad,' said Margaret. 'His mother says he's very gay.'

'He may have changed vastly within two years. Do you think,' the old man added, after a pause, 'that he looks like a man in love?'

'I don't know,' said Margaret, in a low voice. 'I never saw one.'

'Never?' said the priest, with an earnestness which surprised the young girl.

She blushed a little. 'Never, Father Herbert.'

The priest's dark eyes were fixed on her with a strange intensity of expression. 'I hope, my child, you never may,' he said, solemnly.

The tone of his voice was not unkind, but it seemed to Margaret as if there were something cruel and chilling in the wish. 'Why not I as well as another?' she asked.

The old man shrugged his shoulders. 'O, it's a long story,' he said.

The summer passed away and flushed into autumn, and the autumn slowly faded, and finally expired in the cold embrace of

December. Mrs De Grey had written to her son of her having taken Margaret into her service. At this time came a letter in which the young man was pleased to express his satisfaction at this measure. 'Present my compliments to Miss Aldis,' he wrote, 'and assure her of my gratitude for the comfort she has given my dear mother – of which, indeed, I hope before very long to inform her in person.' In writing these good-natured words Paul De Grey little suspected the infinite reverberation they were to have in poor Margaret's heart. A month later arrived a letter, which was handed to Mrs De Grey at breakfast. 'You will have received my letter of December 3rd,' it began (a letter which had miscarried and failed to arrive), 'and will have formed your respective opinions of its contents.' As Mrs De Grey read these words, Father Herbert looked at Margaret; she had turned pale. 'Favourable or not,' the letter continued, 'I am sorry to be obliged to bid you undo them again. But my engage-ment to Miss L. is broken off. It had become impossible. As I made no attempt to give you a history of it, or to set forth my motives, so I shall not now attempt to go into the logic of the rupture. But it's broken clean off, I assure you. Amen.' And the letter passed to other matters, leaving our friends sadly perplexed. They awaited the arrival of the missing letter; but all in vain; it never came. Mrs De Grey immediately wrote to her son, urgently requesting an explanation of the events to which he had referred. His next letter, however, contained none of the desired information. Mrs De Grey repeated her request. Whereupon Paul wrote that he would tell her the story when he had reached home. He hated to talk about it. 'Don't be uneasy, dear mother,' he added; 'Heaven has insured me against a relapse. Miss L. died three weeks ago at Naples.' As Mrs De Grey read these words, she laid down the letter and looked at Father Herbert, who had been called to hear it. His pale face turned ghastly white, and he returned the old woman's gaze with compressed lips and a stony immobility in his eyes. Then, suddenly, a fierce, inarticulate cry broke from his throat, and, doubling up his fist, he brought it down with a terrible blow on the table. Margaret sat watching him, amazed. He rose to his feet, seized her in his arms, and pressed her on his neck.

'My child! my child!' he cried, in a broken voice, 'I have always loved you! I have been harsh and cold and crabbed. I was fearful. The thunder has fallen! Forgive me, child. I'm myself again.' Margaret, frightened, disengaged herself, but he kept her hand. 'Poor boy!' he cried, with a tremulous sigh.

Mrs De Grey sat smelling her vinaigrette, but not visibly discomposed. 'Poor boy!' she repeated, but without a sigh – which gave the words an ironical sound – 'He had ceased to care for her,' she said.

'Ah, madam!' cried the priest, 'don't blaspheme. Go down on your knees, and thank God that *we* have been spared that hideous sight!'

Mystified and horrified, Margaret drew her hand from his grasp, and looked with wondering eyes at Mrs De Grey. She smiled faintly, touched her forefinger to her forehead, tapped it, raised her eyebrows, and shook her head.

From counting the months that were to elapse before Paul's return, our friends came to counting the weeks, and then the days. The month of May arrived; Paul had sailed from England. At this time Mrs De Grey opened her son's room, and caused it to be prepared for occupation. The contents were just as he had left them; she bade Margaret come in and see it. Margaret looked at her face in his mirror, and sat down a moment on his sofa, and examined the books on his shelves. They seemed a prodigious array; they were in several languages, and gave a deep impression of their owner's attainments. Over the chimney hung a small sketch in pencil, which Margaret made haste to inspect – a likeness of a young girl, skilfully enough drawn. The original had apparently been very handsome, in the dark style; and in the corner of the sketch was written the artist's name – *De Grey*. Margaret looked at the portrait in silence, with quickened heart-beats.

'Is this Mr Paul's?' she asked at last of her companion.

'It belongs to Paul,' said Mrs De Grey. 'He used to be very fond of it, and insisted upon hanging it there. His father sketched it before our marriage.'

Margaret drew a breath of relief. 'And who is the lady?' she asked.

'I hardly know. Some foreign person, I think, that Mr De Grey had been struck with. There's something about her in the other corner.'

In effect, Margaret detected on the opposite side of the sketch, written in minute characters, the word '*obiit*, 1786'.

'You don't know Latin, I take it, my dear,' said Mrs De Grey, as Margaret read the inscription. 'It means that she died thirty-four good years ago.'

'Poor girl!' said Margaret, softly. As they were leaving the room, she lingered on the threshold and looked about her, wishing that she might leave some little memento of her visit. 'If we knew just when he would arrive,' she said, 'I would put some flowers on his table. But they might fade.'

As Mrs De Grey assured her that the moment of his arrival was quite uncertain, she left her fancied nosegay uncut, and spent the rest of the day in a delightful tremor of anticipation, ready to see the dazzling figure of a young man, equipped with strange foreign splendour, start up before her and look at her in cold surprise, and hurry past her in search of his mother. At every sound of footsteps or of an opening door she laid down her work, and listened curiously. In the evening, as if by a common instinct of expectancy, Father Herbert met Mrs De Grey in the front drawing-room – an apartment devoted exclusively to those festivities which never occurred in the annals of this tranquil household.

'A year ago today, madam,' said Margaret, as they all sat silent among the gathering shadows, 'I came into your house. Today ends a very happy year.'

'Let us hope,' said Father Herbert, sententiously, 'that tomorrow will begin another.'

'Ah, my dear lady!' cried Margaret, with emotion; 'my good father – my only friends – what harm can come to me with you?

It was you who rescued me from harm.' Her heart was swollen with gratitude, and her eyes with rising tears. She gave a long shudder at the thought of the life that might have been her fate. But, feeling a natural indisposition to obtrude her peculiar sensations upon the attention of persons so devoutly absorbed in the thought of a coming joy, she left her place, and wandered away into the garden. Before many minutes, a little gate opened in the paling, not six yards from where she stood. A man came in, whom, in the dim light, she knew to be Paul De Grey. Approaching her rapidly, he made a movement as if to greet her, but stopped suddenly, and removed his hat.

'Ah, you're Miss – the young lady,' he said.

He had forgotten her name. This was something other, something less felicitous, than the cold surprise of the figure in Margaret's vision. Nevertheless, she answered him, audibly enough: 'They are in the drawing-room; they expect you.'

He bounded along the path, and entered the house. She followed him slowly to the window, and stood without, listening. The silence of the young man's welcome told of its warmth.

Paul De Grey had made good use of his sojourn in Europe; he had lost none of his old merits, and had gained a number of new ones. He was by nature and culture an intelligent, amiable, accomplished fellow. It was his fortune to possess a peculiar, indefinable charm of person and manner. He was tall and slight of structure, but compact, firm, and active, with a clear, fair complexion, an open, prominent brow, crisp auburn hair, and eyes – a glance, a smile – radiant with youth and intellect. His address was frank, manly, and direct; and yet it seemed to Margaret that his bearing was marked by a certain dignity and elegance – at times even verging upon formalism – which distinguished it from that of other men. It was not, however, that she detected in his character any signs of that strange principle of melancholy which had exerted so powerful an action upon the other members of the household (and, from what she was able to gather, on his father). She fancied, on the contrary, that she had never known less levity associated with a more exquisite mirth. If Margaret had been of a more analytical turn of mind, she would have told herself that Paul De Grey's nature was eminently aristocratic. But the young girl contented herself with understanding it less, and secretly loving it more; and when she was in want of an epithet, she chose a simpler term. Paul was like a ray of splendid sunshine in the dull, colourless lives of the two women; he filled the house with light and heat and joy. He moved, to Margaret's fancy, in a circle of almost supernatural glory. His words, as they fell from his lips, seemed diamonds and pearls; and, in truth, his conversation, for a month after his return, was in the last degree delightful. Mrs De Grey's house was *par excellence* the abode of leisure – a castle of indolence; and Paul in talking, and his companions in listening, were conscious of no jealous stress of sordid duties. The summer days were long, and Paul's daily fund of loquacity was inexhaustible. A week after his arrival, after breakfast, Father Herbert contracted the habit of carrying him off to his study; and Margaret, passing the half-open door, would hear the changeful music of his voice. She begrudged the old man, at these times, the exclusive enjoyment of so much eloquence. She felt that with his tutor, Paul's talk was far wiser and richer than it was possible it should be with two simple-minded women; and the young girl had a pious longing to hear him, to see him, at his best. A brilliant best it was to Father Herbert's mind; for Paul had surpassed his fondest hopes. He had amassed such a store of knowledge; he had learned all the good that the old man had enjoined upon him; and, although he had not wholly ignored the evil against which the priest had warned him, he judged it so wisely and wittily! Women and priests, as a general thing, like a man none the less for not being utterly innocent. Father Herbert took an unutterable satisfaction in the happy development of Paul's character. He was more than the son of his loins: he was the child of his intellect, his patience, and devotion.

The afternoons and evenings Paul was free to devote to his mother, who, out of her own room, never dispensed for an hour with Margaret's attendance. This, thanks to the young girl's delicate tact and sympathy, had now become an absolute necessity. Margaret sat by with her work, while Paul talked, and marvelled at his inexhaustible stock of gossip and anecdote and forcible, vivid description. He made cities and churches and galleries and playhouses swarm and shine before her enchanted senses, and reproduced the people he had met and the scenery through which he had travelled, until the young girl's head turned at the rapid succession of images and pictures. And then, at times, he would seem to grow weary, and would sink into silence; and Margaret, looking up askance from her work, would see his eyes absently fixed, and a faint smile on his face, or else a cold gravity, and she would wonder what far-off memory had called back his thoughts to that unknown European world. Sometimes, less frequently, when she raised her eyes, she found him watching her own figure, her bent head, and the busy movement of her hands. But (as yet, at least) he never turned away his glance in confusion; he let his eyes rest, and justified his scrutiny by some simple and natural remark.

But as the weeks passed by, and the summer grew to its fullness, Mrs De Grey contracted the habit of going after dinner to her own room, where, we may respectfully conjecture, she passed the afternoon in dishabille and slumber. But De Grey and Miss Aldis tacitly agreed together that, in the prime and springtime of life, it was stupid folly to waste in any such fashion the longest and brightest hours of the year; and so they, on their side, contracted the habit of sitting in the darkened drawing-room, and gossiping away the time until within an hour of tea. Sometimes, for a change, they went across the garden into a sort of summer-house, which occupied a central point in the enclosure, and stood with its face averted from the mansion, and looking to the north, and with its sides covered with dense, clustering vines. Within, against the wall, was a deep garden-bench, and in the middle a table, upon which Margaret placed her work-basket, and the young man the book, which, under the pretence of meaning to read, he usually carried in his hand. Within was coolness and deep shade and silence, and without the broad glare of the

immense summer sky. When I say there was silence, I mean that
there was nothing to interrupt the conversation of these happy
idlers. Their talk speedily assumed that desultory, volatile character, which is the sign of great intimacy. Margaret found occasion to ask Paul a great many questions which she had not felt at
liberty to ask in the presence of his mother, and to demand additional light upon a variety of little points which Mrs De Grey
had been content to leave in obscurity. Paul was perfectly
communicative. If Miss Aldis cared to hear, he was assuredly
glad to talk. But suddenly it struck him that her attitude of mind
was a singular provocation to egotism, and that for six weeks, in
fact, he had done nothing but talk about himself – his own adventures, sensations, and opinions.

'I declare, Miss Aldis,' he cried, 'you're making me a monstrous
egotist. That's all you women are good for. I shall not say another
word about Mr Paul De Grey. Now it's your turn.'

'To talk about Mr Paul De Grey?' asked Margaret, with a
smile.

'No, about Miss Margaret Aldis – which, by the way, is a very
pretty name.'

'By the way, indeed!' said Margaret. 'By the way for you,
perhaps. But for me, my pretty name is all I have.'

'If you mean, Miss Aldis,' cried Paul, 'that your beauty is all
in your name—'

'I'm sadly mistaken. Well, then, I don't. The rest is in my
imagination.'

'Very likely. It's certainly not in mine.'

Margaret was, in fact, at this time, extremely pretty; a little pale with the heat, but rounded and developed by rest and prosperity, and animated – half inspired, I may call it – with tender gratitude. Looking at her as he said these words, De Grey was forcibly struck with the interesting character of her face. Yes, most assuredly, her beauty was a potent reality. The charm of her face was forever refreshed and quickened by the deep loveliness of her soul.

'I mean literally, Miss Aldis,' said the young man, 'that I wish you to talk about yourself. I want to hear *your* adventures. I demand it – I need it.'

'My adventures?' said Margaret. 'I have never had any.'

'Good!' cried Paul; 'that in itself is an adventure.'

In this way it was that Margaret came to relate to her companion the short story of her young life. The story was not all told, however, short as it was, in a single afternoon; that is, a whole week after she began, the young girl found herself setting Paul right with regard to a matter of which he had received a false impression.

'Nay, he is married,' said Margaret; 'I told you so.'

'O, he is married?' said Paul.

'Yes; his wife's an immense fat woman.'

'O, his wife's an immense fat woman?'

'Yes; and he thinks all the world of her.'

'O, he thinks all the world of her!'

It was natural that, in this manner, with a running commentary supplied by Paul, the narrative should proceed slowly. But, in addition to the observations here quoted, the young man maintained another commentary, less audible and more profound. As he listened to this frank and fair-haired maiden, and reflected that in the wide world she might turn in confidence and sympathy to other minds than his – as he found her resting her candid thoughts and memories on his judgement, as she might lay her white hand on his arm – it seemed to him that the pure intentions with which she believed his soul to be peopled took in her glance a graver and higher cast. All the gorgeous colour faded out of his recent European reminiscences and regrets, and he was sensible only of Margaret's presence, and of the tender rosy radiance in which she sat and moved, as in a sort of earthly halo. Could it be, he asked himself, that while he was roaming about Europe, in a vague, restless search for his future, his end, his aim, these things were quietly awaiting him at his own deserted hearth-stone, gathered together in the immaculate person of the sweetest and fairest of women? Finally, one day, this view of the case struck him so forcibly, that he cried out in an ecstasy of belief and joy.

'Margaret,' he said, 'my mother found you in church, and there, before the altar, she kissed you and took you into her arms. I have often thought of that scene. It makes it no common adoption.'

'I'm sure I have often thought of it,' said Margaret.

'It makes it sacred and everlasting,' said Paul. 'On that blessed day you came to us for ever and ever.'

Margaret looked at him with a face tremulous between smiles and tears. 'For as long as you will keep me,' she said. 'Ah, Paul!'

For in an instant the young man had expressed all his longing and his passion.

With the greatest affection and esteem for his mother, Paul had always found it natural to give precedence to Father Herbert in matters of appeal and confidence. The old man possessed a delicacy of intellectual tact which made his sympathy and his counsel alike delightful. Some days after the conversation upon a few of the salient points of which I have lightly touched, Paul and Margaret renewed their mutual vows in the summer-house. They now possessed that deep faith in the sincerity of their own feelings, and that undoubting delight in each other's reiterated protests, which left them nothing to do but to take their elders into their confidence. They came through the garden together, and on reaching the threshold Margaret found that she had left her scissors in the garden-hut; whereupon Paul went back in search of them. The young girl came into the house, reached the foot of the staircase, and waited for her lover. At this moment Father Herbert appeared in the open doorway of his study, and looked at Margaret with a melancholy smile. He stood, passing one hand slowly over another, and gazing at her with kindly, darksome looks.

'It seems to me, Mistress Margaret,' he said, 'that you keep all this a marvellous secret from your poor old Dr Herbert.'

In the presence of this gentle and venerable scholar, Margaret felt that she had no need of vulgar blushing and simpering and negation. 'Dear Father Herbert,' she said, with heavenly simpleness, 'I have just been begging Paul to tell you.'

'Ah, my daughter –' and the old man but half stifled a sigh – 'it's all a strange and terrible mystery.'

Paul came in and crossed the hall with the light step of a lover.

'Paul,' said Margaret, 'Father Herbert knows.'

'Father Herbert knows!' repeated the priest – 'Father Herbert knows everything. You're very innocent for lovers.'

'You're very wise, sir, for a priest,' said Paul, blushing.

'I knew it a week ago,' said the old man, gravely.

'Well, sir,' said Paul, 'we love you none the less for loving each other so much more. I hope you'll not love us the less.'

'Father Herbert thinks it's "terrible",' said Margaret, smiling.

'O Lord!' cried Herbert, raising his hand to his head as if in pain. He turned about, and went into his room.

Paul drew Margaret's hand through his arm and followed the priest. 'You suffer, sir,' he said, 'at the thought of losing us – of our leaving you. That certainly needn't trouble you. Where should we go? As long as you live, as long as my mother lives, we shall all make but a single household.'

The old man apepared to have recovered his composure. 'Ah!' he said; 'be happy, no matter where, and I shall be happy. You're very young.'

'Not so young,' said Paul, laughing, but with a natural disinclination to be placed in too boyish a light. 'I'm six-and-twenty. *J'ai vécu* – I've lived.'

'He's been through everything,' said Margaret, leaning on his arm.

'Not quite everything.' And Paul, bending his eyes, with a sober smile, met her upward glance.

'O, he's modest,' murmured Father Herbert.

'Paul's been all but married already,' said Margaret.

The young man made a gesture of impatience. Herbert stood with his eyes fixed on his face.

'Why do you speak of that poor girl?' said Paul. Whatever satisfaction he may have given Margaret on the subject of his projected marriage in Europe, he had since his return declined, on the plea that it was extremely painful, to discuss the matter either with his mother or with his old tutor.

'Miss Aldis is perhaps jealous,' said Herbert, cunningly.

'O Father Herbert!' cried Margaret.

'There is little enough to be jealous of,' said Paul.

'There's a fine young man!' cried Herbert. 'One would think he had never cared for her.'

'It's perfectly true.'

'Oh!' said Herbert, in a tone of deep reproach, laying his hand on the young man's arm. 'Don't say that.'

'Nay, sir, I shall say it. I never said anything less to her. She enchanted me, she entangled me, but, before Heaven, I never loved her!'

'O, God help you!' cried the priest. He sat down, and buried his face in his hands.

Margaret turned deadly pale, and recalled the scene which had occurred on the receipt of Paul's letter, announcing the rupture of his engagement. 'Father Herbert,' she cried, 'what horrible, hideous mystery do you keep locked up in your bosom? If it concerns me – if it concerns Paul – I demand of you to tell us.'

Moved apparently by the young girl's tone of agony to a sense of the needfulness of self-control, Herbert uncovered his face, and directed to Margaret a rapid glance of entreaty. She perceived that it meant that, at any cost, she should be silent. Then, with a sublime attempt at dissimulation, he put out his hands, and laid one on each of his companions' shoulders. 'Excuse me, Paul,' he said, 'I'm a foolish old man. Old scholars are a sentimental, a superstitious race. We believe still that all women are angels, and that all men—'

'That all men are fools,' said Paul, smiling.

'Exactly. Whereas, you see,' whispered Father Herbert, 'there are no fools but ourselves.'

Margaret listened to this fantastic bit of dialogue with a beating heart, fully determined not to content herself with any such flimsy explanation of the old man's tragical allusions. Meanwhile, Herbert urgently besought Paul to defer for a few days making known his engagement to his mother.

The next day but one was Sunday, the last in August. The heat for a week had been oppressive, and the air was now sullen and brooding, as if with an approaching storm. As she left the breakfast-table, Margaret felt her arm touched by Father Herbert.

'Don't go to church,' he said, in a low voice. 'Make a pretext, and stay at home.'

'A pretext—?'

'Say you've letters to write.'

'Letters?' and Margaret smiled half bitterly. 'To whom should I write letters?'

'Dear me, then say you're ill. I give you absolution. When they're gone, come to me.'

At church-time, accordingly, Margaret feigned a slight indisposition; and Mrs De Grey, taking her son's arm, mounted into her ancient deep-seated coach, and rolled away from the door. Margaret immediately betook herself to Father Herbert's apartment. She saw in the old man's face the portent of some dreadful avowal. His whole figure betrayed the weight of an inexorable necessity.

'My daughter,' said the priest, 'you are a brave, pious girl—'

'Ah!' cried Margaret, 'it's something horrible, or you wouldn't say that. Tell me at once!'

'You need all your courage.'

'Doesn't he love me? – Ah, in Heaven's name, speak!'

'If he didn't love you with a damning passion, I should have nothing to say.'

'O, then, say what you please!' said Margaret.

'Well then – you must leave this house.'

'Why? – when? – where must I go?'

'This moment, if possible. You must go anywhere – the further the better – the further from him. Listen, my child,' said the old man, his bosom wrung by the stunned, bewildered look of Margaret's face; 'it's useless to protest, to weep, to resist. It's the voice of fate!'

'And pray, sir,' said Margaret, 'of what do you accuse me?'

'I accuse no one. I don't even accuse Heaven.'

'But there's a reason – there's a motive—'

Herbert laid his hand on his lips, pointed to a seat, and, turning to an ancient chest on the table, unlocked it, and drew from it a small volume, bound in vellum, apparently an old illuminated missal. 'There's nothing for it,' he said, 'but to tell you the whole story.'

He sat down before the young girl, who held herself rigid and expectant. The room grew dark with the gathering storm-clouds, and the distant thunder muttered.

'Let me read you ten words,' said the priest, opening at a fly-leaf of the volume, on which a memorandum or register had been inscribed in a great variety of hands, all minute and some barely legible. 'God be with you!' and the old man crossed himself. Involuntarily, Margaret did the same. '"George De Grey",' he read, '"met and loved, September, 1786, Antonietta Gambini, of Milan. She died October 9th, same year. John De Grey married, April 4th, 1749, Henrietta Spencer. She died May 7th. George De Grey engaged himself October, 1710, to Mary Fortescue. She died October 31st. Paul De Grey, aged nineteen, betrothed June, 1672, at Bristol, England, to Lucretia Lefevre, aged thirty-one, of that place. She died July 27th. John De Grey, affianced January 10th, 1649, to Blanche Ferrars, of Castle Ferrars, Cumberland. She died, by her lover's hand, January

12th. Stephen De Grey offered his hand to Isabel Stirling, October, 1619. She died within the month. Paul De Grey exchanged pledges with Magdalen Scrope, August, 1586. She died in childbirth, September, 1587."' Father Herbert paused. 'Is it enough?' he asked, looking up with glowing eyes. 'There are two pages more. The De Greys are an ancient line; they keep their records.'

Margaret had listened with a look of deepening, fierce, passionate horror – a look more of anger and of wounded pride than of terror. She sprang towards the priest with the lightness of a young cat, and dashed the hideous record from his hand.

'What abominable nonsense is this!' she cried. 'What does it mean? I barely heard it; I despise it; I laugh at it!'

The old man seized her arm with a firm grasp. 'Paul De Grey,' he said, in an awful voice, 'exchanged pledges with Margaret Aldis, August, 1821. She died – with the falling leaves.'

Poor Margaret looked about her for help, inspiration, comfort of some kind. The room contained nothing but serried lines of old parchment-covered books, each seeming a grim repetition of the volume at her feet. A vast peal of thunder resounded through the noon-day stillness. Suddenly her strength deserted her; she felt her weakness and loneliness, the grasp of the hand of fate. Father Herbert put out his arms, she flung herself on his neck, and burst into tears.

'Do you still refuse to leave him?' asked the priest. 'If you leave him, you're saved.'

'Saved?' cried Margaret, raising her head; 'and Paul?'

'Ah, there it is. – He'll forget you.'

The young girl pondered a moment. 'To have him do that,' she said, 'I should apparently have to die.' Then wringing her hands with a fresh burst of grief, 'Is it certain,' she cried, 'that there are no exceptions?'

'None, my child'; and he picked up the volume. 'You see it's the first love, the first passion. After that, they're innocent. Look at Mrs De Grey. The race is accursed. It's an awful, inscrutable mystery. I fancied that you were safe, my daughter, and that that poor Miss L. had borne the brunt. But Paul was at pains to undeceive me. I've searched his life, I've probed his conscience: it's a virgin heart. Ah, my child, I dreaded it from the first. I trembled when you came into the house. I wanted Mrs De Grey to turn you off. But she laughs at it – she calls it an old-wife's tale. *She* was safe enough; her husband didn't care two straws for her. But there's a little dark-eyed maiden buried in Italian soil who could tell her another story. She withered, my child. She was life itself – an incarnate ray of her own Southern sun. She died of De Grey's kisses. Don't ask me how it began, it's always been so. It goes back to the night of time. One of the race, they say, came home from the East, from the crusades, infected with the germs of the plague. He had pledged his love-faith to a young girl before his departure, and it had been arranged that the wedding should immediately succeed his return. Feeling unwell, he consulted an elder brother of the bride, a man versed in fantastic medical lore, and supposed to be gifted with magical skill. By him he was assured that he was plague-stricken, and that he was in duty bound to defer the marriage. The young knight refused to comply, and the physician, infuriated, pronounced a curse upon his race. The marriage took place; within a week the bride expired, in horrible agony; the young man, after a slight illness, recovered; the curse took effect.'

Margaret took the quaint old missal into her hand, and turned to the grisly register of death. Her heart grew cold as she thought of her own sad sisterhood with all those miserable women of the past. Miserable women, but ah! tenfold more miserable men – helpless victims of their own baleful hearts. She remained silent, with her eyes fixed on the book, abstractedly; mechanically, as it were, she turned to another page, and read a familiar orison to the Blessed Virgin. Then raising her head, with her deep-blue eyes shining with the cold light of an immense resolve – a prodigious act of volition – 'Father Herbert,' she said, in low, solemn accents, 'I revoke the curse. I undo it. *I curse it!*'

From this moment, nothing would induce her to bestow a moment's thought on salvation by flight. It was too late, she declared. If she was destined to die, she had already imbibed the fatal contagion. But they should see. She cast no discredit on the existence or the potency of the dreadful charm; she simply assumed, with deep self-confidence which filled the old priest with mingled wonder and anguish, that it would vainly expend its mystic force once and for ever upon her own devoted, impassioned life. Father Herbert folded his trembling hands resignedly.

He had done his duty; the rest was with God. At times, living as he had done for years in dread of the moment which had now arrived, with his whole life darkened by its shadow, it seemed to him among the strange possibilities of nature that this frail and pure young girl might indeed have sprung, at the command of outraged love, to the rescue of the unhappy line to which he had dedicated his manhood. And then at other moments it seemed as if she were joyously casting herself into the dark gulf. At all events, the sense of peril had filled Margaret herself with fresh energy and charm. Paul, if he had not been too enchanted with her feverish gaiety and grace to trouble himself about their motive and origin, would have been at loss to explain their sudden morbid intensity. Forthwith, at her request, he announced his engagement to his mother, who put on a very gracious face, and honoured Margaret with a sort of official kiss.

'Ah me!' muttered Father Herbert, 'and now she thinks she has bound them fast.' And later, the next day, when Mrs De Grey, talking of the matter, avowed that it really did cost her a little to accept as a daughter a girl to whom she had paid a salary – 'A salary, madam!' cried the priest with a bitter laugh; 'upon my word, I think it was the least you could do.'

'*Nous verrons,*' said Mrs De Grey, composedly.

A week passed by, without ill omens. Paul was in a manly ecstasy of bliss. At moments he was almost bewildered by the fullness with which his love and faith had been requited. Margaret was transfigured, glorified, by the passion which burned in her heart. 'Give a plain girl, a common girl, a lover,'

thought Paul, 'and she grows pretty, charming. Give a charming girl a lover –' and if Margaret was present, his eloquent eyes
uttered the conclusion; if she was absent, his restless steps
wandered in search of her. Her beauty within the past ten days
seemed to have acquired an unprecedented warmth and richness. Paul went so far as to fancy that her voice had grown more
deep and mellow. She looked older; she seemed in an instant to
have overleaped a year of her development, and to have arrived
at the perfect maturity of her youth. One might have imagined
that, instead of the further, she stood just on the hither verge of
marriage. Meanwhile Paul grew conscious of he hardly knew
what delicate change in his own emotions. The exquisite feeling
of pity, the sense of her appealing weakness, her heavenly
dependence, which had lent its tender strain to swell the concert
of his affections, had died away, and given place to a vague,
profound instinct of respect. Margaret was, after all, no such
simple body; her nature, too, had its mysteries. In truth, thought
Paul, tenderness, gentleness, is its own reward. He had bent to
pluck this pallid flower of sunless household growth; he had
dipped its slender stem in the living waters of his love, and lo! it
had lifted its head, and spread its petals, and brightened into
splendid purple and green. This glowing potency of loveliness
filled him with a tremor which was almost a foreboding. He
longed to possess her; he watched her with covetous eyes; he
wished to call her utterly his own.

'Margaret,' he said to her, 'you fill me with a dreadful delight.
You grow more beautiful every day. We must be married

immediately, or, at this rate, by our wedding-day, I shall have grown mortally afraid of you. By the soul of my father, I didn't bargain for this! Look at yourself in that glass.' And he turned her about to a long mirror; it was in his mother's dressing-room; Mrs De Grey had gone into the adjoining chamber.

Margaret saw herself reflected from head to foot in the glassy depths, and perceived the change in her appearance. Her head rose with a sort of proud serenity from the full curve of her shoulders; her eyes were brilliant, her lips trembled, her bosom rose and fell with all the insolence of her deep devotion. 'Blanche Ferrars, of Castle Ferrars,' she silently repeated, 'Isabel Stirling, Magdalen Scrope – poor foolish women! You were not women, you were children. It's your fault, Paul,' she cried, aloud, 'if I look other than I should! Why is there such a love between us?' And then, seeing the young man's face beside her own, she fancied he looked pale. 'My Paul,' she said, taking his hands, 'you're pale. What a face for a happy lover! You're impatient. Well-a-day, sir! it shall be when you please.'

The marriage was fixed for the last of September; and the two women immediately began to occupy themselves with the purchase of the bridal garments. Margaret, out of her salary, had saved a sufficient sum to buy a handsome wedding gown; but, for the other articles of her wardrobe, she was obliged to be indebted to the liberality of Mrs De Grey. She made no scruple, indeed, of expending large sums of money, and, when they were expended, of asking for more. She took an active, violent delight in procuring quantities of the richest stuffs. It seemed to her that, for the time, she had parted with all flimsy dignity and conventional reticence and coyness, as if she had flung away her conscience to be picked up by vulgar, happy, unimperilled women. She gathered her marriage finery together in a sort of fierce defiance of impending calamity. She felt excited to outstrip it, to confound it, to stare it out of countenance.

One day she was crossing the hall, with a piece of stuff just sent from the shop. It was a long morsel of vivid pink satin, and, as she held it, a portion of it fell over her arm to her feet. Father Herbert's door stood ajar; she stopped, and went in.

'Excuse me, reverend sir,' said Margaret; 'but I thought it a pity not to show you this beautiful bit of satin. Isn't it a lovely pink? – it's almost red – it's carnation. It's the colour of our love – of my death. Father Herbert,' she cried, with a shrill, resounding laugh, '*it's my shroud!* Don't you think it would be a pretty shroud? – pink satin, and blond-lace, and pearls?'

The old man looked at her with a haggard face. 'My daughter,' he said, 'Paul will have an incomparable wife.'

'Most assuredly, if you compare me with those ladies in your prayer-book. Ah! Paul shall have a wife, at least. That's very certain.'

'Well,' said the old man, 'you're braver than I. You frighten me.'

'Dear Father Herbert, didn't you once frighten me?'

The old man looked at Margaret with mingled tenderness and horror. 'Tell me, child,' he said, 'in the midst of all this, do you ever pray?'

'God forbid!' cried the poor creature. 'I have no heart for prayer.'

She had long talks with Paul about their future pleasures, and the happy life they should lead. He declared that he would set their habits to quite another tune, and that the family should no longer be buried in silence and gloom. It was an absurd state of things, and he marvelled that it should ever have come about. They should begin to live like other people, and occupy their proper place in society. They should entertain company, and travel, and go to the play of an evening. Margaret had never seen a play; after their marriage, if she wished, she should see one every week for a year. 'Have no fears, my dear,' cried Paul, 'I don't mean to bury you alive; I'm not digging your grave. If I expected you to be content to live as my poor mother lives, we might as well be married by the funeral service.'

When Paul talked with this buoyant energy, looking with a firm, undoubting gaze on the long, blissful future, Margaret drew from his words fortitude and joy, and scorn of all danger. Father Herbert's secret seemed a vision, a fantasy, a dream, until, after a while, she found herself again face to face with the old man, and read in his haggard features that to him, at least, it was a deep reality. Nevertheless, among all her feverish transitions from hope to fear, from exaltation to despair, she never, for a moment, ceased to keep a cunning watch upon her physical sensations, and to lie in wait for morbid symptoms. She wondered that, with this ghastly burden on her consciousness, she had not long since been goaded to insanity, or crushed into utter idiocy. She fancied that, sad as it would have been to rest in ignorance of the mystery in which her life had been involved, it was yet more terrible to know it. During the week after her interview with Father Herbert, she had not slept half an hour of the daily twenty-four; and yet, far from missing her sleep, she felt, as I have attempted to show, intoxicated, electrified, by the unbroken vigilance and tension of her will. But she well knew that this could not last for ever. One afternoon, a couple of days after Paul had uttered those brilliant promises, he mounted his horse for a ride. Margaret stood at the gate, watching him regretfully, and, as he galloped away, he kissed her his hand. An hour before tea she came out of her room, and entered the parlour, where Mrs De Grey had established herself for the evening. A moment later, Father Herbert, who was in the act of lighting his study-lamp, heard a piercing shriek resound through the house.

His heart stood still. 'The hour is come,' he said. 'It would be a pity to miss it.' He hurried to the drawing-room, together with the servants, also startled by the cry. Margaret lay stretched on the sofa, pale, motionless, panting, with her eyes closed and her hand pressed to her side. Herbert exchanged a rapid glance with Mrs De Grey, who was bending over the young girl, holding her other hand.

'Let us at least have no scandal,' she said, with dignity, and straightway dismissed the servants. Margaret gradually revived, declared that it was nothing – a mere sudden pain – that she felt better, and begged her companions to make no commotion. Mrs

De Grey went to her room, in search of a phial of smelling-salts, leaving Herbert alone with Margaret. He was on his knees on the floor, holding her other hand. She raised herself to a sitting posture.

'I know what you are going to say,' she cried, 'but it's false. Where's Paul?'

'Do you mean to tell him?' asked Herbert.

'Tell him?' and Margaret started to her feet. 'If I were to die, I should wring his heart; if I were to tell him, I should break it.'

She started up, I say; she had heard and recognized her lover's rapid step in the passage. Paul opened the door and came in precipitately, out of breath and deadly pale. Margaret came towards him with her hand still pressed to her side, while Father Herbert mechanically rose from his kneeling posture. 'What has happened?' cried the young man. 'You've been ill!'

'Who told you that anything has happened?' said Margaret.

'What is Herbert doing on his knees?'

'I was praying, sir,' said Herbert.

'Margaret,' repeated Paul, 'in Heaven's name, what *is* the matter?'

'What's the matter with you, Paul? It seems to me that I should ask the question.'

De Grey fixed a dark, searching look on the young girl, and then closed his eyes, and grasped at the back of a chair, as if his head were turning. 'Ten minutes ago,' he said, speaking slowly, 'I was riding along by the river-side; suddenly I heard in the air the sound of a distant cry, which I knew to be yours. I turned and galloped. I made three miles in eight minutes.'

'A cry, dear Paul? what should I cry about? and to be heard three miles! A pretty compliment to my lungs.'

'Well,' said the young man, 'I suppose, then, it was my fancy. But my horse heard it too; he lifted his ears, and plunged and started.'

'It must have been his fancy too! It proves you an excellent rider – you and your horse feeling as one man!'

'Ah, Margaret, don't trifle!'

'As one horse, then!'

'Well, whatever it may have been, I'm not ashamed to confess that I'm thoroughly shaken. I don't know what has become of my nerves.'

'For pity's sake, then, don't stand there shivering and staggering like a man in an ague-fit. Come, sit down on the sofa.' She took hold of his arm, and led him to the couch. He, in turn, clasped her arm in his own hand, and drew her down beside him. Father Herbert silently made his exit, unheeded. Outside of the door he met Mrs De Grey, with her smelling-salts.

'I don't think she needs them now,' he said. 'She has Paul.' And the two adjourned together to the tea-table. When the meal was half finished, Margaret came in with Paul.

'How do you feel, dear?' said Mrs De Grey.

'He feels much better,' said Margaret, hastily.

Mrs De Grey smiled complacently. 'Assuredly,' she thought, 'my future daughter-in-law has a very pretty way of saying things.'

The next day, going into Mrs De Grey's room, Margaret found Paul and his mother together. The latter's eyes were red, as if she had been weeping; and Paul's face wore an excited look, as if he had been making some painful confession. When Margaret came in, he walked to the window and looked out, without speaking to her. She feigned to have come in search of a piece of needle-work, obtained it, and retired. Nevertheless, she felt deeply wounded. What had Paul been doing, saying? Why had he not spoken to her? Why had he turned his back upon her? It was only the evening before, when they were alone in the drawing-room, that he had been so unutterably tender. It was a cruel mystery; she would have no rest until she learned it – although, in truth, she had little enough as it was. In the afternoon, Paul again ordered his horse, and dressed himself for a ride. She waylaid him as he came downstairs, booted and spurred; and, as his horse was not yet at the door, she made him go with her into the garden.

'Paul,' she said, suddenly, 'what were you telling your mother this morning? Yes,' she continued, trying to smile, but without success, 'I confess it – I'm jealous.'

'O my soul!' cried the young man, wearily, putting both his hands to his face.

'Dear Paul,' said Margaret, taking his arm, 'that's very beautiful, but it's not an answer.'

Paul stopped in the path, took the young girl's hands and looked steadfastly into her face, with an expression that was in truth a look of weariness – of worse than weariness, of despair. 'Jealous, you say?'

'Ah, not now!' she cried, pressing his hands.

'It's the first foolish thing I have heard you say.'

'Well, it was foolish to be jealous of your mother; but I'm still jealous of your solitude – of these pleasures in which I have no share – of your horse – your long rides.'

'You wish me to give up my ride?'

'Dear Paul, where are your wits? To wish it is – to wish it. To say I wish it is to make a fool of myself.'

'My wits are with – with something that's for ever gone!' And he closed his eyes and contracted his forehead as if in pain. 'My youth, my hope – what shall I call it? – my happiness.'

'Ah!' said Margaret, reproachfully, 'you have to shut your eyes to say that.'

'Nay, what is happiness without youth?'

'Upon my word, one would think I was forty,' cried Margaret.

'Well, so long as I'm sixty!'

The young girl perceived that behind these light words there was something very grave. 'Paul,' she said, 'the trouble simply is that you're unwell.'

He nodded assent, and with his assent it seemed to her that an unseen hand had smitten the life out of her heart.

'That is what you told your mother?'

He nodded again.

'And what you were unwilling to tell me?'

He blushed deeply. 'Naturally,' he said.

She dropped his hands and sat down, for very faintness, on a garden-bench. Then rising suddenly, 'Go, and take your ride,' she rejoined. 'But, before you go, kiss me once.'

And Paul kissed her, and mounted his horse. As she went into the house, she met Father Herbert, who had been watching the young man ride away, from beneath the porch, and who was returning to his study.

'My dear child,' said the priest, 'Paul is very ill. God grant that, if you manage not to die, it may not be at his expense!'

For all answer, Margaret turned on him, in her passage, a face so cold, ghastly, and agonized, that it seemed a vivid response to his heart-shaking fears. When she reached her room, she sat down on her little bed, and strove to think clearly and deliberately. The old man's words had aroused a deep-sounding echo in the vast spiritual solitudes of her being. She was to find, then, after her long passion, that the curse was absolute, inevitable, eternal. It could be shifted, but not eluded; in spite of the utmost strivings of human agony, it insatiably claimed its victim. Her own strength was exhausted; what was she to do? All her borrowed splendour of brilliancy and bravery suddenly deserted her, and she sat alone, shivering in her weakness. Deluded fool that she was, for a day, for an hour, to have concealed her sorrow from her lover! The greater her burden, the greater should have been her confidence. What neither might endure alone, they might have surely endured together. But she blindly, senselessly, remorselessly drained the life from his being. As she bloomed and prospered, he drooped and languished. While she was living for him, he was dying of her. Execrable, infernal comedy! What would help her now? She thought of suicide, and she thought of flight; – they were about equivalent. If it were certain that by the sudden extinction of her own life she might liberate, exonerate Paul, it would cost her but an instant's delay to plunge a knife into her heart. But who should say that, enfeebled, undermined as he was, the shock of her death might not give him his own quietus? Worse than all was the suspicion that he had begun to dislike her, and that a dim perception of her noxious influence had already taken possession of her senses. He was cold and distant. Why else, when he had begun really to feel ill, had he not spoken first to her? She was distasteful, loath-some. Nevertheless, Margaret still grasped, with all the avidity of despair, at the idea that it was still not too late to take him into her counsels, and to reveal to him all the horrors of her secret. Then at least, whatever came, death or freedom, they should meet it together.

Now that the enchantment of her fancied triumph had been taken from her, she felt utterly exhausted and overwhelmed. Her whole organism ached with the desire for sleep and forgetful-ness. She closed her eyes, and sank into the very stupor of repose. When she came to her senses, her room was dark. She rose, and went to her window, and saw the stars. Lighting a candle, she found that her little clock indicated nine. She had slept five hours. She hastily dressed herself, and went downstairs.

In the drawing-room, by an open window, wrapped in a shawl, with a lighted candle, sat Mrs De Grey.

'You're happy, my dear,' she cried, 'to be able to sleep so soundly, when we are all in such a state.'

'What state, dear lady?'

'Paul has not come in.'

Margaret made no reply; she was listening intently to the distant sound of a horse's steps. She hurried out of the room, to the front door, and across the courtyard to the gate. There, in the dark starlight, she saw a figure advancing, and the rapid ring of hoofs. The poor girl suffered but a moment's suspense. Paul's horse came dashing along the road – rider-less. Margaret, with a cry, plunged forward, grasping at his bridle; but he swerved, with a loud neigh, and, scarcely slackening his pace, swept into the enclosure at a lower entrance, where Margaret heard him clattering over the stones on the road to the stable, greeted by shouts and ejacu-lations from the hostler.

Madly, precipitately, Margaret rushed out into the darkness, along the road, calling upon Paul's name. She had not gone a quarter of a mile, when she heard an answering voice. Repeating her cry, she recognized her lover's accents.

He was upright, leaning against a tree, and apparently unin-jured, but with his face gleaming through the darkness like a mask of reproach, white with the phosphorescent dews of death. He had suddenly felt weak and dizzy, and in the effort to keep himself in the saddle had frightened his horse, who had fiercely plunged, and unseated him. He leaned on Margaret's shoulder for support, and spoke with a faltering voice.

'I have been riding,' he said, 'like a madman. I felt ill when I went out, but without the shadow of a cause. I was determined to work it off by motion and the open air.' And he stopped, gasping.

'And you feel better, dearest?' murmured Margaret.

'No, I feel worse. I'm a dead man.'

Margaret clasped her lover in her arms with a long, piercing moan, which resounded through the night.

'I'm yours no longer, dear unhappy soul – I belong, by I don't know what fatal, inexorable ties, to darkness and death and nothingness. They stifle me. Do you hear my voice?'

'Ah, senseless clod that I am, I have killed you!'

'I believe it's true. But it's strange. What is it, Margaret? – you're enchanted, baleful, fatal!' He spoke barely above a whisper, as if his voice were leaving him; his breath was cold on her cheek, and his arm heavy on her neck.

'Nay,' she cried, 'in Heaven's name, go on! Say something that will kill me.'

'Farewell, farewell!' said Paul, collapsing.

Margaret's cry had been, for the startled household she had left behind her, an index to her halting-place. Father Herbert drew near hastily, with servants and lights. They found Margaret sitting by the roadside, with her feet in a ditch, clasping her lover's inanimate head in her arms, and covering it with kisses, wildly moaning. The sense had left her mind as completely as his body, and it was likely to come back to one as little as to the other.

*   *   *

A great many months naturally elapsed before Mrs De Grey found herself in the humour to allude directly to the immense calamity which had overwhelmed her house; and when she did so, Father Herbert was surprised to find that she still refused to accept the idea of a supernatural pressure upon her son's life, and that she quietly cherished the belief that he had died of the fall from his horse.

'And suppose Margaret had died? Would to Heaven she had!' said the priest.

'Ah, suppose!' said Mrs De Grey. 'Do you make that wish for the sake of your theory?'

'Suppose that Margaret had had a lover – a passionate lover – who had offered her his heart before Paul had ever seen her; and then that Paul had come, bearing love and death.'

'Well, what then?'

'Which of the three, think you, would have had most cause for sadness?'

'It's always the survivors of a calamity who are to be pitied,' said Mrs De Grey.

'Yes, madam, it's the survivors – even after fifty years.'

The Romance of
Certain Old Clothes

I

TOWARDS THE MIDDLE of the eighteenth century there lived in the Province of Massachusetts a widowed gentle-woman, the mother of three children, by name Mrs Veronica Wingrave. She had lost her husband early in life, and had devoted herself to the care of her progeny. These young persons grew up in a manner to reward her tenderness and to gratify her highest hopes. The first-born was a son, whom she had called Bernard, after his father. The others were daughters – born at an interval of three years apart. Good looks were traditional in the family, and this youthful trio were not likely to allow the tradition to perish. The boy was of that fair and ruddy complexion and that athletic structure which in those days (as in these) were the sign of good English descent – a

frank, affectionate young fellow, a deferential son, a patronizing brother, a steadfast friend. Clever, however, he was not; the
wit of the family had been apportioned chiefly to his sisters.
The late Mr Wingrave had been a great reader of Shakespeare,
at a time when this pursuit implied more freedom of thought
than at the present day, and in a community where it required
much courage to patronize the drama even in the closet: and he
had wished to call attention to his admiration of the great poet
by calling his daughters out of his favourite plays.

Upon the elder he had bestowed the romantic name of
Rosalind, and the younger he had called Perdita, in memory
of a little girl born between them, who had lived but a few
weeks.

When Bernard Wingrave came to his sixteenth year his
mother put a brave face upon it and prepared to execute her
husband's last injunction. This had been a formal command
that, at the proper age, his son should be sent out to England, to
complete his education at the university of Oxford, where he
himself had acquired his taste for elegant literature. It was Mrs
Wingrave's belief that the lad's equal was not to be found in the
two hemispheres, but she had the old traditions of literal obedience. She swallowed her sobs, and made up her boy's trunk and
his simple provincial outfit, and sent him on his way across the
seas. Bernard presented himself at his father's college, and spent
five years in England, without great honour, indeed, but with a
vast deal of pleasure and no discredit. On leaving the university
he made the journey to France.

In his twenty-fourth year he took ship for home, prepared to find poor little New England (New England was very small in those days) a very dull, unfashionable residence. But there had been changes at home, as well as in Mr Bernard's opinions. He found his mother's house quite habitable, and his sisters grown into two very charming young ladies, with all the accomplishments and graces of the young women of Britain, and a certain native-grown originality and wildness, which, if it was not an accomplishment, was certainly a grace the more.

Bernard privately assured his mother that his sisters were fully a match for the most genteel young women in the old country; whereupon poor Mrs Wingrave, you may be sure, bade them hold up their heads. Such was Bernard's opinion, and such, in a tenfold higher degree, was the opinion of Mr Arthur Lloyd. This gentleman was a college-mate of Mr Bernard, a young man of reputable family, of a good person and a handsome inheritance; which latter appurtenance he proposed to invest in trade in the flourishing colony. He and Bernard were sworn friends; they had crossed the ocean together, and the young American had lost no time in presenting him at his mother's house, where he had made quite as good an impression as that which he had received and of which I have just given a hint.

The two sisters were at this time in all the freshness of their youthful bloom; each wearing, of course, this natural brilliancy in the manner that became her best. They were equally dissimilar in appearance and character. Rosalind, the elder – now in her twenty-second year – was tall and white, with calm grey eyes and auburn tresses; a very faint likeness to the Rosalind of Shakespeare's comedy, whom I imagine a brunette (if you will), but a slender, airy creature, full of the softest, quickest impulses. Miss Wingrave, with her slightly lymphatic fairness, her fine arms, her majestic height, her slow utterance, was not cut out for adventures. She would never have put on a man's jacket and hose; and, indeed, being a very plump beauty, she may have had reasons apart from her natural dignity. Perdita, too, might very well have exchanged the sweet melancholy of her name against something more in consonance with her aspect and disposition.

She had the cheek of a gypsy and the eye of an eager child, as well as the smallest waist and lightest foot in all the country of the Puritans. When you spoke to her she never made you wait, as her handsome sister was wont to do (while she looked at you with a cold fine eye), but gave you your choke of a dozen answers before you had uttered half your thought.

The young girls were very glad to see their brother once more; but they found themselves quite able to spare part of their attention for their brother's friend. Among the young men their friends and neighbours, the *belle jeunesse* of the Colony, there were many excellent fellows, several devoted swains, and some two or three who enjoyed the reputation of universal charmers and conquerors. But the home-bred arts and somewhat boister-ous gallantry of these honest colonists were completely eclipsed by the good looks, the fine clothes, the punctilious courtesy, the perfect elegance, the immense information, of Mr Arthur Lloyd.

He was in reality no paragon; he was a capable, honourable, civil youth, rich in pounds sterling, in his health and complacency, and his little capital of uninvested affections. But he was a gentleman; he had a handsome person; he had studied and travelled; he spoke French, he played the flute, and he read verses aloud with very great taste. There were a dozen reasons why Miss Wingrave and her sister should have thought their other male acquaintance made but a poor figure before such a perfect man of the world. Mr Lloyd's anecdotes told our little New England maidens a great deal more of the ways and means of people of fashion in European capitals than he had any idea of doing. It was delightful to sit by and hear him and Bernard talk about the fine people and fine things they had seen. They would all gather round the fire after tea, in the little wainscoted parlour, and the two young men would remind each other, across the rug, of this, that and the other adventure. Rosalind and Perdita would often have given their ears to know exactly what adventure it was, and where it happened, and who was there, and what the ladies had on; but in those days a well-bred young woman was not expected to break into the conversation of her elders, or to ask too many questions; and the poor girls used therefore to sit fluttering behind the more languid — or more discreet — curiosity of their mother.

II

THAT THEY WERE both very fine girls Arthur Lloyd was not slow to discover; but it took him some time to make up his mind whether he liked the big sister or the little sister best. He had a strong presentiment – an emotion of a nature entirely too cheerful to be called a foreboding – that he was destined to stand up before the parson with one of them; yet he was unable to arrive at a preference, and for such a consummation a preference was certainly necessary, for Lloyd had too much young blood in his veins to make a choice by lot and be cheated of the satisfaction of falling in love. He resolved to take things as they came – to let his heart speak. Meanwhile he was on very pleasant footing. Mrs Wingrave showed a dignified indifference to his 'intentions', equally remote from a carelessness of her daughter's honour and from that sharp alacrity to make him come to the point, which, in his quality of young man of property, he had too often encountered in the worldly matrons of his native islands. As for Bernard, all that he asked was that his friend should treat his sisters as his own; and as for the poor girls themselves, however each may have secretly longed that their visitor should do or say something 'marked', they kept a very modest and contented demeanour.

Towards each other, however, they were somewhat more on the offensive. They were good friends enough, and accommodating bed-fellows (they shared the same four-poster), betwixt whom it would take more than a day for the seeds of jealousy to sprout and bear fruit; but they felt that the seeds had been sown on the day that Mr Lloyd came into the house. Each made up her mind that, if she should be slighted, she would bear her grief in silence, and that no one should be any the wiser; for if they had a great deal of ambition, they had also a large share of pride. But each prayed in secret, nevertheless, that upon *her* the selection, the distinction, might fall. They had need of a vast deal of patience, of self-control, of dissimulation. In those days a young girl of decent breeding could make no advances whatever, and barely respond, indeed, to those that were made. She was expected to sit still in her chair, with her eyes on the carpet, watching the spot where the mystic handkerchief should fall. Poor Arthur Lloyd was obliged to carry on his wooing in the little wainscoted parlour, before the eyes of Mrs Wingrave, her son, and his prospective sister-in-law. But youth and love are so cunning that a hundred signs and tokens might travel to and fro, and not one of these three pairs of eyes detect them in their passage. The two maidens were almost always together, and had plenty of chances to betray themselves. That each knew she was being watched, made not a grain of difference in the little offices they mutually rendered, or in the various household tasks they performed in common.

Neither flinched nor fluttered beneath the silent battery of her sister's eyes. The only apparent change in their habits was that they had less to say to each other. It was impossible to talk about Mr Lloyd, and it was ridiculous to talk about anything else. By tacit agreement they began to wear all their choice finery, and to devise such little implements of conquest, in the way of ribbons and top-knots and kerchiefs, as were sanctioned by indubitable modesty. They executed in the same inarticulate fashion a contract of fair play in this exciting game.

'Is it better so?' Rosalind would ask, tying a bunch of ribbons on her bosom, and turning about from her glass to her sister. Perdita would look up gravely from her work and examine the decoration. 'I think you had better give it another loop,' she would say, with great solemnity, looking hard at her sister with eyes that added, 'Upon my honour!' So they were forever stitching and turning their petticoats, and pressing out their muslins, and contriving washes and ointments and cosmetics, like the ladies in the household of the vicar of Wakefield. Some three or four months went by; it grew to be midwinter, and as yet Rosalind knew that if Perdita had nothing more to boast of than she, there was not much to be feared from her rivalry. But Perdita by this time – the charming Perdita – felt that her secret had grown to be tenfold more precious than her sister's.

One afternoon Miss Wingrave sat alone – that was a rare accident – before her toilet-glass, combing out her long hair. It was getting too dark to see; she lit the two candles in their sockets, on the frame of her mirror, and then went to the window to draw her curtains. It was a grey December evening; the landscape was bare and bleak, and the sky heavy with snow-clouds. At the end of the large garden into which her window looked was a wall with a little postern-door, opening into a lane. The door stood ajar, as she could vaguely see in the gathering darkness, and moved slowly to and fro, as if someone were swaying it from the lane without. It was doubtless a servant-maid who had been having a tryst with her sweetheart. But as she was about to drop her curtain Rosalind saw her sister step into the garden and hurry along the path which led to the house. She dropped the curtain, all save a little crevice for her eyes. As Perdita came up the path she seemed to be examining something in her hand, holding it close to her eyes. When she reached the house she stopped a moment, looked intently at the object, and pressed it to her lips.

Poor Rosalind slowly came back to her chair and sat down before her glass where, if she had looked at it less abstractly, she would have seen her handsome features sadly disfigured by jealousy. A moment afterwards the door opened behind her and her sister came into the room, out of breath, her cheeks aglow with the chilly air.

Perdita started. 'Ah,' said she, 'I thought you were with our mother.' The ladies were to go to a tea-party, and on such occasions it was the habit of one of the girls to help their mother to dress.

Instead of coming in, Perdita lingered at the door.

'Come in, come in,' said Rosalind. 'We have more than an hour yet. I should like you very much to give a few strokes to my hair.' She knew that her sister wished to retreat, and that she could see in the glass all her movements in the room. 'Nay, just help me with my hair,' she said, 'and I will go to mamma.'

Perdita came reluctantly, and took the brush. She saw her sister's eyes, in the glass, fastened hard upon her hands. She had not made three passes when Rosalind clapped her own right hand upon her sister's left, and started out of her chair. 'Whose ring is that?' she cried, passionately, drawing her towards the light.

On the young girl's third finger glistened a little gold ring, adorned with a very small sapphire.

Perdita felt that she need no longer keep her secret, yet that she must put a bold face on her avowal. 'It's mine,' she said proudly.

'Who gave it to you?' cried the other.

Perdita hesitated a moment. 'Mr Lloyd.'

'Mr Lloyd is generous, all of a sudden.'

'Ah no,' cried Perdita, with spirit, 'not all of a sudden! He offered it to me a month ago.'

'And you needed a month's begging to take it?' said Rosalind, looking at the little trinket, which indeed was not especially elegant, although it was the best that the jeweller of the Province could furnish. 'I wouldn't have taken it in less than two.'

'It isn't the ring,' Perdita answered, 'it's what it means!'

'It means that you are not a modest girl!' cried Rosalind. 'Pray, does your mother know of your intrigue? does Bernard?'

'My mother has approved my "intrigue", as you call it. My Lloyd has asked for my hand, and mamma has given it. Would you have had him apply to you, dearest sister?'

Rosalind gave her companion a long look, full of passionate envy and sorrow. Then she dropped her lashes on her pale cheeks and turned away. Perdita felt that it had not been a pretty scene; but it was her sister's fault. However, the elder girl rapidly called back her pride, and turned herself about again. 'You have my very best wishes,' she said, with a low curtsy. 'I wish you every happiness, and a very long life.'

Perdita gave a bitter laugh. 'Don't speak in that tone!' she cried. 'I would rather you should curse me outright. Come, Rosy,' she added, 'he couldn't marry both of us.'

'I wish you very great joy,' Rosalind repeated, mechanically, sitting down to her glass again, 'and a very long life, and plenty of children.'

There was something in the sound of these words not at all to Perdita's taste, 'Will you give me a year to live at least?' she said. 'In a year I can have one little boy – or one little girl at least.

If you will give me your brush again I will do your hair.'

'Thank you,' said Rosalind. 'You had better go to mamma. It isn't becoming that a young lady with a promised husband should wait on a girl with none.'

'Nay,' said Perdita good-humouredly, 'I have Arthur to wait upon me. You need my service more than I need yours.'

But her sister motioned her away, and she left the room. When she had gone, poor Rosalind fell on her knees before her dressing-table, buried her head in her arms, and poured out a flood of tears and sobs. She felt very much the better for this effusion of sorrow. When her sister came back she insisted on helping her to dress – on her wearing her prettiest things. She forced upon her acceptance a bit of lace of her own, and declared that now that she was to be married she should do her best to appear worthy of her lover's choice. She discharged these offices in stern silence; but, such as they were, they had to do duty as an apology and an atonement; she never made any other.

Now that Lloyd was received by the family as an accepted suitor nothing remained but to fix the wedding-day. It was appointed for the following April, and in the interval preparations were diligently made for the marriage. Lloyd, on his side, was busy with his commercial arrangements, and with establishing a correspondence with the great mercantile house to which he had attached himself in England. He was therefore not so frequent a visitor at Mrs Wingrave's as during the months of his diffidence and irresolution, and poor Rosalind had less to suffer than she had feared from the sight of the mutual endearments of the young lovers. Touching his future sister-in-law Lloyd had a perfectly clear conscience. There had not been a particle of love-making between them, and he had not the slightest suspicion that he had dealt her a terrible blow. He was quite at his ease; life promised so well, both domestically and financially. The great revolt of the Colonies was not yet in the air, and that his connubial felicity should take a tragic turn it was absurd, it was blasphemous, to apprehend. Meanwhile, at Mrs Wingrave's, there was a greater rustling of silks, a more rapid clicking of scissors and flying of needles, than ever. The good lady had determined that her daughter should carry from home the genteelest outfit that her money could buy or that the country could furnish. All the sage women in the Province were convened, and their united taste was brought to bear on Perdita's wardrobe. Rosalind's situation, at this moment, was assuredly not to be envied. The poor girl had an inordinate love of dress, and the very best taste in the world, as her sister perfectly well knew. Rosalind was tall, she was stately and sweeping, she was made to earn stiff brocade and masses of heavy lace, such as belong to the toilet of a rich man's wife. But Rosalind sat aloof with her beautiful arms folded and her head averted, while her mother and sister and the venerable women aforesaid worried and wondered over their materials, oppressed by the multitude of their resources. One day there came in a beautiful piece of white silk, brocaded with heavenly blue and silver sent by the bridegroom himself – it not being thought amiss in those days that the husband-elect should contribute to the bride's trousseau. Perdita could think of no form or fashion which would do sufficient honour to the splendour of the material.

'Blue's your colour, sister, more than mine,' she said, with appealing eyes. 'It is a pity it's not for you. You would know what to do with it.'

Rosalind got up from her place and looked at the great shining fabric, as it lay spread over the back of a chair. Then she took it up in her hands and felt it – lovingly, as Perdita could see – and turned about towards the mirror with it. She let it roll down to her feet, and flung the other end over her shoulder, gathering it in about her waist with her white arm, which was bare to the elbow. She threw back her head, and looked at her image, and a hanging tress of her auburn hair fell upon the gorgeous surface of the silk. It made a dazzling picture. The women standing about uttered a little 'Look, look!' of admiration. 'Yes, indeed,' said Rosalind, quietly, 'blue is my colour.' But Perdita could see that her fancy had been stirred, and that she would now fall to work and solve all their silken riddles. And indeed she behaved very well, as Perdita, knowing her insatiable love of millinery, was quite ready to declare. Innumerable yards of lustrous silk and satin, of muslin, velvet and lace, passed through her cunning hands, without a jealous word coming from her lips. Thanks to her industry, when the wedding-day came Perdita was prepared to espouse more of the vanities of life than any fluttering young bride who had yet received the sacramental blessing of a New England divine.

It had been arranged that the young couple should go out and spend the first days of their wedded life at the country-house of an English gentleman – a man of rank and a very kind friend to Arthur Lloyd. He was a bachelor; he declared he should be delighted to give up the place to the influence of Hymen. After the ceremony at church – it had been performed by an English clergyman – young Mrs Lloyd hastened back to her mother's house to change her nuptial robes for a riding-dress. Rosalind helped her to effect the change, in the little homely room in which they had spent their undivided younger years. Perdita then hurried off to bid farewell to her mother, leaving Rosalind to follow. Then parting was short; the horses were at the door, and Arthur was impatient to start. But Rosalind had not followed, and Perdita hastened back to her room, opening the door abruptly. Rosalind, as usual, was before the glass, but in a position which caused the other to stand still, amazed. She had dressed herself in Perdita's cast-off wedding veil and wreath, and on her neck she had hung the full string of pearls which the young girl had received from her husband as a wedding-gift. These things had been hastily laid aside, to await their possessor's disposal on her return from the country. Bedizened by this unnatural garb Rosalind stood before the mirror, plunging a long look into its depths and reading Heaven knows what audacious visions. Perdita was horrified. It was a hideous image of their old rivalry come to life again. She made a step towards her sister, as if to pull off the veil and the flowers. But catching her eyes in the glass, she stopped.

'Farewell, sweetheart,' she said. 'You might at least have waited till I had got out of the house!' And she hurried away from the room.

Mr Lloyd had purchased in Boston a house which to the taste of those days appeared as elegant as it was commodious; and here he very soon established himself with his young wife. He was thus separated by a distance of twenty miles from the residence of his mother-in-law. Twenty miles, in that primitive era of roads and conveyances, were as serious a matter as a hundred at the present day, and Mrs Wingrave saw but little of her daughter during the first twelvemonth of her marriage. She suffered in no small degree from Perdita's absence; and her affliction was not diminished by the fact that Rosalind had fallen into terribly low spirits and was not to be roused or cheered but by change of air and company. The real cause of the young lady's dejection the reader will not be slow to suspect. Mrs Wingrave and her gossips, however, deemed her complaint a mere bodily ill, and doubted not that she would obtain relief from the remedy just mentioned. Her mother accordingly proposed, on her behalf, a visit to certain relatives on the paternal side, established in New York, who had long complained that they were able to see so little of their New England cousins. Rosalind was despatched to these good people, under a suitable escort, and remained with them for several months. In the interval her brother Bernard, who had begun the practice of the law, made up his mind to take a wife. Rosalind came home to the wedding, apparently cured of her heartache, with bright roses and lilies in her face and a proud smile on her lips. Arthur Lloyd came over from Boston to see his brother-in-law married, but without his wife, who was expecting very soon to present him with an heir. It was nearly a year since Rosalind had seen him. She was glad – she hardly knew why – that Perdita had stayed at home. Arthur looked happy, but he was more grave and important than before his marriage.

She thought he looked 'interesting' – for although the word, in its modern sense, was not then invented, we may be sure that the idea was. The truth is, he was simply anxious about his wife and her coming ordeal. Nevertheless, he by no means failed to observe Rosalind's beauty and splendour, and to note how she effaced the poor little bride. The allowance that Perdita had enjoyed for her dress had now been transferred to her sister, who turned it to wonderful account.

On the morning after the wedding he had a lady's saddle put on the horse of the servant who had come with him from town, and went out with the young girl for a ride. It was a keen, clear morning in January; the ground was bare and hard, and the horses in good condition – to say nothing of Rosalind, who was charming in her hat and plume, and her dark blue riding-coat, trimmed with fur. They rode all the morning, lost their way and were obliged to stop for dinner at a farmhouse. The early winter dusk had fallen when they got home. Mrs Wingrave met them with a long face. A messenger had arrived at noon from Mrs Lloyd; she was beginning to be ill, she desired her husband's immediate return. The young man, at the thought that he had lost several hours, and that by hard riding he might already have been with his wife, uttered a passionate oath. He barely consented to stop for a mouthful of supper, but mounted the messenger's horse and started off at a gallop.

He reached home at midnight. His wife had been delivered of a little girl. 'Ah, why weren't you with me?' she said, as he came to her bedside.

'I was out of the house when the man came. I was with Rosalind,' said Lloyd, innocently.

Mrs Lloyd made a little moan, and turned away. But she continued to do very well, and for a week her improvement was uninterrupted. Finally, however, through some indiscretion in the way of diet or exposure, it was checked, and the poor lady grew rapidly worse. Lloyd was in despair. It very soon became evident that she was breathing her last. Mrs Lloyd came to a sense of her approaching end, and declared that she was reconciled with death. On the third evening after the change took place she told her husband that she felt she should not get through the night. She dismissed her servants, and also requested her mother to withdraw – Mrs Wingrave having arrived on the preceding day. She had had her infant placed on the bed beside her, and she lay on her side, with the child against her breast, holding her husband's hands. The night-lamp was hidden behind the heavy curtains of the bed, but the room was illuminated with a red glow from the immense fire of logs on the hearth.

'It seems strange not to be warmed into life by such a fire as that,' the young woman said, feebly trying to smile. 'If I had but a little of it in my veins! But I have given all my fire to this little spark of mortality.' And she dropped her eyes on her child. Then raising them she looked at her husband with a long, penetrating gaze. The last feeling which lingered in her heart was one of suspicion. She had not recovered from the shock which Arthur had given her by telling her that in the hour of her agony he had been with Rosalind. She trusted her husband very nearly as well as she loved him; but now that she was called away for ever she felt a cold horror of her sister. She felt in her soul that Rosalind had never ceased to be jealous of her good fortune; and a year of happy security had not effaced the young girl's image, dressed in her wedding-garments, and smiling with simulated triumph. Now that Arthur was to be alone, what might not Rosalind attempt? She was beautiful, she was engaging; what arts might she not use, what impression might she not make upon the young man's saddened heart? Mrs Lloyd looked at her husband in silence. It seemed hard, after all, to doubt of his constancy. His fine eyes were filled with tears; his face was convulsed with weeping; the clasp of his hands was warm and passionate. How noble he looked, how tender, how faithful and devoted! 'Nay,' thought Perdita, 'he's not for such a one as Rosalind. He'll never forget me. Nor does Rosalind truly care for him; she cares only for vanities and finery and jewels.' And she lowered her eyes on her white hands, which her husband's liberality had covered with rings, and on the lace ruffles which trimmed the edge of her nightdress. 'She covets my rings and my laces more than she covets my husband.'

At this moment the thought of her sister's rapacity seemed to cast a dark shadow between her and the helpless figure of her little girl. 'Arthur,' she said, 'you must take off my rings. I shall not be buried in them. One of these days my daughter shall wear them – my rings and my laces and silks. I had them all brought out and shown me today. It's a great wardrobe – there's not such another in the Province; I can say it without vanity, now that I have done with it. It will be a great inheritance for my daughter when she grows into a young woman. There are things there that a man never buys twice, and if they are lost you will never again see the like. So you will watch them well. Some dozen things I have left to Rosalind: I have named them to my mother. I have given her that blue and silver; it was meant for her; I wore it only once, I looked ill in it. But the rest are to be sacredly kept for this little innocent. It's such a providence that she should be my colour; she can wear my gowns; she has her mother's eyes. You know the same fashions come back even twenty years. She can wear my gowns as they are. They will lie there quietly waiting till she grows into them – wrapped in camphor and rose-leaves, and keeping their colours in the sweet-scented darkness. She shall have black hair, she shall wear my carnation satin. Do you promise me, Arthur?'

'Promise you what, dearest?'

'Promise me to keep your poor little wife's old gowns.'

'Are you afraid I shall sell them?'

'No, but that they may get scattered, My mother will have them properly wrapped up, and you shall lay them away under a double-lock. Do you know the great chest in the attic, with the iron bands? There is no end to what it will hold. You can put them all there. My mother and the housekeeper will do it, and give you the key. And you will keep the key in your secretary, and never give it to anyone but your child. Do you promise me?'

'Ah, yes, I promise you,' said Lloyd, puzzled at the intensity with which his wife appeared to cling to this idea.

'Will you swear?' repeated Perdita.

'Yes, I swear.'

'Well – I trust you – I trust you,' said the poor lady, looking into his eyes with eyes in which, if he had suspected her vague apprehensions, he might have read an appeal quite as much as an assurance.

Lloyd bore his bereavement rationally and manfully. A month after his wife's death, in the course of business, circumstances arose which offered him an opportunity of going to England.

He took advantage of it, to change the current of his thoughts. He was absent nearly a year, during which his little girl was tenderly nursed and guarded by her grandmother. On his return he had his house again thrown open, and announced his intention of keeping the same state as during his wife's lifetime. It very soon came to be predicted that he would marry again, and there were at least a dozen young women of whom one may say that it was by no fault of theirs that, for six months after his return, the prediction did not come true. During this interval he still left his little daughter in Mrs Wingrave's hands, the latter assuring him that a change of residence at so tender an age would be full of danger for her health. Finally, however, he declared that his heart longed for his daughter's presence and that she must be brought up to town. He sent his coach and his housekeeper to fetch her home. Mrs Wingrave was in terror lest something should befall her on the road; and, in accordance with this feeling, Rosalind offered to accompany her.

She could return the next day. So she went up to town with her little niece, and Mr Lloyd met her on the threshold of his house, overcome with her kindness and with paternal joy. Instead of returning the next day Rosalind stayed out the week;

and when at last she reappeared, she had only come for her clothes. Arthur would not hear of her coming home, nor would the baby. That little person cried and choked if Rosalind left her; and at the sight of her grief Arthur lost his wits, and swore that she was going to die. In fine, nothing would suit them but that the aunt should remain until the little niece had grown used to strange faces.

It took two months to bring this consummation about; for it was not until this period had elapsed that Rosalind took leave of her brother-in-law. Mrs Wingrave had shaken her head over her daughter's absence; she had declared that it was not becoming, that it was the talk of the whole country. She had reconciled herself to it only because, during the girl's visit, the household enjoyed an unwonted term of peace. Bernard Wingrave had brought his wife home to live, between whom and her sister-in-law there was as little love as you please. Rosalind was perhaps no angel; but in the daily practice of life she was a sufficiently good-natured girl, and if she quarrelled with Mrs Bernard, it was not without provocation. Quarrel, however, she did, to the great annoyance not only of her antagonist, but of the two spectators of these constant altercations. Her stay in the household of her brother-in-law, therefore, would have been delightful, if only because it removed her from contact with the object of her antipathy at home.

It was doubly — it was ten times — delightful, in that it kept her near the object of her early passion. Mrs Lloyd's sharp suspicions had fallen very far short of the truth. Rosalind's sentiment had been a passion at first, and a passion it remained – a passion of whose radiant heat, tempered to the delicate state of his feelings, Mr Lloyd very soon felt the influence. Lloyd, as I have hinted, was not a modern Petrarch; it was not in his nature to practise an ideal constancy. He had not been many days in the house with his sister-in-law before he began to assure himself that she was, in the language of that day, a devilish fine woman. Whether Rosalind really practised those insidious arts that her sister had been tempted to impute to her it is needless to inquire. It is enough to say that she found means to appear to the very best advantage. She used to seat herself every morning before the big fireplace in the dining-room, at work upon a piece of tapestry, with her little niece disporting herself on the carpet at her feet, or on the train of her dress, and playing with her woollen balls. Lloyd would have been a very stupid fellow if he had remained insensible to the rich suggestions of this charming picture. He was exceedingly fond of his little girl, and was never weary of taking her in his arms and tossing her up and down, and making her crow with delight. Very often, however, he would venture upon greater liberties than the young lady was yet prepared to allow, and then she would suddenly vociferate her displeasure.

Rosalind, at this, would drop her tapestry, and put out her handsome hands with the serious smile of the young girl whose virgin fancy has revealed to her all a mother's healing arts. Lloyd would give up the child, their eyes would meet, their hands would touch, and Rosalind would extinguish the little girl's sobs upon the snowy folds of the kerchief that crossed her bosom. Her dignity was perfect, and nothing could be more discreet than the manner in which she accepted her brother-in-law's hospitality. It may almost be said, perhaps, that there was something harsh in her reserve. Lloyd had a provoking feeling that she was in the house and yet was unapproachable. Half an hour after supper, at the very outset of the long winter evenings, she would light her candle, make the young man a most respectful curtsy, and march off to bed. If these were arts, Rosalind was a great artist. But their effect was so gentle, so gradual, they were calculated to work upon the young widower's fancy with a *crescendo* so finely shaded, that, as the reader has seen, several weeks elapsed before Rosalind began to feel sure that her returns would cover her outlay. When this became morally certain she packed up her trunk and returned to her mother's house. For three days she waited: on the fourth Mr Lloyd made his appearance – a respectful but pressing suitor. Rosalind heard him to the end, with great humility, and accepted him with infinite modesty. It is hard to imagine that Mrs Lloyd would have forgiven her husband; but if anything might have disarmed her resentment it would have been the ceremonious continence of this interview. Rosalind imposed upon her lover but a short probation. They were married, as was becoming, with great privacy – almost with secrecy – in the hope perhaps, as was waggishly remarked at the time, that the late Mrs Lloyd wouldn't hear of it.

The marriage was to all appearance a happy one, and each party obtained what each had desired – Lloyd 'a devilish fine woman', and Rosalind – but Rosalind's desires, as the reader will have observed, had remained a good deal of a mystery. There were, indeed, two blots upon their felicity, but time would perhaps efface them. During the first three years of her marriage Mrs Lloyd failed to become a mother, and her husband on his side suffered heavy losses of money.

This latter circumstance compelled a material retrenchment in his expenditure, and Rosalind was perforce less of a fine lady than her sister had been. She contrived, however, to carry it like a woman of considerable fashion. She had long since ascertained that her sister's copious wardrobe had been sequestrated for the benefit of her daughter, and that it lay languishing in thankless gloom in the dusty attic. It was a revolting thought that these exquisite fabrics should await the good pleasure of a little girl who sat in a high chair and ate bread-and-milk with a wooden spoon. Rosalind had the good taste, however, to say nothing about the matter until several months had expired. Then, at last, she timidly broached it to her husband. Was it not a pity that so much finery should be lost? – for lost it would be, what with colours fading, and moths eating it up, and the change of fashions. But Lloyd gave her so abrupt and peremptory a refusal, that she saw, for the present, her attempt was vain. Six months went by, however, and brought with them new needs and new visions. Rosalind's thoughts hovered lovingly about her sister's relics. She went up and looked at the chest in which they lay imprisoned. There was a sullen defiance in its three great padlocks and its iron bands which only quickened her cupidity.

There was something exasperating in its incorruptible immobility. It was like a grim and grizzled old household servant, who locks his jaws over a family secret. And then there was a look of capacity in its vast extent, and a sound as of dense fullness, when Rosalind knocked its side with the toe of her little shoe, which caused her to flush with baffled longing. 'It's absurd,' she cried; 'it's improper, it's wicked'; and she forthwith resolved upon another attack upon her husband. On the following day, after dinner, when he had had his wine, she boldly began it. But he cut her short with great sternness.

'Once for all, Rosalind,' said he, 'it's out of the question. I shall be gravely displeased if you return to the matter.'

'Very good,' said Rosalind. 'I am glad to learn the esteem in which I'm held. Gracious Heaven,' she cried, 'I am a very happy woman! It's an agreeable thing to feel one's self sacrificed to a caprice!' And her eyes filled with tears of anger and disappointment.

Lloyd had a good-natured man's horror of a woman's sobs, and he attempted – I may say he condescended – to explain. 'It's not a caprice, dear, it's a promise,' he said – 'an oath.'

'An oath? It's a pretty matter for oaths! and to whom, pray?'

'To Perdita,' said the young man, raising his eyes for an instant, and immediately dropping them.

'Perdita – ah, Perdita!' and Rosalind's tears broke forth. Her bosom heaved with stormy sobs – sobs which were the long-deferred sequel of the violent fit of weeping in which she had indulged herself on the night when she discovered her sister's betrothal. She had hoped, in her better moments, that she had done with her jealousy; but her temper, on that occasion, had taken an ineffaceable hold, 'And pray, what right had Perdita to dispose of my future?' she cried.

'What right had she to bind you to meanness and cruelty? Ah, I occupy a dignified place, and I make a very fine figure! I am welcome to what Perdita has left! And what has she left? I never knew till now how little! Nothing, nothing, nothing.'

This was very poor logic, but it was very good as a 'scene'. Lloyd put his arm around his wife's waist and tried to kiss her, but she shook him off with magnificent scorn. Poor fellow! he had coveted a 'devilish fine woman', and he had got one. Her scorn was intolerable. He walked away with his ears tingling – irresolute, distracted. Before him was his secretary, and in it the sacred key which with his own hand he had turned in the triple lock. He marched up and opened it, and took the key from a secret drawer, wrapped in a little packet which he had sealed with his own honest bit of blazonry. *Je garde*, said the motto – 'I keep'. But he was ashamed to put it back. He flung it upon the table beside his wife.

'Put it back!' she cried. 'I want it not. I hate it!'

'I wash my hands of it,' cried her husband. 'God forgive me!'

Mrs Lloyd gave an indignant shrug of her shoulders, and swept out of the room, while the young man retreated by another door. Ten minutes later Mrs Lloyd returned, and found the room occupied by her little stepdaughter and the nursery-maid. The key was not on the table. She glanced at the child.

Her little niece was perched on a chair, with the packet in her hands. She had broken the seal with her own small fingers. Mrs Lloyd hastily took possession of the key.

At the habitual supper-hour Arthur Lloyd came back from his counting-room. It was the month of June, and supper was served by daylight. The meal was placed on the table, but Mrs Lloyd failed to make her appearance. The servant whom his master sent to call her came back with the assurance that her room was empty, and that the women informed him that she had not been seen since dinner. They had, in truth, observed her to have been in tears, and, supposing her to be shut up in her chamber, had not disturbed her. Her husband called her name in various parts of the house, but without response. At last it occurred to him that he might find her by taking the way to the attic. The thought gave him a strange feeling of discomfort, and he bade his servants remain behind, wishing no witness in his quest. He reached the foot of the staircase leading to the topmost flat, and stood with his hands on the banisters, pronouncing his wife's name. His voice trembled. He called again louder and more firmly. The only sound which disturbed the absolute silence was a faint echo of his own tones, repeating his question under the great eaves.

He nevertheless felt irresistibly moved to ascend the staircase. It opened upon a wide hall, lined with wooden closets, and terminating in a window which looked westward, and admitted the last rays of the sun. Before the window stood the great chest. Before the chest, on her knees, the young man saw with amazement and horror the figure of his wife. In an instant he crossed the interval between them, bereft of utterance. The lid of the chest stood open, exposing, amid their perfumed napkins, its treasure of stuffs and jewels. Rosalind had fallen backward from a kneeling posture, with one hand supporting her on the floor and the other pressed to her heart.

On her limbs was the stiffness of death, and on her face, in the fading light of the sun, the terror of something more than death. Her lips were parted in entreaty, in dismay, in agony; and on her blanched brow and cheeks there glowed the marks of ten hideous wounds from two vengeful ghostly hands.

A Light Man

And I — what I seem to my friend, you see —
  What I soon shall seem to his love, you guess.
What I seem to myself, do you ask of me?
  No hero, I confess.

'A Light Woman',
Browning's *Men and Women*

April 4th, 1857. — I have changed my sky without changing my mind. I resume these old notes in a new world. I hardly know of what use they are; but it's easier to stick to the habit than to drop it. I have been at home now a week — at home, forsooth! And yet, after all, it is home. I am dejected, I am bored, I am blue. How can a man be more at home than that? Nevertheless, I am the citizen of a great country, and for that matter, of a great city. I walked today some ten miles or so along Broadway, and on the whole I don't blush for my native land. We are a capable race and a good-looking withal; and I don't see why we shouldn't prosper as well as another. This, by the way, ought to be a very encouraging reflection. A capable fellow and a good-looking withal; I don't see why he shouldn't die a millionaire. At all events he must do something. When a man has, at thirty-two, a net income of considerably less than nothing, he can scarcely hope to overtake a fortune before he himself is overtaken by age and philosophy – two deplorable obstructions. I am afraid that one of them has already planted itself in my path. What am I? What do I wish? Whither do I tend? What do I believe? I am constantly beset by these impertinent whisperings. Formerly it was enough that I was Maximus Austin; that I was endowed with a cheerful mind and a good digestion; that one day or another, when I had come to the end, I should return to America and begin at the beginning; that, meanwhile, existence was sweet in – in the Rue Tronchet. But now? Has the sweetness really passed out of life? Have I eaten the plums and left nothing but the bread and milk and corn-starch, or whatever the horrible concoction is? – I had it today for dinner. Pleasure, at least, I imagine – pleasure pure and simple, pleasure crude, brutal, and vulgar – this poor flimsy delusion has lost all its charm. I shall never again care for certain things – and indeed for certain persons. Of such things, of such persons, I firmly maintain, however, that I was never an enthusiastic votary. It would be more to my credit, I suppose, if I had been. More would be forgiven me if I had loved a little more, if into all my folly and egotism I had put a little more *naïveté* and sincerity. Well, I did the best I could, I was at once too bad and too good for it all. At present, it's far enough off; I have put the sea between us; I am stranded. I sit high and dry, scanning the horizon for a friendly sail, or waiting for a high tide to set me afloat. The wave of pleasure has deposited me here in the sand. Shall I owe my rescue to the wave of pain? At moments I feel a kind of longing to expiate my stupid little sins. I see, as through a glass, darkly, the beauty of labour and love. Decidedly, I am willing to work. It's written.

7th. — My sail is in sight; it's at hand; I have all but boarded the vessel. I received this morning a letter from the best man in the world. Here it is:

Dear Max

I see this very moment, in an old newspaper which had already passed through my hands without yielding up its most precious item, the announcement of your arrival in New York. To think of your having perhaps missed the welcome you had a right to expect from me! Here it is, dear Max — as cordial as you please. When I say I have just read of your arrival, I mean that twenty minutes have elapsed by the clock. These have been spent in conversation with my excellent friend Mr Sloane — we having taken the liberty of making you the topic. I haven't time to say more about Frederick Sloane than that he is very anxious to make your acquaintance, and that, if your time is not otherwise engaged, he would like you very much to spend a month with him. He is an excellent host, or I shouldn't be here myself. It appears that he knew your mother very intimately, and he has a taste for visiting the amenities of the parents upon the children; the original ground of my own connection with him was that he had been a particular friend of my father. You may have heard your mother speak of him. He is a very strange old fellow, but you will like him. Whether or no you come for his sake, come for mine.

Yours always,
Theodore Lisle

Theodore's letter is of course very kind, but it's remarkably obscure. My mother may have had the highest regard for Mr Sloane, but she never mentioned his name in my hearing. Who is he, what is he, and what is the nature of his relations with Theodore? I shall learn betimes. I have written to Theodore that I gladly accept (I believe I suppressed the 'gladly' though) his friend's invitation, and that I shall immediately present myself. What can I do that is better? Speaking sordidly, I shall obtain food and lodging while I look about me. I shall have a base of operations. D——, it appears, is a long day's journey, but enchanting when you reach it. I am curious to see an enchanting American town. And to stay a month! Mr Frederick Sloane, whoever you are, *vous faites bien les choses*, and the little that I know of you is very much to your credit. You enjoyed the friendship of my dear mother, you possess the esteem of the virtuous Theodore, you commend yourself to my own affection. At this rate, I shall not grudge it.

*   *   *

D——, 14th. – I have been here since Thursday evening – three days. As we rattled up to the tavern in the village, I perceived from the top of the coach, in the twilight, Theodore beneath the porch, scanning the vehicle, with all his amiable disposition in his eyes. He has grown older, of course, in these five years, but less so than I had expected. His is one of those smooth, unwrinkled souls that keep their bodies fair and fresh. As tall as ever, moreover, and as lean and clean. How short and fat and dark and debauched he makes one feel! By nothing he says or means, of course, but merely by his old unconscious purity and simplicity – that slender straightness which makes him remind you of the spire of an English abbey. He greeted me with smiles, and stares, and alarming blushes. He assures me that he never would have known me, and that five years have altered me – *sehr!* I asked him if it were for the better? He looked at me hard for a moment, with his eyes of blue, and then, for an answer, he blushed again.

On my arrival we agreed to walk over from the village. He dismissed his wagon with my luggage, and we went arm-in-arm through the dusk. The town is seated at the foot of certain mountains, whose names I have yet to learn, and at the head of a big sheet of water, which, as yet, too, I know only as 'the Lake'. The road hitherward soon leaves the village and wanders in rural loveliness by the margin of this expanse. Sometimes the water is hidden by clumps of trees, behind which we heard it lapping and gurgling in the darkness; sometimes it stretches out from your feet in shining vagueness, as if it were tired of making, all day, a million little eyes at the great stupid hills. The walk from the tavern takes some half an hour, and in this interval Theodore made his position a little more clear. Mr Sloane is a rich old widower; his age is seventy-two, and as his health is thoroughly broken, is practically even greater; and his fortune – Theodore, characteristically, doesn't know anything definite about that. It's probably about a million. He has lived much in Europe, and in the 'great world'; he has had adventures and passions and all that sort of thing; and now, in the evening of his days, like an old French diplomatist, he takes it into his head to write his memoirs. To this end he has lured poor Theodore to his gruesome side, to mend his pens for him. He has been a great scribbler, says Theodore, all his days, and he proposes to incorporate a large amount of promiscuous literary matter into these *souvenirs intimes*. Theodore's principal function seems to be to get him to leave things out. In fact, the poor youth seems troubled in conscience. His patron's lucubrations have taken the turn of many other memoirs, and have ceased to address themselves *virginibus puerisque*. On the whole, he declares they are a very odd mixture – a medley of gold and tinsel, of bad taste and a good sense. I can readily understand it. The old man bores me, puzzles me, and amuses me.

He was in waiting to receive me. We found him in his library – which, by the way, is simply the most delightful apartment that I ever smoked a cigar in – a room arranged for a lifetime. At one end stands a great fireplace, with a florid, fantastic mantelpiece in carved white marble – an importation, of course, and, as one may say, an interpolation; the groundwork of the house, the 'fixtures', being throughout plain, solid and domestic. Over the mantel-shelf is a large landscape, a fine Gainsborough, full of the complicated harmonies of an English summer. Beneath it stands a row of bronzes of the Renaissance and potteries of the Orient. Facing the door, as you enter, is an immense window set in a recess, with cushioned seats and large clear panes, stationed as it were at the very apex of the lake (which forms an almost perfect oval) and commanding a view of its whole extent. At the other end, opposite the fireplace, the wall is studded, from floor to ceiling, with choice foreign paintings, placed in relief against the orthodox crimson screen. Elsewhere the walls are covered with books, arranged neither in formal regularity nor quite helter-skelter, but in a sort of genial incongruity, which tells that sooner or later each volume feels sure of leaving the ranks and returning into different company. Mr Sloane makes use of his books. His two passions, according to Theodore, are reading and talking; but to talk he must have a book in his hand. The charm of the room lies in the absence of certain pedantic tones – the browns, blacks and greys – which distinguish most libraries. The apartment is of the feminine gender. There are half a dozen light colours scattered about – pink in the carpet, tender blue in the curtains, yellow in the chairs. The result is a general look of brightness and lightness; it expresses even a certain cynicism. You perceive the place to be the home, not of a man of learning, but of a man of fancy.

He rose from his chair – the man of fancy, to greet me – the man of fact. As I looked at him, in the lamplight, it seemed to me, for the first five minutes, that I had seldom seen an uglier little person. It took me five minutes to get the point of view; then I began to admire. He is diminutive, or at best of my own moderate stature, and bent and contracted with his seventy years; lean and delicate, moreover, and very highly finished. He is curiously pale, with a kind of opaque yellow pallor. Literally, it's a magnificent yellow. His skin is of just the hue and apparent texture of some old crumpled Oriental scroll. I know a dozen painters who would give more than they have to arrive at the exact 'tone' of his thick-veined, bloodless hands, his polished ivory knuckles. His eyes are circled with red, but in the battered little setting of their orbits they have the lustre of old sapphires. His nose, owing to the falling away of other portions of his face, has assumed a grotesque, unnatural prominence; it describes an immense arch, gleaming like a piece of parchment stretched on ivory. He has, apparently, all his teeth, but has muffled his cranium in a dead black wig; of course he's clean-shaven. In his dress he has a muffled, wadded look and an apparent aversion to linen, inasmuch as none is visible on his person. He seems neat enough, but not fastidious. At first, as I say, I fancied him monstrously ugly; but on further acquaintance I perceived that what I had taken for ugliness is nothing but the incomplete remains of remarkable good looks. The line of his features is pure; his nose, *caeteris paribus*, would be extremely handsome; his eyes are the oldest eyes I ever saw, and yet they are wonderfully living. He has something remarkably insinuating.

He offered his two hands, as Theodore introduced me; I gave him my own, and he stood smiling at me like some quaint old image in ivory and ebony, scanning my face with a curiosity which he took no pains to conceal. 'God bless me,' he said, at last, 'how much you look like your father!' I sat down, and for half an hour we talked of many things – of my journey, of my impressions of America, of my reminiscences of Europe, and, by implication, of my prospects. His voice is weak and cracked, but he makes it express everything. Mr Sloane is not yet in his dotage – oh no! He nevertheless makes himself out a poor creature. In reply to an inquiry of mine about his health, he favoured me with a long list of his infirmities (some of which are very trying, certainly) and assured me that he was quite finished.

'I live out of mere curiosity,' he said.

'I have heard of people dying from the same motive.'

He looked at me a moment, as if to ascertain whether I were laughing at him. And then, after a pause, 'Perhaps you don't know that I disbelieve in a future life,' he remarked, blandly.

At these words Theodore got up and walked to the fire.

'Well, we shan't quarrel about that,' said I. Theodore turned round, staring.

'Do you mean that you agree with me?' the old man asked.

'I certainly haven't come here to talk theology! Don't ask me to disbelieve, and I'll never ask you to believe.'

'Come,' cried Mr Sloane, rubbing his hands, 'you'll not persuade me you are a Christian – like your friend Theodore there.'

'Like Theodore – assuredly not.' And then, somehow, I don't know why, at the thought of Theodore's Christianity I burst into a laugh. 'Excuse me, my dear fellow,' I said, 'you know, for the last ten years I have lived in pagan lands.'

'What do you call pagan?' asked Theodore, smiling.

I saw the old man, with his hands locked, eyeing me shrewdly, and waiting for my answer. I hesitated a moment, and then I said, 'Everything that makes life tolerable!'

Hereupon Mr Sloane began to laugh till he coughed. Verily, I thought, if he lives for curiosity, he's easily satisfied.

We went into dinner, and this repast showed me that some of his curiosity is culinary. I observed, by the way, that for a victim of neuralgia, dyspepsia, and a thousand other ills, Mr Sloane plies a most inconsequential knife and fork. Sauces and spices and condiments seem to be the chief of his diet. After dinner he dismissed us, in consideration of my natural desire to see my friend in private. Theodore has capital quarters – a downy bedroom and a snug little *salon*. We talked till near midnight – of ourselves, of each other, and of the author of the memoirs, downstairs. That is, I spoke of myself, and Theodore listened; and then Theodore descanted upon Mr Sloane, and I listened. His commerce with the old man has sharpened his wits. Sloane has taught him to observe and judge, and Theodore turns round, observes, judges – him! He has become quite the critic and analyst. There is something very pleasant in the discriminations of a conscientious mind, in which criticism is tempered by an angelic charity. Only, it may easily end by acting on one's nerves. At midnight we repaired to the library, to take leave of our host till the morrow – an attention which, under all circumstances, he rigidly exacts. As I gave him my hand he held it again and looked at me as he had done on my arrival. 'Bless my soul,' he said, at last, 'how much you look like your mother!'

Tonight, at the end of my third day, I begin to feel decidedly at home. The fact is, I am remarkably comfortable. The house is pervaded by an indefinable, irresistible love of luxury and privacy. Mr Frederick Sloane is a horribly corrupt old mortal. Already in his relaxing presence I have become heartily reconciled to doing nothing. But with Theodore on one side – standing there like a tall interrogation-point – I honestly believe I can defy Mr Sloane on the other. The former asked me this morning, with visible solicitude, in allusion to the bit of dialogue I have quoted above on matters of faith, whether I am really a materialist – whether I don't believe something? I told him I would believe anything he liked. He looked at me awhile, in friendly sadness. 'I hardly know whether you are not worse than Mr Sloane,' he said.

But Theodore is, after all, in duty bound to give a man a long rope in these matters. His own rope is one of the longest. He reads Voltaire with Mr Sloane, and Emerson in his own room. He is the stronger man of the two; he has the larger stomach. Mr Sloane delights, of course, in Voltaire, but he can't read a line of Emerson. Theodore delights in Emerson, and enjoys Voltaire, though he thinks him superficial. It appears that since we parted in Paris, five years ago, his conscience has dwelt in many lands.

C'est tout une histoire – which he tells very prettily. He left college determined to enter the church, and came abroad with his mind full of theology and Tübingen. He appears to have studied, not wisely but too well. Instead of faith full-armed and serene, there sprang from the labour of his brain a myriad sickly questions, piping for answers. He went for a winter to Italy, where, I take it, he was not quite so much afflicted as he ought to have been at the sight of the beautiful spiritual repose that he had missed. It was after this that we spent those three months together in Brittany – the best-spent months of my long residence in Europe. Theodore inoculated me, I think, with some of his seriousness, and I just touched him with my profanity; and we agreed together that there were a few good things left – health, friendship, a summer sky, and the lovely byways of an old French province. He came home, searched the Scriptures once more, accepted a 'call', and made an attempt to respond to it. But the inner voice failed him. His outlook was cheerless enough. During his absence his married sister, the elder one, had taken the other to live with her, relieving Theodore of the charge of contribution to her support. But suddenly, behold the husband, the brother-in-law, dies, leaving a mere figment of property; and the two ladies, with their two little girls, are afloat in the wide world. Theodore finds himself at twenty-six without an income, without a profession, and with a family of four females to support. Well, in his quiet way he draws on his courage. The history of the two years that passed before he came to Mr Sloane is really absolutely edifying. He rescued his sisters and nieces from the deep waters, placed them high and dry, established them somewhere in decent gentility – and then found at last that his strength had left him – had dropped dead like an overridden horse. In short, he had worked himself to the bone. It was now his sisters' turn. They nursed him with all the added tenderness of gratitude for the past and terror of the future, and brought him safely through a grievous malady. Meanwhile Mr Sloane, having decided to treat himself to a private secretary and suffered dreadful mischance in three successive experiments, had heard of Theodore's situation and his merits; had furthermore recognized in him the son of an early and intimate friend, and had finally offered him the very comfortable position he now occupies. There is a decided incongruity between Theodore as a man – as Theodore, in fine – and the dear fellow as the intellectual agent, confidant, complaisant, purveyor, pander – what you will – of a battered old cynic and dilettante – a worldling if there ever was one. There seems at first sight a perfect want of agreement between his character and his function. One is gold and the other brass, or something very like it. But on reflection I can enter into it – his having, under the circumstances, accepted Mr Sloane's offer and been content to do his duties. *Ce que c'est de nous!* Theodore's contentment in such a case is a theme for the moralist – a better moralist than I. The best and purest mortals are an odd mixture, and in none of us does honesty exist on its own terms. Ideally, Theodore hasn't the smallest business *dans cette galère*. It offends my sense of propriety to find him here. I feel that I ought to notify him as a friend that he has knocked at the wrong door, and that he had better retreat before he is brought to the blush. However, I suppose he might as well be here as reading Emerson 'evenings' in the back parlour, to those two very plain sisters — judging from their photographs. Practically it hurts no one not to be too much of a prig. Poor Theodore was weak, depressed, out of work. Mr Sloane offers him a lodging and a salary in return for — after all, merely a little tact. All he has to do is to read to the old man, lay down the book awhile, with his finger in the place, and let him talk; take it up again, read another dozen pages and submit to another commentary. Then to write a dozen pages under his dictation — to suggest a word, polish off a period, or help him out with a complicated idea or a half-remembered fact. This is all, I say; and yet this is much. Theodore's apparent success proves it to be much, as well as the old man's satisfaction. It is a part; he has to simulate. He has to 'make believe' a little — a good deal; he has to put his pride in his pocket and send his conscience to the wash. He has to be accommodating — to listen and pretend and flatter; and he does it as well as many a worse man — does it far better than I. I might bully the old man, but I don't think I could humour him. After all, however, it is not a matter of comparative merit. In every son of woman there are two men — the practical man and the dreamer. We live for our dreams — but, meanwhile, we live by our wits. When the dreamer is a poet, the other fellow is an artist. Theodore, at bottom, is only a man of taste. If he were not destined to become a high priest among moralists, he might be a prince among connoisseurs. He plays his part, therefore, artistically, with spirit, with originality, with all his native refinement. How can Mr Sloane fail to believe that he possesses a paragon? He is no such fool as not to appreciate a *nature distinguée* when it comes in his way. He confidentially assured me this morning that Theodore has the most charming mind in the world, but that it's a pity he's so simple as not to suspect it. If he only doesn't ruin him with his flattery!

19th. – I am certainly fortunate among men. This morning when, tentatively, I spoke of going away, Mr Sloane rose from his seat in horror and declared that for the present I must regard his house as my home. 'Come, come,' he said, 'when you leave this place where do you intend to go?' Where, indeed? I graciously allowed Mr Sloane to have the best of the argument. Theodore assures me that he appreciates these and other affabilities, and that I have made what he calls a 'conquest' of his venerable heart. Poor, battered, bamboozled old organ! he would have one believe that it has a most tragical record of capture and recapture. At all events, it appears that I am master of the citadel. For the present I have no wish to evacuate. I feel, nevertheless, in some far-off corner of my soul, that I ought to shoulder my victorious banner and advance to more fruitful triumphs.

I blush for my beastly laziness. It isn't that I am willing to stay here a month, but that I am willing to stay here six. Such is the charming, disgusting truth. Have I really outlived the age of energy? Have I survived my ambition, my integrity, my self-respect? Verily, I ought to have survived the habit of asking myself silly questions. I made up my mind long ago to go in for nothing but present success; and I don't care for that sufficiently to secure it at the cost of temporary suffering. I have a passion for nothing – not even for life. I know very well the appearance I make in the world. I pass for a clever, accomplished, capable, good-natured fellow, who can do anything if he would only try. I am supposed to be rather cultivated, to have latent talents. When I was younger I used to find a certain entertainment in the spectacle of human affairs. I liked to see men and women hurrying on each other's heels across the stage. But I am sick and tired of them now; not that I am a misanthrope, God forbid! They are not worth hating. I never knew but one creature who was, and her I went and loved. To be consistent, I ought to have hated my mother, and now I ought to detest Theodore. But I don't – truly, on the whole, I don't – any more than I dote on him. I firmly believe that it makes a difference to him, his idea that I *am* fond of him. He believes in that, as he believes in all the rest of it – in my culture, my latent talents, my underlying 'earnestness', my sense of beauty and love of truth. Oh, for a *man* among them all – a fellow with eyes in his head – eyes that would know me for what I am and let me see they had guessed it. Possibly such a fellow as that might get a 'rise' out of me.

In the name of bread and butter, what am I to do? (I was obliged this morning to borrow fifty dollars from Theodore, who remembered gleefully that he has been owing me a trifling sum for the past four years, and in fact has preserved a note to this effect.) Within the last week I have hatched a desperate plan: I have made up my mind to take a wife – a rich one, *bien entendu*. Why not accept the goods of the gods? It is not my fault, after all, if I pass for a good fellow. Why not admit that practically, mechanically – as I may say – maritally, I *may* be a good fellow? I warrant myself kind. I should never beat my wife; I don't think I should even contradict her. Assume that her fortune has the proper number of zeros and that she herself is one of them, and I can even imagine her adoring me. I really think this is my only way. Curiously, as I look back upon my brief career, it all seems to tend to this consummation. It has its graceful curves and crooks, indeed, and here and there a passionate tangent; but on the whole, if I were to unfold it here *à la* Hogarth, what better legend could I scrawl beneath the series of pictures than So-and-So's Progress to a Mercenary Marriage?

Coming events do what we all know with their shadows. My noble fate is, perhaps, not far off. I already feel throughout my person a magnificent languor – as from the possession of many dollars. Or is it simply my sense of well-being in this perfectly appointed house? Is it simply the contact of the highest civilization I have known? At all events, the place is of velvet, and my only complaint of Mr Sloane is that, instead of an old widower, he's not an old widow (or a young maid), so that I might marry him, survive him, and dwell for ever in this rich and mellow home. As I write here, at my bedroom table, I have only to stretch out an arm and raise the window-curtain to see the thick-planted garden budding and breathing and growing in the silvery silence. Far above in the liquid darkness rolls the brilliant ball of the moon; beneath, in its light, lies the lake, in murmuring, troubled sleep; round about, the mountains, looking strange and blanched, seem to bare their heads and undrape their shoulders. So much for midnight. Tomorrow the scene will be lovely with the beauty of day. Under one aspect or another I have it always before me. At the end of the garden is moored a boat, in which Theodore and I have indulged in an immense deal of irregular navigation. What lovely landward coves and bays – what alder-smothered creeks – what lily-sheeted pools – what sheer steep hillsides, making the water dark and quiet where they hang. I confess that in these excursions Theodore looks after the boat and I after the scenery. Mr Sloane avoids the water – on account of the dampness, he says; because he's afraid of drowning, I suspect.

22nd. – Theodore is right. The *bonhomme* has taken me into his favour. I protest I don't see how he was to escape it. *Je l'ai bien soigné*, as they say in Paris. I don't blush for it. In one coin or another I must repay his hospitality – which is certainly very liberal. Theodore dots his *i*'s, crosses his *t*'s, verifies his quotations; while I set traps for that famous 'curiosity'. This speaks vastly well for my powers. He pretends to be surprised at nothing, and to possess in perfection – poor, pitiable old fop – the art of keeping his countenance; but repeatedly, I know, I have made him stare. As for his corruption, which I spoke of above, it's a very pretty piece of wickedness, but it strikes me as a purely intellectual matter. I imagine him never to have had any real senses. He may have been unclean; morally, he's not very tidy now; but he never can have been what the French call a *viveur*. He's too delicate, he's of a feminine turn; and what woman was ever a *viveur*? He likes to sit in his chair and read scandal, talk scandal, make scandal, so far as he may without catching a cold or bringing on a headache. I already feel as if I had known him a lifetime. I read him as clearly as if I had. I know the type to which he belongs; I have encountered, first and last, a good many specimens of it. He's neither more nor less than a gossip – a gossip flanked by a coxcomb and an egotist. He's shallow, vain, cold, superstitious, timid, pretentious, capricious; a pretty list of foibles! And yet, for all this, he has his good points. His caprices are sometimes generous, and his rebellion against the ugliness of life frequently makes him do kind things. His memory (for trifles) is remarkable, and (where his own performances are not involved) his taste is excellent. He has no courage for evil more than for good. He is the victim, however, of more illusions with regard to himself than I ever knew a single brain to shelter. At the age of twenty, poor, ignorant and remarkably handsome, he married a woman of immense wealth, many years his senior. At the end of three years she very considerately took herself off and left him to the enjoyment of his freedom and riches. If he had remained poor he might from time to time have rubbed at random against the truth, and would be able to recognize the touch of it. But he wraps himself in his money as in a wadded dressing-gown, and goes trundling through life on his little gold wheels. The greater part of his career, from the time of his marriage till about ten years ago, was spent in Europe, which, superficially, he knows very well. He has lived in fifty places, known thousands of people, and spent a very large fortune. At one time, I believe, he spent considerably too much, trembled for an instant on the verge of a pecuniary crash, but recovered himself, and found himself more frightened than hurt, yet audibly recommended to lower his pitch. He passed five years in a species of penitent seclusion on the lake of – I forget what (his genius seems to be partial to lakes), and laid the basis of his present magnificent taste for literature. I can't call him anything but magnificent in this respect, so long as he must have his punctuation done by a *nature distinguée*. At the close of this period, by economy, he had made up his losses. His turning the screw during those relatively impecunious years represents, I am pretty sure, the only act of resolution of his life. It was rendered possible by his morbid, his actually pusillanimous dread of poverty; he doesn't feel safe without half a million between him and starvation. Meanwhile he had turned from a young man into an old man; his health was broken, his spirit was jaded, and I imagine, to do him justice, that he began to feel certain natural, filial longings for this dear American mother of us all. They say the most hopeless truants and triflers have come to it. He came to it, at all events; he packed up his books and pictures and gimcracks, and bade farewell to Europe. This house which he now occupies belonged to his wife's estate. She had, for sentimental reasons of her own, commended it to his particular care. On his return he came to see it, liked it, turned a parcel of carpenters and upholsterers into it, and by inhabiting it for nine years transformed it into the perfect dwelling which I find it. Here he has spent all his time, with the exception of a usual winter's visit to New York – a practice recently discontinued, owing to the increase of his ailments and the projection of these famous memoirs. His life has finally come to be passed in comparative solitude. He tells of various distant relatives, as well as intimate friends of both sexes, who used formerly to be entertained at his cost; but with each of them, in the course of time, he seems to have succeeded in quarrelling. Throughout life, evidently, he has had capital fingers for plucking off parasites. Rich, lonely, and vain, he must have been fair game for the race of social sycophants and cormorants; and it's much to the credit of his sharpness and that instinct of self-defence which nature bestows even on the weak, that he has not been despoiled and *exploité*. Apparently they have all been bunglers. I maintain that something is to be done with him still. But one must work in obedience to certain definite laws. Dr Jones, his physician, tells me that in point of fact he has had for the past ten years an unbroken series of favourites, *protégés*, heirs presumptive; but that each, in turn, by some fatally false movement, has spilled his pottage. The doctor declares, moreover, that they were mostly very common people. Gradually the old man seems to have developed a preference for two or three strictly exquisite intimates, over a throng of your vulgar pensioners. His tardy literary schemes, too – fruit of his all but sapless senility – have absorbed more and more of his time and attention. The end of it all is, therefore, that Theodore and I have him quite to ourselves, and that it behooves us to hold our porringers straight.

Poor, pretentious old simpleton! It's not his fault, after all, that he fancies himself a great little man. How are you to judge of the stature of mankind when men have forever addressed you on their knees? Peace and joy to his innocent fatuity! He believes himself the most rational of men; in fact, he's the most superstitious. He fancies himself a philosopher, an inquirer, a discoverer. He has not yet discovered that he is a humbug, that Theodore is a prig, and that I am an adventurer. He prides himself on his good manners, his urbanity, his knowing a rule of conduct for every occasion in life. My private impression is that his skinny old bosom contains unsuspected treasures of impertinence. He takes his stand on his speculative audacity – his direct, undaunted gaze at the universe; in truth, his mind is haunted by a hundred dingy old-world spectres and theological phantasms. He imagines himself one of the most solid of men; he is essentially one of the hollowest. He thinks himself ardent, impulsive, passionate, magnanimous – capable of boundless enthusiasm for an idea or a sentiment. It is clear to me that on no occasion of disinterested action can he ever have done anything in time. He believes, finally, that he has drained the cup of life to the dregs; that he has known, in its bitterest intensity, every emotion of which the human spirit is capable; that he has loved, struggled, suffered. Mere vanity, all of it. He has never loved anyone but himself; he has never suffered from anything but an undigested supper or an exploded pretension; he has never touched with the end of his lips the vulgar bowl from which the mass of mankind quaffs its floods of joy and sorrow. Well, the long and short of it all is, that I honestly pity him. He may have given sly knocks in his life, but he can't hurt anyone now. I pity his ignorance, his weakness, his pusillanimity. He has tasted the real sweetness of life no more than its bitterness; he has never dreamed, nor experimented, nor dared; he has never known any but mercenary affection; neither men nor women have risked aught for *him* — for his good spirits, his good looks, his empty pockets. How I should like to give him, for once, a real sensation!

26th. — I took a row this morning with Theodore a couple of miles along the lake, to a point where we went ashore and lounged away an hour in the sunshine, which is still very comfortable. Poor Theodore seems troubled about many things. For one, he is troubled about me; he is actually more anxious about my future than I myself; he thinks better of me than I do of myself; he is so deucedly conscientious, so scrupulous, so averse to giving offence or to *brusquer* any situation before it has played itself out, that he shrinks from betraying his apprehensions or asking direct questions. But I know that he would like very much to extract from me some intimation that there is something under the sun I should like to do. I catch myself in the act of taking – Heaven forgive me! – a half-malignant joy in confounding his expectations – leading his generous sympathies off the scent by giving him momentary glimpses of my latent wickedness. But in Theodore I have so firm a friend that I shall have a considerable job if I ever find it needful to make him change his mind about me. He admires me – that's absolute; he takes my low moral tone for an eccentricity of genius, and it only imparts an extra flavour – a *haut goût* – to the charm of my intercourse. Nevertheless, I can see that he is disappointed. I have even less to show, after all these years, than he had hoped. Heaven help us! little enough it must strike him as being. What a contradiction there is in our being friends at all! I believe we shall end with hating each other. It's all very well now – our agreeing to differ, for we haven't opposed interests. But if we should *really* clash, the situation would be warm! I wonder, as it is, that Theodore keeps his patience with me. His education since we parted should tend logically to make him despise me. He has studied, thought, suffered, loved – loved those very plain sisters and nieces. Poor me! how should I be virtuous? I have no sisters, plain or pretty! – nothing to love, work for, live for. My dear Theodore, if you are going one of these days to despise me and drop me – in the name of comfort, come to the point at once, and make an end of our state of tension.

He is troubled, too, about Mr Sloane. His attitude toward the *bonhomme* quite passes my comprehension. It's the queerest jumble of contraries. He penetrates him, disapproves of him – yet respects and admires him. It all comes of the poor boy's shrinking New England conscience. He's afraid to give his perceptions a fair chance, lest, forsooth, they should look over his neighbour's wall. He'll not understand that he may as well sacrifice the old reprobate for a lamb as for a sheep. His view of the gentleman, therefore, is a perfect tissue of cobwebs — a jumble of half-way sorrows, and wire-drawn charities, and hair-breadth 'scapes from utter damnation, and sudden platitudes of generosity — fit, all of it, to make an angel curse!

'The man's a perfect egotist and fool,' say I, 'but I like him.' Now Theodore likes him — or rather wants to like him; but he can't reconcile it to his self-respect — fastidious deity! — to like a fool. Why the deuce can't he leave it alone altogether? It's a purely practical matter. He ought to do the duties of his place all the better for having his head clear of officious sentiment. I don't believe in disinterested service; and Theodore is too desperately bent on preserving his disinterestedness. With me it's different. I am perfectly free to love the *bonhomme* — for a fool. I'm neither a scribe nor a Pharisee; I am simply a student of the art of life.

And then, Theodore is troubled about his sisters. He's afraid he's not doing his duty by them. He thinks he ought to be with them — to be getting a larger salary — to be teaching his nieces. I am not versed in such questions. Perhaps he ought.

May 3rd. — This morning Theodore sent me word that he was ill and unable to get up; upon which I immediately went in to see him. He had caught cold, was sick and a little feverish. I urged him to make no attempt to leave his room, and assured him that I would do what I could to reconcile Mr Sloane to his absence. This I found an easy matter. I read to him for a couple of hours, wrote four letters – one in French – and then talked for a while – a good while, I have done more talking, by the way, in the last fortnight, than in any previous twelve months – much of it, too, none of the wisest, nor, I may add, of the most superstitiously veracious. In a little discussion, two or three days ago, with Theodore, I came to the point and let him know that in gossiping with Mr Sloane I made no scruple, for our common satisfaction, of 'colouring' more or less. My confession gave him 'that turn', as Mrs Gamp would say, that his present illness may be the result of it. Nevertheless, poor dear fellow, I trust he will be on his legs tomorrow. This afternoon, somehow, I found myself really in the humour of talking. There was something propitious in the circumstances; a hard, cold rain without, a wood-fire in the library, the *bonhomme* puffing cigarettes in his arm-chair, beside him a portfolio of newly imported prints and photographs, and – Theodore tucked safely away on bed. Finally, when I brought our *tête-à-tête* to a close (taking good care not to overstay my welcome), Mr Sloane seized me by both hands and honoured me with one of his venerable grins. 'Max,' he said – 'you must let me call you Max – you are the most delightful man I ever knew.'

Verily, there's some virtue left in me yet. I believe I almost blushed.

'Why didn't I know you ten years ago?' the old man went on. 'There are ten years lost.'

'Ten years ago I was not worth your knowing,' Max remarked.

'But I did know you!' cried the *bonhomme*. 'I knew you in knowing your mother.'

Ah! my mother again. When the old man begins that chapter I feel like telling him to blow out his candle and go to bed.

'At all events,' he continued, 'we must make the most of the years that remain. I am a rotten old carcase, but I have no intention of dying. You won't get tired of me and want to go away?'

'I am devoted to you, sir,' I said. 'But I must be looking for some occupation, you know.'

'Occupation? bother! I'll give you occupation. I'll give you wages.'

'I am afraid that you will want to give me the wages without the work.' And then I declared that I must go up and look at poor Theodore.

The *bonhomme* still kept my hands. 'I wish very much that I could get you to be as fond of me as you are of poor Theodore.'

'Ah, don't talk about fondness, Mr Sloane. I don't deal much in that article.'

'Don't you like my secretary?'

'Not as he deserves.'

'Nor as he likes you, perhaps?'

'He likes me more than I deserve.'

'Well, Max,' my host pursued, 'we can be good friends all the same. We don't need a hocus-pocus of false sentiment. We are *men*, aren't we? — men of sublime good sense.' And just here, as the old man looked at me, the pressure of his hands deepened to a convulsive grasp, and the bloodless mask of his countenance was suddenly distorted with a nameless fear. 'Ah, my dear young man!' he cried, 'come and be a son to me – the son of my age and desolation! For God's sake, don't leave me to pine and die alone!'

I was greatly surprised – and I may add I was moved. Is it true, then, that this dilapidated organism contains such measureless depths of horror and longing? He has evidently a mortal fear of death. I assured him on my honour that he may henceforth call upon me for any service.

8th. – Theodore's little turn proved more serious than I expected. He has been confined to his room till today. This evening he came down to the library in his dressing-gown. Decidedly, Mr Sloane is an eccentric, but hardly, as Theodore thinks, a 'charming' one. There is something extremely curious in his humours and fancies – the incongruous fits and starts, as it were, of his taste. For some reason, best known to himself, he took it into his head to regard it as a want of delicacy, of respect, of *savoir-vivre* – of Heaven knows what – that poor Theodore, who is still weak and languid, should enter the sacred precinct of his study in the vulgar drapery of a dressing-gown. The sovereign trouble with the *bonhomme* is an absolute lack of the instinct of justice. He's of the real feminine turn – I believe I have written it before – without the redeeming fidelity of the sex. I honestly believe that I might come into his study in my night-shirt and he would smile at it as a picturesque *déshabillé*.

But for poor Theodore tonight there was nothing but scowls and frowns, and barely a civil inquiry about his health. But poor Theodore is not such a fool, either; he will not die of a snubbing; I never said he was a weakling. Once he fairly saw from what quarter the wind blew, he bore the master's brutality with the utmost coolness and gallantry. Can it be that Mr Sloane really wishes to drop him? The delicious old brute! He understands favour and friendship only as a selfish rapture – a reaction, an infatuation, an act of aggressive, exclusive patronage. It's not a bestowal, with him, but a transfer, and half his pleasure in causing his sun to shine is that – being woefully near its setting – it will produce certain long fantastic shadows. He wants to cast my shadow, I suppose, over Theodore; but fortunately I am not altogether an opaque body. Since Theodore was taken ill he has been into his room but once, and has sent him none but a dry little message or two. I, too, have been much less attentive than I should have wished to be; but my time has not been my own. It has been, every moment of it, at the disposal of my host. He actually runs after me; he devours me; he makes a fool of himself, and is trying hard to make one of me. I find that he will bear – that, in fact, he actually enjoys – a sort of unexpected contradiction. He likes anything that will tickle his fancy, give an unusual tone to our relations, remind him of certain historical characters whom he thinks he resembles. I have stepped into Theodore's shoes, and done – with what I feel in my bones to be very inferior skill and taste – all the reading, writing, condensing, transcribing and advising that he has been accustomed to do. I have driven with the *bonhomme*; played chess and cribbage with him; beaten him, bullied him, contradicted him; forced him into going out on the water under my charge. Who shall say, after this, that I haven't done my best to discourage his advances, put myself in a bad light? As yet, my efforts are vain; in fact they quite turn to my own confusion. Mr Sloane is so thankful at having escaped from the lake with his life that he looks upon me as a preserver and protector. Confound it all; it's a bore! But one thing is certain, it can't last for ever. Admit that he *has* cast Theodore out and taken me in. He will speedily discover that he has made a pretty mess of it, and he had much better have left well enough alone. He likes my reading and writing now, but in a month he will begin to hate them. He will miss Theodore's better temper and better knowledge – his healthy impersonal judgement. What an advantage that well-regulated youth has over me, after all! I am for days, he is for years; he for the long run, I for the short. I, perhaps, am intended for success, but he is adapted for happiness. He has in his heart a tiny sacred particle which leavens his whole being and keeps it pure and sound – a faculty of admiration and respect. For him human nature is still a wonder and mystery; it bears a divine stamp – Mr Sloane's tawdry composition as well as the rest.

13th. – I have refused, of course, to supplant Theodore further, in the exercise of his functions, and he has resumed his morning labours with Mr Sloane. I, on my side, have spent these morning hours in scouring the country on that capital black mare, the use of which is one of the perquisites of Theodore's place. The days have been magnificent – the heat of the sun tempered by a murmuring, wandering wind, the whole north a mighty ecstasy of sound and verdure, the sky a far-away vault of bended blue. Not far from the mill at M——, the other end of the lake, I met, for the third time, that very pretty young girl who reminds me so forcibly of A. L. She makes so lavish a use of her eyes that I ventured to stop and bid her good-morning. She seems nothing loath to an acquaintance. She's a pure barbarian in speech, but her eyes are quite articulate. These rides do me good; I was growing too pensive.

There is something the matter with Theodore; his illness seems to have left him strangely affected. He has fits of silent stiffness, alternating with spasms of extravagant gaiety. He avoids me at times for hours together, and then he comes and looks at me with an inscrutable smile, as if he were on the verge of a burst of confidence – which again is swallowed up in the immensity of his dumbness. Is he hatching some astounding benefit to his species? Is he working to bring about my removal to a higher sphere of action? *Nous verrons bien.*

18th. – Theodore threatens departure. He received this morning a letter from one of his sisters – the young widow – announcing her engagement to a clergyman whose acquaintance she has recently made, and intimating her expectation of an immediate union with the gentleman – a ceremony which would require

Theodore's attendance. Theodore, in high good humour, read the letter aloud at breakfast – and, to tell the truth, it was a charming epistle. He then spoke of his having to go on to the wedding, a proposition to which Mr Sloane graciously assented – much more than assented. 'I shall be sorry to lose you, after so happy a connection,' said the old man. Theodore turned pale, stared a moment, and then, recovering his colour and his composure, declared that he should have no objection in life to coming back.

'Bless your soul!' cried the *bonhomme*, 'you don't mean to say you will leave your other sister all alone?'

To which Theodore replied that he would arrange for her and her little girl to live with the married pair. 'It's the only proper thing,' he remarked, as if it were quite settled. Has it come to this, then, that Mr Sloane actually wants to turn him out of the house? The shameless old villain! He keeps smiling an uncanny smile, which means, as I read it, that if the poor young man once departs he shall never return on the old footing – for all his impudence!

20th. – This morning, at breakfast, we had a terrific scene. A letter arrives for Theodore; he opens it, turns white and red, frowns, falters, and then informs us that the clever widow has broken off her engagement. No wedding, therefore, and no departure for Theodore. The *bonhomme* was furious. In his fury he took the liberty of calling poor Mrs Parker (the sister) a very uncivil name. Theodore rebuked him, with perfect good taste, and kept his temper.

'If my opinions don't suit you, Mr Lisle,' the old man broke out, 'and my mode of expressing them displeases you, you know you can easily protect yourself.'

'My dear Mr Sloane,' said Theodore, 'your opinions, as a general thing, interest me deeply, and have never ceased to act beneficially upon the formation of my own. Your mode of expressing them is always brilliant, and I wouldn't for the world, after all our pleasant intercourse, separate from you in bitterness. Only, I repeat, your qualification of my sister's conduct is perfectly uncalled for. If you knew her, you would be the first to admit it.'

There was something in Theodore's look and manner, as he said these words, which puzzled me all the morning. After dinner, finding myself alone with him, I told him I was glad he was not obliged to go away. He looked at me with the mysterious smile I have mentioned, thanked me, and fell into meditation. As this bescribbled chronicle is the record of my follies as well of my *hauts faits*, I needn't hesitate to say that for a moment I was a good deal vexed. What business has this angel of candour to deal in signs and portents, to look unutterable things? What right has he to do so with me especially, in whom he has always professed an absolute confidence? Just as I was about to cry out, 'Come, my dear fellow; this affectation of mystery has lasted quite long enough – favour me at last with the result of your cogitations!' – as I was on the point of thus expressing my impatience of his ominous behaviour, the oracle at last addressed itself to utterance.

'You see, my dear Max,' he said, 'I can't, in justice to myself, go away in obedience to the sort of notice that was served on me this morning. What do you think of my actual footing here?'

Theodore's actual footing here seems to me impossible; of course I said so.

'No, I assure you it's not,' he answered. 'I should, on the contrary, feel very uncomfortable to think that I had come away, except by my own choice. You see a man can't afford to cheapen himself. What are you laughing at?'

'I am laughing, in the first place, my dear fellow, to hear on your lips the language of cold calculation; and in the second place, at your odd notion of the process by which a man keeps himself up in the market.'

'I assure you it's the correct notion. I came here as a particular favour to Mr Sloane; it was expressly understood so. The sort of work was odious to me; I had regularly to break myself in. I had to trample on my convictions, preferences, prejudices. I don't take such things easily; I take them hard; and when once the effort has been made, I can't consent to have it wasted. If Mr Sloane needed me then, he needs me still. I am ignorant of any change having taken place in his intentions, or in his means of satisfying them. I came, not to amuse him, but to do a certain work; I hope to remain until the work is completed. To go away sooner is to make a confession of incapacity which, I protest, costs me too much. I am too conceited, if you like.'

Theodore spoke these words with a face which I have never seen him wear – a fixed, mechanical smile; a hard, dry glitter in his eyes; a harsh, strident tone in his voice – in his whole physiognomy a gleam, as it were, a note of defiance. Now I confess that for defiance I have never been conscious of an especial relish. When I am defied I am beastly. 'My dear man,' I replied, 'your sentiments do you prodigious credit. Your very ingenious theory of your present situation, as well as your extremely pronounced sense of your personal value, are calculated to ensure you a degree of practical success which can very well dispense with the furtherance of my poor good wishes.' Oh, the grimness of his visage as he listened to this, and, I suppose I may add, the grimness of mine! But I have ceased to be puzzled. Theodore's conduct for the past ten days is suddenly illumined with a backward, lurid ray. I will note down here a few plain truths which it behooves me to take to heart – commit to memory. Theodore is jealous of Maximus Austin. Theodore hates the said Maximus. Theodore has been seeking for the past three months to see his name written, last but not least, in a certain testamentary document: 'Finally, I bequeath to my dear young friend, Theodore Lisle, in return for invaluable services and unfailing devotion, the bulk of my property, real and personal, consisting of—' (hereupon follows an exhaustive enumeration of houses, lands, public securities, books, pictures, horses, and dogs). It is for this that he has toiled, and watched, and prayed; submitted to intellectual weariness and spiritual torture; accommodated himself to levity, blasphemy, and insult. For this he sets his teeth and tightens his grasp; for this he'll fight. Dear me, it's an immense weight off one's mind! There

are nothing, then, but vulgar, common laws; no sublime exceptions, no transcendent anomalies. Theodore's a knave, a
hypo— nay, nay; stay, irreverent hand! — Theodore's a *man*!
Well, that's all I want. *He* wants fight — he shall have it, Have I
got, at last, my simple, natural emotion?

21st. — I have lost no time. This evening, late, after I had heard
Theodore go to his room (I had left the library early, on the
pretext of having letters to write), I repaired to Mr Sloane, who
had not yet gone to bed, and informed him I should be obliged
to leave him at once, and pick up a subsistence somehow in New
York. He felt the blow; it brought him straight down on his
marrow-bones. He went through the whole gamut of his arts
and graces; he blustered, whimpered, entreated, flattered. He
tried to drag in Theodore's name; but this I, of course,
prevented. But, finally, why, *why*, WHY, after all my promises of
fidelity, must I thus cruelly desert him? Then came my trump
card: I have spent my last penny; while I stay, I'm a beggar. The
remainder of this extraordinary scene I have no power to
describe: how the *bonhomme*, touched, inflamed, inspired, by
the thought of my destitution, and at the same time annoyed,
perplexed, bewildered at having to commit himself to doing
anything for me, worked himself into a nervous frenzy which
deprived him of a clear sense of the value of his words and his
actions; how I, prompted by the irresistible spirit of my desire to
leap astride of his weakness and ride it hard to the goal of my
dreams, cunningly contrived to keep his spirit at the fever-point,

so that strength and reason and resistance should burn themselves out. I shall probably never again have such a sensation as I enjoyed tonight – actually feel a heated human heart throbbing and turning and struggling in my grasp; know its pants, its spasms, its convulsions, and its final senseless quiescence. At half-past one o'clock Mr Sloane got out of his chair, went to his secretary, opened a private drawer, and took out a folded paper. 'This is my will,' he said, 'made some seven weeks ago. If you will stay with me I will destroy it.'

'Really, Mr Sloane,' I said, 'if you think my purpose is to exert any pressure upon your testamentary inclinations——'

'I will tear it in pieces,' he cried; 'I will burn it up! I shall be as sick as a dog tomorrow; but I will do it. A-a-h!'

He clapped his hand to his side, as if in sudden, overwhelming pain, and sank back fainting into his chair. A single glance ensured me that he was unconscious. I possessed myself of the paper, opened it, and perceived that he had left everything to his saintly secretary. For an instant a savage, puerile feeling of hate popped up in my bosom, and I came within a hair's-breadth of obeying my foremost unpulse – that of stuffing the document into the fire. Fortunately, my reason overtook my passion, though for a moment it was an even race. I put the paper back into the bureau, closed it, and rang the bell for Robert (the old man's servant). Before he came I stood watching the poor, pale remnant of mortality before me, and wondering whether those feeble life-gasps were numbered. He was as white as a sheet, grimacing with pain – horribly ugly. Suddenly he opened his eyes; they met my own; I fell on my knees and took his hands. They closed on mine with a grasp strangely akin to the rigidity of death. Nevertheless, since then he has revived, and has relapsed again into a comparatively healthy sleep. Robert seems to know how to deal with him.

22nd. – Mr Sloane is seriously ill – out of his mind and unconscious of people's identity. The doctor has been here, off and on, all day, but this evening reports improvement. I have kept out of the old man's room, and confined myself to my own, reflecting largely upon the chance of his immediate death. Does Theodore know of the will? Would it occur to him to divide the property? Would it occur to me, in his place? We met at dinner, and talked in a grave, desultory, friendly fashion. After all, he's an excellent fellow. I don't hate him. I don't even dislike him. He jars on me, *il m'agace*; but that's no reason why I should do him an evil turn. Nor shall I. The property is a fixed idea, that's all. I shall get it if I can. We are fairly matched. Before Heaven, no, we are not fairly matched! Theodore has a conscience.

23rd. – I am restless and nervous – and for good reasons. Scribbling here keeps me quiet. This morning Mr Sloane is better; feeble and uncertain in mind, but unmistakably on the rise. I may confess now that I feel relieved of a horrid burden. Last night I hardly slept a wink. I lay awake listening to the pendulum of my clock. It seemed to say, 'He lives – he dies.' I fully expected to hear it stop suddenly at *dies*. But it kept going all the morning, and to a decidedly more lively tune. In the afternoon the old man sent for me. I found him in his great muffled bed, with his face the colour of damp chalk, and his eyes glowing faintly, like torches half stamped out. I was forcibly struck with the utter loneliness of his lot. For all human attendance, my villainous self grinning at his bedside and old Rohen without, listening, doubtless, at the keyhole. The *bonhomme* stared at me stupidly; then seemed to know me, and greeted me with a sickly smile. It was some moments before he was able to speak. At last he faintly bade me to descend into the library, open the secret drawer of the secretary (which he contrived to direct me how to do), possess myself of his will, and burn it up. He appears to have forgotten his having taken it out the night before last. I told him that I had an insurmountable aversion to any personal dealings with the document. He smiled, patted the back of my hand, and requested me, in that case, to get it, at least, and bring it to him. I couldn't deny him that favour? No, I couldn't, indeed. I went down to the library, therefore, and on entering the room found Theodore standing by the fireplace with a bundle of papers. The secretary was open. I stood still, looking from the violated cabinet to the documents in his hand. Among them I recognized, by its shape and size, the paper of which I had intended to possess myself. Without delay I walked straight up to him. He looked surprised, but not confused. 'I am afraid I shall have to trouble you to surrender one of those papers,' I said.

'Surrender, Maximus? To anything of your own you are perfectly welcome. I didn't know that you made use of Mr Sloane's secretary. I was looking for some pages of notes which I have made myself and in which I conceive I have a property.'

'This is what I want, Theodore,' I said; and I drew the will, unfolded, from between his hands. As I did so his eyes fell upon the superscription, '*Last Will and Testament. March. F. S.*' He flushed an extraordinary crimson. Our eyes met. Somehow – I don't know how or why, or for that matter why not – I burst into a violent peal of laughter. Theodore stood staring, with two hot, bitter tears in his eyes.

'Of course you think I came to ferret out that thing,' he said.

I shrugged my shoulders – those of my body only. I confess, morally, I was on my knees with contrition, but there was a fascination in it – a fatality. I remembered that in the hurry of my movements the other evening I had slipped the will simply into one of the outer drawers of the cabinet, among Theodore's own papers. 'Mr Sloane sent me for it,' I remarked.

'Very good; I am glad to hear he's well enough to think of such things.'

'He means to destroy it.'

'I hope, then, he has another made.'

'Mentally, I suppose he has.'

'Unfortunately, his weakness isn't mental – or exclusively so.'

'Oh, he will live to make a dozen more,' I said. 'Do you know the purport of this one?'

Theodore's colour, by this time, had died away into plain white. He shook his head. The doggedness of the movement provoked me, and I wished to arouse his curiosity. 'I have his commission to destroy it.'

Theodore smiled very grandly. 'It's not a task I envy you,' he said.

'I should think not – especially if you knew the import of the will.' He stood with folded arms, regarding me with his cold, detached eyes. I couldn't stand it. 'Come, it's your property! You are sole legatee. I give it to you.' And I thrust the paper into his hand.

He received it mechanically; but after a pause, bethinking himself, he unfolded it and cast his eyes over the contents. Then he slowly smoothed it together and held it a moment with a tremulous hand. 'You say that Mr Sloane directed you to destroy it?' he finally inquired.

'I say so.'

'And that you know the contents?'

'Exactly.'

'And that you were about to do what he asked you?'

'On the contrary, I declined.'

Theodore fixed his eyes for a moment on the superscription and then raised them again to my face. 'Thank you, Max,' he said. 'You have left me a real satisfaction.' He tore the sheet across and threw the bits into the fire. We stood watching them burn. 'Now he can make another,' said Theodore.

'Twenty others,' I replied.

'No,' said Theodore, 'you will take care of that.'

'You are very bitter,' I said, sharply enough.

'No, I am perfectly indifferent. Farewell.' And he put out his hand.

'Are you going away?'

'Of course I am. Good-bye.'

'Good-bye, then. But isn't your departure rather sudden?'

'I ought to have gone three weeks ago – three weeks ago.' I had taken his hand, he pulled it away; his voice was trembling – there were tears in it.

'Is *that* indifference?' I asked.

'It's something you will never know!' he cried. 'It's shame! I am not sorry you should see what I feel. It will suggest to you, perhaps, that my heart had never been in this filthy contest. Let me assure you, at any rate, that it hasn't; that it has had nothing but scorn for the base perversion of my pride and my ambition. I could easily shed tears of joy at their return – the return of the prodigals! Tears of sorrow – sorrow—'

He was unable to go on. He sank into a chair, covering his face with his hands.

'For God's sake, stick to the joy!' I exclaimed.

He rose to his feet again. 'Well,' he said, 'it was for your sake that I parted with my self-respect; with your assistance I recover it.'

'How for my sake?'

'For whom but you would I have gone as far as I did? For what other purpose than that of keeping our friendship whole would I have borne your company into this narrow pass? A man whom I cared for less I would long since have parted with. You were needed – you and something you have about you that always takes me so – to bring me to this. You ennobled, exalted, enchanted the struggle. I *did* value my prospect of coming into Mr Sloane's property. I valued it for my poor sister's sake as well as for my own, so long as it was the natural reward of conscientious service, and not the prize of hypocrisy and cunning. With another man than you I never would have contested such a prize. But you fascinated me, even as my rival. You played with me, deceived me, betrayed me. I held my ground, hoping you would see that what you were doing was not fair. But if you have seen it, it has made no difference with you. For Mr Sloane, from the moment that, under your magical influence, he revealed his nasty little nature, I had nothing but contempt.'

'And for me now?'

'Don't ask me. I don't trust myself.'

'Hate, I suppose.'

'Is that the best you can imagine? Farewell.'

'Is it a serious farewell – farewell for ever?'

'How can there be any other?'

'I am sorry this should be your point of view. It's characteristic. All the more reason then that I should say a word in self-defence. You accuse me of having "played with you, deceived you, betrayed you". It seems to me that you are quite beside the mark. You say you were such a friend of mine; if so, you ought to be one still. It was not to my fine sentiments you attached yourself, for I never had any or pretended to any. In anything I have done recently, therefore, there has been no inconsistency. I never pretended to take one's friendship so seriously. I don't understand the word in the sense you attach to it. I don't understand the feeling of affection between men. To me it means quite another thing. You give it a meaning of your own; you enjoy the profit of your invention; it's no more than just that you should pay the penalty. Only it seems to me rather hard that *I* should pay it.' Theodore remained silent, but he looked quite sick. 'Is it still a "serious farewell"?' I went on. 'It seems a pity. After this clearing up, it appears to me that I shall be on better terms with you, No man can have a deeper appreciation of your excellent parts, a keener enjoyment of your society. I should very much regret the loss of it.'

'Have we, then, all this while understood each other so little?' said Theodore.

'Don't say "we" and "each other". I think I have understood you.'

'Very likely. It's not for my having kept anything back.'

Well, I do you justice. To me you have always been over-generous. Try now and be just.'

Still he stood silent, with his cold, hard frown. It was plain that, if he was to come back to me, it would be from the other world – if there be one! What he was going to answer I know not. The door opened, and Robert appeared, pale, trembling, his eyes starting in his head.

'I verily believe that poor Mr Sloane is dead in his bed!' he cried.

There was a moment's perfect silence. 'Amen,' said I. 'Yes, old boy, try and be just.' Mr Sloane had quietly died in my absence.

24th. – Theodore went up to town this morning, having shaken hands with me in silence before he started. Dr Jones, and Brooks the attorney, have been very officious, and, by their advice, I have telegraphed to a certain Miss Meredith, a maiden lady, by their account the nearest of kin; or, in other words, simply a discarded niece of the defunct. She telegraphs back that she will arrive in person for the funeral. I shall remain till she comes. I have lost a fortune, but have I irretrievably lost a friend? I am sure I can't say. Yes, I shall wait for Miss Meredith.

The Madonna of the Future

W E HAD BEEN talking about the masters who had achieved but a single masterpiece – the artists and poets who but once in their lives had known the divine afflatus, and touched the high level of the best. Our host had been showing us a charming little cabinet picture by a painter whose name we had never heard, and who, after this one spasmodic bid for fame, had apparently relapsed into fatal mediocrity. There was some discussion as to the frequency of this phenomenon; during which, I observed, H— sat silent, finishing his cigar with a meditative air, and looking at the picture, which was being handed round the table. 'I don't know how common a case it is,' he said at last, 'but I've seen it. I've known a poor fellow who painted his one masterpiece, and –' he added with a smile – 'he didn't even paint that. He made his bid for fame, and missed it.' We all knew H— for a clever man who had seen much of men and manners, and had a great stock of reminiscences. Someone immediately questioned him further, and while I was engrossed with the raptures of my neighbour over the little picture, he was induced to tell his tale. If I were to doubt whether it would bear repeating, I should only have to remember how that charming woman, our hostess, who had left the table, ventured back in rustling rose-colour, to pronounce our lingering a want of gallantry, and, finding us a listening circle, had sunk into her chair in spite of our cigars, and heard the story out so graciously, that when the catastrophe was reached she glanced across at me, and showed me a tender tear in each of her beautiful eyes.

It relates to my youth, and to Italy: two fine things! (H—— began). I had arrived late in the evening at Florence, and while I finished my bottle of wine at supper, had fancied that, tired traveller though I was, I might pay the city a finer compliment than by going vulgarly to bed. A narrow passage wandered darkly away out of the little square before my hotel, and looked as if it bored into the heart of Florence. I followed it, and at the end of ten minutes emerged upon a great piazza, filled only with the mild autumn moonlight. Opposite rose the Palazzo Vecchio, like some huge civic fortress, with the great bell-tower springing from its embattled verge like a mountain-pine from the edge of a cliff. At its base, in its projected shadow, gleamed certain dim sculptures which I wonderingly approached. One of the images, on the left of the palace door, was a magnificent colossus, shining through the dusky air like some embodied Defiance. In a moment I recognized him as Michael Angelo's David. I turned with a certain relief from his sinister strength to a slender figure in bronze, stationed beneath the high, light *loggia*, which opposes the free and elegant span of its arches to the dead masonry of the palace; a figure supremely shapely and graceful; gentle, almost, in spite of his holding out with his light nervous arm the snaky head of the slaughtered Gorgon. His name is Perseus, and you may read his story, not in the Greek mythology, but in the memoirs of Benvenuto Cellini. Glancing from one of these fine fellows to the other, I probably uttered some irrepressible commonplace of praise, for, as if provoked by my voice, a man rose from the steps of the *loggia*, where he had been sitting in the shadow, and addressed me in good English – a small, slim personage, clad in a sort of black velvet tunic (as it seemed), and with a mass of auburn hair, which gleamed in the moonlight, escaping from a little mediaeval *berretta*. In a tone of the most insinuating deference, he asked me for my 'impressions'. He seemed picturesque, fantastic, slightly unreal. Hovering there in this consecrated neighbourhood, he might have passed for the genius of aesthetic hospitality – if the genius of aesthetic hospitality were not commonly some shabby little *custode*, flourishing a calico pocket-handkerchief, and openly resentful of the divided franc. This fantasy was made none the less plausible by the brilliant tirade with which he greeted my embarrassed silence.

'I've known Florence long, sir, but I've never known her so lovely as tonight. It's as if the ghosts of her past were abroad in the empty streets. The present is sleeping; the past hovers about us like a dream made visible. Fancy the old Florentines strolling up in couples to pass judgement on the last performance of

Michael, of Benvenuto! We should come in for a precious lesson if we might overhear what they say. The plainest burgher of them, in his cap and gown, had a taste in the matter! That was the prime of art, sir. The sun stood high in heaven, and his broad and equal blaze made the darkest places bright and the dullest eyes clear. We live in the evening of time! We grope in the grey dusk, carrying each our poor little taper of selfish and painful wisdom, holding it up to the great models and to the dim idea, and seeing nothing but overwhelming greatness and dimness. The days of illumination are gone! But do you know I fancy – I fancy –' and he grew suddenly almost familiar in this visionary fervour – 'I fancy the light of that time rests upon us here for an hour! I have never seen the David so grand, the Perseus so fair! Even the inferior productions of John of Bologna and of Baccio Bandinelli seem to realize the artist's dream. I feel as if the moonlit air were charged with the secrets of the masters, and as if, standing here in religious contemplation, we might – we might witness a revelation!' Perceiving at this moment, I suppose, my halting comprehension reflected in my puzzled face, this interesting rhapsodist paused and blushed. Then with a melancholy smile, 'You think me a moonstruck charlatan, I suppose. It's not my habit to hang about the piazza and pounce upon innocent tourists. But tonight, I confess, I'm under the charm. And then, somehow, I fancied you, too, were an artist!'

'I'm not an artist, I'm sorry to say, as you must understand the term. But pray make no apologies. I am also under the charm; your eloquent reflections have only deepened it.'

'If you're not an artist, you're worthy to be one!' he rejoined, with a bow. 'A young man who arrives at Florence late in the evening, and, instead of going prosaically to bed, or hanging over the travellers' book at his hotel, walks forth without loss of time to pay his devoirs to the beautiful, is a young man after my own heart!'

The mystery was suddenly solved; my friend was an American! He must have been, to take the picturesque so prodigiously to heart. 'None the less so, I trust,' I answered, 'if the young man is a sordid New Yorker.'

'New Yorkers,' he solemnly proclaimed, 'have been munificent patrons of art!'

For a moment I was alarmed. Was this midnight reverie mere Yankee enterprise, and was he simply a desperate brother of the brush who had posted himself here to extort an 'order' from a sauntering tourist? But I was not called to defend myself. A great brazen note broke suddenly from the far-off summit of the bell-tower above us and sounded the first stroke of midnight. My companion started, apologized for detaining me, and prepared to retire. But he seemed to offer so lively a promise of further entertainment, that I was indisposed to part with him, and suggested that we should stroll homeward together. He cordially assented, so we turned out of the piazza, passed down before the statued arcade of the Uffizi, and came out upon the Arno. What course we took I hardly remember, but we roamed slowly about for an hour, my companion delivering by snatches a sort of moon-touched aesthetic lecture. I listened in puzzled fascination, and wondered who the deuce he was. He confessed with a melancholy but all-respectful head-shake to his American origin. 'We are the disinherited of Art!' he cried. 'We are condemned to be superficial! We are excluded from the magic circle. The soil of American perception is a poor little barren, artificial deposit. Yes! we are wedded to imperfection. An American, to excel, has just ten times as much to learn as a European. We lack the deeper sense. We have neither taste, nor tact, nor force. How should we have them? Our crude and garish climate, our silent past, our deafening present, the constant pressure about us of unlovely circumstance, are as void of all that nourishes and prompts and inspires the artist, as my sad heart is void of bitterness in saying so! We poor aspirants must live in perpetual exile.'

'You seem fairly at home in exile,' I answered, 'and Florence seems to me a very pretty Siberia. But do you know my own thought? Nothing is so idle as to talk about our want of a nutritive soil, of opportunity, of inspiration, and all the rest of it. The worthy part is to do something fine! There's no law in our glorious Constitution against that. Invent, create, achieve! No matter if you've to study fifty times as much as one of these! What else are you an artist for? Be you our Moses,' I added, laughing, and laying my hand on his shoulder, 'and lead us out of the house of bondage!'

'Golden words – golden words, young man!' he cried, with a tender smile. ' "Invent, create, achieve!" Yes, that's our business: I know it well. Don't take me, in Heaven's name, for one of your barren complainers – querulous cynics, who have neither talent nor faith! I'm at work!' – and he glanced about him and lowered his voice as if this were a quite peculiar secret – 'I'm at work night and day. I've undertaken a *creation*! I'm no Moses; I'm only a poor, patient artist; but it would be a fine thing if I were to cause some slender stream of beauty to flow in our thirsty land! Don't think me a monster of conceit,' he went on, as he saw me smile at the avidity with which he adopted my fantasy; 'I confess that I'm in one of those moods when great things seem possible! This is one of my nervous nights – I dream waking! When the south-wind blows over Florence at midnight, it seems to coax the soul from all the fair things locked away in her churches and galleries; it comes into my own little studio with the moonlight, and sets my heart beating too deeply for rest. You see I am always adding a thought to my conception! This evening I felt that I couldn't sleep unless I had communed with the genius of Michael!'

He seemed deeply versed in local history and tradition, and he expatiated *con amore* on the charms of Florence. I gathered that he was an old resident, and that he had taken the lovely city into his heart. 'I owe her everything,' he declared. 'It's only since I came here that I have really lived, intellectually. One by one, all profane desires, all mere worldly aims, have dropped away from me, and left me nothing but my pencil, my little note-book' (and he tapped his breast-pocket), 'and the worship of the pure masters – those who were pure because they were innocent, and those who were pure because they were strong!'

'And have you been very productive all this time?' I asked, with amenity.

He was silent awhile before replying. 'Not in the vulgar sense!' he said, at last. 'I have chosen never to manifest myself by imperfection. The good in every performance I have reabsorbed into the generative force of new creations; the bad — there's always plenty of that — I have religiously destroyed. I may say, with some satisfaction, that I have not added a mite to the rubbish of the world. As a proof of my conscientiousness —' and he stopped short, and eyed me with extraordinary candour, as if the proof were to be overwhelming — 'I've never sold a picture! "At least no merchant traffics in my heart!" Do you remember the line in Browning? My little studio has never been profaned by superficial, feverish, mercenary work. It's a temple of labour, but of leisure! Art is long. If we work for ourselves, of course we must hurry. If we work for her, we must often pause. She can wait!'

This had brought us to my hotel door, somewhat to my relief, I confess, for I had begun to feel unequal to the society of a genius of this heroic strain. I left him, however, not without expressing a friendly hope that we should meet again. The next morning my curiosity had not abated; I was anxious to see him by common daylight. I counted upon meeting him in one of the many aesthetic haunts of Florence, and I was gratified without delay. I found him in the course of the morning in the Tribune of the Uffizi — that little treasure-chamber of perfect works. He had turned his back on the Venus de' Medici, and with his arms resting on the railing which protects the pictures, and his head buried in his hands, he was lost in the contemplation of that superb triptych of Andrea Mantegna – a work which has neither the material splendour nor the commanding force of some of its neighbours, but which, glowing there with the loveliness of patient labour, suits possibly a more constant need of the soul. I looked at the picture for some time over his shoulder; at last, with a heavy sigh, he turned away and our eyes met. As he recognized me a deep blush rose to his face; he fancied, perhaps, that he had made a fool of himself overnight. But I offered him my hand with a frankness which assured him I was not a scoffer. I knew him by his ardent *chevelure*; otherwise he was much altered. His midnight mood was over, and he looked as haggard as an actor by daylight. He was far older than I had supposed, and he had less bravery of costume and gesture. He seemed the quite poor, patient artist he had proclaimed himself, and the fact that he had never sold a picture was more obvious than glorious. His velvet coat was threadbare, and his short slouched hat, of an antique pattern, revealed a rustiness which marked it an 'original', and not one of the picturesque reproductions which brethren of his craft affect. His eye was mild and heavy, and his expression singularly gentle and acquiescent; the more so for a certain pallid leanness of visage which I hardly knew whether to refer to the consuming fire of genius or to a meagre diet. A very little talk, however, cleared his brow and brought back his eloquence.

'And this is your first visit to these enchanted halls?' he cried. 'Happy, thrice happy youth!' And taking me by the arm, he prepared to lead me to each of the pre-eminent works in turn and show me the cream of the gallery. But before we left the Mantegna, he pressed my arm and gave it a loving look. 'He was not in a hurry,' he murmured. '*He* knew nothing of "raw Haste, half-sister to Delay"!' How sound a critic my friend was I am unable to say, but he was an extremely amusing one; overflowing with opinions, theories, and sympathies, with disquisition and gossip and anecdote. He was a shade too sentimental for my own sympathies, and I fancied he was rather too fond of superfine discriminations and of discovering subtle intentions in the shallow felicities of chance. At moments, too, he plunged into the sea of metaphysics and floundered awhile in waters too deep for intellectual security. But his abounding knowledge and happy judgement told a touching story of long attentive hours in this worshipful company; there was a reproach to my wasteful saunterings in so devoted a culture of opportunity. 'There are two moods,' I remember his saying, 'in which we may walk through galleries – the critical and the ideal. They seize us at their pleasure, and we can never tell which is to take its turn. The critical mood, oddly, is the genial one, the friendly, the condescending. It relishes the pretty trivialities of art, its vulgar clevernesses, its conscious graces. It has a kindly greeting for anything which looks as if, according to his light, the painter had enjoyed doing it – for the little Dutch cabbages and kettles, for the taper fingers and breezy mantles of late-coming Madonnas, for the little blue-hilled pastoral, sceptical Italian landscapes. Then there are the days of fierce, fastidious longing

– solemn church-feasts of the intellect – when all vulgar effort and all petty success is a weariness, and everything but the best – the best of the best – disgusts. In these hours we are relentless aristocrats of taste. We'll not take Michael for granted, we'll not swallow Raphael whole!'

The gallery of the Uffizi is not only rich in its possessions, but peculiarly fortunate in that fine architectural accident, as one may call it, which unites it – with the breadth of river and city between them – to those princely chambers of the Pitti Palace. The Louvre and the Vatican hardly give you such a sense of sustained enclosure as those long passages projected over street and stream to establish a sort of inviolate transition between the two palaces of art. We passed along the gallery in which those precious drawings by eminent hands hang chaste and grey above the swirl and murmur of the yellow Arno, and reached the ducal saloons of the Pitti. Ducal as they are, it must be confessed that they are imperfect as show-rooms, and that with their deep-set windows and their massive mouldings, it is rather a broken light that reaches the pictured walls. But here the masterpieces hang thick, and you seem to see them in a luminous atmosphere of their own. And the great saloons, with their superb dim ceilings, their outer wall in splendid shadow, and the sombre opposite glow of mellow canvas and dusky gilding, make, themselves, almost as fine a picture as the Titians and Raphaels they imperfectly reveal. We lingered briefly before many a Raphael and Titian; but I saw my friend was impatient, and I suffered him at last to lead me directly to the goal of our journey — the most tenderly fair of Raphael's Virgins, the Madonna in the Chair. Of all the fine pictures of the world, it seemed to me this is the one with which criticism has least to do. None betrays less effort, less of the mechanism of effect and of the irrepressible discord between conception and result, which shows dimly in so many consummate works. Graceful, human, near to our sympathies as it is, it has nothing of manner, of method, nothing, almost, of style; it blooms there in rounded softness, as instinct with harmony as if it were an immediate exhalation of genius. The figure melts away the spectator's mind into a sort of passionate tenderness which he knows not whether he has given to heavenly purity or to earthly charm. He is intoxicated with the fragrance of the tenderest blossom of maternity that ever bloomed on earth.

'That's what I call a fine picture,' said my companion, after we had gazed awhile in silence. 'I have a right to say so, for I've copied it so often and so carefully that I could repeat it now with my eyes shut. Other works are of Raphael: this *is* Raphael himself. Others you can praise, you can qualify, you can measure, explain, account for: this you can only love and admire. I don't know in what seeming he walked among men, while this divine mood was upon him; but after it, surely, he could do nothing but die; this world had nothing more to teach him. Think of it awhile, my friend, and you'll admit that I'm not raving. Think of his seeing that spotless image, not for a moment, for a day, in a happy dream, as a restless fever-fit, not as a poet in a five minutes' frenzy, time to snatch his phrase and scribble his immortal stanza, but for days together, while the slow labour of the brush went on, while the foul vapours of life interposed, and the fancy ached with tension, fixed, radiant, distinct, as we see it now! What a master, certainly! But ah, what a seer!'

'Don't you imagine,' I answered, 'that he had a model, and that some pretty young woman—'

'As pretty a young woman as you please! It doesn't diminish the miracle! He took his hint, of course, and the young woman, possibly, sat smiling before his canvas. But, meanwhile, the painter's idea had taken wings. No lovely human outline could charm it to vulgar fact. He saw the fair form made perfect; he rose to the vision without tremor, without effort of wing; he communed with it face to face, and resolved into finer and love-lier truth the purity which completes it as the perfume completes the rose. That's what they call idealism; the word's vastly abused, but the thing is good. It's my own creed, at any rate. Lovely Madonna, model at once and muse, I call you to witness that I too am an idealist!'

'An idealist, then,' I said, half jocosely, wishing to provoke him to further utterance, 'is a gentleman who says to Nature in the person of a beautiful girl, "Go to, you're all wrong! Your fine is coarse, your bright is dim, your grace is *gaucherie*. This is the way you should have done it!" Isn't the chance against him?'

He turned upon me almost angrily, but perceiving the genial flavour of my sarcasm, he smiled gravely. 'Look at that picture,' he said, 'and cease your irreverent mockery! Idealism is *that*!

There's no explaining it; one must feel the flame! It says nothing to Nature, or to any beautiful girl, that they'll not both forgive! It says to the fair woman, "Accept me as your artist-friend, lend me your beautiful face, trust me, help me, and your eyes shall be half my masterpiece!" No one so loves and respects the rich realities of nature as the artist whose imagination caresses and flatters them. He knows what a fact may hold (whether Raphael knew, you may judge by his portrait behind us there, of Tommaso Inghirami); but his fancy hovers above it, as Ariel above the sleeping prince. There is only one Raphael, but an artist may still be an artist. As I said last night, the days of illumination are gone; visions are rare; we have to look long to see them. But in meditation we may still woo the ideal; round it, smoothe it, perfect it. The result – the result' (here his voice faltered suddenly, and he fixed his eyes for a moment on the picture; when they met my own again they were full of tears) – 'the result may be less than this; but still it may be good, it may be *great*!' he cried with vehemence. 'It may hang somewhere, in after years, in goodly company, and keep the artist's memory warm. Think of being known to mankind after some such fashion as this! of hanging here through the slow centuries in the gaze of an altered world, living on and on in the cunning of an eye and hand that are part of the dust of ages, a delight and a law to remote generations; making beauty a force and purity an example!'

'Heaven forbid!' I said, smiling, 'that I should take the wind out of your sails; but doesn't it occur to you that beside being strong in his genius, Raphael was happy in a certain good faith of which we have lost the trick? There are people, I know, who deny that his spotless Madonnas are anything more than pretty blondes of that period, enhanced by the Raphaelesque touch, which they declare is a profane touch. Be that as it may, people's religious and aesthetic needs went hand in hand, and there was, as I may say, a demand for the Blessed Virgin, visible and adorable, which must have given firmness to the artist's hand. I'm afraid there is no demand now.'

My companion seemed painfully puzzled; he shivered, as it were, in this chilling blast of scepticism. Then shaking his head with sublime confidence: 'There is always a demand!' he cried; 'that ineffable type is one of the eternal needs of man's heart; but pious souls long for it in silence, almost in shame. Let it appear, and this faith grows brave. How *should* it appear in this corrupt generation? It can't be made to order. It could, indeed, when the order came, trumpet-toned, from the lips of the Church herself, and was addressed to genius panting with inspiration. But it can spring now only from the soil of passionate labour and culture. Do you really fancy that while, from time to time, a man of complete artistic vision is born into the world, that image can perish? The man who paints it has painted everything. The subject admits of every perfection – form, colour, expression, composition. It can be as simple as you please, and yet as rich, as broad and pure, and yet as full of delicate detail. Think of the chance for flesh in the little naked, nestling child, irradiating divinity; of the chance for drapery in the chaste and ample garment of the mother! Think of the great story you compress into that simple theme! Think, above all, of the mother's face and its ineffable suggestiveness, of the mingled burden of joy and trouble, the tenderness turned to worship, and the worship turned to far-seeing pity! Then look at it all in perfect line and lovely colour, breathing truth and beauty and mastery!'

'*Anch'io son pittore!*' I cried. 'Unless I'm mistaken, you've a masterpiece on the stocks. If you put all that in, you'll do more than Raphael himself did. Let me know when your picture is finished, and wherever in the wide world I may be, I'll post back to Florence and make my bow to – the *Madonna of the future*!'

He blushed vividly and gave a heavy sigh, half of protest, half of resignation. 'I don't often mention my picture, in so many words. I detest this modern custom of premature publicity. A great work needs silence, privacy, mystery even. And then, do you know, people are so cruel, so frivolous, so unable to imagine a man's wishing to paint a Madonna at this time of day, that I've been laughed at – laughed at, sir!' And his blush deepened to crimson. 'I don't know what has prompted me to be so frank and trustful with you. You look as if you wouldn't laugh at me. My dear young man –' and he laid his hand on my arm – 'I'm worthy of respect. Whatever my talents may be, I'm honest. There's nothing grotesque in a pure ambition, or in a life devoted to it!'

There was something so sternly sincere in his look and tone, that further questions seemed impertinent. I had repeated opportunity to ask them, however; for after this we spent much time together. Daily, for a fortnight, we met by appointment, to see the sights. He knew the city so well, he had strolled and lounged so often through its streets and churches and galleries, he was so deeply versed in its greater and lesser memories, so imbued with the local genius, that he was an altogether ideal *valet de place*, and I was glad enough to leave my Murray at home, and gather facts and opinions alike from his gossiping commentary. He talked of Florence like a lover, and admitted that it was a very old affair; he had lost his heart to her at first sight. 'It's the fashion to talk of all cities as feminine,' he said, 'but, as a rule, it's a monstrous mistake. Is Florence of the same sex as New York, as Chicago? She's the sole true woman of them all; one feels towards her as a lad in his teens feels to some beautiful older woman with a "history". It's a sort of aspiring gallantry she creates.' This disinterested passion seemed to stand my friend in stead of the common social ties; he led a lonely life, apparently, and cared for nothing but his work. I was duly flattered by his having taken my frivolous self into his favour, and by his generous sacrifice of precious hours, as they must have been, to my society. We spent many of these hours among those early paintings in which Florence is so rich, returning ever and anon with restless sympathies to wonder whether these tender blossoms of art had not a vital fragrance and savour more precious than the full-fruited knowledge of the later works. We lingered often in the sepulchral chapel of San Lorenzo, and watched Michael Angelo's dim-visaged warrior sitting there like some awful Genius of Doubt and brooding behind his eternal mask upon the mysteries of life. We stood more than once in the little convent chambers where Fra Angelico wrought as if an angel indeed had held his hand, and gathered that sense of scattered dews and early bird-notes which makes an hour among his relics seem like a morning stroll in some monkish garden. We did all this and much more – wandered into dark chapels, damp courts, and dusty palace-rooms, in quest of lingering hints of fresco and lurking treasures of carving.

I was more and more impressed with my companion's prodigious singleness of purpose. Everything was a pretext for some wildly idealistic rhapsody or reverie. Nothing could be seen or said that did not end sooner or later in a glowing discourse on the true, the beautiful, and the good. If my friend was not a genius, he was certainly a monomaniac; and I found as great a fascination in watching the odd lights and shades of his character as if he had been a creature from another planet. He seemed, indeed, to know very little of this one, and lived and moved altogether in his own little province of art. A creature more unsullied by the world it is impossible to conceive, and I often thought it a flaw in his artistic character that he hadn't a harmless vice or two. It amused me vastly at times to think that he was of our shrewd Yankee race; but, after all, there could be no better token of his American origin than this high aesthetic fever. The very heat of his devotion was a sign of conversion; those born to European opportunity manage better to reconcile enthusiasm with comfort. He had, moreover, all our native mistrust for intellectual discretion and our native relish for sonorous superlatives. As a critic he was vastly more generous than just, and his mildest terms of approbation were 'stupendous', 'transcendent', and 'incomparable'. The small change of admiration seemed to him no coin for a gentleman to handle; and yet, frank as he was intellectually, he was, personally, altogether a mystery. His professions, somehow, were all half-professions, and his allusions to his work and circumstances left something dimly ambiguous in the background. He was modest and proud, and never spoke of his domestic matters. He was evidently poor; yet he must have had some slender independence, since he could afford to make so merry over the fact that his culture of ideal beauty had never brought him a penny. His poverty, I supposed, was his motive for neither inviting me to his lodging nor mentioning its whereabouts. We met either in some public place or at my hotel, where I entertained him as freely as I might without appearing to be prompted by charity. He seemed always hungry, which was his nearest approach to a 'redeeming vice'. I made a point of asking no impertinent questions, but, each time we met, I ventured to make some respectful allusion to the *magnum opus*, to inquire, as it were, as to its health and progress. 'We're getting on, with the Lord's help,' he would say with a grave smile. 'We're doing well. You see I have the grand advantage that I lose no time. These hours I spend with you are pure profit. They're *suggestive*! Just as the truly religious soul is always at worship, the genuine artist is always in labour. He takes his property wherever he finds it, and learns some precious secret from every object that stands up in the light. If you but knew the rapture of observation! I gather with every glance some hint for light, for colour or relief! When I get home, I pour out my treasures into the lap of my Madonna. O, I'm not idle! *Nulla dies sine linea*.'

I was introduced in Florence to an American lady whose drawing-room had long formed an attractive place of reunion for the foreign residents. She lived on a fourth floor, and she was not rich; but she offered her visitors very good tea, little cakes at option, and conversation not quite to match. Her conversation had mainly an aesthetic flavour, for Mrs Coventry was famously 'artistic'. Her apartment was a sort of Pitti Palace *au petit pied*. She possessed 'early masters' by the dozen – a cluster of Peruginos in her dining-room, a Giotto in her boudoir, an Andrea del Sarto over her parlour chimney-piece. Backed by these treasures, and by innumerable bronzes, mosaics, majolica dishes, and little worm-eaten diptychs showing angular saints on gilded panels, our hostess enjoyed the dignity of a sort of high-priestess of the arts. She always wore on her bosom a huge miniature copy of the Madonna della Seggiola. Gaining her ear quietly one evening I asked her whether she knew that remark-able man, Mr Theobald.

'Know him!' she exclaimed; 'know poor Theobald! All Florence knows him, his flame-coloured locks, his black velvet coat, his interminable harangues on the beautiful, and his wondrous Madonna that mortal eye has never seen, and that mortal patience has quite given up expecting.'

'Really,' I cried, 'you don't believe in his Madonna?'

'My dear ingenuous youth,' rejoined my shrewd friend, 'has he made a convert of you? Well, we all believed in him once; he came down upon Florence and took the town by storm. Another Raphael, at the very least, had been born among men, and poor, dear America was to have the credit of him. Hadn't he the very hair of Raphael flowing down on his shoulders? The hair, alas, but not the head! We swallowed him whole, however; we hung upon his lips and proclaimed his genius on the house-tops. The women were all dying to sit to him for their portraits and be made immortal, like Leonardo's Joconde. We decided that his manner was a good deal like Leonardo's – mysterious and inscrutable and fascinating. Mysterious it certainly was; mystery was the beginning and the end of it. The months passed by, and the miracle hung fire; our master never produced his master-piece. He passed hours in the galleries and churches, posturing, musing, and gazing; he talked more than ever about the beauti-ful, but he never put brush to canvas. We had all subscribed, as it were, to the great performance; but as it never came off, people began to ask for their money again. I was one of the last of the faithful; I carried devotion so far as to sit to him for my head. If you could have seen the horrible creature he made of me, you would admit that even a woman with no more vanity than will tie her bonnet straight must have cooled off then. The man didn't know the very alphabet of drawing! His strong point, he intimated, was his sentiment; but is it a consolation, when one has been painted a fright, to know it has been done with peculiar gusto? One by one, I confess, we fell away from the faith, and Mr Theobald didn't lift his little finger to preserve us. At the first hint that we were tired of waiting and that we should like the show to begin, he was off in a huff. "Great work requires time, contemplation, privacy, mystery! O ye of little faith!" We answered that we didn't insist on a great work; that the five-act tragedy might come at his convenience; that we merely asked for something to keep us from yawning, some inexpensive little *lever de rideau*. Hereupon the poor man took his stand as a genius misconceived and persecuted, an *âme méconnue*, and washed his hands of us from that hour! No, I believe he does me the honour to consider me the head and front of the conspiracy formed to nip his glory in the bud – a bud that has taken twenty years to blossom. Ask him if he knows me, and he'd tell you I'm a horribly ugly old woman who has vowed his destruction because he wouldn't paint her portrait as a pendant to Titian's Flora. I fancy that since then he has had none but chance followers, innocent strangers like yourself, who have taken him at his word. The mountain's still in labour; I've not heard that the mouse has been born. I pass him once in a while in the galleries, and he fixes his great dark eyes on me with a sublimity of indifference, as if I were a bad copy of a Sassoferrato! It is a long time ago now that I heard that he was making studies for a Madonna who was to be a *résumé* of all the other Madonnas of the Italian school – like that antique Venus who borrowed a nose from one great image and an ankle from another. It's certainly a masterly idea. The parts may be fine, but when I think of my unhappy portrait I tremble for the whole. He has communicated this striking idea under the pledge of solemn secrecy to fifty chosen spirits, to everyone he has ever been able to buttonhole for five minutes. I suppose he wants to get an order for it, and he's not to blame; for Heaven knows how he lives. I see by your blush,' my hostess frankly continued, 'that you have been honoured with his confidence. You needn't be ashamed, my dear young man; a man of your age is none the worse for a certain generous credulity. Only allow me to give you a word of advice: keep your credulity out of your pockets! Don't pay for the picture till it's delivered. You've not been treated to a peep at it, I imagine. No more have your fifty predecessors in the faith. There are people who doubt whether there is any picture to be seen. I fancy, myself, that if one were to get into his studio, one would find something very like the picture in that tale of Balzac's – a mere mass of incoherent scratches and daubs, a jumble of dead paint!'

I listened to this pungent recital in silent wonder. It had a painfully plausible sound, and was not inconsistent with certain shy suspicions of my own. My hostess was a clever woman, and presumably a generous one. I determined to let my judgement wait upon events. Possibly she was right; but if she was wrong, she was cruelly wrong! Her version of my friend's eccentricities made me impatient to see him again and examine him in the light of public opinion. On our next meeting, I immediately asked him if he knew Mrs Coventry. He laid his hand on my arm and gave me a sad smile. 'Has she taxed *your* gallantry at last?'

he asked. 'She's a foolish woman. She's frivolous and heartless, and she pretends to be serious and kind. She prattles about Giotto's second manner and Vittoria Colonna's liaison with "Michael" – one would think that Michael lived across the way and was expected in to take a hand at whist – but she knows as little about art, and about the conditions of production, as I know about Buddhism. She profanes sacred words,' he added more vehemently, after a pause. 'She cares for you only as some-one to hand teacups in that horrible mendacious little parlour of hers, with its trumpery Peruginos! If you can't dash off a new picture every three days, and let her hand it round among her guests, she tells them in plain English you're an impostor!'

This attempt of mine to test Mrs Coventry's accuracy was made in the course of a late afternoon walk to the quiet old church of San Miniato, on one of the hill-tops which directly overlook the city, from whose gate you are guided to it by a stony and cypress-bordered walk, which seems a most fitting avenue to a shrine. No spot is more propitious to lingering repose than the broad terrace in front of the church, where, lounging against the parapet, you may glance in slow alterna-tion from the black and yellow marbles of the church *façade*, seamed and cracked with time and wind-sown with a tender flora of its own, down to the full domes and slender towers of Florence and over to the blue sweep of the wide-mouthed cup of mountains into whose hollow the little treasure-city has been dropped. I had proposed, as a diversion from the painful mem-ories evoked by Mrs Coventry's name, that Theobald should go with me the next evening to the opera, where some rarely played work was to be given. He declined, as I had half expected, for I had observed that he regularly kept his evenings in reserve, and never alluded to his manner of passing them. 'You have reminded me before,' I said, smiling, 'of that charming speech of the Florentine painter in Alfred de Musset's *Lorenzaccio*: "I do no harm to anyone. I pass my days in my studio. On Sunday, I go to the Annunziata or to Santa Maria; the monks think I have a voice; they dress me in a white gown and a red cap, and I take a share in the choruses, sometimes I do a little solo: these are the only times I go into public. In the evening, I visit my sweetheart; when the night is fine, we pass it on her balcony." I don't know whether you have a sweetheart, or whether she has a balcony. But if you're so happy, it's certainly better than trying to find a charm in a third-rate *prima donna*.'

He made no immediate response, but at last he turned to me solemnly. 'Can you look upon a beautiful woman with reverent eyes?'

'Really,' I said, 'I don't pretend to be sheepish, but I should be sorry to think I was impudent.' And I asked him what in the world he meant. When at last I had assured him that I could undertake to temper admiration with respect, he informed me, with an air of religious mystery, that it was in his power to introduce me to the most beautiful woman in Italy. 'A beauty with a soul!'

'Upon my word,' I cried, 'you're extremely fortunate. I shall rejoice to witness the conjunction.'

'This woman's beauty,' he answered, 'is a lesson, a morality, a poem! It's my daily study.'

Of course, after this, I lost no time in reminding him of what, before we parted, had taken the shape of a promise. 'I feel somehow,' he had said, 'as if it were a sort of violation of that privacy in which I have always contemplated her beauty. This is friendship, my friend. No hint of her existence has ever fallen from my lips. But with too great a familiarity we are apt to lose a sense of the real value of things, and you perhaps will throw some new light upon it and offer a fresher interpretation.' We went accordingly by appointment to a certain ancient house in the heart of Florence – the precinct of the Mercato Vecchio – and climbed a dark, steep staircase to the very summit of the edifice. Theobald's beauty seemed as jealously exalted above the line of common vision as the Belle aux Cheveux d'Or in her tower-top. He passed without knocking into the dark vestibule of a small apartment, and, flinging open an inner door, ushered me into a small saloon. The room seemed mean and sombre, though I caught a glimpse of white curtains swaying gently at an open window. At a table, near a lamp, sat a woman dressed in black, working at a piece of embroidery. As Theobald entered, she looked up calmly, with a smile; but seeing me, she made a movement of surprise, and rose with a kind of stately grace. Theobald stepped forward, took her hand and kissed it, with an indescribable air of immemorial usage. As he bent his head, she looked at me askance, and I thought she blushed.

'Behold the Serafina!' said Theobald, frankly, waving me forward. 'This is a friend, and a lover of the arts,' he added, introducing me. I received a smile, a courtesy, and a request to be seated.

The most beautiful woman in Italy was a person of a generous Italian type and of a great simplicity of demeanour. Seated again at her lamp, with her embroidery, she seemed to have nothing whatever to say. Theobald, bending towards her in a sort of Platonic ecstasy, asked her a dozen paternally tender questions as to her health, her state of mind, her occupations, and the progress of her embroidery, which he examined minutely and summoned me to admire. It was some portion of an ecclesiastical vestment – yellow satin wrought with an elaborate design of silver and gold. She made answer in a full, rich voice, but with a brevity which I hesitated whether to attribute to native reserve or to the profane constraint of my presence. She had been that morning to confession; she had also been to market, and had bought a chicken for dinner. She felt very happy; she had nothing to complain of, except that the people for whom she was making her vestment, and who furnished her materials, should be willing to put such rotten silver thread into the garment, as one might say, of the Lord. From time to time, as she took her slow stitches, she raised her eyes and covered me with a glance which seemed at first to denote a placid curiosity, but in which, as I saw it repeated, I thought I perceived the dim glimmer of an attempt to establish an understanding with me at the expense of our companion. Meanwhile, as mindful as possible of Theobald's injunction of reverence, I considered the lady's personal claims to the fine compliment he had paid her.

That she was indeed a beautiful woman I perceived, after recovering from the surprise of finding her without the freshness of youth. Her beauty was of a sort which, in losing youth, loses little of its essential charm, expressed for the most part as it was in form and structure, and, as Theobald would have said, in 'composition'. She was broad and ample, low-browed and large-eyed, dark and pale. Her thick brown hair hung low beside her cheek and ear, and seemed to drape her head with a covering as chaste and formal as the veil of a nun. The poise and carriage of her head was admirably free and noble, and the more effective that their freedom was at moments discreetly corrected by a little sanctimonious droop, which harmonized admirably with the level gaze of her dark and quiet eye. A strong, serene physical nature and the placid temper which comes of no nerves and no troubles seemed this lady's comfortable portion. She was dressed in plain dull black, save for a sort of dark blue kerchief which was folded across her bosom and exposed a glimpse of her massive throat. Over this kerchief was suspended a little silver cross. I admired her greatly, and yet with a large reserve. A certain mild intellectual apathy belonged properly to her type of beauty, and had always seemed to round and enrich it; but this *bourgeoise* Egeria, if I viewed her right, betrayed a rather vulgar stagnation of mind. There might have been once a dim, spiritual light in her face; but it had long since begun to wane. And furthermore, in plain prose, she was growing stout. My disappointment amounted very nearly to complete disenchantment when Theobald, as if to facilitate my covert inspection, declaring that the lamp was very dim and that she would ruin her eyes without more light, rose and fetched a couple of candles from the mantelpiece, which he placed lighted on the table. In this brighter illumination I perceived that our hostess was decidedly an elderly woman. She was neither haggard nor worn nor grey; she was simply coarse. The 'soul' which Theobald had promised seemed scarcely worth making such a point of; it was no deeper mystery than a sort of matronly mildness of lip and brow. I would have been ready even to declare that that sanctified bend of the head was nothing more than the trick of a person constantly working at embroidery. It occurred to me even that it was a trick of a less innocent sort; for, in spite of the mellow quietude of her wits, this stately needlewoman dropped a hint that she took the situation rather less *au sérieux* than her friend. When he rose to light the candles, she looked across at me with a quick, intelligent smile and tapped her forehead with her forefinger; then, as from a sudden feeling of compassionate loyalty to poor Theobald, I preserved a blank face, she gave a little shrug and resumed her work.

What was the relation of this singular couple? Was he the most ardent of friends or the most reverent of lovers? Did she regard him as an eccentric youth whose benevolent admiration of her beauty she was not ill-pleased to humour at this small cost of having him climb into her little parlour and gossip of summer nights? With her decent and sombre dress, her simple gravity, and that fine piece of priestly needle-work, she looked like some pious lay-member of a sisterhood, living by special permission outside her convent walls. Or was she maintained here aloft by her friend in comfortable leisure, so that he might have before him the perfect, eternal type, uncorrupted and untarnished by the struggle for existence? Her shapely hands, I observed, were very fair and white; they lacked the traces of what is called 'honest toil'.

'And the pictures, how do they come on?' she asked of Theobald, after a long pause.

'Finely, finely! I have here a friend whose sympathy and encouragement give me new faith and ardour.'

Our hostess turned to me, gazed at me a moment rather inscrutably, and then tapping her forehead with the gesture she had used a minute before, 'He has a magnificent genius!' she said, with perfect gravity.

'I'm inclined to think so,' I answered, with a smile.

'Eh, why do you smile?' she cried. 'If you doubt it, you must see the *bambino*!' And she took the lamp and conducted me to the other side of the room, where on the wall, in a plain black frame, hung a large drawing in red chalk. Beneath it was festooned a little bowl for holy-water. The drawing represented a very young child, entirely naked, half nestling back against his mother's gown, but with his two little arms outstretched, as if in the act of benediction. It was executed with singular freedom and power, and yet seemed vivid with the sacred bloom of infancy. A sort of dimpled elegance and grace, mingled with its boldness, recalled the touch of Correggio. 'That's what he can do!' said my hostess. 'It's the blessed little boy whom I lost. It's his very image, and the Signor Teobaldo gave it me as a gift. He has given me many things beside!'

I looked at the picture for some time and admired it vastly. Turning back to Theobald, I assured him that if it were hung among the drawings in the Uffizi and labelled with a glorious name, it would hold its own. My praise seemed to give him extreme pleasure; he pressed my hands, and his eyes filled with tears. It moved him apparently with the desire to expatiate on the history of the drawing, for he rose and made his *adieux* to our companion, kissing her hand with the same mild ardour as before. It occurred to me that the offer of a similar piece of gallantry on my own part might help me to know what manner of woman she was. When she perceived my intention, she withdrew her hand, dropped her eyes solemnly, and made me a severe courtesy. Theobald took my arm and led me rapidly into the street.

'And what do you think of the divine Serafina?' he cried with fervour.

'It's certainly good solid beauty!' I answered.

He eyed me an instant askance, and then seemed hurried along by the current of remembrance. 'You should have seen the mother and the child together, seen them as I first saw them – the mother with her head draped in a shawl, a divine trouble in her face, and the *bambino* pressed to her bosom. You would have said, I think, that Raphael had found his match in common chance. I was coming in, one summer night, from a long walk in the country, when I met this apparition at the city gate. The woman held out her hand. I hardly knew whether to say, "What do you want?" or to fall down and worship. She asked for a little money. I saw that she was beautiful and pale. She might have stepped out of the stable of Bethlehem! I gave her money and helped her on her way into the town. I had guessed her story. She, too, was a maiden mother, and she had been turned out into the world in her shame. I felt in all my pulses that here was my subject marvellously realized. I felt like one of the old convent artists who had had a vision. I rescued the poor creatures, cherished them, watched them as I would have done some precious work of art, some lovely fragment of fresco discovered in a mouldering cloister. In a month – as if to deepen and consecrate the pathos of it all – the poor little child died. When she felt that he was going, she held him up to me for ten minutes, and I made that sketch. You saw a feverish haste in it, I suppose; I wanted to spare the poor little mortal the pain of his position. After that, I doubly valued the mother. She is the simplest, sweetest, most natural creature that ever bloomed in this brave old land of Italy. She lives in the memory of her child, in her gratitude for the scanty kindness I have been able to show her, and in her simple religion! She's not even conscious of her beauty; my admiration has never made her vain. Heaven knows I've made no secret of it. You must have observed the singular transparency of her expression, the lovely modesty of her glance. And was there ever such a truly virginal brow, such a natural classic elegance in the wave of the hair and the arch of the forehead? I've studied her; I may say I know her. I've absorbed her little by little; my mind is stamped and imbued, and I have determined now to clinch the impression; I shall at last invite her to sit for me!'

'"At last – at last"?' I repeated, in much amazement. 'Do you mean that she has never done so yet?'

'I've not really had – a – a sitting,' said Theobald, speaking very slowly. 'I've taken notes, you know; I've got my grand fundamental impression. That's the great thing! But I've not actually had her as a model, posed and draped and lighted, before my easel.'

What had become for the moment of my perception and my tact I am at a loss to say; in their absence, I was unable to repress headlong exclamation. I was destined to regret it. We had stopped at a turning, beneath a lamp. 'My poor friend,' I exclaimed, laying my hand on his shoulder, 'you've *dawdled*! She's an old, old woman – for a Madonna!'

It was as if I had brutally struck him; I shall never forget the long, slow, almost ghastly look of pain with which he answered me. 'Dawdled – old, old!' he stammered. 'Are you joking?'

'Why, my dear fellow, I suppose you don't take the woman for twenty?'

He drew a long breath and leaned against a house, looking at me with questioning, protesting, reproachful eyes. At last, starting forward, and grasping my arm: 'Answer me solemnly: does she seem to you truly old? Is she wrinkled, is she faded, am I blind?'

Then at last I understood the immensity of his illusion; how, one by one, the noiseless years had ebbed away, and left him brooding in charmed inaction, forever preparing for a work forever deferred. It seemed to me almost a kindness now to tell him the plain truth. 'I should be sorry to say you're blind,' I answered, 'but I think you're deceived. You've lost time in effortless contemplation. Your friend was once young and fresh and virginal; but, I protest, that was some years ago. Still, she has *de beaux restes*? By all means make her sit for you!' I broke down; his face was too horribly reproachful.

He took off his hat and stood passing his handkerchief mechanically over his forehead. '*De beaux restes*? I thank you for sparing me the plain English. I must make up my Madonna out of *de beaux restes*! What a masterpiece she'll be! Old – old! Old – old!' he murmured.

'Never mind her age,' I cried, revolted at what I had done, 'never mind my impression of her! You have your memory, your notes, your genius. Finish your picture in a month. I proclaim it beforehand a masterpiece, and I hereby offer you for it any sum you may choose to ask.'

He stared, but he seemed scarcely to understand me. 'Old – old!' he kept stupidly repeating. 'If she is old, what am I? If her beauty has faded, where – where is my strength? Has life been a dream? Have I worshipped too long – have I loved too well?' The charm, in truth, was broken. That the chord of illusion should have snapped at my light, accidental touch showed how it had been weakened by excessive tension. The poor fellow's sense of wasted time, of vanished opportunity, seemed to roll in upon his soul in waves of darkness. He suddenly dropped his head and burst into tears.

I led him homeward with all possible tenderness, but I attempted neither to check his grief, to restore his equanimity, nor to unsay the hard truth. When we reached my hotel I tried to induce him to come in. 'We'll drink a glass of wine,' I said, smiling, 'to the completion of the Madonna.'

With a violent effort he held up his head, mused for a moment with a formidably sombre frown, and then giving me his hand, 'I'll finish it,' he cried, 'in a month! No, in a fortnight! After all, I have it *here*!' And he tapped his forehead. 'Of course she's old! She can afford to have it said of her – a woman who has made twenty years pass like a twelvemonth! Old – old! Why, sir, she shall be eternal!'

I wished to see him safely to his own door, but he waved me back and walked away with an air of resolution, whistling and swinging his cane. I waited a moment, and then followed him at a distance, and saw him proceed to cross the Santa Trinità Bridge. When he reached the middle, he suddenly paused, as if his strength had deserted him, and leaned upon the parapet gazing over into the river. I was careful to keep him in sight; I confess that I passed ten very nervous minutes. He recovered himself at last, and went his way, slowly and with hanging head.

That I should have really startled poor Theobald into a bolder use of his long-garnered stores of knowledge and taste, into the vulgar effort and hazard of production, seemed at first reason enough for his continued silence, and absence; but as day followed day without his either calling or sending me a line, and without my meeting him in his customary haunts, in the galleries, in the chapel at San Lorenzo, or strolling between the Arno-side and the great hedge-screen of verdure which, along the drive of the Cascine, throws the fair occupants of barouche and phaeton into such becoming relief – as for more than a week I got neither tidings nor sight of him, I began to fear that I had fatally offended him, and that, instead of giving wholesome impetus to his talent, I had brutally paralysed it. I had a wretched suspicion that I had made him ill. My stay at Florence was drawing to a close, and it was important that, before resuming my journey, I should assure myself of the truth. Theobald, to the last, had kept his lodging a mystery, and I was altogether at a loss where to look for him. The simplest course was to make inquiry of the beauty of the Mercato Vecchio, and I confess that unsatisfied curiosity as to the lady herself counselled it as well. Perhaps I had done her injustice, and she was as immortally fresh and fair as he conceived her. I was, at any rate, anxious to behold once more the ripe enchantress who had made twenty years pass as a twelvemonth. I repaired accordingly, one morning, to her abode, climbed the interminable staircase, and reached her door. It stood ajar, and as I hesitated whether to enter, a little serving-maid came clattering out with an empty kettle, as if she had just performed some savoury errand. The inner door, too, was open; so I crossed the little vestibule and entered the room in which I had formerly been received. It had not its evening aspect. The table, or one end of it, was spread for a late breakfast, and before it sat a gentleman – an individual, at least, of the male sex – dealing justice upon a beefsteak and onions, and a bottle of wine. At his elbow, in friendly proximity, was placed the lady of the house. Her attitude, as I entered, was not that of an enchantress. With one hand she held in her lap a plate of smoking maccaroni; with the other she had lifted high in air one of the pendulous filaments of this succulent compound, and was in the act of slipping it gently down her throat. On the uncovered end of the table, facing her companion, were ranged half a dozen small statuettes, of some snuff-coloured substance resembling terra-cotta. He, brandishing his knife with ardour, was apparently descanting on their merits.

Evidently I darkened the door. My hostess dropped her maccaroni – into her mouth, and rose hastily with a harsh exclamation and a flushed face. I immediately perceived that the Signora Serafina's secret was even better worth knowing than I had supposed, and that the way to learn it was to take it for granted. I summoned my best Italian, I smiled and bowed and apologized for my intrusion; and in a moment, whether or no I had dispelled the lady's irritation, I had, at least, stimulated her prudence. I was welcome, she said; I must take a seat. This was another friend of hers – also an artist, she declared with a smile which was almost amiable. Her companion wiped his moustache and bowed with great civility. I saw at a glance that he was equal to the situation. He was presumably the author of the statuettes on the table, and he knew a money-spending *forestiere* when he saw one. He was a small, wiry man, with a clever, impudent, tossed-up nose, a sharp little black eye, and waxed ends to his moustache. On the side of his head he wore jauntily a little crimson velvet smoking-cap, and I observed that his feet were encased in brilliant slippers. On Serafina's remarking with dignity that I was the friend of Mr Theobald, he broke out into that fantastic French of which Italians are so insistently lavish, and declared with fervour that Mr Theobald was a magnificent genius.

'I'm sure I don't know,' I answered with a shrug. 'If you're in a position to affirm it, you have the advantage of me. I've seen nothing from his hand but the *bambino* yonder, which certainly is fine.'

He declared that the *bambino* was a masterpiece, a pure Correggio. It was only a pity, he added, with a knowing laugh, that the sketch had not been made on some good bit of honey-combed old panel. The stately Serafina hereupon protested that Mr Theobald was the soul of honour, and that he would never lend himself to a deceit. 'I'm not a judge of genius,' she said, 'and I know nothing of pictures. I'm but a poor simple widow; but I know that the Signor Teobaldo has the heart of an angel and the virtue of a saint. He's my benefactor,' she added sententiously. The after-glow of the somewhat sinister flush with which she had greeted me still lingered in her cheek, and perhaps did not favour her beauty; I could not but fancy it a wise custom of Theobald's to visit her only by candlelight. She was coarse, and her poor adorer was a poet.

'I have the greatest esteem for him,' I said; 'it is for this reason that I have been uneasy at not seeing him for ten days. Have you seen him? Is he perhaps ill?'

'Ill! Heaven forbid!' cried Serafina, with genuine vehemence.

Her companion uttered a rapid expletive, and reproached her with not having been to see him. She hesitated a moment; then she simpered the least bit and bridled. 'He comes to see me — without reproach! But it would not be the same for me to go to him, though, indeed, you may almost call him a man of holy life.'

'He has the greatest admiration for you,' I said. 'He would have been honoured by your visit.'

She looked at me a moment sharply. 'More admiration than you. Admit that!' Of course I protested with all the eloquence at my command, and my mysterious hostess then confessed that she had taken no fancy to me on my former visit, and that, Theobald not having returned, she believed I had poisoned his mind against her. 'It would be no kindness to the poor gentleman, I can tell you that,' she said. 'He has come to see me every evening for years. It's a long friendship! No one knows him as well as I.'

'I don't pretend to know him, or to understand him,' I said. 'He's a mystery! Nevertheless, he seems to me a little—' And I touched my forehead and waved my hand in the air.

Serafina glanced at her companion a moment, as if for inspiration. He contented himself with shrugging his shoulders, as he filled his glass again. The *padrona* hereupon gave me a more softly insinuating smile than would have seemed likely to bloom on so candid a brow. 'It's for that that I love him!' she said. 'The world has so little kindness for such persons. It laughs at them, and despises them, and cheats them. He is too good for this wicked life! It's his fancy that he finds a little Paradise up here in my poor apartment. If he thinks so, how can I help it? He has a strange belief – really, I ought to be ashamed to tell you – that I resemble the Blessed Virgin: Heaven forgive me! I let him think what he pleases, so long as it makes him happy. He was very kind to me once, and I am not one that forgets a favour. So I receive him every evening civilly, and ask after his health, and let him look at me on this side and that! For that matter, I may say it without vanity, I was worth looking at once! And he's not always amusing, poor man! He sits sometimes for an hour without speaking a word, or else he talks away, without stopping, on art and nature, and beauty and duty, and fifty fine things that are all so much Latin to me. I beg you to understand that he has never said a word to me that I mightn't decently listen to. He may be a little cracked, but he's one of the saints.'

'Eh!' cried the man, 'the saints were all a little cracked!'

Serafina, I fancied, left part of her story untold; but she told enough of it to make poor Theobald's own statement seem intensely pathetic in its exalted simplicity. 'It's a strange fortune, certainly,' she went on, 'to have such a friend as this dear man – a friend who's less than a lover and more than a friend.' I glanced at her companion, who preserved an impenetrable smile, twisted the end of his moustache, and disposed of a copious mouthful. Was *he* less than a lover? 'But what will you have?' Serafina pursued. 'In this hard world one mustn't ask too many questions; one must take what comes and keep what one gets. I've kept my good friend for twenty years, and I do hope that, at this time of day, signore, you've not come to turn him against me!'

I assured her that I had no such design, and that I should vastly regret disturbing Mr Theobald's habits or convictions. On the contrary, I was alarmed about him, and I should immediately go in search of him. She gave me his address and a florid account of her sufferings at his non-appearance. She had not been to him, for various reasons; chiefly because she was afraid of displeasing him, as he had always made such a mystery of his home. 'You might have sent this gentleman!' I ventured to suggest.

'Ah,' cried the gentleman, 'he admires the Signora Serafina, but he wouldn't admire me.' And then, confidentially, with his finger on his nose, 'He's a purist!'

I was about to withdraw, on the promise that I would inform the Signora Serafina of my friend's condition, when her companion, who had risen from table and girded his loins apparently for the onset, grasped me gently by the arm, and led me before the row of statuettes. 'I perceive by your conversation, signore, that you are a patron of the arts. Allow me to request your honourable attention for these modest products of my own ingenuity. They are brand-new, fresh from my atelier, and have never been exhibited in public. I have brought them here to receive the verdict of this dear lady, who is a good critic, for all she may pretend to the contrary. I am the inventor of this peculiar style of statuette – of subject, manner, material, everything. Touch them, I pray you; handle them; you needn't fear. Delicate as they look, it is impossible they should break! My various creations have met with great success. They are especially admired by Americans. I have sent them all over Europe – to London, Paris, Vienna! You may have observed some little specimens in Paris, on the Boulevard, in a shop of which they constitute the speciality. There is always a crowd about the window. They form a very pleasing ornament for the mantel-shelf of a gay young bachelor, for the boudoir of a pretty woman. You couldn't make a prettier present to a person with whom you wished to exchange a harmless joke. It is not classic art, signore, of course; but, between ourselves, isn't classic art sometimes rather a bore? Caricature, burlesque, *la charge*, as the French say, has hitherto been confined to paper, to the pen and pencil. Now, it has been my inspiration to introduce it into statuary. For this purpose I have invented a peculiar plastic compound which you will permit me not to divulge. That's my secret, signore! It's as light, you perceive, as cork, and yet as firm as alabaster! I frankly confess that I really pride myself as much on this little stroke of chemical ingenuity as upon the other element of novelty in my creations – my types. What do you say to my types, signore? The idea is bold; does it strike you as happy? Cats and monkeys – monkeys and cats – all human life is there! Human life, of course, I mean, viewed with the eye of the satirist! To combine sculpture and satire, signore, has been my unprecedented ambition. I flatter myself that I have not egregiously failed.'

As this jaunty Juvenal of the chimney-piece delivered himself of his persuasive allocution, he took up his little groups successively from the table, held them aloft, turned them about, rapped them with his knuckles, and gazed at them lovingly with his head on one side. They consisted each of a cat and a monkey, fantastically draped, in some preposterously sentimental conjunction. They exhibited a certain sameness of motive, and illustrated chiefly the different phases of what, in delicate terms, may be called gallantry and coquetry; but they were strikingly clever and expressive, and were at once very perfect cats and monkeys and very natural men and women. I confess, however, that they failed to amuse me. I was doubtless not in a mood to enjoy them, for they seemed to me peculiarly cynical and vulgar. Their imitative felicity was revolting. As I looked askance at the complacent little artist, brandishing them between finger and thumb, and caressing them with an amorous eye, he seemed to me himself little more than an exceptionally intelligent ape. I mustered an admiring grin, however, and he blew another blast. 'My figures are studied from life! I have a little menagerie of monkeys whose frolics I contemplate by the hour. As for the cats, one has only to look out of one's back window! Since I have begun to examine these expressive little brutes, I have made many profound observations. Speaking, signore, to a man of imagination, I may say that my little designs are not without a philosophy of their own. Truly, I don't know whether the cats and monkeys imitate us, or whether it's we who imitate them.' I congratulated him on his philosophy, and he resumed: 'You will do me the honour to admit that I have handled my subjects with delicacy. Eh, it was needed, signore! I have been free, but not too free – eh? Just a hint, you know! You may see as much or as little as you please. These little groups, however, are no measure of my invention. If you will favour me with a call at my studio, I think that you will admit that my combinations are really infinite. I likewise execute figures to command. You have perhaps some little motive – the fruit of your philosophy of life, signore – which you would like to have interpreted. I can promise to work it up to your satisfaction; it shall be as malicious as you please! Allow me to present you with my card, and to remind you that my prices are moderate. Only sixty francs for a little group like that. My statuettes are as durable as bronze – *aere perennius*, signore – and, between ourselves, I think they are more amusing!'

As I pocketed his card, I glanced at Madonna Serafina, wondering whether she had an eye for contrasts. She had picked up one of the little couples and was tenderly dusting it with a feather broom.

What I had just seen and heard had so deepened my compassionate interest in my deluded friend, that I took a summary leave, and made my way directly to the house designated by this remarkable woman. It was in an obscure corner of the opposite side of the town, and presented a sombre and squalid appearance. An old woman in the doorway, on my inquiring for

Theobald, ushered me in with a mumbled blessing and an expression of relief at the poor gentleman having a friend. His lodging seemed to consist of a single room at the top of the house. On getting no answer to my knock, I opened the door, supposing that he was absent; so that it gave me a certain shock to find him sitting there helpless and dumb. He was seated near the single window, facing an easel which supported a large canvas. On my entering, he looked up at me blankly, without changing his position, which was that of absolute lassitude and dejection, his arms loosely folded, his legs stretched before him, his head hanging on his breast. Advancing into the room, I perceived that his face vividly corresponded with his attitude. He was pale, haggard, and unshaven, and his dull and sunken eye gazed at me without a spark of recognition. I had been afraid that he would greet me with fierce reproaches, as the cruelly officious patron who had turned his peace to bitterness, and I was relieved to find that my appearance awakened no visible resentment. 'Don't you know me?' I asked, as I put out my hand. 'Have you already forgotten me?'

He made no response, kept his position stupidly, and left me staring about the room. It spoke most plaintively for itself. Shabby, sordid, naked, it contained, beyond the wretched bed, but the scantiest provision for personal comfort. It was bedroom at once and studio – a grim ghost of a studio. A few dusty casts and prints on the walls, three or four old canvases turned face inward, and a rusty-looking colour-box formed, with the easel at the window, the sum of its appurtenances. The place savoured horribly of poverty. Its only wealth was the picture on the easel, presumably the famous Madonna. Averted as this was from the door, I was unable to see its face; but at last, sickened by the vacant misery of the spot, I passed behind Theobald, eagerly and tenderly. I can hardly say that I was surprised at what I found – a canvas that was a mere dead blank, cracked and discoloured by time. This was his immortal work! Though not surprised, I confess I was powerfully moved, and I think that for five minutes I could not have trusted myself to speak. At last, my silent nearness affected him; he stirred and turned, and then rose and looked at me with a slowly kindling eye. I murmured some kind, ineffective nothings about his being ill and needing advice and care, but he seemed absorbed in the effort to recall distinctly what had last passed between us. 'You were right,' he said with a pitiful smile, 'I'm a dawdler! I'm a failure! I shall do nothing more in this world. You opened my eyes; and, though the truth is bitter, I bear you no grudge. Amen! I've been sitting here for a week, face to face with the truth, with the past, with my weakness and poverty and nullity. I shall never touch a brush! I believe I've neither eaten nor slept. Look at that canvas!' he went on, as I relieved my emotion in the urgent request that he would come home with me and dine. 'That was to have contained my masterpiece! Isn't it a promising foundation? The elements of it are all *here*.' And he tapped his forehead with that mystic confidence which had marked the gesture before. 'If I could only transpose them into some brain that had the hand, the will! Since I've been sitting here taking stock of my intellects, I've come to believe that I have the material for a hundred masterpieces. But my hand is paralysed now, and they'll never be painted. I never began! I waited and waited to be worthier to begin, and wasted my life in preparation. While I fancied my creation was growing, it was dying. I've taken it all too hard! Michael Angelo didn't when he went at the Lorenzo! He did his best at a venture, and his venture is immortal. *That's* mine!' And he pointed with a gesture I shall never forget at the empty canvas. 'I suppose we're a genus by ourselves in the providential scheme – we talents that can't act, that can't do nor dare! We take it out in talk, in plans and promises, in study, in visions! But our visions, let me tell you,' he cried, with a toss of his head, 'have a way of being brilliant, and a man hasn't lived in vain who has seen the things I have! Of course you'll not believe in them when that bit of worm-eaten cloth is all I have to show for them; but to convince you, to enchant and astound the world, I need only the hand of Raphael. I have his brain. A pity, you'll say, I haven't his modesty! Ah, let me babble now; it's all I have left! I'm the half of a genius! Where in the wide world is my other half? Lodged perhaps in the vulgar soul, the cunning, ready fingers of some dull copyist or some trivial artisan who turns out by the dozen his easy prodigies of touch! But it's not for me to sneer at him; he at least does something. He's not a dawdler! Well for me if I had been vulgar and clever and reckless, if I could have shut my eyes and dealt my stroke!'

What to say to the poor fellow, what to do for him, seemed hard to determine; I chiefly felt that I must break the spell of his present inaction, and remove him from the haunted atmosphere of the little room it seemed such cruel irony to call a studio. I cannot say I persuaded him to come out with me; he simply suffered himself to be led, and when we began to walk in the open air I was able to measure his pitifully weakened condition. Nevertheless, he seemed in a certain way to revive, and murmured at last that he would like to go to the Pitti Gallery. I shall never forget our melancholy stroll through those gorgeous halls, every picture on whose walls seemed, even to my own sympathetic vision, to glow with a sort of insolent renewal of strength and lustre. The eyes and lips of the great portraits seemed to smile in ineffable scorn of the dejected pretender who had dreamed of competing with their triumphant authors; the celestial candour, even, of the Madonna in the Chair, as we paused in perfect silence before her, was tinged with the sinister irony of the women of Leonardo. Perfect silence indeed marked our whole progress – the silence of a deep farewell; for I felt in all my pulses, as Theobald, leaning on my arm, dragged one heavy foot after the other, that he was looking his last. When we came out, he was so exhausted that, instead of taking him to my hotel to dine, I called a carriage and drove him straight to his own poor lodging. He had sunk into an extraordinary lethargy; he lay back in the carriage, with his eyes closed, as pale as death, his faint breathing interrupted at intervals by a sudden gasp, like a smothered sob or a vain attempt to speak. With the help of the old woman who had admitted me before, and who emerged from a dark back court, I contrived to lead him up the long steep staircase and lay him on his wretched bed. To her I gave him in charge, while I prepared in all haste to seek a physician. But she followed me out of the room with a pitiful clasping of her hands.

'Poor, dear, blessed gentleman,' she murmured; 'is he dying?'

'Possibly. How long has he been thus?'

'Since a night he passed ten days ago. I came up in the morning to make his poor bed, and found him sitting up in his clothes before that great canvas he keeps there. Poor, dear, strange man, he says his prayers to it! He had not been to bed, nor since then properly! What has happened to him? Has he found out about the Serafina?' she whispered with a glittering eye and a toothless grin.

'Prove at least that one old woman can be faithful,' I said, 'and watch him well till I come back.' My return was delayed, through the absence of the English physician on a round of visits, and my vainly pursuing him from house to house before I overtook him. I brought him to Theobald's bedside none too soon. A violent fever had seized our patient, and the case was evidently grave. A couple of hours later I knew that he had brain-fever. From this moment I was with him constantly, but I am far from wishing to describe his illness. Excessively painful to witness, it was happily brief. Life burned out in delirium. A certain night that I passed at his pillow, listening to his wild snatches of regret, of aspiration, of rapture and awe at the phantasmal pictures with which his brain seemed to swarm, recurs to my memory now like some stray page from a lost masterpiece of tragedy. Before a week was over we had buried him in the little Protestant cemetery on the way to Fiesole. The Signora Serafina, whom I had caused to be informed of his illness, had come in person, I was told, to inquire about its progress; but she was absent from his funeral, which was attended by but a scanty concourse of mourners. Half a dozen old Florentine sojourners, in spite of the prolonged estrangement which had preceded his death, had felt the kindly impulse to honour his grave. Among them was my friend Mrs Coventry, whom I found, on my departure, waiting at her carriage door at the gate of the cemetery.

'Well,' she said, relieving at last with a significant smile the solemnity of our immediate greeting, 'and the great Madonna? Have you seen her, after all?'

'I've seen her,' I said; 'she's mine – by request. But I shall never show her to you.'

'And why not, pray?'

'My dear Mrs Coventry, you'd not understand her!'

'Upon my word, you're polite.'

'Excuse me; I'm sad and vexed and bitter.' And with reprehensible rudeness, I marched away. I was excessively impatient to leave Florence; my friend's dark spirit seemed diffused through all things. I had packed my trunk to start for Rome that night, and meanwhile, to beguile my unrest, I aimlessly paced the streets. Chance led me at last to the church of San Lorenzo. Remembering poor Theobald's phrase about Michael Angelo – 'He did his best at a venture' – I went in and turned my steps to the chapel of the tombs. Viewing in sadness the sadness of its immortal treasures, I fancied, while I stood there, that the scene demanded no ampler commentary. As I passed through the church again to depart, a woman, turning away from one of the side-altars, met me face to face. The black shawl depending from her head draped picturesquely the handsome visage of Madonna Serafina. She stopped as she recognized me, and I saw that she wished to speak. Her eye was bright and her ample bosom heaved in a way that seemed to portend a certain sharpness of reproach. But the expression of my own face, apparently, drew the sting from her resentment, and she addressed me in a tone in which bitterness was tempered by a sort of dogged resignation. 'I know it was you, now, that separated us,' she said. 'It was a pity he ever brought you to see me! Of course, you couldn't think of me as he did. Well, the Lord gave him, the Lord has taken him. I've just paid for a nine days' mass for his soul. And I can tell you this, signore, I never deceived him. Who put it into his head that I was made to live on holy thoughts and fine phrases? It was his own fancy, and it pleased him to think so. Did he suffer much?' she added more softly, after a pause.

'His sufferings were great, but they were short.'

'And did he speak of me?' She had hesitated and dropped her eyes; she raised them with her question, and revealed in their sombre stillness a gleam of feminine confidence which, for the moment, revived and illumined her beauty. Poor Theobald! Whatever name he had given his passion, it was still her fine eyes that had charmed him.

'Be contented, madam,' I answered, gravely.

She dropped her eyes again and was silent. Then exhaling a full, rich sigh, as she gathered her shawl together: 'He was a magnificent genius!'

I bowed, and we separated.

Passing through a narrow side-street on my way back to my hotel, I perceived above a doorway a sign which it seemed to me I had read before. I suddenly remembered that it was identical with the superscription of a card that I had carried for an hour in my waistcoat-pocket. On the threshold stood the ingenious artist whose claims to public favour were thus distinctly signalized, smoking a pipe in the evening air, and giving the finishing polish with a bit of rag to one of his inimitable 'combinations'. I caught the expressive curl of a couple of tails. He recognized me, removed his little red cap with a most obsequious bow, and motioned me to enter his studio. I returned his bow and passed on, vexed with the apparition. For a week afterwards, whenever I was seized among the ruins of triumphant Rome with some peculiarly poignant memory of Theobald's transcendent illusions and deplorable failure, I seemed to hear a fantastic, impertinent murmur, 'Cats and monkeys, monkeys and cats; all human life is there!'

The Last of the Valerii

I HAD HAD OCCASION to declare more than once that if my god-daughter married a foreigner I should refuse to give her away. And yet when the young Conte Valerio was presented to me, in Rome, as her accepted and plighted lover, I found myself looking at the happy fellow, after a momentary stare of amazement, with a certain paternal benevolence; thinking, indeed, that from the picturesque point of view (she with her yellow locks and he with his dusky ones) they were a strikingly well-assorted pair. She brought him up to me half proudly, half timidly, pushing him before her, and begging me with one of her dove-like glances to he very polite. I don't know that I am addicted to rudeness; but she was so deeply impressed with his grandeur that she thought it impossible to do him honour enough. The Conte Valerio's grandeur was perhaps nothing for a young American girl, who had the air and almost the habits of a princess, to sound her trumpet about; but she was desperately in love with him, and not only her heart, but her imagination, was touched. He was extremely handsome, and with a more significant sort of beauty than is common in the handsome Roman race. He had a sort of sunken depth of expression, and a grave, slow smile, suggesting no great quickness of wit, but an unimpassioned intensity of feeling which promised well for Martha's happiness. He had little of the light, inexpensive urbanity of his countrymen, and more of a sort of heavy sincerity in his gaze which seemed to suspend response until he was sure he understood you. He was perhaps a little stupid, and I fancied that to a political or aesthetic question the reply would be particularly slow. 'He is good and strong and brave,' the young girl however assured me; and I easily believed her. Strong the Conte Valerio certainly was; he had a head and throat like some of the busts in the Vatican. To my eye, which has looked at things now so long with the painter's purpose, it was a real perplexity to see such a throat rising out of the white cravat of the period. It sustained a head as massively round as that of the familiar bust of the Emperor Caracalla, and covered with the same dense sculptural crop of curls. The young man's hair grew superbly; it was such hair as the old Romans must have had when they walked bareheaded and bronzed about the world. It made a perfect arch over his low, clear forehead, and prolonged itself on cheek and chin in a close, crisp beard, strong with its own strength and unstiffened by the razor. Neither his nose nor his mouth was delicate; but they were powerful, shapely, and manly. His complexion was of a deep glowing brown which no emotion would alter, and his large lucid eyes seemed to stare at you like a pair of polished agates. He was of middle stature, and his chest was of so generous a girth that you half expected to hear his linen crack with its even respirations. And yet, with his simple human smile, he looked neither like a young bullock nor a gladiator. His powerful voice was the least bit harsh, and his large, ceremonious reply to my compliment had the massive sonority with which civil speeches must have been uttered in the age of Augustus. I had always considered my god-daughter a very American little person, in all delightful meanings of the word, and I doubted if this sturdy young Latin would understand the transatlantic element in her nature; but, evidently, he would make her a loyal and ardent lover. She seemed to me, in her blond prettiness, so tender, so appealing, so bewitching, that it was impossible to believe he had not more thoughts for all this than for the equally pretty fortune which it yet bothered me to believe that he must, like a good Italian, have taken the exact measure of. His own worldly goods consisted of the paternal estate, a villa within the walls of Rome, which his scanty funds had suffered to fall into sombre disrepair. 'It's the Villa she's in love with, quite as much as the Count,' said her mother. 'She dreams of converting the Count; that's all very well. But she dreams of refurnishing the Villa!'

The upholsterers were turned into it, I believe, before the wedding, and there was a great scrubbing and sweeping of saloons and raking and weeding of alleys and avenues. Martha made frequent visits of inspection while these ceremonies were taking place; but one day, on her return, she came into my little studio with an air of amusing horror. She had found them *scraping* the sarcophagus in the great ilex-walk; divesting it of its mossy coat, divesting it of the sacred green mould of the ages! This was their idea of making the Villa comfortable. She had made them transport it to the dampest place they could find; for next after that slow-coming, slow-going smile of her lover, it was the rusty complexion of his patrimonial marbles that she most prized. The young Count's conversion proceeded less rapidly, and indeed I believe that his betrothed brought little zeal to the affair. She loved him so devoutly that she believed no change of faith could better him, and she would have been willing for his sake to say her prayers to the sacred Bambino at Epiphany. But he had the good taste to demand no such sacrifice, and I was struck with the happy promise of a scene of which I was an accidental observer. It was at St Peter's, one Friday afternoon, during the vesper-service which takes place in the Chapel of the Choir. I met my god-daughter wandering happily on her lover's arm, her mother being established on her camp-stool near the chapel door. The crowd was collected thereabouts, and the body of the church was empty. Now and then the high voices of the singers escaped into the outer vastness and melted slowly away in the incense-thickened air. Something in the young girl's step and the clasp of her arm in her lover's told me that her contentment was perfect. As she threw back her head and gazed into the magnificent immensity of vault and dome, I felt that she was in that enviable mood in which all consciousness revolves on a single centre, and that her sense of the splendours around her was one with the ecstasy of her trust.

They stopped before that sombre group of confessionals which proclaims so portentously the world's sinfulness, and Martha seemed to make some almost passionate protestation. A few minutes later I overtook them.

'Don't you agree with me, dear friend,' said the Count, who always addressed me with the most affectionate deference, 'that before I marry so pure and sweet a creature as this, I ought to go into one of those places and confess every sin I ever was guilty of – every evil thought and impulse and desire of my grossly evil nature?'

Martha looked at him, half in deprecation, half in homage, with a look which seemed at once to insist that her lover could have no vices, and to plead that, if he had, there would be something magnificent in them. 'Listen to him!' she said, smiling. 'The list would be long, and if you waited to finish it, you would be late for the wedding! But if you confess your sins for me, it's only fair I should confess mine for you. Do you know what I have been saying to Camillo?' she added, turning to me with the half-filial confidence she had always shown me and with a rosy glow in her cheeks; 'that I want to do something more for him than girls commonly do for their lovers – to take some step, to run some risk, to break some law, even! I'm willing to change my religion, if he bids me. There are moments when I'm terribly tired of simply staring at Catholicism; it will be a relief to come into a church to kneel. That's, after all, what they are meant for? Therefore, *Camillo mio*, if it casts a shade across your heart to think that. I'm a heretic, I'll go and kneel down to that good old priest who has just entered the confessional yonder and say to him, "My father, I repent, I abjure, I believe. Baptize me in the only faith."'

'If it's as a compliment to the Count,' I said, 'it seems to me he ought to anticipate it by turning Protestant.'

She had spoken lightly and with a smile, and yet with an undertone of girlish ardour. The young man looked at her with a solemn, puzzled face and shook his head. 'Keep your religion,' he said. 'Everyone his own. If you should attempt to embrace mine, I'm afraid you would close your arms about a shadow. I'm a poor Catholic! I don't understand all these chants and ceremonies and splendours. When I was a child I never could learn my catechism. My poor old confessor long ago gave me up; he told me I was a good boy but a *pagan*! You must not be a better Catholic than your husband. I don't understand your religion any better, but I beg you not to change it for mine. If it has helped to make you what you are it must be good.' And taking the young girl's hand, he was about to raise it affectionately to his lips; but suddenly remembering that they were in a place unaccordant with profane passions, he lowered it with a comical smile. 'Let us go!' he murmured, passing his hand over his forehead. 'This heavy atmosphere of St Peter's always stupefies me.'

They were married in the month of May, and we separated for the summer, the Contessa's mamma going to illuminate the domestic circle in New York with her reflected dignity. When I returned to Rome in the autumn I found the young couple established at the Villa Valerio, which was being gradually reclaimed from its antique decay. I begged that the hand of improvement might be lightly laid on it, for as an unscrupulous old *genre* painter, with an eye to 'subjects', I preferred that ruin should accumulate. My god-daughter was quite of my way of thinking, and she had a capital sense of the picturesque. Advising with me often as to projected changes, she was sometimes more conservative than myself; and I more than once smiled at her archaelogical zeal, and declared that I believed she had married the Count because he was like a statue of the Decadence. I had a constant invitation to spend my days at the Villa, and my easel was always planted in one of the garden-walks. I grew to have a painter's passion for the place and to be intimate with every tangled shrub and twisted tree, every moss-coated vase and mouldy sarcophagus and sad, disfeatured bust of those grim old Romans who could so ill afford to become more meagre-visaged. The place was of small extent; but though there were many other villas more pretentious and splendid, none seemed to me more deeply picturesque, more romantically idle and untrimmed, more encumbered with precious antique rubbish, and haunted with half-historic echoes. It contained an old ilex-walk in which I used religiously to spend half an hour every day – half an hour being, I confess, just as long as I could stay without beginning to sneeze. The trees arched and intertwisted here along their dusky vista in the quaintest symmetry; and as it was exposed uninterruptedly to the west, the low evening sun used to transfuse it with a sort of golden mist and play through it – over leaves and knotty boughs and mossy marbles – with a

thousand crimson fingers. It was filled with disinterred fragments of sculpture – nameless statues and noseless heads and
rough-hewn sarcophagi, which made it deliciously solemn. The
statues used to stand there in the perpetual twilight like conscious
things, brooding on their gathered memories. I used to linger
about them, half expecting they would speak and tell me their
stony secrets – whisper heavily the whereabouts of their mouldering fellows, still unrecovered from the soil.

My god-daughter was idyllically happy and absolutely in
love. I was obliged to confess that even rigid rules have their
exceptions, and that now and then an Italian count is an honest
fellow. Camillo was one to the core, and seemed quite content to
be adored. Their life was a kind of childlike interchange of
caresses, as candid and unmeasured as those of a shepherd and
shepherdess in a bucolic poem. To stroll in the ilex-walk and
feel her husband's arm about her waist and his shoulder against
her cheek; to roll cigarettes for him while he puffed them in the
great marble-paved rotunda in the centre of the house; to fill his
glass from an old rusty red amphora – these graceful occupations satisfied the young Countess.

She rode with him sometimes in the tufty shadow of aque-
ducts and tombs, and sometimes suffered him to show his beautiful wife at Roman dinners and balls. She played dominoes with
him after dinner, and carried out in a desultory way a daily
scheme of reading him the newspapers. This observance was
subject to fluctuations caused by the Count's invincible tendency
to go to sleep – a failing his wife never attempted to disguise or

palliate. She would sit and brush the flies from him while he lay picturesquely snoozing, and, if I ventured near him, would place her finger on her lips and whisper that she thought her husband was as handsome asleep as awake. I confess I often felt tempted to reply to her that he was at least as entertaining, for the young man's happiness had not multiplied the topics on which he readily conversed. He had plenty of good sense, and his opinions on practical matters were always worth having. He would often come and sit near me while I worked at my easel and offer a friendly criticism. His taste was a little crude, but his eye was excellent, and his measurement of the resemblance between some point of my copy and the original as trustworthy as that of a mathematical instrument. But he seemed to me to have either a strange reserve or a strange simplicity; to be fundamentally unfurnished with 'ideas'. He had no beliefs, or hopes, or fears – nothing but senses, appetites, and serenely luxurious tastes. As I watched him strolling about looking at his fingernails, I often wondered whether he had anything that could properly be termed a soul, and whether good-health and good-nature were not the sum of his attributes. 'It's lucky he's good-natured,' I used to say to myself; 'for if he were not, there is nothing in his conscience to keep him in order. If he had irritable nerves instead of quiet ones, he would strangle us as the young Hercules strangled the poor little snakes. He's the natural man! Happily, his nature is gentle and I can mix my colours at my ease.' I wondered what he thought about and what passed through his mind in the sunny leisure which seemed to shut him in from the modern work-a-day world of which, in spite of my passion for bedaubing old panels with ineffective portraiture of mouldy statues against screens of box, I still flattered myself I was a member. I went so far as to believe that he sometimes withdrew from the world altogether. He had moods in which his consciousness seemed so remote and his mind so irresponsive and dumb, that nothing but a powerful caress or a sudden violence was likely to arouse him. Even his lavish tenderness for his wife had a quality which I but half relished. Whether or no he had a soul himself, he seemed not to suspect that she had one. I took a god-fatherly interest in what it had not always seemed to me crabbed and pedantic to talk of as her moral development. I fondly believed her to be a creature susceptible of the finer spiritual emotions. But what was becoming of her spiritual life in this interminable heathenish honeymoon? Some fine day she would find herself tired of the Count's *beaux yeux*, and make an appeal to his mind. She had, to my knowledge, plans of study, of charity, of worthily playing her part as a Contessa Valerio – a position as to which the family-records furnished the most memorable examples. But if the Count found the newspapers soporific, I doubted if he would turn Dante's pages very fast for his wife, or smile with much zest at the anecdotes of Vasari. How could he advise her, instruct her, sustain her? And if she became a mother, how could he share her responsibilities? He doubtless would assure his little son and heir a stout pair of arms and legs and a magnificent crop of curls, and sometimes remove his cigarette to kiss a dimpled spot; but I found it hard to picture

him lending his voice to teach the lusty urchin his alphabet or
his prayers, or the rudiments of infant virtue. One accomplishment indeed the Count possessed which would make him an
agreeable play-fellow: he carried in his pocket a collection of
precious fragments of antique pavement – bits of porphyry and
malachite and lapis and basalt – disinterred on his own soil and
brilliantly polished by use. With these you might see him occupied by the half-hour, playing the simple game of catch-and-
toss, ranging them in a circle, tossing them in rotation, and
catching them on the back of his hand. His skill was remarkable;
he would send a stone five feet into the air, and pitch and catch
and transpose the rest before he received it again. I watched
with affectionate jealousy for the signs of a dawning sense, on
Martha's part, that she was the least bit strangely mated. Once
or twice, as the weeks went by, I fancied I read them, and that
she looked at me with eyes which seemed to remember certain
old talks of mine in which I had declared – with such verity as
you please – that a Frenchman, an Italian, a Spaniard, might be
a very good fellow, but that he never really respected the woman
he pretended to love; but for the most part, I confess, these
dusky broodings of mine spent themselves easily in the charmed
atmosphere of our fine old Villa. We were out of the modern
world and had no business with modern scruples. The place was
so bright, so still, so sacred to the silent, imperturbable past, that
drowsy contentment seemed a natural law; and sometimes
when, as I sat at my work, I saw my companions passing arm-
in-arm across the end of one of the long-drawn vistas and,

turning back to my palette, found my colours dimmer for the radiant vision, I could easily believe that I was some loyal old chronicler of a perfectly poetical legend.

It was a help to ungrudging feelings that the Count, yielding to his wife's urgency, had undertaken a series of systematic excavations. To excavate is an expensive luxury, and neither Camillo nor his latter forefathers had possessed the means for a disinterested pursuit of archaeology. But his young wife had persuaded herself that the much-trodden soil of the Villa was as full of buried treasures as a bride-cake of plums, and that it would he a pretty compliment to the ancient house which had accepted her as mistress to devote a portion of her dowry to bringing its mouldy honours to the light. I think she was not without a fancy that this liberal process would help to disinfect her Yankee dollars of the impertinent odour of trade. She took learned advice on the subject, and was soon ready to swear to you, proceeding from irrefutable premises, that a colossal gilt-bronze Minerva mentioned by Strabo was placidly awaiting resurrection at a point twenty rods from the north-west angle of the house. She had a couple of grotesque old antiquaries to lunch, whom having plied with unwonted potations, she walked off their legs in the grounds; and though they agreed on nothing else in the world, they individually assured her that properly conducted researches would probably yield an unequalled harvest of discoveries. The Count had been not only indifferent, but even averse, to the scheme, and had more than once arrested his wife's complacent allusions to it by an

unaccustomed acerbity of tone. 'Let them be, the poor disinherited gods, the Minerva, the Apollo, the Ceres, you are so sure
of finding,' he said, 'and don't break their rest. What do you
want of them? We can't worship them. Would you put them on
pedestals to stare and mock at them? If you can't believe in
them, don't disturb them. Peace be with them!' I remember
being a good deal impressed by a vigorous confession drawn
from him by his wife's playfully declaring in answer to some
remonstrances in this strain that he was veritably superstitious.
'Yes, by Bacchus, I *am* superstitious!' he cried. 'Too much so,
perhaps! But I'm an old Italian, and you must take me as you
find me. There have been things seen and done here which leave
strange influences behind! They don't touch you, doubtless,
who come of another race. But they touch me, often, in the
whisper of the leaves and the odour of the mouldy soil and the
blank eyes of the old statues. I can't bear to look the statues in
the face. I seem to see other strange eyes in the empty sockets,
and I hardly know what they say to me. I call the poor old
statues ghosts. In conscience, we've enough on the place
already, lurking and peering in every shady nook. Don't dig up
any more, or I won't answer for my wits!'

This account of Camillo's sensibilities was too fantastic not
to seem to his wife almost a joke; and though I imagined there
was more in it, he made a joke so seldom that I should have been
sorry to cut short the poor girl's smile. With her smile she
carried her point, and in a few days arrived a kind of explorer,
with a dozen workmen armed with pickaxes and spades. For

myself, I was secretly vexed at these energetic measures; for, though fond of disinterred statues, I disliked the disinterment and deplored the profane sounds which were henceforth to break the leisurely stillness of the gardens. I especially objected to the personage who conducted the operations, an ugly little dwarfish man who seemed altogether a subterranean genius, a mouldy gnome of the underworld, and went prying about the grounds with a malicious smile which suggested more delight in the money the Signor Conte was going to bury than in the expected marbles and bronzes. When the first sod had been turned the Count's mood seemed to alter, and his curiosity got the better of his scruples. He sniffed delightedly the odour of the humid earth, and stood watching the workmen as they struck constantly deeper with a kindling wonder in his eyes. Whenever a pickaxe rang against a stone he would utter a sharp cry, and be deterred from jumping into the trench only by the little explorer's assurance that it was a false alarm. The near prospect of discoveries seemed to act upon his nerves, and I met him more than once strolling restlessly among his cedarn alleys, as if at last he had fallen a-thinking; he took me by the arm and made me walk with him, and discoursed ardently of the chance of a 'find'. I rather marvelled at his sudden zeal, and wondered whether he had an eye to the past or to the future – to the beauty of possible Minervas and Apollos or to their market value. Whenever the Count would come and denounce his little army of spadesmen, a set of loitering vagabonds, the little explorer would glance at me with a sarcastic twinkle which seemed to hint that excavations were a snare. We were kept some time in suspense, for several false beginnings were made. The earth was probed in the wrong places. The Count began to be discouraged and to prolong his abbreviated *siesta*. But the little explorer, who had his own ideas, shrewdly continued his labours; and as I sat at my easel I heard the spades ringing against the dislodged stones. Now and then I would pause, with an uncontrollable acceleration of my heart-beats. 'It *may* be,' I would say, 'that some marble masterpiece is stirring there beneath its lightening weight of earth! There are as good fish in the sea – I *may* be summoned to welcome another Antinous back to fame – a Venus, a Faun, an Augustus!'

One morning it seemed to me that I had been hearing for half an hour a livelier movement of voices than usual, but as I was preoccupied with a puzzling bit of work I made no inquiries. Suddenly a shadow fell across my canvas, and I turned round. The little explorer stood beside me, with a glittering eye, cap in hand, his forehead bathed in perspiration. Resting in the hollow of his arm was an earth-stained fragment of marble, In answer to my questioning glance he held it up to me, and I saw it was a woman's shapely hand. 'Come!' he simply said, and led the way to the excavation. The workmen were so closely gathered round the open trench that I saw nothing till he made them divide. Then, full in the sun and flashing it back, almost, in spite of her mouldy incrustations, I beheld, propped up with stones against a heap of earth, a majestic marble image. She seemed to me almost colossal, though I afterwards perceived that she was of perfect human proportions. My pulses began to throb, for I felt she was something great, and that it was great to be among the first to know her. Her marvellous beauty gave her an almost human look, and her absent eyes seemed to wonder back at us. She was amply draped, so that I saw that she was not a Venus. 'She's a Juno,' said the explorer, decisively; and she seemed indeed an embodiment of celestial supremacy and repose. Her beautiful head, bound with a single band, could have bent only to give the nod of command; her eyes looked straight before her; her month was implacably grave; one hand, outstretched, appeared to have held a kind of imperial wand, the arm from which the other had been broken hung at her side with the most classical majesty. The workmanship was of the rarest finish, and though perhaps there was a sort of vaguely modern attempt at character in her expression, she was wrought, as a whole, in the large and simple manner of the great Greek period. She was a masterpiece of skill and a marvel of preservation. 'Does the Count know?' I soon asked, for I had a guilty sense that our eyes were taking something from her.

'The Signor Conte is at his *siesta*,' said the explorer, with his sceptical grin. 'We don't like to disturb him.'

'Here he comes!' cried one of the workmen, and we made way for him. His *siesta* had evidently been suddenly broken, for his face was flushed and his hair disordered.

'Ah, my dream – my dream was right, then!' he cried, and stood staring at the image.

'What was your dream?' I asked, as his face seemed to betray more dismay than delight.

'That they'd found a Juno; and that she rose and came and laid her marble band on mine – eh?' said the Count excitedly.

A kind of awestruck, guttural *a-ah!* burst from the listening workmen.

'This is the hand!' said the little explorer, holding up his perfect fragment. 'I've had it this half-hour, so it can't have touched you.'

'But you're apparently right as to her being a Juno,' I said. 'Admire her at your leisure.' And I turned away; for if the Count was superstitious, I wished to leave him free to relieve himself. I repaired to the house to carry the news to my god-daughter, whom I found slumbering – dreamlessly, it appeared – over a great archaeological octavo. 'They've touched bottom,' I said. 'They've found a Juno of Praxiteles at the very least!' She dropped her octavo, and rang for a parasol. I described the statue, but not graphically, I presume, for Martha gave a little sarcastic grimace.

'A long, fluted *peplum*,' she said. 'How very odd! I don't believe she's beautiful.'

'She's beautiful enough, *figlioccia mia*,' I answered, 'to make you jealous.'

We found the Count standing before the resurgent goddess in fixed contemplation, with folded arms. He seemed to have recovered from the irritation of his dream, but I thought his face betrayed a still deeper emotion. He was pale, and gave no response as his wife caressingly clasped his arm. I'm not sure, however, that his wife's attitude was not a livelier tribute to the perfection of the image. She had been laughing at my rhapsody as we walked from the house, and I had bethought myself of a statement I had somewhere seen, that women lack the perception of the purest beauty. Martha, however, seemed slowly to measure our Juno's infinite stateliness. She gazed a long time silently, leaning against her husband, and then stepped half timidly down on the stones which formed a rough base for the figure. She laid her two rosy, ungloved hands upon the stony fingers of the goddess, and remained for some moments pressing them in her warm grasp, and fixing her living eyes upon the inexpressive brow. When she turned round her eyes were bright with an admiring tear – a tear which her husband was too deeply absorbed to notice. He had apparently given orders that the workmen should he treated to a cask of wine, in honour of their discovery. It was now brought and opened on the spot, and the little explorer, having drawn the first glass, stepped forward, hat in hand, and obsequiously presented it to the Countess. She only moistened her lips with it and passed it to her husband. He raised it mechanically to his own; then suddenly he stopped, held it a moment aloft, and poured it out slowly and solemnly at the feet of the Juno.

'Why, it's a libation!' I cried. He made no answer and walked slowly away.

There was no more work done that day. The labourers lay on the grass, gazing with the native Roman relish of a fine piece of sculpture, but wasting no wine in pagan ceremonies. In the evening the Count paid the Juno another visit, and gave orders that on the morrow she should be transferred to the Casino. The

Casino was a deserted garden-house, built in not ungraceful imitation of an Ionic temple, in which Camillo's ancestors must often have assembled to drink cool syrups from Venetian glasses, and listen to learned madrigals. It contained several dusty fragments of antique sculpture, and it was spacious enough to enclose that richer collection of which I began fondly to regard the Juno as but the nucleus. Here, with short delay, this fine creature was placed, serenely upright, a reversed funereal *cippus* forming a sufficiently solid pedestal. The little explorer, who seemed an expert in all the offices of restoration, rubbed her and scraped her with mysterious art, removed her earthy stains, and doubled the lustre of her beauty. Her mellow substance seemed to glow with a kind of renascent purity and bloom, and, but for her broken hand, you might have fancied she had just received the last stroke of the chisel. Her fame remained no secret. Within two or three days half a dozen inquisitive *conoscenti* posted out to obtain sight of her. I happened to be present when the first of these gentlemen (a German in blue spectacles, with a portfolio under his arm) presented himself at the Villa. The Count, hearing his voice at the door, came forward and eyed him coldly from head to foot.

'Your new Juno, Signor Conte,' began the German, 'is, in my opinion, much more likely to be a certain Proserpine—'

'I've neither a Juno nor a Proserpine to discuss with you,' said the Count, curtly. 'You're misinformed.'

'You've dug up no statue?' cried the German. 'What a scandalous hoax!'

'None worthy of your learned attention. I'm sorry you should have the trouble of carrying your little note-book so far.' The Count had suddenly become witty!

'But you've something, surely. The rumour is running through Rome.'

'The rumour be damned!' cried the Count savagely. 'I've *nothing* – do you understand? Be so good as to say so to your friends.'

The answer was explicit, and the poor archaeologist departed, tossing his flaxen mane. But I pitied him and ventured to remonstrate with the Count. 'She might as well be still in the earth, if no one is to see her,' I said.

'*I* am to see her: that's enough!' he answered with the same unnatural harshness. Then, in a moment, as he caught me eyeing him askance in troubled surprise, 'I hated his great portfolio. He was going to make some hideous drawing of her.'

'Ah, that touches me,' I said. 'I have been planning to make a little sketch.'

He was silent for some moments, after which he turned and grasped my arm, with less irritation, but with extraordinary gravity. 'Go in there towards twilight,' he said, 'and sit for an hour and look at her. I think you'll give up your sketch. If you don't, my good old friend – you're welcome!'

I followed his advice, and, as a friend, I gave up my sketch. But an artist is an artist, and I secretly longed to attempt it. Orders strictly in accordance with the Count's reply to our German friend were given to the servants, who, with an easy

Italian conscience and a gracious Italian persuasiveness, assured all subsequent inquirers that they had been regrettably misinformed. I have no doubt, indeed, that, in default of larger opportunity, they made condolence remunerative. Further excavation was, for the present, suspended, as implying an affront to the incomparable Juno. The workmen departed, but the little explorer still haunted the premises and sounded the soil for his own entertainment. One day he came to me with his usual ambiguous grimace. 'The beautiful hand of the Juno,' he murmured; 'what has become of it?'

'I've not seen it since you called me to look at her. I remember when I went away I saw it lying on the grass near the excavation.'

'Where I placed it myself! After that it disappeared. *Ecco!*'

'Do you suspect one of your workmen? Such a fragment as that would bring more *scudi* than most of them ever looked at.'

'Some, perhaps, are greater thieves than the others. But if I were to call up the worst of them and accuse him, the Count would interfere.'

'He must value that beautiful hand, nevertheless.'

The little expert in disinterment looked about him and winked. 'He values it so much that he himself purloined it. That's my belief, and I think that the less we say about it the better.'

'Purloined it, my dear sir? After all, it's his own property.'

'Not so much as that comes to. So beautiful a creature is more or less the property of everyone; we've all a right to look at her.

But the Count treats her as if she were a sacrosanct image of the Madonna. He keeps her under lock and key, and pays her solitary visits. What does he do, after all? When a beautiful woman is in stone, all you can do is to look at her. And what does he do with that precious hand? He keeps it in a silver box; he has made a relic of it!' And the little explorer began to titter grotesquely and walked away.

He left me musing uncomfortably, and wondering what the deuce he meant. The Count certainly chose to make a mystery of the Juno, but this seemed a natural incident of the first rapture of possession. I was willing to wait for a free access to her, and in the meantime I was glad to find that there was a limit to his constitutional apathy. But as the days elapsed I began to be conscious that his enjoyment was not communicative, but strangely cold and shy and sombre. That he should admire a marble goddess was no reason for his despising mankind, but he really seemed to be making invidious comparisons between us. From this untender proscription his charming wife was not excepted. At moments, when I tried to persuade myself that he was neither worse nor better company than usual, her face condemned my optimism. She said nothing, but she wore a constant look of pathetic perplexity. She sat at times with her eyes fixed on him with a kind of appealing remonstrance and tender curiosity, as if pitying surprise held resentment yet awhile in check. What passed between them in private, I had, of course, no warrant to inquire. Nothing, I imagined, and that was the misery. It was part of the misery, too, that he seemed impenetrable to these mute glances, and looked over her head with an air of superb abstraction. Occasionally he noticed me looking at him in urgent deprecation, and then for a moment his heavy eye would sparkle, half, as it seemed, in defiant irony and half with a strangely stifled impulse to justify himself. But from his wife he kept his face inexorably, cruelly averted; and when she approached him with some persuasive caress, he received it with an ill-concealed shudder. I inwardly protested and raged. I grew to hate the Count and everything that belonged to him. 'I was a thousand times right,' I cried; 'an Italian count may be mighty fine, but he won't *wear*! Give us some wholesome young fellow of our own blood, who'll play us none of these dusky Old World tricks. Painter as I am, I'll never recommend a picturesque husband!' I lost my pleasure in the Villa, in the purple shadows and glowing lights, the mossy marbles and the long-trailing profile of the Alban Hills. My painting stood still; everything looked ugly. I sat and fumbled with my palette, and seemed to be mixing mud with my colours. My head was stuffed with dismal thoughts; an intolerable weight seemed to lie upon my heart. The Count became, to my imagination, a dark efflorescence of the evil germs which history had implanted in his line. No wonder he was foredoomed to be cruel. Was not cruelty a tradition in his race, and crime an example? The unholy passions of his forefathers stirred blindly in his untaught nature and clamoured dumbly for an issue. What a heavy heritage it seemed to me, as I reckoned it up in my melancholy musings, the Count's interminable ancestry! Back to the profligate revival of arts and vices — back to the bloody medley of mediaeval wars — back through the long, fitfully glaring dusk of the early ages to its ponderous origin in the solid Roman state — back through all the darkness of history it seemed to stretch, losing every feeblest claim on my sympathies as it went. Such a record was in itself a curse; and my poor girl had expected it to sit as lightly and gratefully on her consciousness as her feather on her hat! I have little idea how long this painful situation lasted. It seemed the longer from my god-daughter's continued reserve, and my inability to offer her a word of consolation. A sensitive woman, disappointed in marriage, exhausts her own ingenuity before she takes counsel. The Count's preoccupations, whatever they were, made him increasingly restless; he came and went at random, with nervous abruptness; he took long rides alone, and, as I inferred, rarely went through the form of excusing himself to his wife; and still, as time went on, he came no nearer explaining his mystery. With the lapse of time, however, I confess that my apprehensions began to be tempered with pity. If I had expected to see him propitiate his urgent ancestry by a crime, now that his native rectitude seemed resolute to deny them this satisfaction, I felt a sort of comparative gratitude. A man couldn't be so gratuitously sombre without being unhappy. He had always treated me with that antique deference to a grizzled beard for which elderly men reserve the flames of their general tenderness for waning fashions, and I thought it possible he might suffer me to lay a healing hand upon his trouble. One evening, when I had taken leave of my god-daughter and given her my useless blessing in a silent kiss, I came out and found the Count sitting in the garden in the mild starlight, and staring at a mouldy Hermes, nestling in a clump of oleander. I sat down by him and informed him roundly that his conduct needed an explanation. He half turned his head, and his dark pupil gleamed an instant.

'I understand,' he said, 'you think me crazy!' And he tapped his forehead.

'No, not crazy, but unhappy. And if unhappiness runs its course too freely, of course our poor wits are sorely tried.'

He was silent awhile, and then, 'I'm not unhappy!' he cried abruptly. 'I'm prodigiously happy. You wouldn't believe the satisfaction I take in sitting here and staring at that old weather-worn Hermes. Formerly I used to be afraid of him; his frown used to remind me of a little bushy-browed old priest who taught me Latin and looked at me terribly over the book when I stumbled in my Virgil. But now it seems to me the friendliest, jolliest thing in the world, and suggests the most delightful images. He stood pouting his great lips in some old Roman's garden two thousand years ago. He saw the sandalled feet treading the alleys and the rose-crowned heads bending over the wine; he knew the old feasts and the old worship, the old Romans and the old gods. As I sit here he speaks to me, in his own dumb way, and describes it all! No, no, my friend, I'm the happiest of men!'

I had denied that I thought he was crazy, but I suddenly began to suspect it, for I found nothing reassuring in this singular rhapsody. The Hermes, for a wonder, had kept his nose; and when I reflected that my dear Countess was being neglected for this senseless pagan block, I secretly promised myself to come the next day with a hammer and deal him such a lusty blow as would make him too ridiculous for a sentimental *tête-à-tête*. Meanwhile, however, the Count's infatuation was no laughing matter, and I expressed my sincerest conviction when I said, after a pause, that I should recommend him to see either a priest or a physician.

He burst into uproarious laughter. 'A priest! What should I do with a priest, or he with me? I never loved them, and I feel less like beginning than ever. A priest, my dear friend,' he repeated, laying his hand on my arm, 'don't set a priest at me, if you value *his* sanity! My confession would frighten the poor man out of his wits. As for a doctor, I never was better in my life, and unless,' he added abruptly, rising, and eyeing me askance, 'you want to poison me, in Christian charity I advise you to leave me alone.'

Decidedly, the Count *was* unsound, and I had no heart, for some days, to go back to the Villa. How should I treat him, what stand should I take, what course did Martha's happiness and dignity demand? I wandered about Rome, revolving these questions, and one afternoon found myself in the Pantheon. A light spring shower had begun to fall, and I hurried for refuge into the great temple which its Christian altars have but half converted into a church. No Roman monument retains a deeper impress of ancient life, or verifies more forcibly the memory of these old beliefs which we are apt to regard as dim

fables. The huge dusky dome seems to the spiritual ear to hold
a vague reverberation of pagan worship, as a gathered shell
holds the rumour of the sea. Three or four persons were scattered before the various altars; another stood near the centre,
beneath the aperture in the dome. As I drew near I perceived
he was the Count. He was planted with his hands behind him,
looking up first at the heavy rain-clouds, as they crossed the
great bull's-eye, and then down at the besprinkled circle on
the pavement. In those days the pavement was rugged and
cracked and magnificently old, and this ample space, in free
communion with the weather, had become as mouldy and
mossy and verdant as a strip of garden soil. A tender herbage
had sprung up in the crevices of the slabs and the little micro-
scopic shoots were twinkling in the rain. This great weather-
current, through the unclosed apex of the temple, deadens
most effectively the customary odours of incense and tallow,
and transports one to a faith that was on friendly terms with
nature. It seemed to have performed this office for the Count;
his face wore an indefinable expression of ecstasy, and he was
so rapt in contemplation that it was some time before he
noticed me. The sun was struggling through the clouds without, and yet a thin rain continued to fall and came drifting
down into our gloomy enclosure in a sort of illuminated driz-
zle. The Count watched it with the fascinated stare of a child
watching a fountain, and then turned away, pressing his hand
to his brow, and walked over to one of the ornamental altars.
Here he again stood staring, but in a moment wheeled about

and returned to his former place. Just then he recognized me, and perceived, I suppose, the puzzled gaze I must have fixed on him. He saluted me frankly with his hand, and at last came toward me. I fancied that he was in a kind of nervous tremor and was trying to appear calm.

'This is the best place in Rome,' he murmured. 'It's worth fifty St Peter's. But do you know I never came here till the other day? I left it to the *forestieri*. They go about with their red books, and read about this and that, and think they know it. Ah! you must *feel* it – feel the beauty and fitness of that great open skylight. Now, only the wind and the rain, the sun and the cold come down; but of old – of old –' and he touched my arm and gave me a strange smile – 'the pagan gods and goddesses used to come sailing through it and take their places at their altars. What a procession, when the eyes of faith could see it! Those are the things they have given us instead!' And he gave a pitiful shrug. 'I should like to pull down their pictures, overturn their candlesticks, and poison their holy-water!'

'My dear Count,' I said gently, 'you should tolerate people's honest beliefs. Would you renew the Inquisition, and in the interest of Jupiter and Mercury?'

'People wouldn't tolerate my belief, if they guessed it!' he cried. 'There's been a great talk about the pagan persecutions; but the Christians persecuted as well, and the old gods were worshipped in caves and woods as well as the new. And none the worse for that! It was in caves and woods and streams, in earth and air and water, they dwelt. And there – and here, too, in spite of all your Christian lustrations – a son of old Italy may find them still!'

He had said more than he meant, and his mask had fallen. I looked at him hard, and felt a sudden outgush of the compassion we always feel for a creature irresponsibly excited. I seemed to touch the source of his trouble, and my relief was great, for my discovery made me feel like bursting into laughter. But I contented myself with smiling benignantly. He looked back at me suspiciously, as if to judge how far he had betrayed himself; and in his glance I read, somehow, that he had a conscience we could take hold of. In my gratitude, I was ready to thank any gods he pleased. 'Take care, take care,' I said, 'you're saying things which if the sacristan there were to hear and report—!' And I passed my hand through his arm and led him away.

I was startled and shocked, but I was also amused and comforted. The Count had suddenly become for me a delight-fully curious phenomenon, and I passed the rest of the day in meditating on the strange ineffaceability of race-characteristics. A sturdy young Latin I had called Camillo; sturdier, indeed, than I had dreamed him. Discretion was now misplaced, and on the morrow I spoke to my god-daughter. She had lately been hoping, I think, that I would help her to unburden her heart, for she immediately gave way to tears, and confessed that she was miserable. 'At first,' she said, 'I thought it was fancy, and not his tenderness that was growing less, but my exactions that were growing greater. But suddenly it settled upon me like a mortal chill – the conviction that he had ceased to care for me, that something had come between us. And the horrible thing has been the want of possible cause in my own conduct, or of other visible claim on his interest. I have racked my brain to discover what I had said or done or thought to displease him! And yet he goes about like a man too deeply injured to complain. He has never uttered a harsh word or given me a reproachful look. He has simply renounced me. I have dropped out of his life.'

She spoke with such an appealing tremor in her voice that I was on the point of telling her that I had guessed the riddle, and that this was half the battle. But I was afraid of her incredulity. My solution was so fantastic, so apparently far-fetched, so absurd, that I resolved to wait for convincing evidence. To obtain it, I continued to watch the Count, covertly and cautiously, but with a vigilance which disinterested curiosity now made doubly keen. I returned to my painting, and neglected no pretext for hovering about the gardens and the neighbour-hood of the Casino. The Count, I think, suspected my designs, or at least my suspicions, and would have been glad to remem-ber just what he had suffered himself to say to me in the Pantheon. But it deepened my interest in his extraordinary situ-ation that, in so far as I could read his deeply brooding face, he seemed to have grudgingly pardoned me. He gave me a glance occasionally, as he passed me, in which a sort of dumb desire for help appeared to struggle with the instinct of mistrust. I was willing enough to help him, but the case was prodigiously deli-cate, and I wished to master the symptoms. Meanwhile I worked and waited and wondered. Ah! I wondered, you may be sure, with an interminable wonder; and, turn it over as I would, I couldn't get used to my idea. Sometimes it offered itself to me with a perverse fascination which deprived me of all wish to interfere. The Count took the form of a precious psychological study, and refined feeling seemed to dictate a tender respect for his delusion. I envied him the force of his imagination, and I used sometimes to close my eyes with a vague desire that when I opened them I might find Apollo under the opposite tree, lazily kissing his flute, or see Diana hurrying with long steps down the ilex-walk. But for the most part my host seemed to me simply an unhappy young man, with an unwholesome mental twist which should be smoothed away as speedily as possible. If the remedy was to match the disease, however, it would have to be an ingenious compound!

One evening, having bidden my god-daughter good-night, I had started on my usual walk to my lodgings in Rome. Five minutes after leaving the Villa gate I discovered that I had left my eye-glass – an object in constant use – behind me. I immediately remembered that, while painting, I had broken the string which fastened it round my neck, and had hooked it provisionally upon the twig of a flowering-almond tree within arm's reach. Shortly afterwards I had gathered up my things and retired, unmindful of the glass; and now, as I needed it to read the evening paper at the Caffè Greco, there was no alternative but to retrace my steps and detach it from its twig. I easily found it and lingered awhile to note the curious night-aspect of the spot I had been studying by daylight. The night was magnificent, and full-charged with the breath of the early Roman spring. The moon was rising fast and flinging her silver checkers into the heavy masses of shadow. Watching her at work, I strolled farther and suddenly came in sight of the Casino.

Just then the moon, which for a moment had been concealed, touched with a white ray a small marble figure which adorned the pediment of this rather factitious little structure. Its sudden illumination suggested that a rarer spectacle was at hand, and that the same influence must be vastly becoming to the imprisoned Juno. The door of the Casino was, as usual, locked, but the moonlight was flooding the high-placed windows so generously that my curiosity became obstinate and inventive. I dragged a garden-seat round from the portico, placed it on end, and succeeded in climbing to the top of it and bringing myself abreast of one of the windows. The casement yielded to my pressure, turned on its hinges, and showed me the fancied scene – Juno visited by Diana. The beautiful image stood bathed in the radiant flood and shining with a purity which made her most persuasively divine. If by day her mellow complexion suggested faded gold, her substance now might have passed for polished silver. The effect was almost terrible; beauty so eloquent could hardly be inanimate. This was my foremost observation. I leave you to fancy whether my next was less interesting. At some distance from the foot of the statue, just out of the light, I perceived a figure lying flat on the pavement, prostrate apparently with devotion. I can hardly tell you how it completed the impressiveness of the scene. It marked the shining image as a goddess indeed, and seemed to throw a sort of conscious pride into her stony mask. I of course immediately recognized this recumbent worshipper as the Count, and while I stood gazing, as if to help me to read the full meaning of his attitude, the moonlight travelled forward and covered his breast and face. Then I saw that his eyes were closed, and that he was either asleep or swooning. Watching him attentively, I detected his even respirations, and judged there was no reason for alarm. The moonlight blanched his face, which seemed already pale with weariness. He had come into the presence of the Juno in obedience to that extraordinary need of which the symptoms had so woefully perplexed us, and, exhausted either by compliance or resistance, he had sunk down at her feet in a stupid sleep. The bright moonshine soon aroused him, however; he muttered something and raised himself, vaguely staring. Then, recognizing his situation, he rose and stood for some time gazing fixedly at the shining statue with an expression which I fancied was not that of wholly unprotesting devotion. He uttered a string of broken words of which I was unable to catch the meaning, and then, after another pause and a long, melancholy moan, he turned slowly to the door. As rapidly and noiselessly as possible I descended from my post of vigilance and passed behind the Casino, and in a moment I heard the sound of the closing lock and of his departing footsteps.

The next day, meeting the little explorer in the grounds, I shook my finger at him with what I meant he should consider portentous gravity. But he only grinned like the malicious earth-gnome to which I had always likened him, and twisted his moustache as if my menace were a capital joke. 'If you dig any more holes here,' I said, 'you shall be thrust into the deepest of them, and have the earth packed down on top of you. We have made enough discoveries, and we want no more statues. Your Juno has almost ruined us.'

He burst out laughing. 'I expected as much,' he cried, 'I had my notions!'

'What did you expect?'

'That the Signor Conte would begin and say his prayers to her.'

'Good Heavens! Is the case so common? Why did you expect it?'

'On the contrary, the case is rare. But I've fumbled so long in the monstrous heritage of antiquity, that I have learned a multitude of secrets – learned that ancient relics may work modern miracles. There's a pagan element in all of us – I don't speak for you, *illustrissimi forestieri* – and the old gods have still their worshippers. The old spirit still throbs here and there, and the Signor Conte has his share of it. He's a good fellow, but, between ourselves, he's an impossible Christian!' And this singular personage resumed his impertinent hilarity. 'If your previsions were so distinct,' I said, 'you ought to have given me a hint of them. I should have sent your spadesmen walking!'

'Ah, but the Juno is so beautiful!'

'Her beauty be blasted! Can you tell me what has become of the Contessa's? To rival the Juno, she's turning to marble herself.'

He shrugged his shoulders. 'Ah, but the Juno is worth fifty thousand *scudi*!'

'I'd give a hundred thousand,' I said, 'to have her annihilated. Perhaps, after all, I shall want you to dig another hole.'

'At your service!' he answered, with a flourish; and we separated.

A couple of days later I dined, as I often did, with my host and hostess, and met the Count face to face for the first time since his prostration in the Casino. He bore the traces of it, and sat plunged in sombre distraction. I fancied that the path of the old faith was not strewn with flowers, and that the Juno was becoming daily a harder mistress to serve. Dinner was scarcely over before he rose from table and took up his hat. As he did so, passing near his wife, he faltered a moment, stopped and gave her – for the first time, I imagine – that vaguely imploring look which I had often caught. She moved her lips in inarticulate sympathy and put out her hands. He drew her towards him, kissed her with a kind of angry ardour, and strode away. The occasion was propitious, and further delay unnecessary.

'What I have to tell you is very strange,' I said to the Countess, 'very fantastic, very incredible. But perhaps you'll not find it so bad as you feared. Your enemy is the Juno. The Count – how shall I say it? – the Count takes her *au sérieux*.' She was silent; but after a moment she touched my arm with her hand, and I knew she meant that I had spoken her own belief. 'You admired his antique simplicity: you see how far it goes. He has reverted to the faith of his fathers. Dormant through the ages, that imperious statue has silently aroused it. He believes in the pedigrees you used to dog's-ear your School Mythology with trying to get by heart. In a word, dear child, Camillo is a pagan.'

'I suppose you'll be terribly shocked,' she answered, 'if I say that he's welcome to any faith, if he will only share it with me. I'll believe in Jupiter, If he'll bid me! My sorrow's not for that: let my husband be himself! My sorrow is for the gulf of silence and indifference that has burst open between us. His Juno's the reality: I'm the fiction!'

'I've lately become reconciled to this gulf of silence, and to your wearing for a while a fabulous character. After the fable the moral! The poor fellow has but half succumbed: the other half protests. The modern man is shut out in the darkness with his incomparable wife. How can he have failed to feel — vaguely and grossly, if it must have been, but in every throb of his heart — that you are a more perfect experiment of nature, a riper fruit of time, than those primitive persons for whom Juno was a terror and Venus an example? He pays you the compliment of believing you an inconvertible modern. He has crossed the Acheron, but he has left you behind, as a pledge to the present. We'll bring him back to redeem it. The old ancestral ghosts ought to be propitiated when a pretty creature like you has sacrificed the roses of her life. He has proved himself one of the Valerii; we shall see to that he is the last, and yet that his decease shall leave the Conte Camillo in excellent health.'

I spoke with a confidence which I had partly felt, for it seemed to me that if the Count was to be touched it must be by the sense that his strange, spiritual excursion had not made his wife detest him. We talked long and to a hopeful end, for before I went away my god-daughter expressed the desire to go out and look at the Juno. 'I was afraid of her almost from the first,' she said, 'and have hardly seen her since she was set up in the Casino. Perhaps I can learn a lesson from her and guess the secret of her influence.'

For a moment I hesitated, with the fear that we might intrude upon the Count's devotions. Then, as something in the young girl's face suggested that she had thought of this and felt a sudden impulse to pluck victory from the heart of danger, I bravely offered her my arm. The night was cloudy, and on this occasion apparently the triumphant goddess was to depend upon her own lustre. But as we approached the Casino I saw that the door was ajar, and that there was lamplight within. The lamp was suspended in front of the image, and it showed us that the place was empty. But the Count had lately been there. Before the statue stood a roughly extemporized altar, composed of a nameless fragment of antique marble, engraved with an illegible Greek inscription. We seemed really to stand in a pagan temple, and we gazed at the serene divinity with an impulse of spiritual reverence. It ought to have been deepened, I suppose, but it was rudely checked, by our observing a curious glitter on the face of the low altar. A second glance showed us it was blood!

My companion looked at me in pale horror, and turned away with a cry. A swarm of hideous conjectures pressed into my mind, and for a moment I was sickened. But at last I remembered that there is blood and blood, and the later Latins were not the anthropophagi.

'Be sure it's very innocent,' I said, 'a lamb, a kid, or a sucking calf!' But it was enough for her nerves and her conscience that it was a crimson trickle, and she returned to the house in great agitation. The rest of the night was not passed in a way to restore her to calmness. The Count had not come in, and she sat up for him from hour to hour. I remained with her and smoked my cigar as composedly as I might; but internally I wondered what in horror's name had become of him. Gradually, as the hours wore away, I shaped a vague interpretation of those dusky portents – an interpretation none the less valid and devoutly desired for its being tolerably cheerful. The blood-drops on the altar, I mused, were the last instalment of his debt and the end of his delusion. They had been a happy necessity, for he was, after all, too gentle a creature not to hate himself for having shed them, not to abhor so cruelly insistent an idol. He had wandered away to recover himself in solitude, and he would come back to us with a repentant heart and an inquiring mind! I should certainly have believed all this more easily, however, if I could have heard his footstep in the hall. Toward dawn, as scepticism threatened to creep in with the grey light, I restlessly betook myself to the portico. Here in a few moments I saw him cross the grass, heavy-footed, splashed with mud, and evidently excessively tired. He must have been walking all night; and his face denoted that his spirit had been as restless as his body. He paused near me, and before he entered the house he stopped, looked at me a moment, and then held out his hand. I grasped it warmly, and it seemed to me to throb with all that he could not speak.

'Will you see your wife?' I asked.

He passed his hand over his eyes and shook his head. 'Not now – not yet – some time!' he answered.

I was disappointed, but I convinced her, I think, that he had cast out the devil. She felt, poor girl, a pardonable desire to celebrate the event. I returned to my lodging, spent the day in Rome, and came back to the Villa toward dusk. I was told that the Countess was in the grounds. I looked for her cautiously at first, for I thought it just possible I might interrupt the natural consequences of a reconciliation; but failing to meet her, I turned toward the Casino, and found myself face to face with the little explorer.

'Does your excellency happen to have twenty yards of stout rope about him?' he asked, gravely.

'Do you want to hang yourself for the trouble you've stood sponsor to?' I answered.

'It's a hanging matter, I promise you. The Countess has given orders. You'll find her in the Casino. Sweet-voiced as she is, she knows how to make her orders understood.'

At the door of the Casino stood half a dozen of the labourers on the place, looking vaguely solemn, like outlying dependants at a superior funeral. The Countess was within, in a position which was an answer to the surveyor's riddle. She stood with her eyes fixed on the Juno, who had been removed from her pedestal and lay stretched in her magnificent length upon a rude litter.

'Do you understand?' she said. 'She's beautiful, she's noble, she's precious, but she must go back!' And, with a passionate gesture, she seemed to indicate an open grave.

I was hugely delighted, but I thought it discreet to stroke my chin and look sober. 'She's worth fifty thousand *scudi.*'

She shook her head sadly. 'If we were to sell her to the Pope and give the money to the poor, it wouldn't profit us. She must go back – she must go back! We must smother her beauty in the dreadful earth. It makes me feel almost as if she were alive; but it came to me last night with overwhelming force, when my husband came in and refused to see me, that he'll not be himself as long as she is above ground. To cut the knot we must bury her! If I had only thought of it before!'

Not before!' I said, shaking my head in turn, 'Heaven reward our sacrifice now!'

The little surveyor, when he reappeared, seemed hardly like an agent of the celestial influences, but he was deft and active, which was more to the point. Every now and then he uttered some half-articulate lament, by way of protest against the Countess's cruelty; but I saw him privately scanning the recumbent image with an eye which seemed to foresee a malicious glee in standing on a certain unmarked spot on the turf and grinning till people stared. He had brought back an abundance of rope, and having summoned his assistants, who vigorously lifted the litter, he led the way to the original excavation, which had been left unclosed with the project of further researches. By the time we reached the edge of the grave the evening had fallen and the beauty of our marble victim was shrouded in a dusky veil. No one spoke – if not exactly for shame, at least for regret. Whatever our plea, our performance looked, at least, monstrously profane. The ropes were adjusted and the Juno was slowly lowered into her earthy bed. The Countess took a handful of earth and dropped it solemnly on her breast. 'May it lie lightly, but for ever!' she said.

'Amen!' cried the little surveyor with a strange, mocking inflection; and he gave us a bow, as he departed, which betrayed an agreeable consciousness of knowing where fifty thousand *scudi* were buried. His underlings had another cask of wine, the result of which, for them, was a suspension of all consciousness, and a subsequent irreparable confusion of memory as to where they had plied their spades.

The Countess had not yet seen her husband, who had again apparently betaken himself to communion with the great god Pan. I was of course unwilling to leave her to encounter alone the results of her momentous deed. She wandered into the drawing-room and pretended to occupy herself with a bit of embroidery, but in reality she was bravely composing herself for an 'explanation'. I took up a book, but it held my attention as feebly. As the evening wore away I heard a movement on the threshold and saw the Count lifting the tapestried curtain which masked the door, and looking silently at his wife. His eyes were brilliant, but not angry. He had missed the Juno – and rejoiced! The Countess kept her eyes fixed on her work, and drew her silken stitches like an image of wifely contentment. The image seemed to fascinate him: he came in slowly, almost on tiptoe, walked to the chimney-piece, and stood there in a sort of rapt contemplation. What had passed, what was passing, in his mind, I leave to your own apprehension. My god-daughter's hand trembled as it rose and fell, and the colour came into her cheek. At last she raised her eyes and sustained the gaze in which all his returning faith seemed concentrated. He hesitated a moment, as if her very forgiveness kept the gulf open between them, and then he strode forward, fell on his two knees and buried his head in her lap. I departed as the Count had come in, on tiptoe.

He never became, if you will, a thoroughly modern man; but one day, years after, when a visitor to whom he was showing his cabinet became inquisitive as to a marble hand, suspended in one of its inner recesses, he looked grave and turned the lock on it. 'It is the hand of a beautiful creature,' he said, 'whom I once greatly admired.'

'Ah – a Roman?' said the gentleman, with a smirk.

'A Greek,' said the Count, with a frown.

Madame de Mauves

I

THE VIEW FROM the terrace at Saint-Germain-en-Laye is immense and famous. Paris lies spread before you in dusky vastness, domed and fortified, glittering here and there through her light vapours, and girdled with her silver Seine. Behind you is a park of stately symmetry, and behind that a forest, where you may lounge through turfy avenues and light-chequered glades, and quite forget that you are within half an hour of the boulevards. One afternoon, however, in mid-spring, some five years ago, a young man seated on the terrace had chosen not to forget this. His eyes were fixed in idle wistfulness on the mighty human hive before him. He was fond of rural things, and he had come to Saint-Germain a week before to meet the spring half-way; but though he could boast of a six months' acquaintance with the great city, he never looked at it from his present stand-point without a feeling of painfully unsatisfied curiosity. There were moments when it seemed to him that not to be there just then was to miss some thrilling chapter of experience. And yet his winter's experience had been rather fruitless, and he had closed the book almost with a yawn. Though not in the least a cynic, he was what one may call a disappointed observer; and he never chose the right-hand road without beginning to suspect after an hour's wayfaring that the left would have been the interesting one. He now had a dozen minds to go to Paris for the evening, to dine at the Café Brébant, and to repair afterwards to the Gymnase and listen to the latest exposition of the duties of the injured husband. He would probably have risen to execute this project, if he had not observed a little girl who, wandering along the terrace, had suddenly stopped short and begun to gaze at him with round-eyed frankness. For a moment he was simply amused, for the child's face denoted helpless wonderment; the next he was agreeably surprised. 'Why, this is my friend Maggie,' he said; 'I see you have not forgotten me.'

Maggie, after a short parley, was induced to seal her remembrance with a kiss. Invited then to explain her appearance at Saint-Germain, she embarked on a recital in which the general, according to the infantine method, was so fatally sacrificed to the particular, that Longmore looked about him for a superior source of information. He found it in Maggie's mamma, who was seated with another lady at the opposite end of the terrace; so, taking the child by the hand, he led her back to her companions.

Maggie's mamma was a young American lady, as you would immediately have perceived, with a pretty and friendly face and an expensive spring toilet. She greeted Longmore with surprised cordiality, mentioned his name to her friend, and bade him bring a chair and sit with them. The other lady, who, though equally young and perhaps even prettier, was dressed more soberly, remained silent, stroking the hair of the little girl, whom she had drawn against her knee. She had never heard of Longmore, but she now perceived that her companion had crossed the ocean with him, had met him afterwards in travelling, and (having left her husband in Wall Street) was indebted to him for various small services.

Maggie's mamma turned from time to time and smiled at her friend with an air of invitation; the latter smiled back, and continued gracefully to say nothing.

For ten minutes Longmore felt a revival of interest in his inter-locutress; then (as riddles are more amusing than commonplaces) it gave way to curiosity about her friend. His eyes wandered; her volubility was less suggestive than the latter's silence.

The stranger was perhaps not obviously a beauty nor obvi-ously an American, but essentially both, on a closer scrutiny. She was slight and fair, and, though naturally pale, delicately flushed, apparently with recent excitement. What chiefly struck Longmore in her face was the union of a pair of beautifully gentle, almost languid grey eyes, with a mouth peculiarly expressive and firm. Her forehead was a trifle more expansive than belongs to classic types, and her thick brown hair was dressed out of the fashion, which was just then very ugly. Her throat and bust were slender, but all the more in harmony with certain rapid, charming movements of the head, which she had a way of throwing back every now and then, with an air of attention and a sidelong glance from her dove-like eyes. She seemed at once alert and indifferent, contemplative and restless; and Longmore very soon discovered that if she was not a brilliant beauty, she was at least an extremely interesting one. This very impression made him magnanimous. He perceived that he had interrupted a confidential conversation, and he judged it discreet to withdraw, having first learned from Maggie's mamma – Mrs Draper – that she was to take the six o'clock train back to Paris. He promised to meet her at the station.

He kept his appointment, and Mrs Draper arrived betimes, accompanied by her friend. The latter, however, made her farewells at the door and drove away again, giving Longmore time only to raise his hat. 'Who is she?' he asked with visible ardour, as he brought Mrs Draper her tickets.

'Come and see me tomorrow at the Hôtel de l'Empire,' she answered, 'and I will tell you all about her.' The force of this offer in making him punctual at the Hôtel de l'Empire Longmore doubtless never exactly measured; and it was perhaps well that he did not, for he found his friend, who was on the point of leaving Paris, so distracted by procrastinating milliners and perjured *lingères* that she had no wits left for disinterested narrative. 'You must find Saint-Germain dreadfully dull,' she said, as he was going. 'Why won't you come with me to London?'

'Introduce me to Madame de Mauves,' he answered, 'and Saint-Germain will satisfy me.' All he had learned was the lady's name and residence.

'Ah! she, poor woman, will not make Saint-Germain cheerful for you. She's very unhappy.'

Longmore's further inquiries were arrested by the arrival of a young lady with a bandbox; but he went away with the promise of a note of introduction, to be immediately despatched to him at Saint-Germain.

He waited a week, but the note never came; and he declared that it was not for Mrs Draper to complain of her milliner's treachery. He lounged on the terrace and walked in the forest, studied suburban street life, and made a languid attempt to investigate the records of the court of the exiled Stuarts; but he spent most of his time in wondering where Madame de Mauves lived, and whether she never walked on the terrace. Sometimes, he finally discovered; for one afternoon toward dusk he perceived her leaning against the parapet, alone. In his momentary hesitation to approach her, it seemed to him that there was almost a shade of trepidation; but his curiosity was not diminished by the consciousness of this result of a quarter of an hour's acquaintance. She immediately recognized him on his drawing near, with the manner of a person unaccustomed to encounter a confusing variety of faces. Her dress, her expression, were the same as before; her charm was there, like that of sweet music on a second hearing. She soon made conversation easy by asking him for news of Mrs Draper. Longmore told her that he was daily expecting news, and, after a pause, mentioned the promised note of introduction.

'It seems less necessary now,' he said – 'for me, at least. But for you – I should have liked you to know the flattering things Mrs Draper would probably have said about me.'

'If it arrives at last,' she answered, 'you must come and see me and bring it. If it doesn't, you must come without it.'

Then, as she continued to linger in spite of the thickening twilight, she explained that she was waiting for her husband, who was to arrive in the train from Paris, and who often passed along the terrace on his way home. Longmore well remembered that Mrs Draper had pronounced her unhappy, and he found it convenient to suppose that this same husband made her so. Edified by his six months in Paris – 'What else is possible,' he asked himself, 'for a sweet American girl who marries an unclean Frenchman?'

But this tender expectancy of her lord's return undermined his hypothesis, and it received a further check from the gentle eagerness with which she turned and greeted an approaching figure. Longmore beheld in the fading light a stoutish gentleman, on the fair side of forty, in a high light hat, whose countenance, indistinct against the sky, was adorned by a fantastically pointed moustache. M. de Mauves saluted his wife with punctilious gallantry, and having bowed to Longmore, asked her several questions in French. Before taking his proffered arm to walk to their carriage, which was in waiting at the terrace gate, she introduced our hero as a friend of Mrs Draper, and a fellow-countryman, whom she hoped to see at home. M. de Mauves responded briefly, but civilly, in very fair English, and led his wife away.

Longmore watched him as he went, twisting his picturesque moustache, with a feeling of irritation which he certainly would have been at a loss to account for. The only conceivable cause was the light which M. de Mauves's good English cast upon his own bad French. For reasons involved apparently in the very structure of his being, Longmore found himself unable to speak the language tolerably. He admired and enjoyed it, but the very genius of awkwardness controlled his phraseology. But he reflected with satisfaction that Madame de Mauves and he had a common idiom, and his vexation was effectually dispelled by his finding on his table that evening a letter from Mrs Draper. It enclosed a short, formal missive to Madame de Mauves, but the epistle itself was copious and confidential. She had deferred writing till she reached London, where for a week, of course, she had found other amusements.

'I think it is these distracting Englishwomen,' she wrote, 'with their green barege gowns and their white-stitched boots, who have reminded me in self-defence of my graceful friend at Saint-Germain and my promise to introduce you to her. I believe I told you that she was unhappy, and I wondered afterwards whether I had not been guilty of a breach of confidence. But you would have found it out for yourself, and besides, she told me no secrets. She declared she was the happiest creature in the world, and then, poor thing, she burst into tears, and I prayed to be delivered from such happiness. It's the miserable story of an American girl, born to be neither a slave nor a toy, marrying a profligate Frenchman, who believes that a woman must be one or the other. The silliest American woman is too good for the best foreigner, and the poorest of us have moral needs a Frenchman can't appreciate. She was romantic and wilful, and thought Americans were vulgar. Matrimonial felicity perhaps is vulgar; but I think nowadays she wishes she were a little less elegant. M. de Mauves cared, of course, for nothing but her money, which he's spending royally on his *menus plaisirs*. I hope you appreciate the compliment I pay you when I recommend you to go and console an unhappy wife. I have never given a man such a proof of esteem, and if you were to disappoint me I should renounce the world. Prove to Madame de Mauves that an American friend may mingle admiration and respect better than a French husband. She avoids society and lives quite alone, seeing no one but a horrible French sister-in-law. Do let me hear that you have drawn some of the sadness from that desperate smile of hers. Make her smile with a good conscience.'

These zealous admonitions left Longmore slightly disturbed. He found himself on the edge of a domestic tragedy from which he instinctively recoiled. To call upon Madame de Mauves with his present knowledge seemed a sort of fishing in troubled waters. He was a modest man, and yet he asked himself whether the effect of his attentions might not be to add to her tribulation. A flattering sense of unwonted opportunity, however, made him, with the lapse of time, more confident – possibly more reckless. It seemed a very inspiring idea to draw the sadness from his fair countrywoman's smile, and at least he hoped to persuade her that there was such a thing as an agreeable American. He immediately called upon her.

II

SHE HAD BEEN placed for her education, fourteen years before, in a Parisian convent, by a widowed mamma, fonder of Homburg and Nice than of letting out tucks in the frocks of a vigorously growing daughter. Here, besides various elegant accomplishments – the art of wearing a train, of composing a bouquet, of presenting a cup of tea – she acquired a certain turn of the imagination which might have passed for a sign of precocious worldliness. She dreamed of marrying a title – not for the pleasure of hearing herself called Mme la Vicomtesse (for which it seemed to her that she should never greatly care), but because she had a romantic belief that the best birth is the guaranty of an ideal delicacy of feeling. Romances are rarely shaped in such perfect good faith, and Euphemia's excuse was in the radical purity of her imagination. She was profoundly incorruptible, and she cherished this pernicious conceit as if it had been a dogma revealed by a white-winged angel. Even after experience had given her a hundred rude hints, she found it easier to believe in fables, when they had a certain nobleness of meaning, than in well-attested but sordid facts. She believed that a gentleman with a long pedigree must be of necessity a very fine fellow, and that the consciousness of a picturesque family tradition imparts an exquisite tone to the character. *Noblesse oblige*, she thought, as regards yourself, and insures, as regards your wife. She had never spoken to a nobleman in her life, and these convictions were but a matter of transcendent theory. They were the fruit, in part, of the perusal of various ultramontane works of fiction – the only ones admitted to the convent library – in which the hero was always a legitimist vicomte who fought duels by the dozen, but went twice a month to confession; and in part of the perfumed gossip of her companions, many of them *filles de haut lieu*, who in the convent garden, after Sundays at home, depicted their brothers and cousins as Prince Charmings and young Paladins. Euphemia listened and said nothing; she shrouded her visions of matrimony under a coronet in religious mystery. She was not of that type of young lady who is easily induced to declare that her husband must be six feet high and a little near-sighted, part his hair in the middle, and have amber lights in his beard. To her companions she seemed to have a very pallid fancy; and even the fact that she was a sprig of the transatlantic democracy never sufficiently explained her apathy on social questions. She had a mental image of that son of the Crusaders who was to suffer her to adore him, but like many an artist who has produced a masterpiece of idealization, she shrank from exposing it to public criticism. It was the portrait of a gentleman rather ugly than handsome, and rather poor than rich. But his ugliness was to be nobly expressive, and his poverty delicately proud. Euphemia had a fortune of her own, which, at the proper time, after fixing on her in eloquent silence those fine eyes which were to soften the feudal severity of his visage, he was to accept with a world of stifled protestations. One condition alone she was to make – that his blood should be of the very finest strain. On this she would stake her happiness.

It so chanced that circumstances were to give convincing colour to this primitive logic.

Though little of a talker, Euphemia was an ardent listener, and there were moments when she fairly hung upon the lips of Mademoiselle Marie de Mauves. Her intimacy with this chosen schoolmate was, like most intimacies, based on their points of difference. Mademoiselle de Mauves was very positive, very shrewd, very ironical, very French – everything that Euphemia felt herself unpardonable in not being. During her Sundays *en ville* she had examined the world and judged it, and she imparted her impressions to our attentive heroine with an agreeable mixture of enthusiasm and scepticism. She was moreover a handsome and well-grown person, on whom Euphemia's ribbons and trinkets had a trick of looking better than on their slender proprietress. She had, finally, the supreme merit of being a rigorous example of the virtue of exalted birth, having, as she did, ancestors honourably mentioned by Joinville and Commines, and a stately grandmother with a hooked nose, who came up with her after the holidays from a veritable *castel* in Auvergne. It seemed to Euphemia that these attributes made her friend more at home in the world than if she had been the daughter of even the most prosperous grocer. A certain aristocratic impudence Mademoiselle de Mauves abundantly possessed, and her raids among her friend's finery were quite in the spirit of her baronial ancestors in the twelfth century – a spirit which Euphemia considered but a large way of understanding friendship – a freedom from small deference to the world's opinions which would sooner or later justify itself in acts of surprising magnanimity. Mademoiselle de Mauves perhaps enjoyed but slightly that easy attitude toward society which Euphemia envied her. She proved herself later in life such an accomplished schemer that her sense of having further heights to scale must have awakened early. Our heroine's ribbons and trinkets had much to do with the other's sisterly patronage, and her appealing pliancy of character even more; but the concluding motive of Marie's writing to her grandmamma to invite Euphemia for a three weeks' holiday to the *castel* in Auvergne, involved altogether superior considerations. Mademoiselle de Mauves was indeed at this time seventeen years of age, and presumably capable of general views; and Euphemia, who was hardly less, was a very well-grown subject for experiment, besides being pretty enough almost to pre-assure success. It is a proof of the sincerity of Euphemia's aspirations that the *castel* was not a shock to her faith. It was neither a cheerful nor a luxurious abode, but the young girl found it as delightful as a play. It had battered towers and an empty moat, a rusty draw-bridge and a court paved with crooked, grass-grown slabs, over which the antique coach-wheels of the old lady with the hooked nose seemed to awaken the echoes of the seventeenth century.

Euphemia was not frightened out of her dream; she had the pleasure of seeing it assume the consistency of a flattering presentiment. She had a taste for old servants, old anecdotes, old furniture, faded household colours, and sweetly stale odours – musty treasures in which the Château de Mauves abounded. She made a dozen sketches in water-colours, after her conventual pattern; but sentimentally, as one may say, she was forever sketching with a freer hand.

Old Madame de Mauves had nothing severe but her nose, and she seemed to Euphemia, as indeed she was, a graciously venerable relic of a historic order of things. She took a great fancy to the young American, who was ready to sit all day at her feet and listen to anecdotes of the *bon temps* and quotations from the family chronicles. Madame de Mauves was a very honest old woman, and uttered her thoughts with antique plainness. One day, after pushing back Euphemia's shining locks and blinking at her with some tenderness from under her spectacles, she declared, with an energetic shake of the head, that she didn't know what to make of her. And in answer to the young girl's startled blush – 'I should like to advise you,' she said, 'but you seem to me so all of a piece that I am afraid that if I advise you, I shall spoil you. It's easy to see that you're not one of us. I don't know whether you're better, but you seem to me to listen to the murmur of your own young spirit, rather than to the voice from behind the confessional or to the whisper of opportunity. Young girls, in my day, when they were stupid, were very docile, but when they were clever, were very sly. You're clever enough, I imagine, and yet if I guessed all your secrets at this moment, is there one I should have to frown at? I can tell you a wickeder one than any you have discovered for yourself. If you expect to live in France, and you want to be happy, don't listen too hard to that little voice I just spoke of – the voice that is neither the curé's nor the world's. You'll fancy it saying things that it won't help your case to hear. They'll make you sad, and when you're sad you'll grow plain, and when you're plain you'll grow bitter, and when you're bitter you'll be very disagreeable. I was brought up to think that a woman's first duty was to please, and the happiest women I've known have been the ones who performed this duty faithfully. As you're not a Catholic, I suppose you can't be a *dévote*; and if you don't take life as a fifty years' mass, the only way to take it is as a game of skill. Listen: not to lose, you must – I don't say cheat; but don't be too sure your neighbour won't, and don't be shocked out of your self-possession if he does. Don't lose, my dear; I beseech you, don't lose. Be neither suspicious nor credulous; but if you find your neighbour peeping, don't cry out, but very politely wait your own chance. I've had my *revanche* more than once in my day, but I'm not sure that the sweetest I could take against life as a whole would be to have your blessed innocence profit by my experience.'

This was rather awful advice, but Euphemia understood it too little to be either edified or frightened. She sat listening to it very much as she would have listened to the speeches of an old lady in a comedy, whose diction should picturesquely correspond to the pattern of her mantilla and the fashion of her headdress. Her indifference was doubly dangerous, for Madame de Mauves spoke at the prompting of coming events, and her words were the result of a somewhat troubled conscience – a conscience which told her at once that Euphemia was too tender a victim to be sacrificed to an ambition, and that the prosperity of her house was too precious a heritage to be sacrificed to a scruple. The prosperity in question had suffered repeated and grievous breaches, and the house of De Mauves had been pervaded by the cold comfort of an establishment in which people were obliged to balance dinner-table allusions to feudal ancestors against the absence of side dishes; a state of things the more regrettable as the family was now mainly represented by a gentleman whose appetite was large, and who justly maintained that its historic glories were not established by underfed heroes.

Three days after Euphemia's arrival, Richard de Mauves came down from Paris to pay his respects to his grandmother, and treated our heroine to her first encounter with a *gentilhomme* in the flesh. On coming in he kissed his grandmother's hand, with a smile which caused her to draw it away with dignity, and set Euphemia, who was standing by, wondering what had happened between them. Her unanswered wonder was but the beginning of a life of bitter perplexity, but the reader is free to know that the smile of M. de Mauves was a reply to a certain postscript affixed by the old lady to a letter promptly addressed to him by her granddaughter, after Euphemia had been admitted to justify the latter's promises. Mademoiselle de Mauves brought her letter to her grandmother for approval, but obtained no more than was expressed in a frigid nod. The old lady watched her with a sombre glance as she proceeded to seal the letter, and suddenly bade her open it again and bring her a pen.

'Your sister's flatteries are all nonsense,' she wrote; 'the young lady is far too good for you, *mauvais sujet*. If you have a conscience you'll not come and take possession of an angel of innocence.'

The young girl, who had read these lines, made up a little face as she redirected the letter; but she laid down her pen with a confident nod, which might have seemed to mean that, to the best of her belief, her brother had not a conscience.

'If you meant what you said,' the young man whispered to his grandmother on the first opportunity, 'it would have been simpler not to let her send the letter!'

It was perhaps because she was wounded by this cynical insinuation, that Madame de Mauves remained in her own apartment during a greater part of Euphemia's stay, so that the latter's angelic innocence was left entirely to the Baron's mercy. It suffered no worse mischance, however, than to be prompted to intenser communion with itself. M. de Mauves was the hero of the young girl's romance made real, and so completely accordant with this creature of her imagination, that she felt afraid of him, very much as she would have been of a supernatural apparition. He was thirty-five years old – young enough to suggest possibilities of ardent activity, and old enough to have formed opinions which a simple woman might deem it an intellectual privilege to listen to. He was perhaps a trifle handsomer than Euphemia's rather grim, Quixotic ideal, but a very few days reconciled her to his good looks, as they would have reconciled her to his ugliness. He was quiet, grave, and eminently distinguished. He spoke little, but his speeches, without being sententious, had a certain nobleness of tone which caused them to re-echo in the young girl's ears at the end of the day. He paid her very little direct attention, but his chance words — if he only asked her if she objected to his cigarette — were accompanied by a smile of extraordinary kindness.

It happened that shortly after his arrival, riding an unruly horse, which Euphemia with shy admiration had watched him mount in the castle yard, he was thrown with a violence which, without disparaging his skill, made him for a fortnight an interesting invalid, lounging in the library with a bandaged knee. To beguile his confinement, Euphemia was repeatedly induced to sing to him, which she did with a little natural tremor in her voice, which might have passed for an exquisite refinement of art. He never overwhelmed her with compliments, but he listened with unwandering attention, remembered all her melodies, and sat humming them to himself. While his imprisonment lasted, indeed, he passed hours in her company, and made her feel not unlike some unfriended artist who has suddenly gained the opportunity to devote a fortnight to the study of a great model. Euphemia studied with noiseless diligence what she supposed to be the 'character' of M. de Mauves, and the more she looked the more fine lights and shades she seemed to behold in this masterpiece of nature. M. de Mauves's character indeed, whether from a sense of being generously scrutinized, or for reasons which bid graceful defiance to analysis, had never been so amiable; it seemed really to reflect the purity of Euphemia's interpretation of it. There had been nothing especially to admire in the state of mind in which he left Paris – a hard determination to marry a young girl whose charms might or might not justify his sister's account of them, but who was mistress, at the worst, of a couple of hundred thousand francs a year. He had not counted out sentiment; if she pleased him, so much the better; but he had left a meagre margin for it, and he would hardly have admitted that so excellent a match could be improved by it. He was a placid sceptic, and it was a singular fate for a man who believed in nothing to be so tenderly believed in. What his original faith had been he could hardly have told you; for as he came back to his childhood's home to mend his fortunes by pretending to fall in love, he was a thoroughly perverted creature, and overlaid with more corruptions than a summer day's questioning of his conscience would have released him from. Ten years' pursuit of pleasure, which a bureau full of unpaid bills was all he had to show for, had pretty well stifled the natural lad, whose violent will and generous temper might have been shaped by other circumstances to a result which a romantic imagination might fairly accept as a late-blooming flower of hereditary honour. The Baron's violence had been subdued, and he had learned to be irreproachably polite; but he had lost the edge of his generosity, and his politeness, which in the long run society paid for, was hardly more than a form of luxurious egotism, like his fondness for cambric handkerchiefs, lavender gloves, and other fopperies by which shopkeepers remained out of pocket. In after years he was terribly polite to his wife. He had formed himself, as the phrase was, and the form prescribed to him by the society into which his birth and his tastes introduced him was marked by some peculiar features. That which mainly concerns us is its classification of the fairer half of humanity as objects not essentially different – say from the light gloves one soils in an evening and throws away. To do M. de Mauves justice, he had in the course of time encountered such plentiful evidence of this pliant, glove-like quality in the feminine character, that idealism naturally seemed to him a losing game.

Euphemia, as he lay on his sofa, seemed by no means a refutation; she simply reminded him that very young women, are generally innocent, and that this, on the whole, was the most charming stage of their development. Her innocence inspired him with profound respect, and it seemed to him that if he shortly became her husband it would be exposed to a danger the less. Old Madame de Mauves, who flattered herself that in this whole matter she was being laudably rigid, might have learned a lesson from his gallant consideration. For a fortnight the Baron was almost a blushing boy again. He watched from behind the *Figaro*, and admired, and held his tongue. He was not in the least disposed toward a flirtation; he had no desire to trouble the waters he proposed to transfuse into the golden cup of matrimony. Sometimes a word, a look, a movement of

Euphemia's, gave him the oddest sense of being, or of seeming at least, almost bashful; for she had a way of not dropping her eyes, according to the mysterious virginal mechanism, of not fluttering out of the room when she found him there alone, of treating him rather as a benignant than as a pernicious influence — a radiant frankness of demeanour, in fine, in spite of an evident natural reserve, which it seemed equally graceless not to make the subject of a compliment and indelicate not to take for granted. In this way there was wrought in the Baron's mind a vague, unwonted resonance of soft impressions, as we may call it, which indicated the transmutation of 'sentiment' from a contingency into a fact. His imagination enjoyed it; he was very fond of music, and this reminded him of some of the best he had ever heard. In spite of the bore of being laid up with a lame knee, he was in a better humour than he had known for months; he lay smoking cigarettes and listening to the nightingales, with the comfortable smile of one of his country neighbours whose big ox should have taken the prize at a fair. Every now and then, with an impatient suspicion of the resemblance, he declared that he was pitifully *bête*; but he was under a charm which braved even the supreme penalty of seeming ridiculous. One morning he had half an hour's *tête-à-tête* with his grandmother's confessor, a soft-voiced old abbé, whom, for reasons of her own, Madame de Mauves had suddenly summoned, and had left waiting in the drawing-room while she rearranged her curls. His reverence, going up to the old lady, assured her that M. le Baron was in a most edifying state of mind, and a promising subject for the operation of grace. This was a pious interpretation of the Baron's momentary good-humour. He had always lazily wondered what priests were good for, and he now remembered, with a sense of especial obligation to the abbé, that they were excellent for marrying people.

A day or two after this he left off his bandages, and tried to walk. He made his way into the garden and hobbled successfully along one of the alleys; but in the midst of his progress he was seized with a spasm of pain which forced him to stop and call for help. In an instant Euphemia came tripping along the path and offered him her arm with the frankest solicitude.

'Not to the house,' he said, taking it; 'farther on, to the bosquet.' This choice was prompted by her having immediately confessed that she had seen him leave the house, had feared an accident, and had followed him on tiptoe.

'Why didn't you join me?' he had asked, giving her a look in which admiration was no longer disguised, and yet felt itself half at the mercy of her replying that a *jeune fille* should not be seen following a gentleman. But it drew a breath which filled its lungs for a long time afterward, when she replied simply that if she had overtaken him he might have accepted her arm out of politeness, whereas she wished to have the pleasure of seeing him walk alone.

The bosquet was covered with an odorous tangle of blossoming vines, and a nightingale overhead was shaking out love-notes with a profuseness which made the Baron consider his own conduct the perfection of propriety.

'In America,' he said, 'I have always heard that when a man wishes to marry a young girl, he offers himself simply, face to face, without any ceremony – without parents, and uncles, and cousins sitting round in a circle.'

'Why, I believe so,' said Euphemia, staring, and too surprised to be alarmed.

'Very well, then,' said the Baron, 'suppose our bosquet here to be America. I offer you my hand, *à l'Américaine*. It will make me intensely happy to have you accept it.'

Whether Euphemia's acceptance was in the American manner is more than I can say; I incline to think that for fluttering, grateful, trustful, softly amazed young hearts, there is only one manner all over the world.

That evening, in the little turret chamber which it was her happiness to inhabit, she wrote a dutiful letter to her mamma, and had just sealed it when she was sent for by Madame de Mauves. She found this ancient lady seated in her boudoir, in a lavender satin gown, with all her candles lighted, as if to celebrate her grandson's betrothal. 'Are you very happy?' Madame de Mauves demanded, making Euphemia sit down before her.

'I'm almost afraid to say so,' said the young girl, 'lest I should wake myself up.'

'May you never wake up, *belle enfant*,' said the old lady, solemnly. 'This is the first marriage ever made in our family in this way – by a Baron de Mauves proposing to a young girl in an arbour, like Jeannot and Jeannette. It has not been our way of doing things, and people may say it wants frankness. My grandson tells me he considers it the perfection of frankness. Very good. I'm a very old woman, and if your differences should ever be as frank as your agreement, I shouldn't like to see them. But I should be sorry to die and think you were going to be unhappy. You can't be, beyond a certain point; because, though in this world the Lord sometimes makes light of our expectations, he never altogether ignores our deserts. But you're very young and innocent, and easy to deceive. There never was a man in the world – among the saints themselves – as good as you believe the Baron. But he's a *galant homme* and a gentleman, and I've been talking to him tonight. To you I want to say this – that you're to forget the worldly rubbish I talked the other day about frivolous women being happy. It's not the kind of happiness that would suit you. Whatever befalls you, promise me this: to be yourself. The Baronne de Mauves will be none the worse for it. Yourself, understand, in spite of everything – bad precepts and bad examples, bad usage even. Be persistently and patiently yourself, and a De Mauves will do you justice!'

Euphemia remembered this speech in after years, and more than once, wearily closing her eyes, she seemed to see the old woman sitting upright in her faded finery and smiling grimly, like one of the Fates who sees the wheel of fortune turning up her favourite event. But at the moment it seemed to her simply to have the proper gravity of the occasion; this was the way, she supposed, in which lucky young girls were addressed on their engagement by wise old women of quality.

At her convent, to which she immediately returned, she found a letter from her mother, which shocked her far more than the remarks of Madame de Mauves. Who were these people, Mrs Cleve demanded, who had presumed to talk to her daughter of marriage without asking her leave? Questionable gentlefolk, plainly; the best French people never did such things. Euphemia would return straightway to her convent, shut herself up, and await her own arrival.

It took Mrs Cleve three weeks to travel from Nice to Paris, and during this time the young girl had no communication with her lover beyond accepting a bouquet of violets, marked with his initials and left by a female friend. 'I've not brought you up with such devoted care,' she declared to her daughter at their first interview, 'to marry a penniless Frenchman. I will take you straight home, and you will please to forget M. de Mauves.'

Mrs Cleve received that evening at her hotel a visit from the Baron which mitigated her wrath, but failed to modify her decision. He had very good manners, but she was sure he had horrible morals; and Mrs Cleve, who had been a very good-natured censor on her own account, felt a genuine spiritual need to sacrifice her daughter to propriety. She belonged to that large class of Americans who make light of America in familiar discourse, but are startled back into a sense of moral responsibility when they find Europeans taking them at their word. 'I know the type, my dear,' she said to her daughter with a sagacious nod. 'He'll not beat you; sometimes you'll wish he would.'

Euphemia remained solemnly silent; for the only answer she felt capable of making her mother was that her mind was too small a measure of things, and that the Baron's 'type' was one which it took some mystical illumination to appreciate. A person who confounded him with the common throng of her watering-place acquaintance was not a person to argue with. It seemed to Euphemia that she had no cause to plead; her cause was in the Lord's hands and her lover's.

M. de Mauves had been irritated and mortified by Mrs Cleve's opposition, and hardly knew how to handle an adversary who failed to perceive that a De Mauves of necessity gave more than he received. But he had obtained information on his return to Paris which exalted the uses of humility. Euphemia's fortune, wonderful to say, was greater than its fame, and in view of such a prize, even a De Mauves could afford to take a snubbing.

The young man's tact, his deference, his urbane insistence, won a concession from Mrs Cleve. The engagement was to be suspended and her daughter was to return home, be brought out and receive the homage she was entitled to, and which would but too surely take a form dangerous to the Baron's suit. They were to exchange neither letters, nor mementos, nor messages; but if at the end of two years Euphemia had refused offers enough to attest the permanence of her attachment, he should receive an invitation to address her again.

This decision was promulgated in the presence of the parties interested. The Baron bore himself gallantly, and looked at the young girl, expecting some tender protestation. But she only looked at him silently in return, neither weeping, nor smiling, nor putting out her hand. On this they separated; but as the Baron walked away, he declared to himself that, in spite of the confounded two years, he was a very happy fellow – to have a fiancée who, to several millions of francs, added such strangely beautiful eyes.

How many offers Euphemia refused but scantily concerns us – and how the Baron wore his two years away. He found that he needed pastimes, and, as pastimes were expensive, he added heavily to the list of debts to be cancelled by Euphemia's millions. Sometimes, in the thick of what he had once called pleasure with a keener conviction than now, he put to himself the case of their failing him after all; and then he remembered that last mute assurance of her eyes, and drew a long breath of such confidence as he felt in nothing else in the world save his own punctuality in an affair of honour.

At last, one morning, he took the express to Havre with a letter of Mrs Cleve's in his pocket, and ten days later made his bow to mother and daughter in New York. His stay was brief, and he was apparently unable to bring himself to view what Euphemia's uncle, Mr Butterworth, who gave her away at the altar, called our great experiment in democratic self-government in a serious light. He smiled at everything, and seemed to regard the New World as a colossal *plaisanterie*. It is true that a perpetual smile was the most natural expression of countenance for a man about to marry Euphemia Cleve.

III

LONGMORE'S FIRST VISIT seemed to open to him so large an opportunity for tranquil enjoyment, that he very soon paid a second, and, at the end of a fortnight, had spent a great many hours in the little drawing-room which Madame de Mauves rarely quitted except to drive or walk in the forest. She lived in an old-fashioned pavilion, between a high-walled court and an excessively artificial garden, beyond whose enclosure you saw a long line of tree-tops. Longmore liked the garden, and in the mild afternoons used to move his chair through the open window to the little terrace which overlooked it, while his hostess sat just within. After a while she came out and wandered through the narrow alleys and beside the thin-spouting fountain, and last introduced him to a little gate in the garden-wall, opening upon a lane which led into the forest. Hitherward, more than once, she wandered with him, bareheaded and meaning to go but twenty rods, but always strolling good-naturedly farther, and often taking a generous walk. They discovered a vast deal to talk about, and to the pleasure of finding the hours tread inaudibly away, Longmore was able to add the satisfaction of suspecting that he was a 'resource' for Madame de Mauves. He had made her acquaintance with the sense, not altogether comfortable, that she was a woman with a painful secret, and that seeking her acquaintance would be like visiting at a house where there was an invalid who could bear no noise. But he very soon perceived that her sorrow, since sorrow it was, was not an aggressive one; that it was not fond of attitudes and ceremonies, and that her earnest wish was to forget it. He felt that even if Mrs Draper had not told him she was unhappy, he would have guessed it; and yet he could hardly have pointed to his evidence. It was chiefly negative – she never alluded to her husband. Beyond this it seemed to him simply that her whole being was pitched on a lower key than harmonious Nature meant; she was like a powerful singer who had lost her high notes. She never drooped nor sighed nor looked unutterable things; she indulged in no dusky sarcasms against fate; she had, in short, none of the coquetry of unhappiness. But Longmore was sure that her gentle gaiety was the result of strenuous effort, and that she was trying to interest herself in his thoughts to escape from her own. If she had wished to irritate his curiosity and lead him to take her confidence by storm, nothing could have served her purpose better than this ingenuous reserve. He declared to himself that there was a rare magnanimity in such ardent self-effacement, and that but one woman in ten thousand was capable of merging an intensely personal grief in thankless outward contemplation. Madame de Mauves, he instinctively felt, was not sweeping the horizon for a compensation or a consoler; she had suffered a personal deception which had disgusted her with persons. She was not striving to balance her sorrow with some strongly flavoured joy; for the present, she was trying to live with it, peaceably, reputably, and without scandal – turning the key on it occasionally, as you would on a companion liable to attacks of insanity. Longmore was a man of fine senses and of an active imagination, whose leading-strings had never been slipped. He began to regard his hostess as a figure haunted by a shadow which was somehow her intenser, more authentic self. This hovering mystery came to have for him an extraordinary charm. Her delicate beauty acquired to his eye the serious cast of certain blank-browed Greek statues, and sometimes, when his imagination, more than his ear, detected a vague tremor in the tone in which she attempted to make a friendly question seem to have behind it none of the hollow resonance of absent-mindedness, his marvelling eyes gave her an answer more eloquent, though much less to the point, than the one she demanded.

She gave him indeed much to wonder about, and, in his ignorance, he formed a dozen experimental theories upon the history of her marriage. She had married for love and staked her whole soul on it; of that he was convinced. She had not married a Frenchman to be near Paris and her base of supplies of millinery; he was sure she had seen conjugal happiness in a light of which her present life, with its conveniences for shopping and its moral aridity, was the absolute negation. But by what extraordinary process of the heart – through what mysterious intermission of that moral instinct which may keep pace with the heart, even when that organ is making unprecedented time – had she fixed her affections on an arrogantly frivolous Frenchman? Longmore needed no telling; he knew M. de Mauves was frivolous; it was stamped on his eyes, his nose, his mouth, his carriage. For French women Longmore had but a scanty kindness, or at least (what with him was very much the same thing) but a scanty gallantry; they all seemed to belong to the type of a certain fine lady to whom he had ventured to present a letter of introduction, and whom, directly after his first visit to her, he had set down in his note-book as 'metallic'. Why should Madame de Mauves have chosen a French woman's lot – she whose character had a perfume which doesn't belong to even the brightest metals? He asked her one day frankly if it had cost her nothing to transplant herself – if she was not oppressed with a sense of irreconcilable difference from 'all these people'. She was silent awhile, and he fancied that she was hesitating as to whether she should resent so unceremonious an allusion to her husband. He almost wished she would; it would seem a proof that her deep reserve of sorrow had a limit.

'I almost grew up here,' she said at last, 'and it was here for me that those dreams of the future took shape that we all have when we cease to be very young. As matters stand, one may be very American and yet arrange it with one's conscience to live in Europe. My imagination perhaps – I had a little when I was younger – helped me to think I should find happiness here. And after all, for a woman, what does it signify? This is not America, perhaps, about me, but it's quite as little France. France is out there, beyond the garden, in the town, in the forest; but here, close about me, in my room and –' she paused a moment – 'in my mind, it's a nameless country of my own. It's not her country,' she added, 'that makes a woman happy or unhappy.'

Madame Clairin, Euphemia's sister-in-law, might have been supposed to have undertaken the graceful task of making

Longmore ashamed of his uncivil jottings about her sex and nation. Mademoiselle de Mauves, bringing example to the confirmation of precept, had made a remunerative match and sacrificed her name to the millions of a prosperous and aspiring wholesale druggist – a gentleman liberal enough to consider his fortune a moderate price for being towed into circles unpervaded by pharmaceutic odours. His system, possibly, was sound, but his own application of it was unfortunate. M. Clairin's head was turned by his good luck. Having secured an aristocratic wife, he adopted an aristocratic vice and began to gamble at the Bourse. In an evil hour he lost heavily and staked heavily to recover himself. But he overtook his loss only by a greater one. Then he let everything go – his wits, his courage, his probity – everything that had made him what his ridiculous marriage had so promptly unmade. He walked up the Rue Vivienne one day with his hands in his empty pockets, and stood for half an hour staring confusedly up and down the glittering boulevard. People brushed against him, and half a dozen carriages almost ran over him, until at last a policeman, who had been watching him for some time, took him by the arm and led him gently away. He looked at the man's cocked hat and sword with tears in his eyes; he hoped he was going to interpret to him the wrath of Heaven – to execute the penalty of his dead-weight of self-abhorrence. But the *sergent de ville* only stationed him in the embrasure of a door, out of harm's way, and walked away to supervise a financial contest between an old lady and a cabman. Poor M. Clairin had only been married a year, but he had had time to measure the lofty spirit of a De Mauves. When night had fallen, he repaired to the house of a friend and asked for a night's lodging; and as his friend, who was simply his old head book-keeper and lived in a small way, was put to some trouble to accommodate him — 'You must excuse me,' Clairin said, 'but I can't go home. I'm afraid of my wife!' Toward morning he blew his brains out. His widow turned the remnants of his property to better account than could have been expected, and wore the very handsomest mourning. It was for this latter reason, perhaps, that she was obliged to retrench at other points and accept a temporary home under her brother's roof.

Fortune had played Madame Clairin a terrible trick, but had found an adversary and not a victim. Though quite without beauty, she had always had what is called the grand air, and her air from this time forward was grander than ever. As she trailed about in her sable furbelows, tossing back her well-dressed head, and holding up her vigilant eye-glass, she seemed to be sweeping the whole field of society and asking herself where she should pluck her revenge. Suddenly she espied it, ready made to her hand, in poor Longmore's wealth and amiability. American dollars and American complaisance had made her brother's fortune; why shouldn't they make hers? She overestimated Longmore's wealth and misinterpreted his amiability; for she was sure that a man could not be so contented without being rich, nor so unassuming without being weak. He encountered her advances with a formal politeness which covered a great deal of unflattering discomposure. She made him feel acutely uncomfortable; and though he was at a loss to conceive how he could be an object of interest to a shrewd Parisienne, he had an indefinable sense of being enclosed in a magnetic circle, like the victim of an incantation. If Madame Clairin could have fathomed his Puritanic soul, she would have laid by her wand and her book and admitted that he was an impossible subject. She gave him a kind of moral chill, and he never mentally alluded to her save as that dreadful woman – that terrible woman. He did justice to her grand air, but for his pleasure he preferred the small air of Madame de Mauves; and he never made her his bow, after standing frigidly passive for five minutes to one of her gracious overtures to intimacy, without feeling a peculiar desire to ramble away into the forest, fling himself down on the warm grass, and, staring up at the blue sky, forget that there were any women in nature who didn't please like the swaying tree-tops. One day, on his arrival, she met him in the court and told him that her sister-in-law was shut up with a headache, and that his visit must be for her. He followed her into the drawing-room with the best grace at his command, and sat twirling his hat for half an hour. Suddenly he understood her; the caressing cadence of her voice was a distinct invitation to solicit the incomparable honour of her hand. He blushed to the roots of his hair and jumped up with uncontrollable alacrity; then, dropping a glance at Madame Clairin, who sat watching him with hard eyes over the edge of her smile, as it were, perceived on her brow a flash of unforgiving wrath. It was not becoming, but his eyes lingered a moment, for it seemed to illuminate her character. What he saw there frightened him, and he felt himself murmuring, 'Poor Madame de Mauves!' His departure was abrupt, and this time he really went into the forest and lay down on the grass.

After this he admired Madame de Mauves more than ever; she seemed a brighter figure, dogged by a darker shadow. At the end of a month he received a letter from a friend with whom he had arranged a tour through the Low Countries, reminding him of his promise to meet him promptly at Brussels. It was only after his answer was posted that he fully measured the zeal with which he had declared that the journey must either be deferred or abandoned – that he could not possibly leave Saint-Germain. He took a walk in the forest, and asked himself if this was irrevocably true. If it was, surely his duty was to march straight home and pack his trunk. Poor Webster, who, he knew, had counted ardently on this excursion, was an excellent fellow; six weeks ago he would have gone through fire and water to join Webster. It had never been in his books to throw overboard a friend whom he had loved for ten years for a married woman whom for six weeks he had – admired. It was certainly beyond question that he was lingering at Saint-Germain because this admirable married woman was there; but in the midst of all this admiration what had become of prudence? This was the conduct of a man prepared to fall utterly in love. If she was as unhappy as he believed, the love of such a man would help her very little more than his indifference; if she was less so, she needed no help and could dispense with his friendly offices. He was sure, moreover, that if she knew he was staying on her account, she would be extremely annoyed. But this very feeling had much to do with making it hard to go; her displeasure would only enhance the gentle stoicism which touched him to the heart. At moments, indeed, he assured himself that to linger was simply impertinent; it was indelicate to make a daily study of such a shrinking grief. But inclination answered that some day her self-support would fail, and he had a vision of this admirable creature calling vainly for help. He would be her friend, to any length; it was unworthy of both of them to think about conse‑ quences. But he was a friend who carried about with him a muttering resentment that he had not known her five years earlier, and a brooding hostility to those who had anticipated him. It seemed one of fortune's most mocking strokes, that she should be surrounded by persons whose only merit was that they threw the charm of her character into radiant relief.

Longmore's growing irritation made it more and more diffi‑ cult for him to see any other merit than this in the Baron de Mauves. And yet, disinterestedly, it would have been hard to give a name to the portentous vices which such an estimate implied, and there were times when our hero was almost persuaded against his finer judgement that he was really the most considerate of husbands, and that his wife liked melan‑ choly for melancholy's sake. His manners were perfect, his urbanity was unbounded, and he seemed never to address her but, sentimentally speaking, hat in hand. His tone to Longmore (as the latter was perfectly aware) was that of a man of the world to a man not quite of the world; but what it lacked in deference it made up in easy friendliness. 'I can't thank you enough for having overcome my wife's shyness,' he more than once declared. 'If we left her to do as she pleased, she would bury herself alive. Come often, and bring someone else. She'll have nothing to do with my friends, but perhaps she'll accept yours.'

The Baron made these speeches with a remorseless placidity very amazing to our hero, who had an innocent belief that a man's head may point out to him the shortcomings of his heart and make him ashamed of them. He could not fancy him capable both of neglecting his wife and taking an almost humorous view of her suffering. Longmore had, at any rate, an exasperating sense that the Baron thought rather less of his wife than more, for that very same fine difference of nature which so deeply stirred his own sympathies. He was rarely present during Longmore's visits, and made a daily journey to Paris, where he had 'business', as he once mentioned – not in the least with a tone of apology. When he appeared, it was late in the evening, and with an imperturbable air of being on the best of terms with everyone and everything, which was peculiarly annoying if you happened to have a tacit quarrel with him. If he was a good fellow, he was surely a good fellow spoiled. Something he had, however, which Longmore vaguely envied – a kind of superb positiveness – a manner rounded and polished by the traditions of centuries – an amenity exercised for his own sake and not his neighbours' – which seemed the result of something better than a good conscience – of a vigorous and unscrupulous temperament. The Baron was plainly not a moral man, and poor Longmore, who was, would have been glad to learn the secret of his luxurious serenity. What was it that enabled him, without being a monster with visibly cloven feet, exhaling brimstone, to misprise so cruelly a lovely wife, and to walk about the world with a smile under his moustache? It was the essential grossness of his imagination, which had nevertheless helped him to turn so many neat compliments. He could be very polite, and he could doubtless be supremely impertinent; but he was as unable to draw a moral inference of the finer strain, as a school-boy who has been playing truant for a week to solve a problem in algebra. It was ten to one he didn't know his wife was unhappy; he and his brilliant sister had doubtless agreed to consider their companion a Puritanical little person, of meagre aspirations and slender accomplishments, contented with looking at Paris from the terrace, and, as an especial treat, having a countryman very much like herself to supply her with homely transatlantic gossip. M. de Mauves was tired of his companion: he relished a higher flavour in female society. She was too modest, too simple, too delicate; she had too few arts, too little coquetry, too much charity. M. de Mauves, some day, lighting a cigar, had probably decided she was stupid. It was the same sort of taste, Longmore moralized, as the taste for Gérôme in painting, and for M. Gustave Flaubert in literature. The Baron was a pagan and his wife was a Christian, and between them, accordingly, was a gulf. He was by race and instinct a *grand seigneur*. Longmore had often heard of this distinguished social type, and was properly grateful for an opportunity to examine it closely. It had certainly a picturesque boldness of outline, but it was fed from spiritual sources so remote from those of which he felt the living gush in his own soul, that he found himself gazing at it, in irreconcilable antipathy, across a dim historic mist. 'I'm a modern *bourgeois*,' he said, 'and not perhaps so good a judge of how far a pretty woman's tongue may go at supper without prejudice to her reputation. But I've not met one of the sweetest of women without recognizing her and discovering that a certain sort of character offers better entertainment than Thérésa's songs, sung by a dissipated duchess. Wit for wit, I think mine carries me further.' It was easy indeed to perceive that, as became a *grand seigneur*, M. de Mauves had a stock of rigid notions. He would not especially have desired, perhaps, that his wife should compete in amateur operettas with the duchesses in question, chiefly of recent origin; but he held that a gentleman may take his amusement where he finds it, that he is quite at liberty not to find it at home; and that the wife of a De Mauves who should hang her head and have red eyes, and allow herself to make any other response to officious condolence than that her husband's amusements were his own affair, would have forfeited every claim to having her finger-tips bowed over and kissed. And yet in spite of these sound principles, Longmore fancied that the Baron was more irritated than gratified by his wife's irreproachable reserve. Did it dimly occur to him that it was self-control and not self-effacement? She was a model to all the inferior matrons of his line, past and to come, and an occasional 'scene' from her at a convenient moment would have something reassuring – would attest her stupidity a trifle more forcibly than her inscrutable tranquillity.

Longmore would have given much to know the principle of her submissiveness, and he tried more than once, but with rather awkward timidity, to sound the mystery. She seemed to him to have been long resisting the force of cruel evidence, and, though she had succumbed to it at last, to have denied herself the right to complain, because if faith was gone her heroic generosity remained. He believed even that she was capable of reproaching herself with having expected too much, and of trying to persuade herself out of her bitterness by saying that her hopes had been illusions and that this was simply – life. 'I hate tragedy,' she once said to him; 'I have a really pusillanimous dread of moral suffering. I believe that – without base concessions – there is always some way of escaping from it. I had almost rather never smile all my life than have a single violent explosion of grief.' She lived evidently in nervous apprehension of being fatally convinced – of seeing to the end of her deception. Longmore, when he thought of this, felt an immense longing to offer her something of which she could be as sure as of the sun in heaven.

IV

HIS FRIEND WEBSTER lost no time in accusing him of the basest infidelity, and asking him what he found at Saint-Germain to prefer to Van Eyck and Memling, Rubens and Rembrandt. A day or two after the receipt of Webster's letter, he took a walk with Madame de Mauves in the forest. They sat down on a fallen log, and she began to arrange into a bouquet the anemones and violets she had gathered. 'I have a letter,' he said at last, 'from a friend whom I some time ago promised to join at Brussels. The time has come – it has passed. It finds me terribly unwilling to leave Saint-Germain.'

She looked up with the candid interest which she always displayed in his affairs, but with no disposition, apparently, to make a personal application of his words. 'Saint-Germain is pleasant enough,' she said; 'but are you doing yourself justice? Won't you regret in future days that instead of travelling and seeing cities and monuments and museums and improving your mind, you sat here – for instance – on a log, pulling my flowers to pieces?'

'What I shall regret in future days,' he answered after some hesitation, 'is that I should have sat here and not spoken the truth on the matter. I am fond of museums and monuments and of improving my mind, and I'm particularly fond of my friend Webster. But I can't bring myself to leave Saint-Germain without asking you a question. You must forgive me if it's unfortunate, and be assured that curiosity was never more respectful. Are you really as unhappy as I imagine you to be?'

She had evidently not expected his question, and she greeted it with a startled blush. 'If I strike you as unhappy,' she said, 'I have been a poorer friend to you than I wished to be.'

'I, perhaps, have been a better friend of yours than you have supposed. I've admired your reserve, your courage, your studied gaiety. But I have felt the existence of something beneath them that was more you – more you as I wished to know you – than they were; something that I have believed to be a constant sorrow.'

She listened with great gravity, but without an air of offence, and he felt that while he had been timorously calculating the last consequences of friendship, she had placidly accepted them. 'You surprise me,' she said slowly, and her blush still lingered. 'But to refuse to answer you would confirm an impression which is evidently already too strong. An unhappiness that one can sit comfortably talking about, is an unhappiness with distinct limitations. If I were examined before a board of commissioners for investigating the felicity of mankind, I'm sure I should be pronounced a very fortunate woman.'

There was something delightfully gentle to him in her tone, and its softness seemed to deepen as she continued: 'But let me add, with all gratitude for your sympathy, that it's my own affair altogether. It needn't disturb you, Mr Longmore, for I have often found myself in your company a very contented person.'

'You're a wonderful woman,' he said, 'and I admire you as I never have admired anyone. You're wiser than anything I, for one, can say to you; and what I ask of you is not to let me advise or console you, but simply thank you for letting me know you.' He had intended no such outburst as this, but his voice rang loud, and he felt a kind of unfamiliar joy as he uttered it.

She shook her head with some impatience. 'Let us be friends – as I supposed we were going to be – without protestations and fine words. To have you making bows to my wisdom — that would be real wretchedness. I can dispense with your admiration better than the Flemish painters can — better than Van Eyck and Rubens, in spite of all their worshippers. Go join your friend — see everything, enjoy everything, learn everything, and write me an excellent letter, brimming over with your impressions. I'm extremely fond of the Dutch painters,' she added with a slight faltering of the voice, which Longmore had noticed once before, and which he had interpreted as the sudden weariness of a spirit self-condemned to play a part.

'I don't believe you care about the Dutch painters at all,' he said with an unhesitating laugh. 'But I shall certainly write you a letter.'

She rose and turned homeward, thoughtfully rearranging her flowers as she walked. Little was said; Longmore was asking himself, with a tremor in the unspoken words, whether all this meant simply that he was in love. He looked at the rooks wheeling against the golden-hued sky, between the tree-tops, but not at his companion, whose personal presence seemed lost in the felicity she had created. Madame de Mauves was silent and grave, because she was painfully disappointed. A sentimental friendship she had not desired; her scheme had been to pass with Longmore as a placid creature with a good deal of leisure, which she was disposed to devote to profitable conversation of an impersonal sort. She liked him extremely, and felt that there was something in him to which, when she made up her girlish mind, that a needy French baron was the ripest fruit of time, she had done very scanty justice. They went through the little gate in the garden-wall and approached the house. On the terrace Madame Clairin was entertaining a friend – a little elderly gentleman with a white moustache, and an order in his button-hole. Madame de Mauves chose to pass round the house into the court; whereupon her sister-in-law, greeting Longmore with a commanding nod, lifted her eye-glass and stared at them as they went by. Longmore heard the little old gentleman uttering some old-fashioned epigram about '*la vieille galanterie française*', and then, by a sudden impulse, he looked at Madame de Mauves and wondered what she was doing in such a world. She stopped before the house, without asking him to come in. 'I hope,' she said, 'you'll consider my advice, and waste no more time at Saint-Germain.'

For an instant there rose to his lips some faded compliment about his time not being wasted, but it expired before the simple sincerity of her look. She stood there as gently serious as the angel of disinterestedness, and Longmore felt as if he should insult her by treating her words as a bait for flattery. 'I shall start in a day or two,' he answered, 'but I won't promise you not to come back.'

'I hope not,' she said simply. 'I expect to be here a long time.'

'I shall come and say good-bye,' he rejoined; on which she nodded with a smile, and went in.

He turned away, and walked slowly homeward by the terrace. It seemed to him that to leave her thus, for a gain on which she herself insisted, was to know her better and admire her more.

But he was in a vague ferment of feeling which her evasion of his question half an hour before had done more to deepen than to allay. Suddenly, on the terrace, he encountered M. de Mauves, who was leaning against the parapet finishing a cigar. The Baron, who, he fancied, had an air of peculiar affability, offered him his fair, plump hand. Longmore stopped; he felt a sudden angry desire to cry out to him that he had the loveliest wife in the world; that he ought to be ashamed of himself not to know it; and that for all his shrewdness he had never looked into the depths of her eyes. The Baron, we know, considered that he had; but there was something in Euphemia's eyes now that was not there five years before. They talked for a while about various things, and M. de Mauves gave a humorous account of his visit to America. His tone was not soothing to Longmore's excited sensibilities. He seemed to consider the country a gigantic joke, and his urbanity only went so far as to admit that it was not a bad one. Longmore was not, by habit, an aggressive apologist for our institutions; but the Baron's narrative confirmed his worst impressions of French superficiality. He had understood nothing, he had felt nothing, he had learned nothing; and our hero, glancing askance at his aristocratic profile, declared that if the chief merit of a long pedigree was to leave one so vaingloriously stupid, he thanked his stars that the Longmores had emerged from obscurity in the present century, in the person of an enterprising lumber merchant. M. de Mauves dwelt of course on that prime oddity of ours — the liberty allowed to young girls; and related the history of his researches into the 'opportunities' it presented to French noblemen – researches in which, during a fortnight's stay, he seemed to have spent many agreeable hours. 'I am bound to admit,' he said, 'that in every case I was disarmed by the extreme candour of the young lady, and that they took care of themselves to better purpose than I have seen some mammas in France take care of them.' Longmore greeted this handsome concession with the grimmest of smiles, and damned his impertinent patronage.

Mentioning at last that he was about to leave Saint-Germain, he was surprised, without exactly being flattered, by the Baron's quickened attention. 'I'm very sorry,' the latter cried. 'I hoped we had you for the summer.' Longmore murmured something civil, and wondered why M. de Mauves should care whether he stayed or went. 'You were a diversion to Madame de Mauves,' the Baron added. 'I assure you I mentally blessed your visits.'

'They were a great pleasure to me,' Longmore said gravely. 'Some day I expect to come back.'

'Pray do,' and the Baron laid his hand urgently on his arm. 'You see I have confidence in you!' Longmore was silent for a moment, and the Baron puffed his cigar reflectively and watched the smoke. 'Madame de Mauves,' he said at last, 'is a rather singular person.'

Longmore shifted his position, and wondered whether he was going to 'explain' Madame de Mauves.

'Being as you are her fellow-countryman,' the Baron went on, 'I don't mind speaking frankly. She's just a little morbid – the most charming woman in the world, as you see, but a little fanciful – a little *exaltée*. Now you see she has taken this extraordinary fancy for solitude. I can't get her to go anywhere – to see anyone. When my friends present themselves she's polite, but she's freezing. She doesn't do herself justice, and I expect every day to hear two or three of them say to me, "Your wife's *jolie à croquer*: what a pity she hasn't a little *esprit*." You must have found out that she has really a great deal. But to tell the whole truth, what she needs is to forget herself. She sits alone for hours poring over her English books and looking at life through that terrible brown fog which they always seem to me to fling over the world. I doubt if your English authors,' the Baron continued, with a serenity which Longmore afterwards characterized as sublime, 'are very sound reading for young married women. I don't pretend to know much about them; but I remember that, not long after our marriage, Madame de Mauves undertook to read me one day a certain Wordsworth – a poet highly esteemed, it appears, *chez vous*. It seemed to me that she took me by the nape of the neck and forced my head for half an hour over a basin of *soupe aux choux*, and that one ought to ventilate the drawing-room before anyone called. But I suppose you know him – *ce génie là*. I think my wife never forgave me, and that it was a real shock to her to find she had married a man who had very much the same taste in literature as in cookery. But you're a man of general culture,' said the Baron, turning to Longmore and fixing his eyes on the seal on his watch-guard. 'You can talk about everything, and I'm sure you like Alfred de Musset as well as Wordsworth. Talk to her about everything, Alfred de Musset included. Bah! I forgot you're going. Come back then as soon as possible and talk about your travels. If Madame de Mauves too would travel for a couple of months, it would do her good. It would enlarge her horizon –' and M. de Mauves made a series of short nervous jerks with his stick in the air – 'it would wake up her imagination. She's too rigid, you know – it would show her that one may bend a trifle without breaking.' He paused a moment and gave two or three vigorous puffs. Then turning to his companion again, with a little nod and a confidential smile: 'I hope you admire my candour. I wouldn't say all this to one of us.'

Evening was coming on, and the lingering light seemed to float in the air in faintly golden motes. Longmore stood gazing at these luminous particles; he could almost have fancied them a swarm of humming insects, murmuring as a refrain, 'She has a great deal of *esprit* – she has a great deal of *esprit*.' 'Yes, she has a great deal,' he said mechanically, turning to the Baron. M. de Mauves glanced at him sharply, as if to ask what the deuce he was talking about. 'She has a great deal of intelligence,' said Longmore, deliberately, 'a great deal of beauty, a great many virtues.'

M. de Mauves busied himself for a moment in lighting another cigar, and when he had finished, with a return of his confidential smile, 'I suspect you of thinking,' he said, 'that I don't do my wife justice. Take care – take care, young man; that's a dangerous assumption. In general, a man always does his wife justice. More than justice,' cried the Baron with a laugh – 'that we keep for the wives of other men!'

Longmore afterwards remembered it in favour of the Baron's grace of address that he had not measured at this moment the dusky abyss over which it hovered. But a sort of deepening subterranean echo lingered on his spiritual ear. For the present his keenest sensation was a desire to get away and cry aloud that M. de Mauves was an arrogant fool. He bade him an abrupt good-night, which must serve also, he said, as good-bye.

'Decidedly, then, you go?' said M. de Mauves, almost peremptorily.

'Decidedly.'

'Of course you'll come and say good-bye to Madame de Mauves.' His tone implied that the omission would be most uncivil; but there seemed to Longmore something so ludicrous in his taking a lesson in consideration from M. de Mauves, that he burst into a laugh. The Baron frowned, like a man for whom it was a new and most unpleasant sensation to be perplexed. 'You're a queer fellow,' he murmured, as Longmore turned away, not foreseeing that he would think him a very queer fellow indeed before he had done with him.

Longmore sat down to dinner at his hotel with his usual good intentions; but as he was lifting his first glass of wine to his lips, he suddenly fell to musing and set down his wine untasted. His reverie lasted long, and when he emerged from it, his fish was cold; but this mattered little, for his appetite was gone. That evening he packed his trunk with a kind of indignant energy. This was so effective that the operation was accomplished before bedtime, and as he was not in the least sleepy, he devoted the interval to writing two letters; one was a short note to Madame de Mauves, which he entrusted to a servant, to be delivered the next morning. He had found it best, he said, to leave Saint-Germain immediately, but he expected to be back in Paris in the early autumn. The other letter was the result of his having remembered a day or two before that he had not yet complied with Mrs Draper's injunction to give her an account of his impressions of her friend. The present occasion seemed propitious, and he wrote half a dozen pages. His tone, however, was grave, and Mrs Draper, on receiving them, was slightly disappointed – she would have preferred a stronger flavour of rhapsody. But what chiefly concerns us is the concluding sentences.

'The only time she ever spoke to me of her marriage,' he wrote, 'she intimated that it had been a perfect love-match. With all abatements, I suppose most marriages are; but in her case this would mean more, I think, than in that of most women; for her love was an absolute idealization. She believed her husband was a hero of rose-coloured romance, and he turns out to be not even a hero of very sad-coloured reality. For some time now she has been sounding her mistake, but I don't believe she has touched the bottom of it yet. She strikes me as a person who is begging off from full knowledge – who has struck a truce with painful truth, and is trying awhile the experiment of living with closed eyes. In the dark she tries to see again the gilding on her idol. Illusion of course is illusion, and one must always pay for it; but there is something truly tragical in seeing an earthly penalty levied on such divine folly as this. As for M. de Mauves, he's a Frenchman to his fingers' ends; and I confess I should dislike him for this if he were a much better man. He can't forgive his wife for having married him too sentimentally and loved him too well; for in some uncorrupted corner of his being he feels, I suppose, that as she saw him, so he ought to have been. It's a perpetual vexation to him that a little American *bourgeoise* should have fancied him a finer fellow than he is, or than he at all wants to be. He hasn't a glimmering of real acquaintance with his wife; he can't understand the stream of passion flowing so clear and still. To tell the truth, I hardly can myself; but when I see the spectacle I can admire it furiously. M. de Mauves, at any rate, would like to have the comfort of feeling that his wife was as corruptible as himself; and you'll hardly believe me when I tell you that he goes about intimating to gentlemen whom he deems worthy of the knowledge, that it would be a convenience to him to have them make love to her.'

V

ON REACHING PARIS, Longmore straightway purchased a Murray's *Belgium*, to help himself to believe that he would start on the morrow for Brussels; but when the morrow came, it occurred to him that, by way of preparation, he ought to acquaint himself more intimately with the Flemish painters in the Louvre. This took a whole morning, but it did little to hasten his departure. He had abruptly left Saint-Germain, because it seemed to him that respect for Madame de Mauves demanded that he should allow her husband no reason to suppose that he had understood him; but now that he had satisfied this immediate need of delicacy, he found himself thinking more and more ardently of Euphemia. It was a poor expression of ardour to be lingering irresolutely on the deserted boulevards, but he detested the idea of leaving Saint-Germain five hundred miles behind him. He felt very foolish, nevertheless, and wandered about nervously, promising himself to take the next train; but a dozen trains started, and Longmore was still in Paris. This sentimental tumult was more than he had bargained for, and, as he looked in the shop windows, he wondered whether it was a 'passion'. He had never been fond of the word, and had grown up with a kind of horror of what it represented. He had hoped that when he fell in love, he should do it with an excellent conscience, with no greater agitation than a mild general glow of satisfaction. But here was a sentiment compounded of pity and anger, as well as admiration, and bristling with scruples and doubts. He had come abroad to enjoy the Flemish painters and all others; but what fair-tressed saint of Van Eyck or Memling was so appealing a figure as Madame de Mauves? His restless steps carried him at last out of the long villa-bordered avenue which leads to the Bois de Boulogne.

Summer had fairly begun, and the drive beside the lake was empty, but there were various loungers on the benches and chairs, and the great café had an air of animation. Longmore's walk had given him an appetite, and he went into the establishment and demanded a dinner, remarking for the hundredth time, as he observed the smart little tables disposed in the open air, how much better they ordered this matter in France.

'Will monsieur dine in the garden, or in the salon?' asked the waiter. Longmore chose the garden; and observing that a great vine of June roses was trained over the wall of the house, placed himself at a table near by, where the best of dinners was served him on the whitest of linen, in the most shining of porcelain. It so happened that his table was near a window, and that as he sat he could look into a corner of the salon. So it was that his attention rested on a lady seated just within the window, which was open, face to face apparently to a companion who was concealed by the curtain. She was a very pretty woman, and Longmore looked at her as often as was consistent with good manners. After a while he even began to wonder who she was, and to suspect that she was one of those ladies whom it is no breach of good manners to look at as often as you like. Longmore, too, if he had been so disposed, would have been the more free to give her all his attention, that her own was fixed upon the person opposite to her. She was what the French call a *belle brune*, and though our hero, who had rather a conservative taste in such matters, had no great relish for her bold outlines and even bolder colouring, he could not help admiring her expression of basking contentment.

She was evidently very happy, and her happiness gave her an air of innocence. The talk of her friend, whoever he was, abundantly suited her humour, for she sat listening to him with a broad, lazy smile, and interrupted him occasionally, while she crunched her *bon-bons*, with a murmured response, presumably as broad, which seemed to deepen his eloquence. She drank a great deal of champagne and ate an immense number of strawberries, and was plainly altogether a person with an impartial relish for strawberries, champagne, and what she would have called *bêtises*.

They had half finished dinner when Longmore sat down, and he was still in his place when they rose. She had hung her bonnet on a nail above her chair, and her companion passed round the table to take it down for her. As he did so, she bent her head to look at a wine stain on her dress, and in the movement exposed the greater part of the back of a very handsome neck. The gentleman observed it, and observed also, apparently, that the room beyond them was empty; that he stood within eyeshot of Longmore, he failed to observe. He stooped suddenly and imprinted a gallant kiss on the fair expanse. Longmore then recognized M. de Mauves. The recipient of this vigorous tribute put on her bonnet, using his flushed smile as a mirror, and in a moment they passed through the garden on their way to their carriage.

Then, for the first time, M. de Mauves perceived Longmore. He measured with a rapid glance the young man's relation to the open window, and checked himself in the impulse to stop and speak to him. He contented himself with bowing with great gravity as he opened the gate for his companion.

That evening Longmore made a railway journey, but not to Brussels. He had effectually ceased to care about Brussels; the only thing he now cared about was Madame de Mauves. The atmosphere of his mind had had a sudden clearing up; pity and anger were still throbbing there, but they had space to rage at their pleasure, for doubts and scruples had abruptly departed. It was little, he felt, that he could interpose between her resignation and the unsparing harshness of her position; but that little, if it involved the sacrifice of everything that bound him to the tranquil past, it seemed to him that he could offer her with a rapture which at last made reflection a woefully halting substitute for faith. Nothing in his tranquil past had given such a zest to consciousness as the sense of tending with all his being to a single aim which bore him company on his journey to Saint-Germain. How to justify his return, how to explain his ardour, troubled him little. He was not sure, even, that he wished to be understood; he wished only to feel that it was by no fault of his that Madame de Mauves was alone with the ugliness of fate. He was conscious of no distinct desire to 'make love' to her; if he could have uttered the essence of his longing, he would have said that he wished her to remember that in a world coloured grey to her vision by disappointment, there was one vividly honest man. She might certainly have remembered it, however, without his coming back to remind her; and it is not to be denied that, as he packed his valise that evening, he wished immensely to hear the sound of her voice.

He waited the next day till his usual hour of calling – the late afternoon; but he learned at the door that Madame de Mauves was not at home. The servant offered the information that she was walking in the forest. Longmore went through the garden and out of the little door into the lane, and, after half an hour's vain exploration, saw her coming toward him at the end of a green by-path. As he appeared, she stopped for a moment, as if to turn aside; then recognizing him, she slowly advanced, and he was soon shaking hands with her.

'Nothing has happened,' she said, looking at him fixedly. 'You're not ill?'

'Nothing, except that when I got to Paris I found how fond I had grown of Saint-Germain.'

She neither smiled nor looked flattered; it seemed indeed to Longmore that she was annoyed. But he was uncertain, for he immediately perceived that in his absence the whole character of her face had altered. It told him that something momentous had happened. It was no longer self-contained melancholy that he read in her eyes, but grief and agitation which had lately struggled with that passionate love of peace of which she had spoken to him, and forced it to know that deep experience is never peaceful. She was pale, and she had evidently been shedding tears. He felt his heart beating hard; he seemed now to know her secrets. She continued to look at him with a contracted brow, as if his return had given her a sense of responsibility too great to be disguised by a commonplace welcome. For some moments, as he turned and walked beside her, neither spoke;

then abruptly – 'Tell me truly, Mr Longmore,' she said, 'why you have come back.'

He turned and looked at her with an air which startled her into a certainty of what she had feared. 'Because I've learned the real answer to the question I asked you the other day. You're not happy – you're too good to be happy on the terms offered you. Madame de Mauves,' he went on with a gesture which protested against a gesture of her own, 'I can't be happy if you're not. I don't care for anything so long as I see such a depth of unconquerable sadness in your eyes. I found during three dreary days in Paris that the thing in the world I most care for is this daily privilege of seeing you. I know it's absolutely brutal to tell you I admire you; it's an insult to you to treat you as if you had complained to me or appealed to me. But such a friendship as I waked up to there –' and he tossed his head toward the distant city – 'is a potent force, I assure you; and when forces are compressed they explode. But if you had told me every trouble in your heart, it would have mattered little; I couldn't say more than I must say now – that if that in life from which you've hoped most has given you least, my devoted respect will refuse no service and betray no trust.'

She had begun to make marks in the earth with the point of her parasol; but she stopped and listened to him in perfect immobility. Rather, her immobility was not perfect; for when he stopped speaking a faint flush had stolen into her cheek. It told Longmore that she was moved, and his first perceiving it was the happiest instant of his life. She raised her eyes at last, and looked at him with what at first seemed a pleading dread of excessive emotion.

'Thank you – thank you!' she said, calmly enough; but the next moment her own emotion overcame her calmness, and she burst into tears. Her tears vanished as quickly as they came, but they did Longmore a world of good. He had always felt indefinably afraid of her; her being had somehow seemed fed by a deeper faith and a stronger will than his own; but her half-dozen smothered sobs showed him the bottom of her heart, and assured him that she was weak enough to be grateful.

'Excuse me,' she said; 'I'm too nervous to listen to you. I believe I could have faced an enemy today, but I can't endure a friend.'

'You're killing yourself with stoicism – that's my belief,' he cried. 'Listen to a friend for his own sake, if not for yours. I have never ventured to offer you an atom of compassion, and you can't accuse yourself of an abuse of charity.'

She looked about her with a kind of weary confusion which promised a reluctant attention. But suddenly perceiving by the wayside the fallen log on which they had rested a few evenings before, she went and sat down on it in impatient resignation, and looked at Longmore, as he stood silent, watching her, with a glance which seemed to urge that, if she was charitable now, he must be very wise.

'Something came to my knowledge yesterday,' he said as he sat down beside her, 'which gave me a supreme sense of your moral isolation. You are truth itself, and there is no truth about you. You believe in purity and duty and dignity, and you live in a world in which they are daily belied. I sometimes ask myself with a kind of rage how you ever came into such a world – and why the perversity of fate never let me know you before.'

'I like my "world" no better than you do, and it was not for its own sake I came into it. But what particular group of people is worth pinning one's faith upon? I confess it sometimes seems to me that men and women are very poor creatures. I suppose I'm romantic. I have a most unfortunate taste for poetic fitness. Life is hard prose, which one must learn to read contentedly. I believe I once thought that all the prose was in America, which was very foolish. What I thought, what I believed, what I expected, when I was an ignorant girl, fatally addicted to falling in love with my own theories, is more than I can begin to tell you now. Sometimes, when I remember certain impulses, certain illusions of those days, they take away my breath, and I wonder my bedazzled visions didn't lead me into troubles greater than any I have now to lament. I had a conviction which you would probably smile at if I were to attempt to express it to you. It was a singular form for passionate faith to take, but it had all of the sweetness and the ardour of passionate faith. It led me to take a great step, and it lies behind me now in the distance like a shadow melting slowly in the light of experience. It has faded, but it has not vanished. Some feelings, I am sure, die only with ourselves; some illusions are as much the condition of our life as our heart-beats. They say that life itself is an illusion – that this world is a shadow of which the reality is yet to come. Life is all of a piece, then, and there is no shame in being miserably human. As for my "isolation", it doesn't greatly matter; it's the fault, in part, of my obstinacy. There have been times when I have been frantic- ally distressed, and, to tell you the truth, wretchedly homesick, because my maid – a jewel of a maid – lied to me with every second breath. There have been moments when I have wished I was the daughter of a poor New England minister, living in a little white house under a couple of elms, and doing all the housework.'

She had begun to speak slowly, with an air of effort; but she went on quickly, as if talking were a relief. 'My marriage intro- duced me to people and things which seemed to me at first very strange and then very horrible, and then, to tell the truth, very contemptible. At first I expended a great deal of sorrow and dismay and pity on it all; but there soon came a time when I began to wonder whether it was worth one's tears. If I could tell you the eternal friendships I've seen broken, the inconsolable woes consoled, the jealousies and vanities leading off the dance, you would agree with me that tempers like yours and mine can under- stand neither such losses nor such compensations. A year ago, while I was in the country, a friend of mine was in despair at the infidelity of her husband; she wrote me a most tragical letter, and on my return to Paris I went immediately to see her. A week had elapsed, and, as I had seen stranger things, I thought she might have recovered her spirits. Not at all; she was still in despair – but at what? At the conduct, the abandoned, shameless conduct of Mme de T. You'll imagine, of course, that Mme de T. was the lady whom my friend's husband preferred to his wife. Far from it; he had never seen her. Who, then, was Mme de T.? Mme de T. was cruelly devoted to M. de V. And who was M. de V.? M. de V. — in two words, my friend was cultivating two jealousies at once. I hardly know what I said to her; something, at any rate, that she found unpardonable, for she quite gave me up. Shortly afterward my husband proposed we should cease to live in Paris, and I gladly assented, for I believe I was falling into a state of mind that made me a detestable companion. I should have preferred to go quite into the country, into Auvergne, where my husband has a place. But to him Paris, in some degree, is necessary, and Saint-Germain has been a sort of compromise.'

'A sort of compromise!' Longmore repeated. 'That's your whole life.'

'It's the life of many people, of most people of quiet tastes, and it is certainly better than acute distress. One is at loss theoretically to defend a compromise; but if I found a poor creature clinging to one from day to day, I should think it poor friendship to make him lose his hold.' Madame de Mauves had no sooner uttered these words than she smiled faintly, as if to mitigate their personal application.

'Heaven forbid,' said Longmore, 'that one should do that unless one has something better to offer. And yet I am haunted by a vision of a life in which you should have found no compromises, for they are a perversion of natures that tend only to goodness and rectitude. As I see it, you should have found happiness serene, profound, complete; a *femme de chambre* not a jewel perhaps, but warranted to tell but one fib a day; a society possibly rather provincial, but (in spite of your poor opinion of mankind) a good deal of solid virtue; jealousies and vanities very tame, and no particular inquities and adulteries. A husband,' he added after a moment – 'a husband of your own faith and race and spiritual substance, who would have loved you well.'

She rose to her feet, shaking her head. 'You are very kind to go to the expense of visions for me. Visions are vain things; we must make the best of the reality.'

'And yet,' said Longmore, provoked by what seemed the very wantonness of her patience, 'the reality, if I'm not mistaken, has very recently taken a shape that keenly tests your philosophy.'

She seemed on the point of replying that his sympathy was too zealous; but a couple of impatient tears in his eyes proved that it was founded on a devotion to which it was impossible not to defer. 'Philosophy?' she said. 'I have none. Thank Heaven!' she cried, with vehemence, 'I have none. I believe, Mr Longmore,' she added in a moment, 'that I have nothing on earth but a conscience – it's a good time to tell you so – nothing but a dogged, clinging, inexpugnable conscience. Does that prove me to be indeed of your faith and race, and have you one for which you can say as much? I don't say it in vanity, for I believe that if my conscience will prevent me from doing anything very base, it will effectually prevent me from doing anything very fine.'

'I am delighted to hear it,' cried Longmore. 'We are made for each other. It's very certain I too shall never do anything fine. And yet I have fancied that in my case this inexpugnable organ you so eloquently describe might be blinded and gagged awhile, in a fine cause, if not turned out of doors. In yours,' he went on with the same appealing irony, 'is it absolutely invincible?'

But her fancy made no concession to his sarcasm. 'Don't laugh at your conscience,' she answered gravely; 'that's the only blasphemy I know.'

She had hardly spoken when she turned suddenly at an unexpected sound, and at the same moment Longmore heard a footstep in an adjacent by-path which crossed their own at a short distance from where they stood.

'It's M. de Mauves,' said Euphemia directly, and moved slowly forward. Longmore, wondering how she knew it, had overtaken her by the time her husband advanced into sight. A solitary walk in the forest was a pastime to which M. de Mauves was not addicted, but he seemed on this occasion to have resorted to it with some equanimity. He was smoking a fragrant cigar, and his thumb was thrust into the armhole of his waistcoat, with an air of contemplative serenity. He stopped short with surprise on seeing his wife and her companion, and Longmore considered his surprise impertinent. He glanced rapidly from one to the other, fixed Longmore's eye sharply for a single instant, and then lifted his hat with formal politeness.

'I was not aware,' he said, turning to Madame de Mauves, 'that I might congratulate you on the return of monsieur.'

'You should have known it,' she answered gravely, 'if I had expected Mr Longmore's return.'

She had become very pale, and Longmore felt that this was a first meeting after a stormy parting. 'My return was unexpected to myself,' he said. 'I came last evening.'

M. de Mauves smiled with extreme urbanity. 'It's needless for me to welcome you. Madame de Mauves knows the duties of hospitality.' And with another bow he continued his walk.

Madame de Mauves and her companion returned slowly home, with few words, but, on Longmore's part at least, many thoughts. The Baron's appearance had given him an angry chill; it was a dusky cloud reabsorbing the light which had begun to shine between himself and his companion.

He watched Euphemia narrowly as they went, and wondered what she had last had to suffer. Her husband's presence had checked her frankness, but nothing indicated that she had accepted the insulting meaning of his words. Matters were evidently at a crisis between them, and Longmore wondered vainly what it was on Euphemia's part that prevented an absolute rupture. What did she suspect? – how much did she know? To what was she resigned? – how much had she forgiven? How, above all, did she reconcile with knowledge, or with suspicion, that ineradicable tenderness of which she had just now all but assured him? 'She has loved him once,' Longmore said with a sinking of the heart, 'and with her to love once is to commit one's being for ever. Her husband thinks her too rigid! What would a poet call it?'

He relapsed with a kind of aching impotence into the sense of her being somehow beyond him, unattainable, immeasurable by his own fretful spirit. Suddenly he gave three passionate switches in the air with his cane, which made Madame de Mauves look round. She could hardly have guessed that they meant that where ambition was so vain, it was an innocent compensation to plunge into worship.

Madame de Mauves found in her drawing-room the little elderly Frenchman, M. de Chalumeau, whom Longmore had observed a few days before on the terrace. On this occasion, too, Madame Clairin was entertaining him, but as her sister-in-law came in she surrendered her post and addressed herself to our hero. Longmore, at thirty, was still an ingenuous youth, and there was something in this lady's large coquetry which had the power of making him blush. He was surprised at finding he had not absolutely forfeited her favour by his deportment at their last interview, and a suspicion of her meaning to approach him on another line completed his uneasiness.

'So you've returned from Brussels,' she said, 'by way of the forest.'

'I've not been to Brussels. I returned yesterday from Paris by the only way – by the train.'

Madame Clairin stared and laughed. 'I've never known a young man to be so fond of Saint-Germain. They generally declare it's horribly dull.'

'That's not very polite to you,' said Longmore, who was vexed at his blushes, and determined not to be abashed.

'Ah, what am I?' demanded Madame Clairin, swinging open her fan. 'I'm the dullest thing here. They've not had your success with my sister-in-law.'

'It would have been very easy to have it. Madame de Mauves is kindness itself.'

'To her own countrymen!'

Longmore remained silent; he hated the talk. Madame Clairin looked at him a moment, and then turned her head and surveyed Euphemia, to whom M. de Chalumeau was serving up another epigram, which she was receiving with a slight droop of the head and her eyes absently wandering through the window. 'Don't pretend to tell me,' she murmured suddenly, 'that you're not in love with that pretty woman.'

'*Allons donc!*' cried Longmore, in the best French he had ever uttered. He rose the next minute, and took a hasty farewell.

VI

HE ALLOWED SEVERAL days to pass without going back; it seemed delicate not to appear to regard his friend's frankness during their last interview as a general invitation. This cost him a great effort, for hopeless passions are not the most defer-ential; and he had, moreover, a constant fear, that if, as he believed, the hour of supreme 'explanations' had come, the magic of her magnanimity might convert M. de Mauves. Vicious men, it was abundantly recorded, had been so converted as to be acceptable to God, and the something divine in Euphemia's temper would sanctify any means she should choose to employ. Her means, he kept repeating, were no business of his, and the essence of his admiration ought to be to respect her freedom; but he felt as if he should turn away into a world out of which most of the joy had departed, if her freedom, after all, should spare him only a murmured 'Thank you'.

When he called again he found to his vexation that he was to run the gantlet of Madame Clairin's officious hospitality. It was one of the first mornings of perfect summer, and the drawing-room, through the open windows, was flooded with a sweet confusion of odours and bird-notes which filled him with the hope that Madame de Mauves would come out and spend half the day in the forest. But Madame Clairin, with her hair not yet dressed, emerged like a brassy discord in a maze of melody.

At the same moment the servant returned with Euphemia's regrets; she was indisposed and unable to see Mr Longmore. The young man knew that he looked disappointed, and that Madame Clairin was observing him, and this consciousness impelled her to give him a glance of almost aggressive frigidity. This was apparently what she desired. She wished to throw him off his balance, and, if he was not mistaken, she had the means.

'Put down your hat, Mr Longmore,' she said, 'and be polite for once. You were not at all polite the other day when I asked you that friendly question about the state of your heart.'

'I have no heart – to talk about,' said Longmore, uncompromisingly.

'As well say you've none at all. I advise you to cultivate a little eloquence; you may have use for it. That was not an idle question of mine; I don't ask idle questions. For a couple of months now that you've been coming and going among us, it seems to me that you have had very few to answer of any sort.'

'I have certainly been very well treated,' said Longmore.

Madame Clairin was silent a moment, and then – 'Have you never felt disposed to ask any?' she demanded.

Her look, her tone, were so charged with roundabout meanings that it seemed to Longmore as if even to understand her would savour of dishonest complicity. 'What is it you have to tell me?' he asked, frowning and blushing.

Madame Clairin flushed. It is rather hard, when you come bearing yourself very much as the sibyl when she came to the Roman king, to be treated as something worse than a vulgar gossip. 'I might tell you, Mr Longmore,' she said, 'that you have as bad a *ton* as any young man I ever met. Where have you lived – what are your ideas? I wish to call your attention to a fact which it takes some delicacy to touch upon. You have noticed, I supposed, that my sister-in-law is not the happiest woman in the world.'

Longmore assented with a gesture.

Madame Clairin looked slightly disappointed at his want of enthusiasm. Nevertheless – 'You have formed, I suppose,' she continued, 'your conjectures on the causes of her – dissatisfaction.'

'Conjecture has been superfluous. I have seen the causes – or at least a specimen of them – with my own eyes.'

'I know perfectly what you mean. My brother, in a single word, is in love with another woman. I don't judge him; I don't judge my sister-in-law. I permit myself to say that in her position I would have managed otherwise. I would have kept my husband's affection, or I would have frankly done without it, before this. But my sister is an odd compound; I don't profess to understand her. Therefore it is, in a measure, that I appeal to you, her fellow-countryman. Of course you'll be surprised at my way of looking at the matter, and I admit that it's a way in use only among people whose family traditions compel them to take a superior view of things.' Madame Clairin paused, and Longmore wondered where her family traditions were going to lead her.

'Listen,' she went on. 'There has never been a De Mauves who has not given his wife the right to be jealous. We know our history for ages back, and the fact is established. It's a shame if you like, but it's something to have a shame with such a pedigree. The De Mauves are real Frenchmen, and their wives – I may say it – have been worthy of them. You may see all their portraits in our Château de Mauves; every one of them an "injured" beauty, but not one of them hanging her head. Not one of them had the bad taste to be jealous, and yet not one in a dozen was guilty of an escapade – not one of them was talked about. There's good sense for you! How they managed – go and look at the dusky, faded canvases and pastels, and ask. They were *femmes d'esprit*. When they had a headache, they put on a little rouge and came to supper as usual; and when they had a heart-ache, they put a little rouge on their hearts. These are fine traditions, and it doesn't seem to me fair that a little American *bourgeoise* should come in and interrupt them, and should hang her photograph, with her obstinate little *air penché*, in the gallery of our shrewd fine ladies. A De Mauves must be a De Mauves. When she married my brother, I don't suppose she took him for a member of a *societé de bonnes œuvres*. I don't say we're right; who is right? But we're as history has made us, and if anyone is to change, it had better be Madame de Mauves herself.' Again Madame Clairin paused and opened and closed her fan. 'Let her conform!' she said, with amazing audacity.

Longmore's reply was ambiguous; he simply said, 'Ah!'

Madame Clairin's pious retrospect had apparently imparted an honest zeal to her indignation. 'For a long time,' she continued, 'my sister has been taking the attitude of an injured woman, affecting a disgust with the world, and shutting herself up to read the *Imitation*. I've never remarked on her conduct, but I've quite lost patience with it. When a woman with her prettiness lets her husband wander, she deserves her fate. I don't wish you to agree with me – on the contrary; but I call such a woman a goose. She must have bored him to death. What has passed between them for many months needn't concern us; what provocation my sister has had – monstrous, if you wish – what ennui my brother has suffered. It's enough that a week ago, just after you had ostensibly gone to Brussels, something happened to produce an explosion. She found a letter in his pocket – a photograph – a trinket – *que sais-je?* At any rate, the scene was terrible. I didn't listen at the keyhole, and I don't know what was said; but I have reason to believe that my brother was called to account as I fancy none of his ancestors have ever been – even by injured sweethearts.'

Longmore had leaned forward in silent attention with his elbows on his knees, and instinctively he dropped his face into his hands. 'Ah, poor woman!' he groaned.

'*Voilà!*' said Madame Clairin. 'You pity her.'

'Pity her?' cried Longmore, looking up with ardent eyes and forgetting the spirit of Madame Clairin's narrative in the miserable facts. 'Don't you?'

'A little. But I'm not acting sentimentally; I'm acting politically. I wish to arrange things – to see my brother free to do as he chooses – to see Euphemia contented. Do you understand me?'

'Very well, I think. You're the most immoral person I've lately had the privilege of conversing with.'

Madame Clairin shrugged her shoulders. 'Possibly. When was there a great politician who was not immoral?'

'Nay,' said Longmore in the same tone. 'You're too superficial to be a great politician. You don't begin to know anything about Madame de Mauves.'

Madame Clairin inclined her head to one side, eyed Longmore sharply, mused a moment, and then smiled with an excellent imitation of intelligent compassion. 'It's not in my interest to contradict you.'

'It would be in your interest to learn, Madame Clairin,' the young man went on with unceremonious candour, 'what honest men most admire in a woman – and to recognize it when you see it.'

Longmore certainly did injustice to her talents for diplomacy, for she covered her natural annoyance at this sally with a pretty piece of irony. 'So you *are* in love!' she quietly exclaimed.

Longmore was silent awhile. 'I wonder if you would understand me,' he said at last, 'if I were to tell you that I have for Madame de Mauves the most devoted friendship?'

'You underrate my intelligence. But in that case you ought to exert your influence to put an end to these painful domestic scenes.'

'Do you suppose,' cried Longmore, 'that she talks to me about her domestic scenes?'

Madame Clairin stared. 'Then your friendship isn't returned?' And as Longmore turned away, shaking his head – 'Now, at least,' she added, 'she will have something to tell you. I happen to know the upshot of my brother's last interview with his wife.' Longmore rose to his feet as a sort of protest against the indelicacy of the position into which he was being forced; but all that made him tender made him curious, and she caught in his averted eyes an expression which prompted her to strike her blow. 'My brother is monstrously in love with a certain person in Paris; of course he ought not to be; but he wouldn't be a De Mauves if he were not. It was this unsanctified passion that spoke. "Listen, madam," he cried at last: "let us live like people who understand life! It's unpleasant to be forced to say such things outright, but you have a way of bringing one down to the rudiments. I'm faithless, I'm heartless, I'm brutal, I'm everything horrible – it's understood. Take your revenge, console yourself; you're too pretty a woman to have anything to complain of. Here's a handsome young man sighing himself into a consumption for you. Listen to the poor fellow, and you'll find that virtue is none the less becoming for being good-natured. You'll see that it's not after all such a doleful world, and that there is even an advantage in having the most impudent of husbands."' Madame Clairin paused; Longmore had turned very pale. 'You may believe it,' she said; 'the speech took place in my presence; things were done in order. And now, Mr Longmore –' this with a smile which he was too troubled at the moment to appreciate, but which he remembered later with a kind of awe – 'we count upon you!'

'He said this to her, face to face, as you say it to me now?' Longmore asked slowly, after a silence.

'Word for word, and with the greatest politeness.'

'And Madame de Mauves – what did she say?'

Madame Clairin smiled again. 'To such a speech as that a woman says – nothing. She had been sitting with a piece of needle-work, and I think she had not seen her husband since their quarrel the day before. He came in with the gravity of an ambassador, and I'm sure that when he made his *demande en mariage* his manner was not more respectful. He only wanted white gloves!' said Madame Clairin. 'Euphemia sat silent a few moments drawing her stitches, and then without a word, without a glance, she walked out of the room. It was just what she should have done!'

'Yes,' Longmore repeated, 'it was just what she should have done.'

'And I, left alone with my brother, do you know what I said?'
Longmore shook his head. '*Mauvais sujet!*' he suggested.

' "You've done me the honour," I said, "to take this step in my presence. I don't pretend to qualify it. You know what you're about, and it's your own affair. But you may confide in my discretion." Do you think he has had reason to complain of it?' She received no answer, Longmore was slowly turning away and passing his gloves mechanically round the band of his hat. 'I hope,' she cried, 'you're not going to start for Brussels!'

Plainly, Longmore was deeply disturbed, and Madame Clairin might flatter herself on the success of her plea for old-fashioned manners. And yet there was something that left her more puzzled than satisfied in the reflective tone with which he answered, 'No, I shall remain here for the present.' The processes of his mind seemed provokingly subterranean, and she would have fancied for a moment that he was linked with her sister in some monstrous conspiracy of asceticism.

'Come this evening,' she boldly resumed. 'The rest will take care of itself. Meanwhile I shall take the liberty of telling my sister-in-law that I have repeated – in short, that I have put you *au fait.*'

Longmore started and coloured, and she hardly knew whether he was going to assent or demur. 'Tell her what you please. Nothing you can tell her will affect her conduct.'

'*Voyons!* Do you mean to tell me that a woman, young, pretty, sentimental, neglected – insulted, if you will——? I see you don't believe it. Believe simply in your own opportunity! But for heaven's sake, if it's to lead anywhere, don't come back with that *visage de croquemort*. You look as if you were going to bury your heart – not to offer it to a pretty woman. You're much better when you smile. Come, do yourself justice.'

'Yes,' he said, 'I must do myself justice.' And abruptly, with a bow, he took his departure.

VII

HE FELT, WHEN he found himself unobserved, in the open air, that he must plunge into violent action, walk fast and far, and defer the opportunity for thought. He strode away into the forest, swinging his cane, throwing back his head, gazing away into the verdurous vistas, and following the road without a purpose. He felt immensely excited, but he could hardly have said whether his emotion was a pain or a joy. It was joyous as all increase of freedom is joyous; something seemed to have been knocked down across his path; his destiny appeared to have rounded a cape and brought him into sight of an open sea. But his freedom resolved itself somehow into the need of despising all mankind, with a single exception; and the fact of Madame de Mauves inhabiting a planet contaminated by the presence of this baser multitude kept his elation from seeming a pledge of ideal bliss.

But she was there, and circumstance now forced them to be intimate. She had ceased to have what men call a secret for him, and this fact itself brought with it a sort of rapture. He had no prevision that he should 'profit', in the vulgar sense, by the extraordinary position into which they had been thrown; it might be but a cruel trick of destiny to make hope a harsher mockery and renunciation a keener suffering. But above all this rose the conviction that she could do nothing that would not deepen his admiration.

It was this feeling that circumstance – unlovely as it was in itself – was to force the beauty of her character into more perfect relief, that made him stride along as if he were celebrating a kind of spiritual festival. He rambled at random for a couple of hours, and found at last that he had left the forest behind him and had wandered into an unfamiliar region. It was a perfectly rural scene, and the still summer day gave it a charm for which its meagre elements but half accounted.

Longmore thought he had never seen anything so characteristically French; all the French novels seemed to have described it, all the French landscapists to have painted it. The fields and trees were of a cool metallic green; the grass looked as if it might stain your trousers, and the foliage your hands. The clear light had a sort of mild greyness; the sunbeams were of silver rather than gold. A great red-roofed, high-stacked farm-house, with whitewashed walls and a straggling yard, surveyed the high road, on one side, from behind a transparent curtain of poplars. A narrow stream, half choked with emerald rushes and edged with grey aspens, occupied the opposite quarter. The meadows rolled and sloped away gently to the low horizon, which was barely concealed by the continuous line of clipped and marshalled trees. The prospect was not rich, but it had a frank homeliness which touched the young man's fancy. It was full of light atmosphere and diffused sunshine, and if it was prosaic, it was soothing.

Longmore was disposed to walk further, and he advanced along the road beneath the poplars. In twenty minutes he came to a village which straggled away to the right, among orchards and *potagers*. On the left, at a stone's throw from the road, stood a little pink-faced inn, which reminded him that he had not breakfasted, having left home with a prevision of hospitality from Madame de Mauves. In the inn he found a brick-tiled parlour and a hostess in sabots and a white cap, whom, over the omelette she speedily served him – borrowing licence from the bottle of sound red wine which accompanied it – he assured that she was a true artist. To reward his compliment, she invited him to smoke his cigar in her little garden behind the house.

Here he found a *tonnelle* and a view of ripening crops, stretching down to the stream. The *tonnelle* was rather close, and he preferred to lounge on a bench against the pink wall, in the sun, which was not too hot. Here, as he rested and gazed and mused, he fell into a train of thought which, in an indefinable fashion, was a soft influence from the scene about him. His heart, which had been beating fast for the past three hours, gradually checked its pulses and left him looking at life with a rather more level gaze. The homely tavern sounds coming out through the open windows, the sunny stillness of the fields and crops, which covered so much vigorous natural life, suggested very little that was transcendental, had very little to say about renunciation – nothing at all about spiritual zeal. They seemed to utter a message from plain ripe nature, to express the unperverted reality of things, to say that the common lot is not brilliantly amusing, and that the part of wisdom is to grasp frankly at experience, lest you miss it altogether. What reason there was for his falling a-wondering after this whether a deeply wounded heart might be soothed and healed by such a scene, it would be difficult to explain; certain it is that, as he sat there, he had a waking dream of an unhappy woman strolling by the slow-flowing stream before him, and pulling down the blossoming boughs in the orchards. He mused and mused, and at last found himself feeling angry that he could not somehow think worse of Madame de Mauves – or at any rate think otherwise. He could fairly claim that in a sentimental way he asked very little of life – he made modest demands on passion; why then should his only passion be born to ill-fortune? why should his first – his last – glimpse of positive happiness be so indissolubly linked with renunciation?

It is perhaps because, like many spirits of the same stock, he had in his composition a lurking principle of asceticism to whose authority he had ever paid an unquestioning respect, that he now felt all the vehemence of rebellion. To renounce – to renounce again – to renounce for ever – was this all that youth and longing and resolve were meant for? Was experience to be muffled and mutilated, like an indecent picture? Was a man to sit and deliberately condemn his future to be the blank memory of a regret, rather than the long reverberation of a joy? Sacrifice? The word was a trap for minds muddled by fear, an ignoble refuge of weakness. To insist now seemed not to dare, but simply to be, to live on possible terms.

His hostess came out to hang a cloth to dry on the hedge, and, though her guest was sitting quietly enough, she seemed to see in his kindled eyes a flattering testimony to the quality of her wine.

As she turned back into the house, she was met by a young man whom Longmore observed in spite of his preoccupation. He was evidently a member of that jovial fraternity of artists whose very shabbiness has an affinity with the element of pictur-esqueness and unexpectedness in life which provokes a great deal of unformulated envy among people foredoomed to be respectable.

Longmore was struck first with his looking like a very clever man, and then with his looking like a very happy one. The combination, as it was expressed in his face, might have arrested the attention of even a less cynical philosopher. He had a slouched hat and a blond beard, a light easel under one arm, and an unfinished sketch in oils under the other.

He stopped and stood talking for some moments to the land-lady with a peculiarly good-humoured smile. They were discussing the possibilities of dinner; the hostess enumerated some very savoury ones, and he nodded briskly, assenting to everything. It couldn't be, Longmore thought, that he found such soft contentment in the prospect of lamb chops and spinach and a *tarte à la crême*. When the dinner had been ordered, he turned up his sketch, and the good woman fell a-wondering and looking off at the spot by the stream-side where he had made it.

Was it his work, Longmore wondered, that made him so happy? Was a strong talent the best thing in the world? The landlady went back to her kitchen, and the young painter stood as if he were waiting for something, beside the gate which opened upon the path across the fields. Longmore sat brooding and asking himself whether it was better to cultivate an art than to cultivate a passion. Before he had answered the question the painter had grown tired of waiting. He picked up a pebble, tossed it lightly into an upper window, and called, 'Claudine!'

Claudine appeared; Longmore heard her at the window, bidding the young man to have patience. 'But I'm losing my light,' he said; 'I must have my shadows in the same place as yesterday.'

'Go without me, then,' Claudine answered; 'I will join you in ten minutes.' Her voice was fresh and young; it seemed to say to Longmore that she was as happy as her companion.

'Don't forget the Chénier,' cried the young man; and turning away, he passed out of the gate and followed the path across the fields until he disappeared among the trees by the side of the stream. Who was Claudine? Longmore vaguely wondered; and was she as pretty as her voice? Before long he had a chance to satisfy himself; she came out of the house with her hat and parasol, prepared to follow her companion. She had on a pink muslin dress and a little white hat, and she was as pretty as a Frenchwoman needs to be to be pleasing. She had a clear brown skin and a bright dark eye, and a step which seemed to keep time to some slow music, heard only by herself. Her hands were encumbered with various articles which she seemed to intend to carry with her. In one arm she held her parasol and a large roll of needle-work, and in the other a shawl and a heavy white umbrella, such as painters use for sketching. Meanwhile she was trying to thrust into her pocket a paper-covered volume which Longmore saw to be the Poems of André Chénier; but in the effort she dropped the large umbrella, and uttered a half-smiling exclamation of disgust. Longmore stepped forward with a bow and picked up the umbrella, and as she, protesting her gratitude, put out her hand to take it, it seemed to him that she was unbecomingly overburdened.

'You have too much to carry,' he said; 'you must let me help you.'

'You're very good, monsieur,' she answered. 'My husband always forgets something. He can do nothing without his umbrella. He is *d'une étourderie*—'

'You must allow me to carry the umbrella,' Longmore said. 'It's too heavy for a lady.'

She assented, after many compliments to his politeness; and he walked by her side into the meadow. She went lightly and rapidly, picking her steps and glancing forward to catch a glimpse of her husband. She was graceful, she was charming, she had an air of decision and yet of sweetness, and it seemed to Longmore that a young artist would work none the worse for having her seated at his side, reading Chénier's iambics. They were newly married, he supposed, and evidently their path of life had none of the mocking crookedness of some others. They asked little; but what need one ask more than such quiet summer days, with the creature one loves, by a shady stream, with art and books and a wide, unshadowed horizon? To spend such a morning, to stroll back to dinner in the red-tiled parlour of the inn, to ramble away again as the sun got low – all this was a vision of bliss which floated before him, only to torture him with a sense of the impossible. All Frenchwomen are not coquettes, he remarked, as he kept pace with his companion. She uttered a word now and then, for politeness' sake, but she never looked at him, and seemed not in the least to care that he was a well-favoured young man. She cared for nothing but the young artist in the shabby coat and the slouched hat, and for discovering where he had set up his easel.

This was soon done. He was encamped under the trees, close to the stream, and, in the diffused green shade of the little wood, seemed to be in no immediate need of his umbrella. He received a vivacious rebuke, however, for forgetting it, and was informed of what he owed to Longmore's complaisance. He was duly grateful; he thanked our hero warmly, and offered him a seat on the grass. But Longmore felt like a marplot, and lingered only long enough to glance at the young man's sketch, and to see it was a very clever rendering of the silvery stream and the vivid green rushes. The young wife had spread her shawl on the grass at the base of a tree, and meant to seat herself when Longmore had gone, and murmur Chénier's verses to the music of the gurgling river. Longmore looked awhile from one to the other, barely stifled a sigh, bade them good-morning, and took his departure.

He knew neither where to go nor what to do; he seemed afloat on the sea of ineffectual longing. He strolled slowly back to the inn, and in the doorway met the landlady coming back from the butcher's with the lamb chops for the dinner of her lodgers.

'Monsieur has made the acquaintance of the *dame* of our young painter,' she said with a broad smile – a smile too broad for malicious meanings. 'Monsieur has perhaps seen the young man's picture. It appears that he has a great deal of talent.'

'His picture was very pretty,' said Longmore, 'but his *dame* was prettier still.'

'She's a very nice little woman; but I pity her all the more.'

'I don't see why she's to be pitied,' said Longmore; 'they seem a very happy couple.'

The landlady gave a knowing nod.

Don't trust to it, monsieur! Those artists – *ça n'a pas de principes!* From one day to another he can plant her there! I know them, *allez*. I've had them here very often; one year with one, another year with another.'

Longmore was puzzled for a moment. Then, 'You mean she's not his wife?' he asked.

She shrugged her shoulders. 'What shall I tell you? They are not *des hommes sérieux*, those gentlemen! They don't engage themselves for an eternity. It's none of my business, and I've no wish to speak ill of madame. She's a very nice little woman, and she loves her *jeune homme* to distraction.'

'Who is she?' asked Longmore. 'What do you know about her?'

'Nothing for certain; but it's my belief that she's better than he. I've even gone so far as to believe that she's a lady – a true lady – and that she has given up a great many things for him. I do the best I can for them, but I don't believe she's been obliged all her life to content herself with a dinner of two courses.' And she turned over her lamb chops tenderly, as if to say that though a good cook could imagine better things, yet if you could have but one course, lamb chops had much in their favour. 'I shall cook them with bread crumbs. *Voilà les femmes, monsieur!*'

Longmore turned away with the feeling that women were indeed a measureless mystery, and that it was hard to say whether there was greater beauty in their strength or in their weakness. He walked back to Saint-Germain, more slowly than he had come, with less philosophic resignation to any event, and more of the urgent egotism of the passion which philosophers call the supremely selfish one. Every now and then the episode of the happy young painter and the charming woman who had given up a great many things for him rose vividly in his mind, and seemed to mock his moral unrest like some obtrusive vision of unattainable bliss.

The landlady's gossip cast no shadow on its brightness; her voice seemed that of the vulgar chorus of the uninitiated, which stands always ready with its gross prose rendering of the inspired passages in human action. Was it possible a man could take that from a woman – take all that lent lightness to that other woman's footstep and intensity to her glance – and not give her the absolute certainty of a devotion as unalterable as the process of the sun? Was it possible that such a rapturous union had the seeds of trouble – that the charm of such a perfect accord could be broken by anything but death? Longmore felt an immense desire to cry out a thousand times 'No!' for it seemed to him at last that he was somehow spiritually the same as the young painter, and that the latter's companion had the soul of Euphemia de Mauves.

The heat of the sun, as he walked along, became oppressive and when he re-entered the forest he turned aside into the deepest shade he could find, and stretched himself on the mossy ground at the foot of a great beech. He lay for a while staring up into the verdurous dusk overhead, and trying to conceive Madame de Mauves hastening toward some quiet stream-side where he waited, as he had seen that trusting creature do an hour before. It would be hard to say how well he succeeded; but the effort soothed him rather than excited him, and as he had

had a good deal both of moral and physical fatigue, he sank at last into a quiet sleep.

While he slept he had a strange, vivid dream. He seemed to be in a wood, very much like the one on which his eyes had lately closed; but the wood was divided by the murmuring stream he had left an hour before. He was walking up and down, he thought, restlessly and in intense expectation of some momentous event. Suddenly, at a distance, through the trees, he saw the gleam of a woman's dress, and hurried forward to meet her. As he advanced he recognized her, but he saw at the same time that she was on the opposite bank of the river. She seemed at first not to notice him, but when they were opposite each other she stopped and looked at him very gravely and pityingly. She made him no motion that he should cross the stream, but he wished greatly to stand by her side. He knew the water was deep, and it seemed to him that he knew that he should have to plunge, and that he feared that when he rose to the surface she would have disappeared. Nevertheless, he was going to plunge, when a boat turned into the current from above and came swiftly toward them, guided by an oarsman, who was sitting so that they could not see his face. He brought the boat to the bank where Longmore stood; the latter stepped in, and with a few strokes they touched the opposite shore. Longmore got out, and, though he was sure he had crossed the stream, Madame de Mauves was not there. He turned with a kind of agony and saw that now she was on the other bank – the one he had left. She gave him a grave, silent glance, and walked away up the stream.

The boat and the boatman resumed their course, but after going a short distance they stopped, and the boatman turned back and looked at the still divided couple. Then Longmore recognized him — just as he had recognized him a few days before at the café in the Bois de Boulogne.

VIII

HE MUST HAVE slept some time after he ceased dreaming, for he had no immediate memory of his dream. It came back to him later, after he had roused himself and had walked nearly home. No great ingenuity was needed to make it seem a rather striking allegory, and it haunted and oppressed him for the rest of the day. He took refuge, however, in his quickened conviction that the only sound policy in life is to grasp unsparingly at happiness; and it seemed no more than one of the vigorous measures dictated by such a policy, to return that evening to Madame de Mauves. And yet when he had decided to do so, and had carefully dressed himself, he felt an irresistible nervous tremor which made it easier to linger at his open window, wondering, with a strange mixture of dread and desire, whether Madame Clairin had told her sister-in-law that she had told him . . . His presence now might be simply a gratuitous cause of suffering; and yet his absence might seem to imply that it was in the power of circumstances to make them ashamed to meet each other's eyes. He sat a long time with his head in his hands, lost in a painful confusion of hopes and questionings. He felt at moments as if he could throttle Madame Clairin, and yet he could not help asking himself whether it was not possible that she might have done him a service. It was late when he left the hotel, and as he entered the gate of the other house his heart was beating so that he was sure his voice would show it.

The servant ushered him into the drawing-room, which was empty, with the lamp burning low. But the long windows were open, and their light curtains swaying in a soft, warm wind, and Longmore stepped out upon the terrace. There he found Madame de Mauves alone, slowly pacing up and down. She was dressed in white, very simply, and her hair was arranged, not as she usually wore it, but in a single loose coil, like that of a person unprepared for company.

She stopped when she saw Longmore, seemed slightly startled, uttered an exclamation, and stood waiting for him to speak. He looked at her, tried to say something, but found no words. He knew it was awkward, it was offensive, to stand silent, gazing; but he could not say what was suitable, and he dared not say what he wished.

Her face was indistinct in the dim light, but he could see that her eyes were fixed on him, and he wondered what they expressed. Did they warn him, did they plead, or did they confess to a sense of provocation? For an instant his head swam; he felt as if it would make all things clear to stride forward and fold her in his arms. But a moment later he was still standing looking at her; he had not moved; he knew that she had spoken, but he had not understood her.

'You were here this morning,' she continued, and now, slowly, the meaning of her words came to him. 'I had a bad headache and had to shut myself up.' She spoke in her usual voice.

Longmore mastered his agitation and answered her without betraying himself: 'I hope you are better now.'

'Yes, thank you, I'm better – much better.'

He was silent a moment, and she moved away to a chair and seated herself. After a pause he followed her and stood before her, leaning against the balustrade of the terrace. 'I hoped you might have been able to come out for the morning into the forest. I went alone; it was a lovely day, and I took a long walk.'

'It was a lovely day,' she said absently, and sat with her eyes lowered, slowly opening and closing her fan. Longmore, as he watched her, felt more and more sure that her sister-in-law had seen her since her interview with him; that her attitude toward him was changed. It was this same something that chilled the ardour with which he had come, or at least converted the dozen passionate speeches which kept rising to his lips into a kind of reverential silence. No, certainly, he could not clasp her to his arms now, any more than some early worshipper could have clasped the marble statue in his temple. But Longmore's statue spoke at last, with a full human voice, and even with a shade of human hesitation. She looked up, and it seemed to him that her eyes shone through the dusk.

'I'm very glad you came this evening,' she said. 'I have a particular reason for being glad. I half expected you, and yet I thought it possible you might not come.'

'As I have been feeling all day,' Longmore answered, 'it was impossible I should not come. I have spent the day in thinking of you.'

She made no immediate reply, but continued to open and close her fan thoughtfully. At last – 'I have something to say to you,' she said abruptly. 'I want you to know to a certainty that I have a very high opinion of you.' Longmore started and shifted his position. To what was she coming? But he said nothing, and she went on.

'I take a great interest in you; there's no reason why I should not say it – I have a great friendship for you.'

He began to laugh; he hardly knew why, unless that this seemed the very mockery of coldness. But she continued without heeding him.

'You know, I suppose, that a great disappointment always implies a great confidence – a great hope?'

'I have hoped,' he said, 'hoped strongly; but doubtless never rationally enough to have a right to bemoan my disappointment.'

'You do yourself injustice. I have such confidence in your reason, that I should be greatly disappointed if I were to find it wanting.'

'I really almost believe that you are amusing yourself at my expense,' cried Longmore. 'My reason? Reason is a mere word! The only reality in the world is *feeling*!'

She rose to her feet and looked at him gravely. His eyes by this time were accustomed to the imperfect light, and he could see that her look was reproachful, and yet that it was beseechingly kind. She shook her head impatiently, and laid her fan upon his arm with a strong pressure.

'If that were so, it would be a weary world. I know your feeling, however, nearly enough. You needn't try to express it. It's enough that it gives me the right to ask a favour of you – to make an urgent, a solemn request.'

'Make it; I listen.'

'*Don't disappoint me.* If you don't understand me now, you will tomorrow, or very soon. When I said just now that I had a very high opinion of you, I meant it very seriously. It was not a vain compliment. I believe that there is no appeal one may make to your generosity which can remain long unanswered. If this were to happen – if I were to find you selfish where I thought you generous, narrow where I thought you large –' and she spoke slowly, with her voice lingering with emphasis on each of these words – 'vulgar where I thought you rare – I should think worse of human nature. I should suffer – I should suffer keenly. I should say to myself in the dull days of the future, "There was one man who might have done so and so; and he, too, failed." But this shall not be. You have made too good an impression on me not to make the very best. If you wish to please me for ever, there's a way.'

She was standing close to him, with her dress touching him, her eyes fixed on his. As she went on her manner grew strangely intense, and she had the singular appearance of a woman preaching reason with a kind of passion. Longmore was confused, dazzled, almost bewildered. The intention of her words was all remonstrance, refusal, dismissal; but her presence there, so close, so urgent, so personal, seemed a distracting contradiction of it. She had never been so lovely. In her white dress, with her pale face and deeply lighted eyes, she seemed the very spirit of the summer night. When she had ceased speaking, she drew a long breath; Longmore felt it on his cheek, and it stirred in his whole being a sudden, rapturous conjecture. Were her words in their soft severity a mere delusive spell, meant to throw into relief her almost ghostly beauty, and was this the only truth, the only reality, the only law?

He closed his eyes and felt that she was watching him, not without pain and perplexity herself. He looked at her again, met her own eyes, and saw a tear in each of them. Then this last suggestion of his desire seemed to die away with a stifled murmur, and her beauty, more and more radiant in the darkness, rose before him as a symbol of something vague which was yet more beautiful than itself.

'I may understand you tomorrow,' he said, 'but I don't understand you now.'

'And yet I took counsel with myself today and asked myself how I had best speak to you. On one side, I might have refused to see you at all.' Longmore made a violent movement, and she added: 'In that case I should have written to you. I might see you, I thought, and simply say to you that there were excellent reasons why we should part, and that I begged this visit should be your last. This I inclined to do; what made me decide otherwise was – simply friendship! I said to myself that I should be glad to remember in future days, not that I had dismissed you, but that you had gone away out of the fullness of your own wisdom.'

'The fullness – the fullness!' cried Longmore.

'I'm prepared, if necessary,' Madame de Mauves continued after a pause, 'to fall back upon my strict right. But, as I said before, I shall be greatly disappointed, if I am obliged to.'

'When I hear you say that,' Longmore answered, 'I feel so angry, so horribly irritated, that I wonder it is not easy to leave you without more words.'

'If you should go away in anger, this idea of mine about our parting would be but half realized. No, I don't want to think of you as angry; I don't want even to think of you as making a serious sacrifice. I want to think of you as—'

'As a creature who never has existed – who never can exist! A creature who knew you without loving you – who left you without regretting you!'

She turned impatiently away and walked to the other end of the terrace. When she came back, he saw that her impatience had become a cold sternness. She stood before him again, looking at him from head to foot, in deep reproachfulness, almost in scorn. Beneath her glance he felt a kind of shame. He coloured; she observed it and withheld something she was about to say. She turned away again, walked to the other end of the terrace, and stood there looking away into the garden. It seemed to him that she had guessed he understood her, and slowly – slowly – half as the fruit of his vague self-reproach – he did understand her. She was giving him a chance to do gallantly what it seemed unworthy of both of them he should do meanly.

She liked him, she must have liked him greatly, to wish so to spare him, to go to the trouble of conceiving an ideal of conduct for him. With this sense of her friendship – her strong friendship she had just called it – Longmore's soul rose with a new flight, and suddenly felt itself breathing a clearer air. The words ceased to seem a mere bribe to his ardour; they were charged with ardour themselves; they were a present happiness. He moved rapidly toward her with a feeling that this was something he might immediately enjoy.

They were separated by two-thirds of the length of the terrace, and he had to pass the drawing-room window. As he did so he started with an exclamation. Madame Clairin stood posted there, watching him. Conscious, apparently, that she might be suspected of eavesdropping, she stepped forward with a smile and looked from Longmore to his hostess.

'Such a *tête-à-tête* as that,' she said, 'one owes no apology for interrupting. One ought to come in for good manners.'

Madame de Mauves turned round, but she answered nothing. She looked straight at Longmore, and her eyes had extraordinary eloquence. He was not exactly sure, indeed, what she meant them to say; but they seemed to say plainly something of this kind: 'Call it what you will, what you have to urge upon me is the thing which this woman can best conceive. What I ask of you is something she can't!' They seemed, somehow, to beg him to suffer her to be herself, and to intimate that that self was as little as possible like Madame Clairin. He felt an immense answering desire not to do anything which would seem natural to this lady. He had laid his hat and cane on the parapet of the terrace. He took them up, offered his hand to Madame de Mauves with a simple good-night, bowed silently to Madame Clairin, and departed.

IX

HE WENT HOME and without lighting his candle flung himself on his bed. But he got no sleep till morning; he lay hour after hour tossing, thinking, wondering; his mind had never been so active. It seemed to him that Euphemia had laid on him in those last moments an inspiring commission, and that she had expressed herself almost as largely as if she had listened assentingly to an assurance of his love. It was neither easy nor delightful thoroughly to understand her; but little by little her perfect meaning sank into his mind and soothed it with a sense of opportunity, which somehow stifled his sense of loss. For, to begin with, she meant that she could love him in no degree nor contingency, in no imaginable future. This was absolute; he felt that he could alter it no more than he could transpose the constellations he lay gazing at through his open window. He wondered what it was, in the background of her life, that she grasped so closely: a sense of duty, unquenchable to the end? a love that no offence could trample out? 'Good Heavens!' he thought, 'is the world so rich in the purest pearls of passion, that such tenderness as that can be wasted for ever – poured away without a sigh into bottomless darkness?' Had she, in spite of the detestable present, some precious memory which contained the germ of a shrinking hope? Was she prepared to submit to everything and yet to believe? Was it strength, was it weakness, was it a vulgar fear, was it conviction, conscience, constancy?

Longmore sank back with a sigh and an oppressive feeling that it was vain to guess at such a woman's motives. He only felt that those of Madame de Mauves were buried deep in her soul, and that they must be of some fine temper, not of a base one. He had a dim, overwhelming sense of a sort of invulnerable constancy being the supreme law of her character – a constancy which still found a foothold among crumbling ruins. 'She has loved once,' he said to himself as he rose and wandered to his window; 'that's for ever. Yes, yes – if she loved again she would be *common*.' He stood for a long time looking out into the starlit silence of the town and the forest, and thinking of what life would have been if *his* constancy had met hers unpledged. But life was this, now, and he must live. It was living keenly to stand there with a petition from such a woman to revolve. He was not to disappoint her, he was to justify a conception which it had beguiled her weariness to shape. Longmore's imagination swelled; he threw back his head and seemed to be looking for Madame de Mauves's conception among the blinking, mocking stars. But it came to him rather on the mild night-wind, as it wandered in over the house-tops which covered the rest of so many heavy human hearts. What she asked he felt that she was asking, not for her own sake (she feared nothing, she needed nothing), but for that of his own happiness and his own character. He must assent to destiny. Why else was he young and strong, intelligent and resolute? He must not give it to her to reproach him with thinking that she had a moment's attention for his love – to plead, to argue, to break off in bitterness; he must see everything from above, her indifference and his own ardour; he must prove his strength, he must do the handsome thing; he must decide that the handsome thing was to submit to the inevitable, to be supremely delicate, to spare her all pain, to stifle his passion, to ask no compensation, to depart without delay and try to believe that wisdom is its own reward. All this, neither more nor less, it was a matter of friendship with Madame de Mauves to expect of him. And what should he gain by it? He should have pleased her! . . . He flung himself on his bed again, fell asleep at last, and slept till morning.

Before noon the next day he had made up his mind that he would leave Saint-Germain at once. It seemed easier to leave without seeing her, and yet if he might ask a grain of 'compensation', it would be five minutes face to face with her. He passed a restless day. Wherever he went he seemed to see her standing before him in the dusky halo of evening, and looking at him with an air of still negation more intoxicating than the most passionate self-surrender. He must certainly go, and yet it was hideously hard. He compromised and went to Paris to spend the rest of the day. He strolled along the boulevards and looked at the shops, sat awhile in the Tuileries gardens, and looked at the shabby unfortunates for whom this only was nature and summer; but simply felt, as a result of it all, that it was a very dusty, dreary, lonely world into which Madame de Mauves was turning him away.

In a sombre mood he made his way back to the boulevards and sat down at a table on the great plain of hot asphalt, before a café. Night came on, the lamps were lighted, the tables near him found occupants, and Paris began to wear that peculiar evening look of hers which seems to say, in the flare of windows and theatre doors, and the muffled rumble of swift-rolling carriages, that this is no world for you unless you have your pockets lined and your scruples drugged. Longmore, however, had neither scruples nor desires; he looked at the swarming city for the first time with an easy sense of repaying its indifference. Before long a carriage drove up to the pavement directly in front of him, and remained standing for several minutes without its occupant getting out. It was one of those neat, plain coupés, drawn by a single powerful horse, in which one is apt to imagine a pale, handsome woman, buried among silk cushions, and yawning as she sees the gas-lamps glittering in the gutters. At last the door opened and out stepped M. de Mauves. He stopped and leaned on the window for some time, talking in an excited manner to a person within. At last he gave a nod and the carriage rolled away.

He stood swinging his cane and looking up and down the boulevard, with the air of a man fumbling, as one may say, with the loose change of time. He turned toward the café and was apparently, for want of anything better worth his attention, about to seat himself at one of the tables, when he perceived Longmore. He wavered an instant, and then, without a change in his nonchalant gait, strolled toward him with a bow and a vague smile.

It was the first time they had met since their encounter in the forest after Longmore's false start for Brussels. Madame Clairin's revelations, as we may call them, had not made the Baron especially present to his mind; he had another office for his emotions than disgust. But as M. de Mauves came toward him he felt deep in his heart that he abhorred him. He noticed, however, for the first time, a shadow upon the Baron's cool placidity, and his delight at finding that somewhere at last the shoe pinched *him*, mingled with his impulse to be as exasperatingly impenetrable as possible, enabled him to return the other's greeting with all his own self-possession.

M. de Mauves sat down, and the two men looked at each other across the table, exchanging formal greetings which did little to make their mutual scrutiny seem gracious. Longmore had no reason to suppose that the Baron knew of his sister's revelations. He was sure that M. de Mauves cared very little about his opinions, and yet he had a sense that there was that in his eyes which would have made the Baron change colour if keener suspicion had helped him to read it. M. de Mauves did not change colour, but he looked at Longmore with a half-defiant intentness, which betrayed at once an irritating memory of the episode in the Bois de Boulogne, and such vigilant curiosity as was natural to a gentleman who had entrusted his 'honour' to another gentleman's magnanimity – or to his artlessness. It would appear that Longmore seemed to the Baron to possess these virtues in rather scantier measure than a few days before; for the cloud deepened on his face, and he turned away and frowned as he lighted a cigar.

The person in the coupé, Longmore thought, whether or no the same person as the heroine of the episode of the Bois de Boulogne, was not a source of unalloyed delight. Longmore had dark blue eyes, of admirable lucidity – truth-telling eyes which had in his childhood always made his harshest task-masters smile at his nursery fibs. An observer watching the two men, and knowing something of their relations, would certainly have said that what he saw in those eyes must not a little have puzzled and tormented M. de Mauves. They judged him, they mocked him, they eluded him, they threatened him, they triumphed over him, they treated him as no pair of eyes had ever treated him. The Baron's scheme had been to make no one happy but himself, and here was Longmore already, if looks were to be trusted, primed for an enterprise more inspiring than the finest of his own achievements. Was this candid young barbarian but a *faux bonhomme* after all? He had puzzled the Baron before, and this was once too often.

M. de Mauves hated to seem preoccupied, and he took up the evening paper to help himself to look indifferent. As he glanced over it he uttered some cold commonplace on the political situation, which gave Longmore an easy opportunity of replying by an ironical sally which made him seem for the moment aggressively at his ease. And yet our hero was far from being master of the situation. The Baron's ill-humour did him good, so far as it pointed to a want of harmony with the lady in the coupé; but it disturbed him sorely as he began to suspect that it possibly meant jealousy of himself. It passed through his mind that jealousy is a passion with a double face, and that in some of its moods it bears a plausible likeness to affection. It recurred to him painfully that the Baron might grow ashamed of his political compact with his wife, and he felt that it would be far more tolerable in the future to think of his continued turpitude than of his repentance. The two men sat for half an hour exchanging stinted small-talk, the Baron feeling a nervous need of playing the spy, and Longmore indulging a ferocious relish of his discomfort. These rigid courtesies were interrupted however by the arrival of a friend of M. de Mauves — a tall, pale, consumptive-looking dandy, who filled the air with the odour of heliotrope. He looked up and down the boulevard wearily, examined the Baron's toilet from head to foot, then surveyed his own in the same fashion, and at last announced languidly that the Duchess was in town! M. de Mauves must come with him to call; she had abused him dreadfully a couple of evenings before — a sure sign she wanted to see him.

'I depend upon you,' said M. de Mauves's friend with an infantine drawl, 'to put her *en train*.'

M. de Mauves resisted, and protested that he was *d'une humeur massacrante*; but at last he allowed himself to be drawn to his feet, and stood looking awkwardly – awkwardly for M. de Mauves – at Longmore. 'You'll excuse me,' he said dryly; 'you, too, probably, have occupation for the evening?'

'None but to catch my train,' Longmore answered, looking at his watch.

'Ah, you go back to Saint-Germain?'

'In half an hour.'

M. de Mauves seemed on the point of disengaging himself from his companion's arm, which was locked in his own; but on the latter uttering some persuasive murmur, he lifted his hat stiffly and turned away.

Longmore packed his trunk the next day with dogged heroism and wandered off to the terrace, to try and beguile the restlessness with which he waited for evening; for he wished to see Madame de Mauves for the last time at the hour of long shadows and pale pink-reflected lights, as he had almost always seen her. Destiny, however, took no account of this humble plea for poetic justice; it was his fortune to meet her on the terrace sitting under a tree, alone. It was an hour when the place was almost empty; the day was warm, but as he took his place beside her a light breeze stirred the leafy edges on the broad circle of shadow in which she sat. She looked at him with candid anxiety, and he immediately told her that he should leave Saint-Germain that evening – that he must bid her farewell. Her eye expanded and brightened for a moment as he spoke; but she said nothing and turned her glance away toward distant Paris, as it lay twinkling and flashing through its hot exhalations. 'I have a request to make of you,' he added. 'That you think of me as a man who has felt much and claimed little.'

She drew a long breath, which almost suggested pain. 'I can't think of you as unhappy. It's impossible. You have a life to lead, you have duties, talents, and interests. I shall hear of your career. And then,' she continued after a pause and with the deepest seriousness, 'one can't be unhappy through having a better opinion of a friend, instead of a worse.'

For a moment he failed to understand her. 'Do you mean that there can be varying degrees in my opinion of you?'

She rose and pushed away her chair. 'I mean,' she said quickly, 'that it's better to have done nothing in bitterness – nothing in passion.' And she began to walk.

Longmore followed her, without answering. But he took off his hat and with his pocket-handkerchief wiped his forehead. 'Where shall you go? what shall you do?' he asked at last, abruptly.

'Do? I shall do as I've always done – except perhaps that I shall go for a while to Auvergne.'

'I shall go to America. I have done with Europe for the present.'

She glanced at him as he walked beside her after he had spoken these words, and then bent her eyes for a long time on the ground. At last, seeing that she was going far, she stopped and put out her hand. 'Good-bye,' she said; 'may you have all the happiness you deserve!'

He took her hand and looked at her, but something was passing in him that made it impossible to return her hand's light pressure. Something of infinite value was floating past him, and he had taken an oath not to raise a finger to stop it. It was borne by the strong current of the world's great life and not of his own small one. Madame de Mauves disengaged her hand, gathered her shawl, and smiled at him almost as you would do at a child you should wish to encourage. Several moments later he was still standing watching her receding figure. When it had disappeared, he shook himself, walked rapidly back to his hotel, and without waiting for the evening train paid his bill and departed.

Later in the day M. de Mauves came into his wife's drawing-room, where she sat waiting to be summoned to dinner. He was dressed with a scrupulous freshness which seemed to indicate an intention of dining out. He walked up and down for some moments in silence, then rang the bell for a servant, and went out into the hall to meet him. He ordered the carriage to take him to the station, paused a moment with his hand on the knob of the door, dismissed the servant angrily as the latter lingered observing him, re-entered the drawing-room, resumed his restless walk, and at last stepped abruptly before his wife, who had taken up a book. 'May I ask the favour,' he said with evident effort, in spite of a forced smile of easy courtesy, 'of having a question answered?'

'It's a favour I never refused,' Madame de Mauves replied.

'Very true. Do you expect this evening a visit from Mr Longmore?'

'Mr Longmore,' said his wife, 'has left Saint-Germain.' M. de Mauve started and his smile expired. 'Mr Longmore,' his wife continued, 'has gone to America.'

M. de Mauves stared a moment, flushed deeply, and turned away. Then recovering himself – 'Had anything happened?' he asked, 'Had he a sudden call?'

But his question received no answer. At the same moment the servant threw open the door and announced dinner; Madame Clairin rustled in, rubbing her white hands, Madame de Mauves passed silently into the dining-room, and he stood frowning and wondering. Before long he went out upon the terrace and continued his uneasy walk. At the end of a quarter of an hour the servant came to inform him that the carriage was at the door. 'Send it away,' he said curtly. 'I shall not use it.' When the ladies had half finished dinner he went in and joined them, with a formal apology to his wife for his tardiness.

The dishes were brought back, but he hardly tasted them; on the other hand, he drank a great deal of wine. There was little talk; what there was, was supplied by Madame Clairin. Twice she saw her brother's eyes fixed on her own, over his wineglass, with a piercing, questioning glance. She replied by an elevation of the eyebrows, which did the office of a shrug of the shoulders. M. de Mauves was left alone to finish his wine; he sat over it for more than an hour, and let the darkness gather about him. At last the servant came in with a letter and lighted a candle. The letter was a telegram, which M. de Mauves, when he had read it, burned at the candle. After five minutes' meditation, he wrote a message on the back of a visiting-card and gave it to the servant to carry to the office. The man knew quite as much as his master suspected about the lady to whom the telegram was addressed; but its contents puzzled him; they consisted of the single word '*Impossible*'. As the evening passed without her brother reappearing in the drawing-room, Madame Clairin came to him where he sat, by his solitary candle. He took no notice of her presence for some time; but he was the one person to whom she allowed this licence. At last, speaking in a peremptory tone, 'The American has gone home at an hour's notice,' he said. 'What does it mean?'

Madame Clairin now gave free play to the shrug she had been obliged to suppress at the table. 'It means that I have a sister-in-law whom I haven't the honour to understand.'

He said nothing more, and silently allowed her to depart, as if it had been her duty to provide him with an explanation and he was disgusted with her levity. When she had gone, he went into the garden and walked up and down, smoking. He saw his wife sitting alone on the terrace, but remained below strolling along the narrow paths. He remained a long time. It became late and Madame de Mauves disappeared. Toward midnight he dropped upon a bench, tired, with a kind of angry sigh. It was sinking into his mind that he, too, did not understand Madame Clairin's sister-in-law.

Longmore was obliged to wait a week in London for a ship. It was very hot, and he went out for a day to Richmond. In the garden of the hotel at which he dined he met his friend Mrs Draper, who was staying there. She made eager inquiry about Madame de Mauves, but Longmore at first, as they sat looking out at the famous view of the Thames, parried her questions and confined himself to small-talk. At last she said she was afraid he had something to conceal; whereupon, after a pause, he asked her if she remembered recommending him, in the letter she sent to him at Saint-Germain, to draw the sadness from her friend's smile. 'The last I saw of her was her smile,' said he – 'when I bade her good-bye.'

'I remember urging you to "console" her,' Mrs Draper answered, 'and I wondered afterwards whether – a model of discretion as you are – I hadn't given you rather foolish advice.'

'She has her consolation in herself,' he said; 'she needs none that anyone else can offer her. That's for troubles for which – be it more, be it less – our own folly has to answer. Madame de Mauves has not a grain of folly left.'

'Ah, don't say that!' murmured Mrs Draper. 'Just a little folly is very graceful.'

Longmore rose to go, with a quick nervous movement. 'Don't talk of grace,' he said, 'till you have measured her reason.'

For two years after his return to America he heard nothing of Madame de Mauves. That he thought of her intently, constantly, I need hardly say: most people wondered why such a clever young man should not 'devote' himself to something; but to himself he seemed absorbingly occupied. He never wrote to her; he believed that she preferred it. At last he heard that Mrs Draper had come home, and he immediately called on her. 'Of course,' she said after the first greetings, 'you are dying for news of Madame de Mauves. Prepare yourself for something strange.

I heard from her two or three times during the year after your return. She left Saint-Germain and went to live in the country, on some old property of her husband's. She wrote me very kind little notes, but I felt somehow that – in spite of what you said about "consolation" – they were the notes of a very sad woman. The only advice I could have given her was to leave her wretch of a husband and come back to her own land and her own people. But this I didn't feel free to do, and yet it made me so miserable not to be able to help her that I preferred to let our correspondence die a natural death. I had no news of her for a year. Last summer, however, I met at Vichy a clever young Frenchman whom I accidentally learned to be a friend of Euphemia's lovely sister-in-law, Madame Clairin. I lost no time in asking him what he knew about Madame de Mauves – a countrywoman of mine and an old friend. "I congratulate you on possessing her friendship," he answered. "That's the charming little woman who killed her husband." You may imagine that I promptly asked for an explanation, and he proceeded to relate to me what he called the whole story. M. de Mauves had fait *quelques folies*, which his wife had taken absurdly to heart. He had repented and asked her forgiveness, which she had inexorably refused. She was very pretty, and severity, apparently, suited her style; for whether or no her husband had been in love with her before, he fell madly in love with her now. He was the proudest man in France, but he had begged her on his knees to be readmitted to favour. All in vain! She was stone, she was ice, she was outraged virtue. People noticed a great change in him:

he gave up society, ceased to care for anything, looked shockingly. One fine day they learned that he had blown out his brains. My friend had the story of course from Madame Clairin.'

Longmore was strongly moved, and his first impulse after he had recovered his composure was to return immediately to Europe. But several years have passed, and he still lingers at home. The truth is, that in the midst of all the ardent tenderness of his memory of Madame de Mauves, he has become conscious of a singular feeling – a feeling for which awe would be hardly too strong a name.

The Ghostly Rental

I WAS IN MY twenty-second year, and I had just left college. I
was at liberty to choose my career, and I chose it with much
promptness. I afterward renounced it, in truth, with equal
ardour, but I have never regretted those two youthful years of
perplexed and excited, but also of agreeable and fruitful experiment. I had a taste for theology, and during my college term I
had been an admiring reader of Dr Channing. This was theology of a greatful and succulent savour; it seemed to offer one
the rose of faith delightfully stripped of its thorns. And then
(for I rather think this had something to do with it), I had taken
a fancy to the old Divinity School. I have always had an eye to
the back scene in the human drama, and it seemed to me that I
might play my part with a fair chance of applause (from myself
at least), in that detached and tranquil home of mild casuistry,
with its respectable avenue on one side, and its prospect of green
fields and contact with acres of woodland on the other.
Cambridge, for the lovers of woods and fields, has changed for
the worse since those days, and the precinct in question has

forfeited much of its mingled pastoral and scholastic quietude. It was then a College-hall in the woods – a charming mixture. What it is now has nothing to do with my story; and I have no doubt that there are still doctrine-haunted young seniors who, as they stroll near it in the summer dusk, promise themselves, later, to taste of its fine leisurely quality. For myself, I was not disappointed. I established myself in a great square, low-browed room, with deep window-benches; I hung prints from Overbeck and Ary Scheffer on the walls; I arranged my books, with great refinement of classification, in the alcoves beside the high chimney-shelf, and I began to read Plotinus and St Augustine. Among my companions were two or three men of ability and of good fellowship, with whom I occasionally brewed a fireside bowl; and with adventurous reading, deep discourse, potations conscientiously shallow, and long country walks, my initiation into the clerical mystery progressed agreeably enough.

With one of my comrades I formed an especial friendship, and we passed a great deal of time together. Unfortunately he had a chronic weakness of one of his knees, which compelled him to lead a very sedentary life, and as I was a methodical pedestrian, this made some difference in our habits. I used often to stretch away for my daily ramble, with no companion but the stick in my hand or the book in my pocket. But in the use of my legs and the sense of unstinted open air, I have always found company enough. I should, perhaps, add that in the enjoyment of a very sharp pair of eyes, I found something of a social pleasure. My eyes and I were on excellent terms; they were indefatigable observers of all wayside incidents, and so long as they were amused I was contented. It is, indeed, owing to their inquisitive habits that I came into possession of this remarkable story. Much of the country about the old college town is pretty now, but it was prettier thirty years ago. That multitudinous eruption of domiciliary pasteboard which now graces the landscape, in the direction of the low, blue Waltham Hills, had not yet taken place; there were no genteel cottages to put the shabby meadows and scrubby orchards to shame – a juxtaposition by which, in later years, neither element of the contrast has gained. Certain crooked crossroads, then, as I remember them, were more deeply and naturally rural, and the solitary dwellings on the long grassy slopes beside them, under the tall, customary elm that curved its foliage in mid-air like the outward dropping ears of a girdled wheat-sheaf, sat with their shingled hoods well pulled down on their ears, and no prescience whatever of the fashion of French roofs – weather-wrinkled old peasant women, as you might call them, quietly wearing the native coif, and never dreaming of mounting bonnets, and indecently exposing their venerable brows. That winter was what is called an 'open' one; there was much cold, but little snow; the roads were firm and free, and I was rarely compelled by the weather to forego my exercise. One grey December afternoon I had sought it in the direction of the adjacent town of Medford, and I was retracing my steps at an even pace, and watching the pale, cold tints – the transparent amber and faded rose-colour – which curtained, in wintry fashion, the western sky, and reminded me of a sceptical smile on the lips of a beautiful woman. I came, as dusk was falling, to a narrow road which I had never traversed and which I imagined offered me a short cut homeward. I was about three miles away; I was late, and would have been thankful to make them two. I diverged, walked some ten minutes, and then perceived that the road had a very unfrequented air. The wheel-ruts looked old; the stillness seemed peculiarly sensible. And yet down the road stood a house, so that it must in some degree have been a thoroughfare. On one side was a high, natural embankment, on the top of which was perched an apple-orchard, whose tangled boughs made a stretch of coarse black lace-work, hung across the coldly rosy west. In a short time I came to the house, and I immediately found myself interested in it. I stopped in front of it gazing hard, I hardly knew why, but with a vague mixture of curiosity and timidity. It was a house like most of the houses thereabouts, except that it was decidedly a handsome specimen of its class. It stood on a grassy slope, it had its tall, impartially drooping elm beside it, and its old black well-cover at its shoulder. But it was of very large proportions, and it had a striking look of solidity and stoutness of timber. It had lived to a good old age, too, for the wood-work on its doorway and under its eaves, carefully and abundantly carved, referred it to the middle, at the latest, of the last century. All this had once been painted white, but the broad back of time, leaning against the door-posts for a hundred years, had laid bare the grain of the wood. Behind the house stretched an orchard of apple-trees, more gnarled and fantastic than usual, and wearing, in the deepening dusk, a blighted and exhausted aspect. All the windows of the house had rusty shutters, without slats, and these were closely drawn. There was no sign of life about it; it looked blank, bare and vacant, and yet, as I lingered near it, it seemed to have a familiar meaning – an audible eloquence. I have always thought of the impression made upon me at first sight, by that grey colonial dwelling, as a proof that induction may sometimes be near akin to divination; for after all, there was nothing on the face of the matter to warrant the very serious induction that I made. I fell back and crossed the road. The last red light of the sunset disengaged itself, as it was about to vanish, and rested faintly for a moment on the time-silvered front of the old house. It touched, with perfect regularity, the series of small panes in the fan-shaped window above the door, and twinkled there fantastically. Then it died away, and left the place more intensely sombre. At this moment, I said to myself with the accent of profound conviction – 'The house is simply haunted!'

Somehow, immediately, I believed it, and so long as I was not shut up inside, the idea gave me pleasure. It was implied in the aspect of the house, and it explained it. Half an hour before, if I had been asked, I would have said, as befitted a young man who was explicitly cultivating cheerful views of the supernatural, that there were no such things as haunted houses. But the dwelling before me gave a vivid meaning to the empty words; it had been spiritually blighted.

The longer I looked at it, the intenser seemed the secret that it held. I walked all round it, I tried to peep here and there, through a crevice in the shutters, and I took a puerile satisfaction in laying my hand on the door-knob and gently turning it. If the door had yielded, would I have gone in? – would I have penetrated the dusky stillness? My audacity, fortunately, was not put to the test. The portal was admirably solid, and I was unable even to shake it. At last I turned away, casting many looks behind me. I pursued my way, and, after a longer walk than I had bargained for, reached the high-road. At a certain distance below the point at which the long lane I have mentioned entered it, stood a comfortable, tidy dwelling, which might have offered itself as the model of the house which is in no sense haunted – which has no sinister secrets, and knows nothing but blooming prosperity. Its clean white paint stared placidly through the dusk, and its vine-covered porch had been dressed in straw for the winter. An old, one-horse chaise, freighted with two departing visitors, was leaving the door, and through the undraped windows, I saw the lamp-lit sitting-room, and the table spread with the early 'tea', which had been improvised for the comfort of the guests. The mistress of the house had come to the gate with her friends; she lingered there after the chaise had wheeled creakingly away, half to watch them down the road, and half to give me, as I passed in the twilight, a questioning look. She was a comely, quick young woman, with a sharp, dark eye, and I ventured to stop and speak to her.

'That house down that side-road,' I said, 'about a mile from here – the only one – can you tell me whom it belongs to?'

She stared at me a moment, and, I thought, coloured a little. 'Our folks never go down that road,' she said, briefly.

'But it's a short way to Medford,' I answered.

She gave a little toss of her head. 'Perhaps it would turn out a long way. At any rate, we don't use it.'

This was interesting. A thrifty Yankee household must have good reasons for this scorn of time-saving processes. 'But you know the house, at least?' I said.

'Well, I have seen it.'

'And to whom does it belong?'

She gave a little laugh and looked away, as if she were aware that, to a stranger, her words might seem to savour of agricultural superstition. 'I guess it belongs to them that are in it.'

'But is there anyone in it? It is completely closed.'

'That makes no difference. They never come out, and no one ever goes in.' And she turned away.

But I laid my hand on her arm, respectfully. 'You mean,' I said, 'that the house is haunted?'

She drew herself away, coloured, raised her finger to her lips, and hurried into the house, where, in a moment, the curtains were dropped over the windows.

For several days, I thought repeatedly of this little adventure, but I took some satisfaction in keeping it to myself. If the house was not haunted, it was useless to expose my imaginative whims, and if it was, it was agreeable to drain the cup of horror without assistance. I determined, of course, to pass that way again; and a week later – it was the last day of the year – I retraced my steps. I approached the house from the opposite direction, and found myself before it at about the same hour as before. The light was failing, the sky low and grey; the wind wailed along the hard, bare ground, and made slow eddies of the frost-blackened leaves. The melancholy mansion stood there, seeming to gather the winter twilight around it, and mask itself in it, inscrutably. I hardly knew on what errand I had come, but I had a vague feeling that if this time the door-knob were to turn and the door to open, I should take my heart in my hands, and let them close behind me. Who were the mysterious tenants to whom the good woman at the corner had alluded? What had been seen or heard – what was related? The door was as stubborn as before, and my impertinent fumblings with the latch caused no upper window to be thrown open, nor any strange, pale face to be thrust out. I ventured even to raise the rusty knocker and give it half a dozen raps, but they made a flat, dead sound, and aroused no echo. Familiarity breeds contempt; I don't know what I should have done next, if, in the distance, up the road (the same one I had followed), I had not seen a solitary figure advancing. I was unwilling to be observed hanging about this ill-famed dwelling, and I sought refuge among the dense shadows of a grove of pines near by, where I might peep forth, and yet remain invisible. Presently, the new-comer drew near, and I perceived that he was making straight for the house. He was a little, old man, the most striking feature of whose appearance was a voluminous cloak, of a sort of military cut. He carried a walking-stick, and advanced in a slow, painful, somewhat hobbling fashion, but with an air of extreme resolution. He turned off from the road, and followed the vague wheel-track, and within a few yards of the house he paused. He looked up at it, fixedly and searchingly, as if he were counting the windows, or noting certain familiar marks. Then he took off his hat, and bent over slowly and solemnly, as if he were performing an obeisance. As he stood uncovered, I had a good look at him. He was, as I have said, a diminutive old man, but it would have been hard to decide whether he belonged to this world or to the other. His head reminded me, vaguely, of the portraits of Andrew Jackson. He had a crop of grizzled hair, as stiff as a brush, a lean, pale, smooth-shaven face, and an eye of intense brilliancy, surmounted with thick brows, which had remained perfectly black. His face, as well as his cloak, seemed to belong to an old soldier; he looked like a retired military man of a modest rank; but he struck me as exceeding the classic privilege of even such a personage to be eccentric and grotesque. When he had finished his salute, he advanced to the door, fumbled in the folds of his cloak, which hung down much further in front than behind, and produced a key. This he slowly and carefully inserted into the lock, and then, apparently, he turned it. But the door did not immediately open; first he bent his head, turned his ear, and stood listening, and then he looked up and down the road. Satisfied or reassured, he applied his aged shoulder to one of the deep-set panels, and pressed a moment. The door yielded – opening into perfect darkness. He stopped again on the threshold, and again removed his hat and made his bow. Then he went in, and carefully closed the door behind him.

Who in the world was he, and what was his errand? He might have been a figure out of one of Hoffmann's tales. Was he vision or a reality – an inmate of the house, or a familiar, friendly visitor? What had been the meaning, in either case, of his mystic genuflexions, and how did he propose to proceed, in that inner darkness? I emerged from my retirement, and observed narrowly, several of the windows. In each of them, at an interval, a ray of light became visible in the chink between the two leaves of the shutters. Evidently, he was lighting up; was he going to give a party – a ghostly revel? My curiosity grew intense, but I was quite at a loss how to satisfy it. For a moment I thought of rapping peremptorily at the door; but I dismissed this idea as unmannerly, and calculated to break the spell, if spell there was. I walked round the house and tried, without violence, to open one of the lower windows. It resisted, but I had better fortune, in a moment, with another. There was a risk, certainly, in the trick I was playing – a risk of being seen from within, or (worse) seeing, myself, something that I should repent of seeing. But curiosity, as I say, had become an inspiration, and the risk was highly agreeable. Through the parting of the shutters I looked into a lighted room – a room lighted by two candles in old brass flambeaux, placed upon the mantel-shelf. It was apparently a sort of back parlour, and it had retained all its furniture. This was of a homely, old-fashioned pattern, and consisted of hair-cloth chairs and sofas, spare mahogany tables, and framed samplers hung upon the walls. But although the room was furnished, it had a strangely uninhabited look; the tables and chairs were in rigid positions, and no small, familiar objects were visible. I could not see everything, and I could only guess at the existence, on my right, of a large folding-door. It was apparently open, and the light of the neighbouring room passed through it. I waited for some time, but the room remained empty. At last I became conscious that a large shadow was projected upon the wall opposite the folding-door – the shadow, evidently, of a figure in the adjoining room. It was tall and grotesque, and seemed to represent a person sitting perfectly motionless, in profile. I thought I recognized the perpendicular bristles and far-arching nose of my little old man. There was a strange fixedness in his posture; he appeared to be seated, and looking intently at something. I watched the shadow a long time, but it never stirred. At last, however, just as my patience began to ebb, it moved slowly, rose to the ceiling, and became indistinct. I don't know what I should have seen next, but by an irresistible impulse, I closed the shutter. Was it delicacy? – was it pusillanimity? I can hardly say. I lingered, nevertheless, near the house, hoping that my friend would reappear. I was not disappointed; for he at last emerged, looking just as when he had gone in, and taking his leave in the same ceremonious fashion. (The lights, I had already observed, had disappeared from the crevice of each of the windows.) He faced about before the door, took off his hat, and made an obsequious bow. As he turned away I had a hundred minds to speak to him, but I let him depart in peace. This, I may say, was pure delicacy; – you will answer, perhaps, that it came too late. It seemed to me that he had a right to resent my observation; though my own right to exercise it (if ghosts were in the question) struck me as equally positive. I continued to watch him as he hobbled softly down the bank, and along the lonely road. Then I musingly retreated in the opposite direction. I was tempted to follow him, at a distance, to see what became of him; but this, too, seemed indelicate; and I confess, moreover, that I felt the inclination to coquet a little, as it were, with my discovery — to pull apart the petals of the flower one by one.

I continued to smell the flower, from time to time, for its oddity of perfume had fascinated me. I passed by the house on the cross-road again, but never encountered the old man in the cloak, or any other wayfarer. It seemed to keep observers at a distance, and I was careful not to gossip about it: one inquirer, I said to myself, may edge his way into the secret, but there is no room for two. At the same time, of course, I would have been thankful for any chance side-light that might fall across the matter — though I could not well see whence it was to come. I hoped to meet the old man in the cloak elsewhere, but as the days passed by without his reappearing, I ceased to expect it. And yet I reflected that he probably lived in that neighbour-hood, inasmuch as he had made his pilgrimage to the vacant house on foot. If he had come from a distance, he would have been sure to arrive in some old deep-hooded gig with yellow wheels — a vehicle as venerably grotesque as himself. One day I took a stroll in Mount Auburn cemetery — an institution at that period in its infancy, and full of a sylvan charm which it has now completely forfeited. It contained more maple and birch than willow and cypress, and the sleepers had ample elbow room. It was not a city of the dead, but at the most a village, and a meditative pedestrian might stroll there without too importunate reminder of the grotesque side of our claims to posthumous consideration. I had come out to enjoy the first foretaste of spring – one of those mild days of late winter, when the torpid earth seems to draw the first long breath that marks the rupture of the spell of sleep. The sun was veiled in haze, and yet warm, and the frost was oozing from its deepest lurking-places. I had been treading for half an hour the winding ways of the cemetery, when suddenly I perceived a familiar figure seated on a bench against a southward-facing evergreen hedge. I call the figure familiar, because I had seen it often in memory and in fancy; in fact, I had beheld it but once. Its back was turned to me, but it wore a voluminous cloak, which there was no mistaking. Here, at last, was my fellow-visitor at the haunted house, and here was my chance, if I wished to approach him! I made a circuit, and came toward him from in front. He saw me, at the end of the alley, and sat motionless, with his hands on the head of his stick, watching me from under his black eyebrows as I drew near. At a distance these black eyebrows looked formidable; they were the only thing I saw in his face. But on a closer view I was reassured, simply because I immediately felt that no man could really be as fantastically fierce as this poor old gentleman looked. His face was a kind of caricature of martial truculence. I stopped in front of him, and respectfully asked leave to sit and rest upon his bench. He granted it with a silent gesture, of much dignity, and I placed myself beside him. In this position I was able, covertly, to observe him. He was quite as much an oddity in the morning sunshine, as he had been in the dubious twilight. The lines in his face were as rigid as if they had been hacked out of a block by a clumsy woodcarver. His eyes were flamboyant, his nose terrific, his mouth implacable. And yet, after a while, when he slowly turned and looked at me, fixedly, I perceived that in spite of this portentous mask, he was a very mild old man. I was sure he even would have been glad to smile, but, evidently, his facial muscles were too stiff – they had taken a different fold, once for all. I wondered whether he was demented, but I dismissed the idea; the fixed glitter in his eye was not that of insanity. What his face really expressed was deep and simple sadness; his heart perhaps was broken, but his brain was intact. His dress was shabby but neat, and his old blue cloak had known half a century's brushing.

I hastened to make some observation upon the exceptional softness of the day, and he answered me in a gentle, mellow voice, which it was almost startling to hear proceed from such bellicose lips.

'This is a very comfortable place,' he presently added.

'I am fond of walking in graveyards,' I rejoined deliberately; flattering myself that I had struck a vein that might lead to something.

I was encouraged; he turned and fixed me with his duskily glowing eyes. Then very gravely – 'Walking, yes. Take all your exercise now. Some day you will have to settle down in a grave-yard in a fixed position.'

'Very true,' said I. 'But you know there are some people who are said to take exercise even after that day.'

He had been looking at me still; at this he looked away.

'You don't understand?' I said, gently.

He continued to gaze straight before him.

'Some people, you know, walk about after death,' I went on.

At last he turned, and looked at me more portentously than ever. 'You don't believe that,' he said simply.

'How do you know I don't?'

'Because you are young and foolish.' This was said without acerbity – even kindly; but in the tone of an old man whose consciousness of his own heavy experience made everything else seem light.

'I am certainly young,' I answered; 'but I don't think that, on the whole, I am foolish. But say I don't believe in ghosts – most people would be on my side.'

'Most people are fools!' said the old man.

I let the question rest, and talked of other things. My companion seemed on his guard, he eyed me defiantly, and made brief answers to my remarks; but I nevertheless gathered an impression that our meeting was an agreeable thing to him, and even a social incident of some importance. He was evidently a lonely creature, and his opportunities for gossip were rare. He had had troubles, and they had detached him from the world, and driven him back upon himself; but the social chord in his antiquated soul was not entirely broken, and I was sure he was gratified to find that it could still feebly resound. At last, he began to ask questions himself; he inquired whether I was a student.

'I am a student of divinity,' I answered.

'Of divinity?'

'Of theology. I am studying for the ministry.'

At this he eyed me with peculiar intensity – after which his gaze wandered away again. 'There are certain things you ought to know, then,' he said at last.

'I have a great desire for knowledge,' I answered. 'What things do you mean?'

He looked at me again awhile, but without heeding my question.

'I like your appearance,' he said. 'You seem to me a sober lad.'

'Oh, I am perfectly sober!' I exclaimed – yet departing for a moment from my soberness.

'I think you are fair-minded,' he went on.

'I don't any longer strike you as foolish, then?' I asked.

'I stick to what I said about people who deny the power of departed spirits to return. They *are* fools!' And he rapped fiercely with his staff on the earth.

I hesitated a moment, and then, abruptly, 'You have seen a ghost!' I said.

He appeared not at all startled.

'You are right, sir!' he answered with great dignity. 'With me it's not a matter of cold theory – I have not had to pry into old books to learn what to believe. *I know!* With these eyes I have beheld the departed spirit standing before me as near as you are!' And his eyes, as he spoke, certainly looked as if they had rested upon strange things.

I was irresistibly impressed – I was touched with credulity.

'And was it very terrible?' I asked.

'I am an old soldier – I am not afraid!'

'When was it? – where was it?' I asked.

He looked at me mistrustfully, and I saw that I was going too fast.

'Excuse me from going into particulars,' he said. 'I am not at liberty to speak more fully. I have told you so much, because I cannot bear to hear this subject spoken of lightly. Remember in future, that you have seen a very honest old man who told you – on his honour – that he had seen a ghost!' And he got up, as if he thought he had said enough. Reserve, shyness, pride, the fear of being laughed at, the memory, possibly, of former strokes of sarcasm – all this, on one side, had its weight with him; but I suspected that on the other, his tongue was loosened by the garrulity of old age, the sense of solitude, and the need of sympathy – and perhaps, also, by the friendliness which he had been so good as to express toward myself. Evidently it would be unwise to press him, but I hoped to see him again.

'To give greater weight to my words,' he added, 'let me mention my name – Captain Diamond, sir. I have seen service.'

'I hope I may have the pleasure of meeting you again,' I said.

'The same to you, sir!' And brandishing his stick portentously – though with the friendliest intentions – he marched stiffly away.

I asked two or three persons – selected with discretion – whether they knew anything about Captain Diamond, but they were quite unable to enlighten me. At last, suddenly, I smote my forehead, and, dubbing myself a dolt, remembered that I was neglecting a source of information to which I had never applied in vain. The excellent person at whose table I habitually dined, and who dispensed hospitality to students at so much a week, had a sister as good as herself, and of conversational powers more varied. This sister, who was known as Miss Deborah, was an old maid in all the force of the term. She was deformed, and she never went out of the house; she sat all day at the window, between a bird-cage and a flower-pot, stitching small linen articles – mysterious bands and frills. She wielded, I was assured, an exquisite needle, and her work was highly prized. In spite of her deformity and her confinement, she had a little, fresh, round face, and an imperturbable serenity of spirit. She had also a very quick little wit of her own, she was extremely observant, and she had a high relish for a friendly chat. Nothing pleased her so much as to have you – especially, I think, if you were a young divinity student – move your chair near her sunny window, and settle yourself for twenty minutes' 'talk'. 'Well, sir,' she used always to say, 'what is the latest monstrosity in Biblical criticism?' – for she used to pretend to be horrified at the rationalistic tendency of the age. But she was an inexorable little philosopher, and I am convinced that she was a keener rationalist than any of us, and that, if she had chosen, she could have propounded questions that would have made the boldest of us wince. Her window commanded the whole town – or rather, the whole country. Knowledge came to her as she sat singing, with her little, cracked voice, in her low rocking-chair. She was the first to learn everything, and the last to forget it. She had the town gossip at her fingers' ends, and she knew everything about people she had never seen. When I asked her how she had acquired her learning, she said simply – 'Oh, I observe!' 'Observe closely enough,' she once said, 'and it doesn't matter where you are. You may be in a pitch-dark closet. All you want is something to start with; one thing leads to another, and all things are mixed up. Shut me up in a dark closet and I will observe after a while, that some places in it are darker than others. After that (give me time), and I will tell you what the President of the United States is going to have for dinner.' Once I paid her a compliment. 'Your observation,' I said, 'is as fine as your needle, and your statements are as true as your stitches.'

Of course Miss Deborah had heard of Captain Diamond. He had been much talked about many years before, but he had survived the scandal that attached to his name.

'What was the scandal?' I asked.

'He killed his daughter.'

'Killed her?' I cried; 'How so?'

'Oh, not with a pistol, or a dagger, or a dose of arsenic! With his tongue. Talk of women's tongues! He cursed her – with some horrible oath – and she died!'

'What had she done?'

'She had received a visit from a young man who loved her, and whom he had forbidden the house.'

'The house,' I said – 'ah yes! The house is out in the country, two or three miles from here, on a lonely cross-road.'

Miss Deborah looked sharply at me, as she bit her thread.

'Ah, you know about the house?' she said.

'A little,' I answered; 'I have seen it. But I want you to tell me more.'

But here Miss Deborah betrayed an incommunicativeness which was most unusual.

'You wouldn't call me superstitious, would you?' she asked.

'You? – you are the quintessence of pure reason.'

'Well, every thread has its rotten place, and every needle its grain of rust. I would rather not talk about that house.'

'You have no idea how you excite my curiosity!' I said.

'I can feel for you. But it would make me very nervous.'

'What harm can come to you?' I asked.

'Some harm came to a friend of mine.' And Miss Deborah gave a very positive nod.

'What had your friend done?'

'She had told me Captain Diamond's secret, which he had told her with a mighty mystery. She had been an old flame of his, and he took her into his confidence. He bade her tell no one, and assured her that if she did, something dreadful would happen to her.'

'And what happened to her?'

'She died.'

'Oh, we are all mortal!' I said. 'Had she given him a promise?'

'She had not taken it seriously, she had not believed him. She repeated the story to me, and three days afterward, she was taken with inflammation of the lungs. A month afterward, here where I sit now, I was stitching her grave-clothes. Since then, I have never mentioned what she told me.'

'Was it very strange?'

'It was strange, but it was ridiculous too. It is a thing to make you shudder and to make you laugh, both. But you can't worry it out of me. I am sure that if I were to tell you, I should immediately break a needle in my finger, and die the next week of lock-jaw.'

I retired, and urged Miss Deborah no further; but every two or three days, after dinner, I came and sat down by her rocking-chair. I made no further allusion to Captain Diamond; I sat silent, clipping tape with her scissors. At last, one day, she told me I was looking poorly. I was pale.

'I am dying of curiosity,' I said. 'I have lost my appetite. I have eaten no dinner.'

'Remember Bluebeard's wife!' said Miss Deborah.

'One may as well perish by the sword as by famine!' I answered.

Still she said nothing, and at last I rose with a melodramatic sigh and departed. As I reached the door she called me and pointed to the chair I had vacated. 'I never was hard-hearted,' she said. 'Sit down, and if we are to perish, may we at least perish together.' And then, in very few words, she communicated what she knew of Captain Diamond's secret. 'He was a very high-tempered old man, and though he was very fond of his daughter, his will was law. He had picked out a husband for her, and given her due notice. Her mother was dead, and they lived alone together. The house had been Mrs Diamond's own marriage portion; the Captain, I believe, hadn't a penny. After his marriage they had come to live there, and he had begun to work the farm. The poor girl's lover was a young man with whiskers from Boston. The Captain came in one evening and found them together; he collared the young man, and hurled a terrible curse at the poor girl. The young man cried that she was his wife, and he asked her if it was true. She said, No! Thereupon Captain Diamond, his fury growing fiercer, repeated his imprecation, ordered her out of the house, and disowned her for ever. She swooned away, but her father went raging off and left her. Several hours later, he came back and found the house empty. On the table was a note from the young man telling him that he had killed his daughter, repeating the assurance that she was his own wife, and declaring that he himself claimed the sole right to commit her remains to earth. He had carried the body away in a gig! Captain Diamond wrote him a dreadful note in answer, saying that he didn't believe his daughter was dead, but that, whether or no, she was dead to him. A week later, in the middle of the night, he saw her ghost. Then, I suppose, he was convinced. The ghost reappeared several times, and finally began regularly to haunt the house. It made the old man very uncomfortable, for little by little his passion had passed away, and he was given up to grief. He determined at last to leave the place, and tried to sell it or rent it; but meanwhile the story had gone abroad, the ghost had been seen by other persons, the house had a bad name, and it was impossible to dispose of it. With the farm, it was the old man's only property, and his only means of subsistence; if he could neither live in it nor rent it he was beggared. But the ghost had no mercy, as he had had none. He struggled for six months, and at last he broke down. He put on his old blue cloak and took up his staff, and prepared to wander away and beg his bread. Then the ghost relented, and proposed a compromise. "Leave the house to me!" it said; "I have marked it for my own. Go off and live elsewhere. But to enable you to live, I will be your tenant, since you can find no other. I will hire the house of you and pay you a certain rent." And the ghost named a sum. The old man consented, and he goes every quarter to collect his rent!'

I laughed at this recital, but I confess I shuddered too, for my own observation had exactly confirmed it. Had I not been witness of one of the Captain's quarterly visits, had I not all but seen him sit watching his spectral tenant count out the rent-money, and when he trudged away in the dark, had he not a little bag of strangely gotten coin hidden in the folds of his old blue cloak? I imparted none of these reflections to Miss Deborah, for I was determined that my observations should have a sequel, and I promised myself the pleasure of treating her to my story in its full maturity. 'Captain Diamond,' I asked, 'has no other known means of subsistence?'

'None whatever. He toils not, neither does he spin – his ghost supports him. A haunted house is valuable property!'

'And in what coin does the ghost pay?'

'In good American gold and silver. It has only this peculiarity – that the pieces are all dated before the young girl's death. It's a strange mixture of matter and spirit!'

'And does the ghost do things handsomely; is the rent large?'

'The old man, I believe, lives decently, and has his pipe and his glass. He took a little house down by the river; the door is sidewise to the street, and there is a little garden before it. There he spends his days, and has an old coloured woman to do for him. Some years ago, he used to wander about a good deal, he was a familiar figure in the town, and most people knew his legend. But of late he has drawn back into his shell; he sits over his fire, and curiosity has forgotten him. I suppose he is falling into his dotage. But I am sure, I trust,' said Miss Deborah in conclusion, 'that he won't outlive his faculties or his powers of locomotion, for, if I remember rightly, it was part of the bargain that he should come in person to collect his rent.'

We neither of us seemed likely to suffer any especial penalty for Miss Deborah's indiscretion; I found her, day after day, singing over her work, neither more nor less active than usual. For myself, I boldly pursued my observations. I went again, more than once, to the great graveyard, but I was disappointed in my hope of finding Captain Diamond there. I had a prospect, however, which afforded me compensation. I shrewdly inferred that the old man's quarterly pilgrimages were made upon the last day of the old quarter. My first sight of him had been on the 31st of December, and it was probable that he would return to his haunted home on the last day of March. This was near at hand; at last it arrived. I betook myself late in the afternoon to the old house on the cross-road, supposing that the hour of twilight was the appointed season. I was not wrong. I had been hovering about for a short time, feeling very much like a restless ghost myself, when he appeared in the same manner as before, and wearing the same costume. I again concealed myself, and saw him enter the house with the ceremonial which he had used on the former occasion. A light appeared successively in the crevice of each pair of shutters, and I opened the window which had yielded to my importunity before. Again I saw the great shadow on the wall, motionless and solemn. But I saw nothing else. The old man reappeared at last, made his fantastic salaam before the house, and crept away into the dusk.

One day, more than a month after this, I met him again at Mount Auburn. The air was full of the voice of spring; the birds had come back and were twittering over their winter's travels, and a mild west wind was making a thin murmur in the raw verdure. He was seated on a bench in the sun, still muffled in his enormous mantle, and he recognized me as soon as I approached him. He nodded at me as if he were an old Bashaw giving the signal for my decapitation, but it was apparent that he was pleased to see me.

'I have looked for you here more than once,' I said. 'You don't come often.'

'What did you want of me?' he asked.

'I wanted to enjoy your conversation. I did so greatly when I met you here before.'

'You found me amusing?'

'Interesting!' I said.

'You didn't think me cracked?'

'Cracked? – My dear sir –!' I protested.

'I'm the sanest man in the country. I know that is what insane people always say; but generally they can't prove it. I can!'

'I believe it,' I said. 'But I am curious to know how such a thing can be proved.'

He was silent awhile.

'I will tell you. I once committed, unintentionally, a great crime. Now I pay the penalty. I give up my life to it. I don't shirk it; I face it squarely, knowing perfectly what it is. I haven't tried to bluff it off; I haven't begged off from it; I haven't run away from it. The penalty is terrible, but I have accepted it. I have been a philosopher! If I were a Catholic, I might have turned monk, and spent the rest of my life in fasting and praying. That is no penalty; that is an evasion. I might have blown my brains out – I might have gone mad. I wouldn't do either. I would simply face the music, take the consequences. As I say, they are awful! I take them on certain days, four times a year. So it has been these twenty years; so it will be as long as I last. It's my business; it's my avocation. That's the way I feel about it. I call that reasonable!'

'Admirably so!' I said. 'But you fill me with curiosity and with compassion.'

'Especially with curiosity,' he said, cunningly.

'Why,' I answered, 'if I know exactly what you suffer I can pity you more.'

'I'm much obliged. I don't want your pity; it won't help me. I'll tell you something, but it's not for myself; it's for your own sake.' He paused a long time and looked all round him, as if for chance eavesdroppers. I anxiously awaited his revelation, but he disappointed me. 'Are you still studying theology?' he asked.

'Oh, yes,' I answered, perhaps with a shade of irritation. 'It's a thing one can't learn in six months.'

'I should think not, so long as you have nothing but your books. Do you know the proverb, "A grain of experience is worth a pound of precept"? I'm a great theologian.'

'Ah, you have had experience,' I murmured sympathetically.

'You have read about the immortality of the soul; you have seen Jonathan Edwards and Dr Hopkins chopping logic over it, and deciding, by chapter and verse, that it is true. But I have seen it with these eyes; I have touched it with these hands!' And the old man held up his rugged old fists and shook them portentously. 'That's better!' he went on; 'but I have bought it dearly. You had better take it from the books – evidently you always will. You are a very good young man; you will never have a crime on your conscience.'

I answered with some juvenile fatuity, that I certainly hoped I had my share of human passions, good young man and prospective Doctor of Divinity as I was.

'Ah, but you have a nice, quiet little temper,' he said. 'So have I – now! But once I was very brutal – very brutal. You ought to know that such things are. I killed my own child.'

'Your own child?'

'I struck her down to the earth and left her to die. They could not hang me, for it was not with my hand I struck her. It was with foul and damnable words. That makes a difference; it's a grand law we live under! Well, sir, I can answer for it that her soul is immortal. We have an appointment to meet four times a year, and then I catch it!'

'She has never forgiven you?'

'She has forgiven me as the angels forgive! That's what I can't stand – the soft, quiet way she looks at me. I'd rather she twisted a knife about in my heart – O Lord, Lord, Lord!' and Captain Diamond bowed his head over his stick, and leaned his forehead on his crossed hands.

I was impressed and moved, and his attitude seemed for the moment a check to further questions. Before I ventured to ask him anything more, he slowly rose and pulled his old cloak around him. He was unused to talking about his troubles, and his memories overwhelmed him. 'I must go my way,' he said; 'I must be creeping along.'

'I shall perhaps meet you here again,' I said.

'Oh, I'm a stiff-jointed old fellow,' he answered, 'and this is rather far for me to come. I have to reserve myself. I have sat sometimes a month at a time smoking my pipe in my chair. But I should like to see you again.' And he stopped and looked at me, terribly and kindly. 'Some day, perhaps, I shall be glad to be able to lay my hand on a young, unperverted soul. If a man can make a friend, it is always something gained. What is your name?'

I had in my pocket a small volume of Pascal's *Thoughts*, on the fly-leaf of which were written my name and address. I took it out and offered it to my old friend. 'Pray keep this little book,' I said. 'It is one I am very fond of, and it will tell you something about me.'

He took it and turned it over slowly, then looking up at me with a scowl of gratitude, 'I'm not much of a reader,' he said; 'but I won't refuse the first present I shall have received since – my troubles; and the last. Thank you, sir!' And with the little book in his hand he took his departure.

I was left to imagine him for some weeks after that sitting solitary in his arm-chair with his pipe. I had not another glimpse of him. But I was awaiting my chance, and on the last day of June, another quarter having elapsed, I deemed that it had come. The evening dusk in June falls late, and I was impatient for its coming. At last, toward the end of a lovely summer's day, I revisited Captain Diamond's property. Everything now was green around it save the blighted orchard in its rear, but its own immitigable greyness and sadness were as striking as when I had first beheld it beneath a December sky. As I drew near it, I saw that I was late for my purpose, for my purpose had simply been to step forward on Captain Diamond's arrival, and bravely ask him to let me go in with him. He had preceded me, and there were lights already in the windows. I was unwilling, of course, to disturb him during his ghostly interview, and I waited till he came forth. The lights disappeared in the course of time; then the door opened and Captain Diamond stole out. That evening he made no bow to the haunted house, for the first object he beheld was his fair-minded young friend planted, modestly but firmly, near the door-step. He stopped short, looking at me, and this time his terrible scowl was in keeping with the situation.

'I knew you were here,' I said. 'I came on purpose.'

He seemed dismayed, and looked round at the house uneasily.

'I beg your pardon if I have ventured too far,' I added, 'but you know you have encouraged me.'

'How did you know I was here?'

'I reasoned it out. You told me half your story, and I guessed the other half. I am a great observer, and I had noticed this house in passing. It seemed to me to have a mystery. When you kindly confided to me that you saw spirits, I was sure that it could only be here that you saw them.'

'You are mighty clever,' cried the old man. 'And what brought you here this evening?'

I was obliged to evade this question.

'Oh, I often come; I like to look at the house — it fascinates me.'

He turned and looked up at it himself. 'It's nothing to look at outside.' He was evidently quite unaware of its peculiar outward appearance, and this odd fact, communicated to me thus in the twilight, and under the very brow of the sinister dwelling, seemed to make his vision of the strange things within more real.

'I have been hoping,' I said, 'for a chance to see the inside. I thought I might find you here, and that you would let me go in with you. I should like to see what you see.'

He seemed confounded by my boldness, but not altogether displeased. He laid his hand on my arm. 'Do you know what I see?' he asked.

'How can I know, except as you said the other day, by experience? I want to have the experience. Pray, open the door and take me in.'

Captain Diamond's brilliant eyes expanded beneath their dusky brows, and after holding his breath a moment, he indulged in the first and last apology for a laugh by which I was to see his solemn visage contorted. It was profoundly grotesque, but it was perfectly noiseless. 'Take you in?' he softly growled. 'I wouldn't go in again before my time's up for a thousand times that sum.' And he thrust out his hand from the folds of his cloak and exhibited a small agglommeration of coin, knotted into the corner of an old silk pocket-handkerchief. 'I stick to my bargain no less, but no more!'

'But you told me the first time I had the pleasure of talking with you that it was not so terrible.'

'I don't say it's terrible – now. But it's damned disagreeable!'

This adjective was uttered with a force that made me hesitate and reflect. While I did so, I thought I heard a slight movement of one of the window-shutters above us. I looked up, but every-thing seemed motionless. Captain Diamond, too, had been thinking; suddenly he turned toward the house. 'If you will go in alone,' he said, 'you are welcome.'

'Will you wait for me here?'

'Yes, you will not stop long.'

'But the house is pitch dark. When you go you have lights.'

He thrust his hand into the depths of his cloak and produced some matches. 'Take these,' he said. 'You will find two candle-sticks with candles on the table in the hall. Light them, take one in each hand and go ahead.'

'Where shall I go?'

'Anywhere – everywhere. You can trust the ghost to find you.'

I will not pretend to deny that by this time my heart was beat-ing. And yet I imagine I motioned the old man with a sufficiently dignified gesture to open the door. I had made up my mind that there was in fact a ghost. I had conceded the premise. Only I had assured myself that once the mind was prepared, and the thing was not a surprise, it was possible to keep cool. Captain Diamond turned the lock, flung open the door, and bowed low to me as I passed in. I stood in the darkness, and heard the door close behind me. For some moments, I stirred neither finger nor toe; I stared bravely into the impenetrable dusk. But I saw noth-ing and heard nothing, and at last I struck a match. On the table were two old brass candlesticks rusty from disuse. I lighted the candles and began my tour of exploration.

A wide staircase rose in front of me, guarded by an antique balustrade of that rigidly delicate carving which is found so often in old New England houses. I postponed ascending it, and turned into the room on my right. This was an old-fashioned parlour, meagrely furnished, and musty with the absence of human life. I raised my two lights aloft and saw nothing but its empty chairs and its blank walls. Behind it was the room into which I had peeped from without, and which, in fact, communicated with it, as I had supposed, by folding-doors. Here, too, I found myself confronted by no menacing spectre. I crossed the hall again, and visited the rooms on the other side; a dining-room in front, where I might have written my name with my finger in the deep dust of the great square table; a kitchen behind with its pots and pans eternally cold. All this was hard and grim, but it was not formidable. I came back into the hall, and walked to the foot of the staircase, holding up my candles; to ascend required a fresh effort, and I was scanning the gloom above. Suddenly, with an inexpressible sensation, I became aware that this gloom was animated; it seemed to move and gather itself together. Slowly – I say slowly, for to my tense expectancy the instants appeared ages – it took the shape of a large, definite figure, and this figure advanced and stood at the top of the stairs. I frankly confess that by this time I was conscious of a feeling to which I am in duty bound to apply the vulgar name of fear. I may poetize it and call it Dread, with a capital letter; it was at any rate the feeling that makes a man yield ground. I measured it as it grew, and it seemed perfectly irresistible; for it did not

appear to come from within but from without, and to be embodied in the dark image at the head of the staircase. After a
fashion I reasoned – I remember reasoning. I said to myself, 'I
had always thought ghosts were white and transparent; this is a
thing of thick shadows, densely opaque.' I reminded myself that
the occasion was momentous, and that if fear were to overcome
me I should gather all possible impressions while my wits
remained. I stepped back, foot behind foot, with my eyes still on
the figure and placed my candles on the table. I was perfectly
conscious that the proper thing was to ascend the stairs reso-
lutely, face to face with the image, but the soles of my shoes
seemed suddenly to have been transformed into leaden weights.
I had got what I wanted; I was seeing the ghost. I tried to look
at the figure distinctly so that I could remember it, and fairly
claim, afterward, not to have lost my self-possession. I even
asked myself how long it was expected I should stand looking,
and how soon I could honourably retire. All this, of course,
passed through my mind with extreme rapidity, and it was
checked by a further movement on the part of the figure. Two
white hands appeared in the dark perpendicular mass, and were
slowly raised to what seemed to be the level of the head. Here
they were pressed together, over the region of the face, and then
they were removed, and the face was disclosed. It was dim,
white, strange, in every way ghostly. It looked down at me for
an instant, after which one of the hands was raised again, slowly,
and waved to and fro before it. There was something very
singular in this gesture; it seemed to denote resentment and

dismissal, and yet it had a sort of trivial, familiar motion. Familiarity on the part of the haunting Presence had not entered into my calculations, and did not strike me pleasantly. I agreed with Captain Diamond that it was 'damned disagreeable'. I was pervaded by an intense desire to make an orderly, and, if possible, a graceful retreat. I wished to do it gallantly, and it seemed to me that it would be gallant to blow out my candles. I turned and did so, punctiliously, and then I made my way to the door, groped a moment and opened it. The outer light, almost extinct as it was, entered for a moment, played over the dusty depths of the house, and showed me the solid shadow.

Standing on the grass, bent over his stick, under the early glimmering stars, I found Captain Diamond. He looked up at me fixedly for a moment, but asked no questions, and then he went and locked the door. This duty performed, he discharged the other – made his obeisance like the priest before the altar – and then without heeding me further, took his departure.

A few days later, I suspended my studies and went off for the summer's vacation. I was absent for several weeks, during which I had plenty of leisure to analyse my impressions of the supernatural. I took some satisfaction in the reflection that I had not been ignobly terrified; I had not bolted nor swooned – I had proceeded with dignity. Nevertheless, I was certainly more comfortable when I had put thirty miles between me and the scene of my exploit, and I continued for many days to prefer the daylight to the dark. My nerves had been powerfully excited; of this I was particularly conscious when, under the influence of the drowsy air of the seaside, my excitement began slowly to ebb. As it disappeared, I attempted to take a sternly rational view of my experience. Certainly I had seen *something* – that was not fancy; but what had I seen? I regretted extremely now that I had not been bolder, that I had not gone nearer and inspected the apparition more minutely. But it was very well to talk; I had done as much as any man in the circumstances would have dared; it was indeed a physical impossibility that I should have advanced. Was not this paralysation of my powers in itself a supernatural influence? Not necessarily, perhaps, for a sham ghost that one accepted might do as much execution as a real ghost. But why had I so easily accepted the sable phantom that waved its hand? Why had it so impressed itself? Unquestionably, true or false, it was a very clever phantom. I greatly preferred that it should have been true – in the first place because I did not care to have shivered and shaken for nothing, and in the second place because to have seen a well-authenticated goblin is, as things go, a feather in a quiet man's cap. I tried, therefore, to let my vision rest and to stop turning it over. But an impulse stronger than my will recurred at intervals and set a mocking question on my lips. Granted that the apparition was Captain Diamond's daughter; if it was she it certainly was her spirit. But was it not her spirit and something more?

The middle of September saw me again established among the theologic shades, but I made no haste to revisit the haunted house.

The last of the month approached – the term of another quarter with poor Captain Diamond – and found me indisposed to disturb his pilgrimage on this occasion; though I confess that I thought with a good deal of compassion of the feeble old man trudging away, lonely, in the autumn dusk, on his extraordinary errand. On the thirtieth of September, at noon-day, I was drowsing over a heavy octavo, when I heard a feeble rap at my door. I replied with an invitation to enter, but as this produced no effect I repaired to the door and opened it. Before me stood an elderly negress with her head bound in a scarlet turban, and a white handkerchief folded across her bosom. She looked at me intently and in silence; she had that air of supreme gravity and decency which aged persons of her race so often wear. I stood interrogative, and at last, drawing her hand from her ample pocket, she held up a little book. It was the copy of Pascal's *Thoughts* that I had given to Captain Diamond.

'Please, sir,' she said, very mildly, 'do you know this book?'

'Perfectly,' said I, 'my name is on the fly-leaf.'

'It is your name – no other?'

'I will write my name if you like, and you can compare them,' I answered.

She was silent a moment and then, with dignity – 'It would be useless, sir,' she said, 'I can't read. If you will give me your word that is enough. I come,' she went on, 'from the gentleman to whom you gave the book. He told me to carry it as a token – a token – that is what he called it. He is right down sick, and he wants to see you.'

'Captain Diamond – sick?' I cried. 'Is his illness serious?'

'He is very bad – he is all gone.'

I expressed my regret and sympathy, and offered to go to him immediately, if his sable messenger would show me the way. She assented deferentially, and in a few moments I was following her along the sunny streets, feeling very much like a personage in *The Arabian Nights*, led to a postern gate by an Ethiopian slave. My own conductress directed her steps toward the river and stopped at a decent little yellow house in one of the streets that descend to it. She quickly opened the door and led me in, and I very soon found myself in the presence of my old friend. He was in bed, in a darkened room, and evidently in a very feeble state. He lay back on his pillow staring before him, with his bristling hair more erect than ever, and his intensely dark and bright old eyes touched with the glitter of fever. His apartment was humble and scrupulously neat, and I could see that my dusky guide was a faithful servant. Captain Diamond, lying there rigid and pale on his white sheets, resembled some ruggedly carven figure on the lid of a Gothic tomb. He looked at me silently, and my companion withdrew and left us alone.

'Yes, it's you,' he said, at last, 'it's you, that good young man. There is no mistake, is there?'

'I hope not; I believe I'm a good young man. But I am very sorry you are ill. What can I do for you?'

'I am very bad, very bad; my poor old bones ache so!' and, groaning portentously, he tried to turn toward me.

I questioned him about the nature of his malady and the length of time he had been in bed, but he barely heeded me; he seemed impatient to speak of something else. He grasped my sleeve, pulled me toward him, and whispered quickly:

'You know my time's up!'

'Oh, I trust not,' I said, mistaking his meaning. 'I shall certainly see you on your legs again.'

'God knows!' he cried. 'But I don't mean I'm dying; not yet a bit. What I mean is, I'm due at the house. This is rent-day.'

'Oh, exactly! But you can't go.'

'I can't go. It's awful. I shall lose my money. If I am dying, I want it all the same. I want to pay the doctor. I want to be buried like a respectable man.'

'It is this evening?' I asked.

'This evening at sunset, sharp.'

He lay staring at me, and, as I looked at him in return, I suddenly understood his motive in sending for me. Morally, as it came into my thought, I winced. But, I suppose I looked unperturbed, for he continued in the same tone. 'I can't lose my money. Someone else must go. I asked Belinda; but she won't hear of it.'

'You believe the money will be paid to another person?'

'We can try, at least. I have never failed before and I don't know. But, if you say I'm as sick as a dog, that my old bones ache, that I'm dying, perhaps she'll trust you. She don't want me to starve!'

'You would like me to go in your place, then?'

'You have been there once; you know what it is. Are you afraid?'

I hesitated.

'Give me three minutes to reflect,' I said, 'and I will tell you.' My glance wandered over the room and rested on the various objects that spoke of the threadbare, decent poverty of its occupant. There seemed to be a mute appeal to my pity and my resolution in their cracked and faded sparseness. Meanwhile Captain Diamond continued, feebly:

'I think she'd trust you, as I have trusted you; she'll like your face; she'll see there is no harm in you. It's a hundred and thirty-three dollars, exactly. Be sure you put them into a safe place.'

'Yes,' I said at last, 'I will go, and, so far as it depends upon me, you shall have the money by nine o'clock tonight.'

He seemed greatly relieved; he took my hand and faintly pressed it, and soon afterward I withdrew. I tried for the rest of the day not to think of my evening's work, but, of course, I thought of nothing else. I will not deny that I was nervous; I was, in fact, greatly excited, and I spent my time in alternately hoping that the mystery should prove less deep than it appeared, and yet fearing that it might prove too shallow. The hours passed very slowly, but, as the afternoon began to wane, I started on my mission. On the way, I stopped at Captain Diamond's modest dwelling, to ask how he was doing, and to receive such last instructions as he might desire to lay upon me. The old negress, gravely and inscrutably placid, admitted me, and, in answer to my inquiries, said that the Captain was very low; he had sunk since the morning.

'You must be right smart,' she said, 'if you want to get back before he drops off.'

A glance assured me that she knew of my projected expedition, though, in her own opaque black pupil, there was not a gleam of self-betrayal.

'But why should Captain Diamond drop off?' I asked. 'He certainly seems very weak; but I cannot make out that he has any definite disease.'

'His disease is old age,' she said, sententiously.

'But he is not so old as that; sixty-seven or sixty-eight, at most.'

She was silent a moment.

'He's worn out; he's used up; he can't stand it any longer.'

'Can I see him a moment?' I asked; upon which she led me again to his room.

He was lying in the same way as when I had left him, except that his eyes were closed. But he seemed very 'low', as she had said, and he had very little pulse. Nevertheless, I further learned the doctor had been there in the afternoon and professed himself satisfied. 'He don't know what's been going on,' said Belinda, curtly.

The old man stirred a little, opened his eyes, and after some time recognized me.

'I'm going, you know,' I said. 'I'm going for your money. Have you anything more to say?' He raised himself slowly, and with a painful effort, against his pillows; but he seemed hardly to understand me. 'The house, you know,' I said. 'Your daughter.'

He rubbed his forehead, slowly, awhile, and at last, his comprehension awoke. 'Ah, yes,' he murmured, 'I trust you. A hundred and thirty-three dollars. In old pieces – all in old pieces.' Then he added more vigorously, and with a brightening eye: 'Be very respectful – be very polite. If not – if not—' and his voice failed again.

'Oh, I certainly shall be,' I said, with a rather forced smile. 'But, if not?'

'If not, I shall know it!' he said, very gravely. And with this, his eyes closed and he sunk down again.

I took my departure and pursued my journey with a sufficiently resolute step. When I reached the house, I made a propitiatory bow in front of it, in emulation of Captain Diamond. I had timed my walk so as to be able to enter without delay; night had already fallen. I turned the key, opened the door and shut it behind me. Then I struck a light, and found the two candlesticks I had used before, standing on the tables in the entry. I applied a match to both of them, took them up and went into the parlour. It was empty, and though I waited awhile, it remained empty. I passed then into the other rooms on the same floor, and no dark image rose before me to check my steps. At last, I came out into the hall again, and stood weighing the question of going upstairs. The staircase had been the scene of my discomfiture before, and I approached it with profound mistrust. At the foot, I paused, looking up, with my hand on the balustrade. I was acutely expectant, and my expectation was justified. Slowly, in the darkness above, the black figure that I had seen before took shape. It was not an illusion; it was a figure, and the same. I gave it time to define itself, and watched it stand and look down at me with its hidden face. Then, deliberately, I lifted up my voice and spoke.

'I have come in place of Captain Diamond, at his request,' I said. 'He is very ill; he is unable to leave his bed. He earnestly begs that you will pay the money to me; I will immediately carry it to him.' The figure stood motionless, giving no sign. 'Captain Diamond would have come if he were able to move,' I added, in a moment, appealingly; 'but, he is utterly unable.'

At this the figure slowly unveiled its face and showed me a dim, white mask; then it began slowly to descend the stairs. Instinctively I fell back before it, retreating to the door of the front sitting-room. With my eyes still fixed on it, I moved backward across the threshold; then I stopped in the middle of the room and set down my lights. The figure advanced; it seemed to be that of a tall woman, dressed in vaporous black crape. As it drew near, I saw that it had a perfectly human face, though it looked extremely pale and sad. We stood gazing at each other; my agitation had completely vanished; I was only deeply interested.

'Is my father dangerously ill?' said the apparition.

At the sound of its voice – gentle, tremulous, and perfectly human – I started forward; I felt a rebound of excitement. I drew a long breath, I gave a sort of cry, for what I saw before me was not a disembodied spirit, but a beautiful woman, an audacious actress. Instinctively, irresistibly, by the force of reaction against my credulity, I stretched out my hand and seized the long veil that muffled her head. I gave it a violent jerk, dragged it nearly off, and stood staring at a large fair person, of about five-and-thirty. I comprehended her at a glance; her long black dress, her pale, sorrow-worn face, painted to look paler, her very fine eyes – the colour of her father's – and her sense of outrage at my movement.

'My father, I suppose,' she cried, 'did not send you here to insult me!' and she turned away rapidly, took up one of the candles and moved toward the door. Here she paused, looked at me again, hesitated, and then drew a purse from her pocket and flung it down on the floor. 'There is your money!' she said, majestically.

I stood there, wavering between amazement and shame, and saw her pass out into the hall. Then I picked up the purse. The next moment, I heard a loud shriek and a crash of something dropping, and she came staggering back into the room without her light.

'My father – my father!' she cried; and with parted lips and dilated eyes, she rushed toward me.

'Your father – where?' I demanded.

'In the hall, at the foot of the stairs.'

I stepped forward to go out, but she seized my arm.

'He is in white,' she cried, 'in his shirt. It's not he!'

'Why, your father is in his house, in his bed, extremely ill,' I answered.

She looked at me fixedly, with searching eyes.

'Dying?'

'I hope not,' I stuttered.

She gave a long moan and covered her face with her hands.

'Oh, Heavens, I have seen his ghost!' she cried.

She still held my arm; she seemed too terrified to release it.

'His ghost!' I echoed, wondering.

'It's the punishment of my long folly!' she went on.

'Ah,' said I, 'it's the punishment of my indiscretion – of my violence!'

'Take me away, take me away!' she cried, still clinging to my arm. 'Not there –' as I was turning toward the hall and the front door – 'not there, for pity's sake! By this door – the back entrance.' And snatching the other candles from the table, she led me through the neighbouring room into the back part of the house. Here was a door opening from a sort of scullery into the orchard. I turned the rusty lock and we passed out and stood in the cool air, beneath the stars. Here my companion gathered her black drapery about her, and stood for a moment, hesitating. I had been infinitely flurried, but my curiosity touching her was uppermost. Agitated, pale, picturesque, she looked, in the early evening light, very beautiful.

'You have been playing all these years a most extraordinary game,' I said.

She looked at me sombrely, and seemed disinclined to reply. 'I came in perfect good faith,' I went on. 'The last time – three months ago – you remember? – you greatly frightened me.'

'Of course it was an extraordinary game,' she answered at last. 'But it was the only way.'

'Had he not forgiven you?'

'So long as he thought me dead, yes. There have been things in my life he could not forgive.'

I hesitated and then – 'And where is your husband?' I asked.

'I have no husband – I have never had a husband.'

She made a gesture which checked further questions, and moved rapidly away. I walked with her round the house to the road, and she kept murmuring – 'It was he – it was he!' When we reached the road she stopped, and asked me which way I was going. I pointed to the road by which I had come, and she said – 'I take the other. You are going to my father's?' she added.

'Directly,' I said.

'Will you let me know tomorrow what you have found?'

'With pleasure. But how shall I communicate with you?'

She seemed at a loss, and looked about her. 'Write a few words,' she said, 'and put them under that stone.' And she pointed to one of the lava slabs that bordered the old well. I gave her my promise to comply, and she turned away. 'I know my road,' she said. 'Everything is arranged. It's an old story.'

She left me with a rapid step, and as she receded into the darkness, resumed, with the dark flowing lines of her drapery, the phantasmal appearance with which she had at first appeared to me. I watched her till she became invisible, and then I took my own leave of the place. I returned to town at a swinging pace, and marched straight to the little yellow house near the river. I took the liberty of entering without a knock, and, encountering no interruption, made my way to Captain Diamond's room. Outside the door, on a low bench, with folded arms, sat the sable Belinda.

'How is he?' I asked.

'He's gone to glory.'

'Dead?' I cried.

She rose with a sort of tragic chuckle.

'He's as big a ghost as any of them now!'

I passed into the room and found the old man lying there irredeemably rigid and still. I wrote that evening a few lines which I proposed on the morrow to place beneath the stone, near the well; but my promise was not destined to be executed. I slept that night very ill – it was natural – and in my restlessness left my bed to walk about the room. As I did so I caught sight, in passing my window, of a red glow in the north-western sky. A house was on fire in the country, and evidently burning fast. It lay in the same direction as the scene of my evening's adventures, and as I stood watching the crimson horizon I was startled by a sharp memory. I had blown out the candle which lighted me, with my companion, to the door through which we escaped, but I had not accounted for the other light, which she had carried into the hall and dropped – Heaven knew where – in her consternation. The next day I walked out with my folded letter and turned into the familiar cross-road. The haunted house was a mass of charred beams and smouldering ashes; the well-cover had been pulled off, in quest of water, by the few neighbours who had had the audacity to contest what they must have regarded as a demon-kindled blaze, the loose stones were completely displaced, and the earth had been trampled into puddles.

A Bundle of Letters

I

From Miss Miranda Hope, *in Paris, to*
Mrs Abraham C. Hope, *at Bangor, Maine*

September 5th, 1879

My Dear Mother

I have kept you posted as far as Tuesday week last, and, although my letter will not have reached you yet, I will begin another, before my news accumulates too much. I am glad you show my letters round in the family, for I like them all to know what I am doing, and I can't write to everyone, though I try to answer all reasonable expectations. But there are a great many unreasonable ones, as I suppose you know — not yours, dear mother, for I am bound to say that you never required of me more than was natural. You see you are reaping your reward: I write to you before I write to anyone else.

There is one thing, I hope – that you don't show any of my letters to William Platt. If he wants to see any of my letters, he knows the right way to go to work. I wouldn't have him see one of these letters, written for circulation in the family, for anything in the world. If he wants one for himself, he has got to write to me first. Let him write to me first, and then I will see about answering him. You can show him this if you like; but if you show him anything more, I will never write to you again.

I told you in my last about my farewell to England, my crossing the channel, and my first impressions of Paris. I have thought a great deal about that lovely England since I left it, and all the famous historic scenes I visited; but I have come to the conclusion that it is not a country in which I should care to reside. The position of woman does not seem to me at all satisfactory, and that is a point, you know, on which I feel very strongly. It seems to me that in England they play a very faded-out part, and those with whom I conversed had a kind of depressed and humiliated tone; a little dull, tame look, as if they were used to being snubbed and bullied, which made me want to give them a good shaking. There are a great many people – and a great many things, too – over here that I should like to perform that operation upon. I should like to shake the starch out of some of them, and the dust out of the others. I know fifty girls in Bangor that come much more up to my notion of the stand a truly noble woman should take, than those young ladies in England. But they had a most lovely way of speaking (in England), and the men are *remarkably handsome*. (You can show this to William Platt, if you like.)

I gave you my first impressions of Paris, which quite came up to my expectations, much as I had heard and read about it. The objects of interest are extremely numerous, and the climate is remarkably cheerful and sunny. I should say the position of woman here was considerably higher, though by no means coming up to the American standard. The manners of the people are in some respects extremely peculiar, and I feel at last that I am indeed in *foreign parts*. It is, however, a truly elegant city (very superior to New York), and I have spent a great deal of time in visiting the various monuments and palaces. I won't give you an account of all my wanderings, though I have been most indefatigable; for I am keeping, as I told you before, a most *exhaustive* journal, which I will allow you the *privilege* of reading on my return to Bangor. I am getting on remarkably well, and I must say I am sometimes surprised at my universal good fortune. It only shows what a little energy and common-sense will accomplish. I have discovered none of these objections to a young lady travelling in Europe by herself, of which we heard so much before I left, and I don't expect I ever shall, for I certainly don't mean to look for them. I know what I want and I always manage to get it.

I have received a great deal of politeness – some of it really most pressing, and I have experienced no drawbacks whatever. I have made a great many pleasant acquaintances in travelling round (both ladies and gentlemen), and had a great many most interesting talks. I have collected a great deal of information, for which I refer you to my journal. I assure you my journal is going to be a splendid thing. I do just exactly as I do in Bangor, and I find I do perfectly right; and at any rate, I don't care if I don't. I didn't come to Europe to lead a merely conventional life; I could do that at Bangor. You know I never *would* do it at Bangor, so it isn't likely I am going to make myself miserable over here. So long as I accomplish what I desire, and make my money hold out, I shall regard the thing as a success. Sometimes I feel rather lonely, especially in the evening; but I generally manage to interest myself in something or in someone. In the evening I usually read up about the objects of interest I have visited during the day, or I post up my journal. Sometimes I go to the theatre; or else I play the piano in the public parlour. The public parlour at the hotel isn't much; but the piano is better than that fearful old thing at the Sebago House. Sometimes I go downstairs and talk to the lady who keeps the books – a French lady, who is remarkably polite. She is very pretty, and always wears a black dress, with the most beautiful fit; she speaks a little English; she tells me she had to learn it in order to converse with the Americans who come in such numbers to this hotel. She has given me a great deal of information about the position of woman in France, and much of it is very encouraging. But she has told me at the same time some things that I should not like to write to you (I am hesitating even about putting them into my journal), especially if my letters are to be handed round in the family. I assure you they appear to talk about things here that we never think of mentioning at Bangor, or even of thinking about. She seems to think she can tell me everything, because I told her I was travelling for general culture. Well, I *do* want to know so much that it seems sometimes as if I wanted to know everything; and yet there are some things that I think I don't want to know. But, as a general thing, everything is intensely interesting; I don't mean only everything that this French lady tells me, but everything I see and hear for myself. I feel really as if I should gain all I desire.

I meet a great many Americans, who, as a general thing, I must say, are not as polite to me as the people over here. The people over here – especially the gentlemen – are much more what I should call *attentive*. I don't know whether Americans are more *sincere*; I haven't yet made up my mind about that. The only drawback I experience is when Americans sometimes express surprise that I should be travelling round alone; so you see it doesn't come from Europeans. I always have my answer ready: 'For general culture, to acquire the languages, and to see Europe for myself'; and that generally seems to satisfy them. Dear mother, my money holds out very well, and it *is* real interesting.

II

From the Same to the Same

September 16th

Since I last wrote to you I have left that hotel, and come to live in a French family. It's a kind of boarding-house combined with a kind of school; only it's not like an American boarding-house, nor like an American school either. There are four or five people here that have come to learn the language – not to take lessons, but to have an opportunity for conversation. I was very glad to come to such a place, for I had begun to realize that I was not making much progress with the French. It seemed to me that I should feel ashamed to have spent two months in Paris, and not to have acquired more insight into the language. I had always heard so much of French conversation, and I found I was having no more opportunity to practise it than if I had remained at Bangor. In fact, I used to hear a great deal more at Bangor, from those French Canadians that came down to cut the ice, than I saw I should ever hear at that hotel. The lady that kept the books seemed to want so much to talk to me in English (for the sake of practice, too, I suppose), that I couldn't bear to let her know I didn't like it. The chambermaid was Irish, and all the waiters were German, so that I never heard a word of French spoken. I suppose you might hear a great deal in the shops; only, as I don't buy anything – I prefer to spend my money for purposes of culture – I don't have that advantage.

I have been thinking some of taking a teacher, but I am well acquainted with the grammar already, and teachers always keep you bothering over the verbs. I was a good deal troubled, for I felt as if I didn't want to go away without having, at least, got a general idea of French conversation. The theatre gives you a good deal of insight, and, as I told you in my last, I go a good deal to places of amusement. I find no difficulty whatever in going to such places alone, and am always treated with the politeness which, as I told you before, I encounter everywhere. I see plenty of other ladies alone (mostly French), and they generally seem to be enjoying themselves as much as I. But, at the theatre, everyone talks so fast that I can scarcely make out what they say; and, besides, there are a great many vulgar expressions which it is unnecessary to learn. But it was the theatre, nevertheless, that put me on the track. The very next day after I wrote to you last, I went to the Palais Royal, which is one of the principal theatres in Paris. It is very small, but it is very celebrated, and in my guide-book it is marked with *two stars*, which is a sign of importance attached only to *first-class* objects of interest. But after I had been there half an hour I found I couldn't understand a single word of the play, they gabbled it off so fast, and they made use of such peculiar expressions. I felt a good deal disappointed and troubled – I was afraid I shouldn't gain all I had come for. But while I was thinking it over – thinking what I *should* do – I heard two gentlemen talking behind me. I was between the acts, and I couldn't help listening to what they said. They were talking English, but I guess they were Americans.

'Well,' said one of them, 'it all depends on what you are after. I'm after French; that's what I'm after.'

'Well,' said the other, 'I'm after Art.'

'Well,' said the first, 'I'm after Art too; but I'm after French most.'

Then, dear mother, I am sorry to say the second one swore a little. He said, 'Oh, damn French!'

No, I won't damn French,' said his friend. 'I'll acquire it —
that's what I'll do with it. I'll go right into a family.'

'What family'll you go into?'

'Into some French family. That's the only way to do — to go
to some place where you can talk. If you're after Art, you want
to stick to the galleries; you want to go right through the Louvre,
room by room; you want to take a room a day, or something of
that sort. But, if you want to acquire French, the thing is to look
out for a family. There are lots of French families here that take
you to board and teach you. My second cousin — that young
lady I told you about — she got in with a crowd like that, and
they booked her right up in three months. They just took her
right in and they talked to her. That's what they do to you; they
set you right down and they talk *at* you. You've got to understand them; you can't help yourself. That family my cousin was
with has moved away somewhere, or I should try and get in
with them. They were very smart people, that family; after she
left, my cousin corresponded with them in French. But I mean
to find some other crowd, if it takes a lot of trouble!'

I listened to all this with great interest, and when he spoke
about his cousin I was on the point of turning around to ask him
the address of the family that she was with; but the next moment
he said they had moved away; so I sat still. The other gentleman, however, didn't seem to be affected in the same way as I
was.

'Well,' he said, 'you may follow up that if you like; I mean to
follow up the pictures. I don't believe there is ever going to be

any considerable demand in the United States for French; but I can promise you that in about ten years there'll be a big demand for Art! And it won't be temporary either.'

That remark may be very true, but I don't care anything about the demand; I want to know French for its own sake. I don't want to think I have been all this while without having gained an insight . . . The very next day, I asked the lady who kept the books at the hotel whether she knew of any family that could take me to board and give me the benefit of their conversation. She instantly threw up her hands, with several little shrill cries (in their French way, you know), and told me that her dearest friend kept a regular place of that kind. If she had known I was looking out for such a place she would have told me before; she had not spoken of it herself, because she didn't wish to injure the hotel by being the cause of my going away. She told me this was a charming family, who had often received American ladies (and others as well) who wished to follow up the language, and she was sure I should be delighted with them. So she gave me their address, and offered to go with me to introduce me. But I was in such a hurry that I went off by myself, and I had no trouble in finding these good people. They were delighted to receive me, and I was very much pleased with what I saw of them. They seemed to have plenty of conversation, and there will be no trouble about that.

I came here to stay about three days ago, and by this time I have seen a great deal of them. The price of board struck me as rather high; but I must remember that a quantity of conversation is thrown in. I have a very pretty little room – without any carpet, but with seven mirrors, two clocks, and five curtains. I was rather disappointed after I arrived to find that there are several other Americans here for the same purpose as myself. At least there are three Americans and two English people; and also a German gentleman. I am afraid, therefore, our conversation will be rather mixed, but I have not yet time to judge. I try to talk with Madame de Maisonrouge all I can (she is the lady of the house, and the real family consists only of herself and her two daughters). They are all most elegant, interesting women, and I am sure we shall become intimate friends. I will write you more about them in my next. Tell William Platt I don't care what he does.

III

From Miss Violet Ray, *in Paris,*
to Miss Agnes Rich, *in New York*

September 21st

We had hardly got here when father received a telegram saying he would have to come right back to New York. It was for something about his business – I don't know exactly what; you know I never understand those things, never want to. We had just got settled at the hotel, in some charming rooms, and mother and I, as you may imagine, were greatly annoyed. Father is extremely fussy, as you know, and his first idea, as soon as he found he should have to go back, was that we should go back with him. He declared he would never leave us in Paris alone, and that we must return and come out again. I don't know what he thought would happen to us; I suppose he thought we should be too extravagant. It's father's theory that we are always running up bills, whereas a little observation would show him that we wear the same *old rags* FOR MONTHS. But father has no observation; he has nothing but theories. Mother and I, however, have, fortunately, a great deal of *practice*, and we succeeded in making him understand that we wouldn't budge from Paris, and that we would rather be chopped into small pieces than cross that dreadful ocean again. So, at last, he decided to go back alone, and to leave us here for three months. But, to show you how fussy he is, he refused to let us stay at the hotel, and insisted that we should go into a *family*. I don't know what put such an idea into his head, unless it was some advertisement that he saw in one of the American papers that are published here.

There are families here who receive American and English people to live with them, under the pretence of teaching them French. You may imagine what people they are — I mean the families themselves. But the Americans who choose this peculiar manner of seeing Paris must be actually just as bad. Mother and I were horrified, and declared that *main force* should not remove us from the hotel. But father has a way of arriving at his ends which is more efficient than violence. He worries and fusses; he 'nags', as we used to say at school; and, when mother and I are quite worn out, his triumph is assured. Mother is usually worn out more easily than I, and she ends by siding with father; so that, at last, when they combine their forces against poor little me, I have to succumb. You should have heard the way father went on about this 'family' plan; he talked to everyone he saw about it; he used to go round to the banker's and talk to the people there – the people in the post-office; he used to try and exchange ideas about it with the waiters at the hotel. He said it would be more safe, more respectable, more economical; that I should perfect my French; that mother would learn how a French household is conducted; that he should feel more easy, and five hundred reasons more. They were none of them good, but that made no difference. It's all humbug, his talking about economy, when everyone knows that business in America has completely recovered, that the prostration is all over, and that *immense fortunes* are being made. We have been economizing for the last five years, and I supposed we came abroad to reap the benefits of it.

As for my French, it is quite as perfect as I want it to be. (I assure you I am often surprised at my own fluency, and, when I get a little more practice in the genders and the idioms, I shall do very well in this respect.) To make a long story short, however, father carried his point, as usual; mother basely deserted me at the last moment, and, after holding out alone for three days, I told them to do with me what they pleased! Father lost three steamers in succession by remaining in Paris to argue with me.

You know he is like the schoolmaster in Goldsmith's 'Deserted Village' – 'e'en though vanquished, he would argue still'. He and mother went to look at some seventeen families (they had got the addresses somewhere), while I retired to my sofa, and would have nothing to do with it. At last they made arrangements, and I was transported to the establishment from which I now write you. I write you from the bosom of a Parisian ménage – from the depths of a second-rate boarding-house.

Father only left Paris after he had seen us what he calls comfortably settled here, and had informed Madame de Maisonrouge (the mistress of the establishment – the head of the 'family') that he wished my French pronunciation especially attended to. The pronunciation, as it happens, is just what I am most at home in; if he had said my genders or my idioms there would have been some sense. But poor father has no tact, and this defect is especially marked since he has been in Europe. He will be absent, however, for three months, and mother and I shall breathe more freely; the situation will be less intense. I must confess that we breathe more freely than I expected, in this place, where we have been for about a week. I was sure, before we came, that it would prove to be an establishment of the *lowest description*; but I must say that, in this respect, I am agreeably disappointed. The French are so clever that they know even how to manage a place of this kind. Of course it is very disagreeable to live with strangers, but as, after all, if I were not staying with Madame de Maisonrouge I should not be living in the Faubourg Saint-Germain, I don't know that from the point of view of exclusiveness it is any great loss to be here.

Our rooms are very prettily arranged, and the table is remarkably good. Mamma thinks the whole thing – the place and the people, the manners and customs – very amusing; but mamma is very easily amused. As for me, you know, all that I ask is to be let alone, and not to have people's society *forced upon me*. I have never wanted for society of my own choosing, and, so long as I retain possession of my faculties, I don't suppose I ever shall. As I said, however, the place is very well managed, and I succeed in doing as I please, which, you know, is my most cherished pursuit. Madame de Maisonrouge has a great deal of tact – much more than poor father. She is what they call here a *belle femme*, which means that she is a tall, ugly woman, with style. She dresses very well, and has a great deal of talk; but, though she is a very good imitation of a lady, I never see her behind the dinner-table, in the evening, smiling and bowing, as the people come in, and looking all the while at the dishes and the servants, without thinking of a *dame de comptoir* blooming in a corner of a shop or a restaurant. I am sure that, in spite of her fine name, she was once a *dame de comptoir*. I am also sure that, in spite of her smiles and the pretty things she says to everyone, she hates us all, and would like to murder us. She is a hard, clever Frenchwoman, who would like to amuse herself and enjoy her Paris, and she must be bored to death at passing all her time in the midst of stupid English people who mumble broken French at her. Some day she will poison the soup or the *vin rouge*; but I hope that will not be until after mother and I shall have left her. She has two daughters, who, except that one is decidedly pretty, are meagre imitations of herself.

The 'family', for the rest, consists altogether of our beloved compatriots, and of still more beloved Englanders. There is an Englishman here, with his sister, and they seem to be rather nice people. He is remarkably handsome, but excessively affected and patronizing, especially to us Americans; and I hope to have a chance of biting his head off before long. The sister is very pretty, and, apparently, very nice; but, in costume, she is Britannia incarnate. There is a very pleasant little Frenchman – when they are nice they are charming – and a German doctor, a big, blond man, who looks like a great white bull; and two Americans, besides mother and me. One of them is a young man from Boston – an aesthetic young man, who talks about its being 'a real Corot day', etc., and a young woman – a girl, a female, I don't know what to call her – from Vermont, or Minnesota, or some such place. This young woman is the most extraordinary specimen of artless Yankeeism that I ever encountered; she is really too horrible, I have been three times to Clémentine about your underskirt, etc.

IV

My dear Harvard

I have carried out my plan, of which I gave you a hint in my last, and I only regret that I should not have done it before. It is human nature, after all, that is the most interesting thing in the world, and it only reveals itself to the truly earnest seeker. There is a want of earnestness in that life of hotels and railroad trains, which so many of our countrymen are content to lead in this strange Old World, and I was distressed to find how far I, myself, had been led along the dusty, beaten track. I had, however, constantly wanted to turn aside into more unfrequented ways; to plunge beneath the surface and see what I should discover. But the opportunity had always been missing; somehow, I never meet those opportunities that we hear about and read about – the things that happen to people in novels and biographies. And yet I am always on the watch to take advantage of any opening that may present itself; I am always looking out for experiences, for sensations – I might almost say for adventures.

The great thing is to *live*, you know – to feel, to be conscious of one's possibilities; not to pass through life mechanically and insensibly, like a letter through the post-office. There are times, my dear Harvard, when I feel as if I were really capable of everything – *capable de tout*, as they say here – of the greatest excesses as well as the greatest heroism. Oh, to be able to say that one has lived – *qu'on a vécu*, as they say here – that idea exercises an indefinable attraction for me. You will, perhaps, reply, it is easy to say it; but the thing is to make people believe you! And, then, I don't want any second-hand, spurious sensations; I want the knowledge that leaves a trace – that leaves strange scars and stains and reveries behind it! But I am afraid I shock you, perhaps even frighten you.

If you repeat my remarks to any of the West Cedar Street circle, be sure you tone them down as your discretion will suggest. For yourself, you will know that I have always had an intense desire to see something of *real French life*. You are acquainted with my great sympathy with the French; with my natural tendency to enter into the French way of looking at life. I sympathize with the artistic temperament; I remember you used sometimes to hint to me that you thought my own temperament too artistic. I don't think that in Boston there is any real sympathy with the artistic temperament; we tend to make everything a matter of right and wrong. And in Boston one can't live – *on ne peut pas vivre*, as they say here. I don't mean one can't reside – for a great many people manage that; but one can't live, aesthetically – I may almost venture to say, sensuously. This is why I have always been so much drawn to the French, who are so aesthetic, so sensuous. I am so sorry that Théophile Gautier has passed away; I should have liked so much to go and see him, and tell him all that I owe him. He was living when I was here before; but, you know, at that time I was travelling with the Johnsons, who are not aesthetic, and who used to make me feel rather ashamed of my artistic temperament. If I had gone to see the great apostle of beauty, I should have had to go clandestinely – *en cachette*, as they say here; and that is not my nature; I like to do everything frankly, freely, *naïvement, au grand jour*. That is the great thing – to be free, to be frank, to be *naïf*. Doesn't Matthew Arnold say that somewhere – or is it Swinburne, or Pater?

When I was with the Johnsons everything was superficial; and, as regards life, everything was brought down to the question of right and wrong. They were too didactic; art should never be didactic; and what is life but an art? Pater has said that so well, somewhere. With the Johnsons I am afraid I lost many opportunities; the tone was grey and cottony, I might almost say woolly. But now, as I tell you, I have determined to take right hold for myself; to look right into European life, and judge it without Johnsonian prejudices. I have taken up my residence in a French family, in a real Parisian house. You see I have the courage of my opinions; I don't shrink from carrying out my theory that the great thing is to *live*.

You know I have always been intensely interested in Balzac, who never shrank from the reality, and whose almost *lurid* pictures of Parisian life have often haunted me in my wanderings through the old wicked-looking streets on the other side of the river. I am only sorry that my new friends – my French family – do not live in the old city – *au cœur du vieux Paris*, as they say here. They live only in the Boulevard Haussman, which is less picturesque; but in spite of this they have a great deal of the Balzac tone. Madame de Maisonrouge belongs to one of the oldest and proudest families in France; but she has had reverses which have compelled her to open an establishment in which a limited number of travellers, who are weary of the beaten track, who have the sense of local colour – she explains it herself, she expresses it so well – in short, to open a sort of boarding-house. I don't see why I should not, after all, use that expression, for it is the correlative of the term *pension bourgeoise*, employed by Balzac in the *Père Goriot*. Do you remember the *pension bourgeoise* of Madame Vauquer *née* de Conflans? But this establishment is not at all like that: and indeed it is not at all *bourgeois*; there is something distinguished, something aristo-cratic, about it. The Pension Vauquer was dark, brown, sordid, *graisseuse*; but this is in quite a different tone, with high, clear, lightly draped windows, tender, subtle, almost morbid, colours, and furniture in elegant, studied, reed-like lines. Madame de Maisonrouge reminds me of Madame Hulot – do you remember '*la belle Madame Hulot*'? – in *Les Parents Pauvres*. She has a great charm; a little artificial, a little fatigued, with a little suggestion of hidden things in her life; but I have always been sensitive to the charm of fatigue, of duplicity.

I am rather disappointed, I confess, in the society I find here; it is not so local, so characteristic, as I could have desired.

Indeed, to tell the truth, it is not local at all; but, on the other hand, it is cosmopolitan, and there is a great advantage in that. We are French, we are English, we are American, we are German: and, I believe, there are some Russians and Hungarians expected. I am much interested in the study of national types; in comparing, contrasting, seizing the strong points, the weak points, the point of view of each. It is interesting to shift one's point of view — to enter into strange, exotic ways of looking at life.

The American types here are not, I am sorry to say, so interesting as they might be, and, excepting myself, are exclusively feminine. We are *thin*, my dear Harvard; we are pale, we are sharp. There is something meagre about us; our line is wanting in roundness, our composition in richness. We lack temperament; we don't know how to live; *nous ne savons pas vivre*, as they say here. The American temperament is represented (putting myself aside, and I often think that my temperament is not at all American) by a young girl and her mother, and another young girl without her mother — without her mother or any attendant or appendage whatever. These young girls are rather curious types; they have a certain interest, they have a certain grace, but they are disappointing too; they don't go far; they don't keep all they promise; they don't satisfy the imagination. They are cold, slim, sexless; the physique is not generous, not abundant; it is only the drapery, the skirts and furbelows (that is, I mean in the young lady who has her mother) that are abundant. They are very different: one of them all elegance, all expensiveness, with an air of high fashion, from New York; the other a plain, pure, clear-eyed, straight-waisted, straight-stepping maiden from the heart of New England. And yet they are very much alike too – more alike than they would care to think themselves; for they eye each other with cold, mistrustful, deprecating looks. They are both specimens of the emancipated young American girl – practical, positive, passionless, subtle, and knowing, as you please, either too much or too little. And yet, as I say, they have a certain stamp, a certain grace; I like to talk with them, to study them.

The fair New Yorker is, sometimes, very amusing; she asks me if everyone in Boston talks like me – if everyone is as 'intellectual' as your poor correspondent. She is forever throwing Boston up at me; I can't get rid of Boston. The other one rubs it into me too; but in a different way; she seems to feel about it as a good Mahommedan feels toward Mecca, and regards it as a kind of focus of light for the whole human race. Poor little Boston, what nonsense is talked in thy name! But this New England maiden is, in her way, a strange type: she is travelling all over Europe alone – 'to see it,' she says, 'for herself'. For herself! What can that stiff, slim self of hers do with such sights, such visions! She looks at everything, goes everywhere, passes her way, with her clear, quiet eyes wide open; skirting the edge of obscene abysses without suspecting them; pushing through brambles without tearing her robe; exciting, without knowing it, the most injurious suspicions; and always holding her course, passionless, stainless, fearless, charmless! It is a little figure in which, after all, if you can get the right point of view, there is something rather striking.

By way of contrast, there is a lovely English girl, with eyes as shy as violets, and a voice as sweet! She has a sweet Gainsborough head, and a great Gainsborough hat, with a mighty plume in front of it, which makes a shadow over her quiet English eyes. Then she has a sage-green robe, 'mystic, wonderful', all embroidered with subtle devices and flowers, and birds of tender tint; very straight and tight in front, and adorned behind, along the spine, with large, strange, iridescent buttons. The revival of taste, of the sense of beauty, in England, interests me deeply; what is there in a simple row of spinal buttons to make one dream – to *donner à rêver*, as they say here? I think that a great aesthetic renascence is at hand, and that a great light will be kindled in England, for all the world to see. There are spirits there that I should like to commune with; I think they would understand me.

This gracious English maiden, with her clinging robes, her amulets and girdles, with something quaint and angular in her step, her carriage, something mediaeval and Gothic in the details of her person and dress, this lovely Evelyn Vane (isn't it a beautiful name?) is deeply, delightfully picturesque. She is much a woman – *elle est bien femme*, as they say here; simpler, softer, rounder, richer than the young girls I spoke of just now. Not much talk – a great, sweet silence. Then the violet eye – the very eye itself seems to blush; the great shadowy hat, making the brow so quiet; the strange, clinging, clutching, pictured raiment! As I say, it is a very gracious, tender type. She has her brother with her, who is a beautiful, fair-haired, grey-eyed young Englishman. He is purely objective; and he, too, is very plastic.

V

From Miranda Hope *to her* Mother

September 26th

You must not be frightened at not hearing from me oftener; it is not because I am in any trouble, but because I am getting on so well. If I were in any trouble I don't think I should write to you; I should just keep quiet and see it through myself. But that is not the case at present; and, if I don't write to you, it is because I am so deeply interested over here that I don't seem to find time. It was a real providence that brought me to this house, where, in spite of all obstacles, I am able to do much good work. I wonder how I find the time for all I do; but when I think that I have only got a year in Europe, I feel as if I wouldn't sacrifice a single hour.

The obstacles I refer to are the disadvantages I have in learning French, there being so many persons around me speaking English, and that, as you may say, in the very bosom of a French family. It seems as if you heard English everywhere; but I certainly didn't expect to find it in a place like this. I am not discouraged, however, and I talk French all I can, even with the other English boarders, Then I have a lesson every day from Miss Maisonrouge (the elder daughter of the lady of the house), and French conversation every evening in the *salon*, from eight to eleven, with Madame herself, and some friends of hers that often come in. Her cousin, Mr Verdier, a young French gentleman, is fortunately staying with her, and I make a point of talking with him as much as possible. I have *extra private lessons* from him, and I often go out to walk with him. Some night, soon, he is to accompany me to the opera. We have also a most interesting plan of visiting all the galleries in Paris together. Like most of the French, he converses with great fluency, and I feel as if I should really gain from him. He is remarkably handsome, and extremely polite – paying a great many compliments, which, I am afraid, are not always *sincere*. When I return to Bangor I will tell you some of the things he has said to me. I think you will consider them extremely curious, and very beautiful *in their way*.

The conversation in the parlour (from eight to eleven) is often remarkably brilliant, and I often wish that you, or some of the Bangor folks, could be there to enjoy it. Even though you couldn't understand it I think you would like to hear the way they go on; they seem to express so much. I sometimes think that at Bangor they don't express enough (but it seems as if over there, there was less to express). It seems as if, at Bangor, there were things that folks never *tried* to say; but here, I have learned from studying French that you have no idea what you *can* say, before you try. At Bangor they seem to give it up beforehand; they don't make any effort. (I don't say this in the least for William Platt, *in particular*.)

I am sure I don't know what they will think of me when I get back. It seems as if, over here, I had learned to come out with everything. I suppose they will think I am not sincere; but isn't it more sincere to come out with things than to conceal them? I have become very good friends with everyone in the house — that is (you see, I *am* sincere), with *almost* everyone. It is the most interesting circle I ever was in. There's a girl here, an American, that I don't like so much as the rest; but that is only because she won't let me. I should like to like her, ever so much, because she is most lovely and most attractive; but she doesn't seem to want to know me or to like me. She comes from New York, and she is remarkably pretty, with beautiful eyes and the most delicate features; she is also remarkably elegant — in this respect would bear comparison with anyone I have seen over here. But it seems as if she didn't want to recognize me, or associate with me; as if she wanted to make a difference between us. It is like people they call 'haughty' in books. I have never seen anyone like that before — anyone that wanted to make a difference; and at first I was right down interested, she seemed to me so like a proud young lady in a novel. I kept saying to myself all day, 'Haughty, haughty,' and I wished she would keep on so. But she did keep on; she kept on too long; and then I began to feel hurt. I couldn't think what I have done, and I can't think yet. It's as if she had got some idea about me, or had heard someone say something. If some girls should behave like that I shouldn't make any account of it; but this one is so refined, and looks as if she might be so interesting if I once got to know her, that I think about it a good deal. I am bound to find out what her reason is – for of course she has got some reason; I am right down curious to know.

I went up to her to ask her the day before yesterday; I thought that was the best way. I told her I wanted to know her better, and would like to come and see her in her room – they tell me she has got a lovely room – and that if she had heard anything against me, perhaps she would tell me when I came. But she was more distant than ever, and she just turned it off; said that she had never heard me mentioned, and that her room was too small to receive visitors. I suppose she spoke the truth, but I am sure she has got some reason, all the same. She has got some idea, and I am bound to find out before I go, if I have to ask every-body in the house. I am right down curious. I wonder if she doesn't think me refined – or if she had ever heard anything against Bangor? I can't think it is that. Don't you remember when Clara Barnard went to visit in New York, three years ago, how much attention she received? And you know Clara *is* Bangor, to the soles of her shoes. Ask William Platt – so long as he isn't a native – if he doesn't consider Clara Barnard refined.

Apropos, as they say here, of refinement, there is another American in the house – a gentleman from Boston – who is just crowded with it. His name is Mr Louis Leverett (such a beautiful name, I think), and he is about thirty years old. He is rather small, and he looks pretty sick; he suffers from some affection of the liver. But his conversation is remarkably interesting, and I delight to listen to him – he has such beautiful ideas. I feel as if it were hardly right, not being in French; but, fortunately, he uses a great many French expressions. It's in a different style from the conversation of Mr Verdier – not so complimentary, but more intellectual. He is intensely fond of pictures, and has given me a great many ideas about them which I should never have gained without him; I shouldn't have known where to look for such ideas. He thinks everything of pictures; he thinks we don't make near enough of them. They seem to make a good deal of them here; but I couldn't help telling him the other day that in Bangor I really don't think we do.

If I had any money to spend I would buy some and take them back, to hang up. Mr Leverett says it would do them good – not the pictures, but the Bangor folks. He thinks everything of the French, too, and says we don't make nearly enough of *them*. I couldn't help telling him the other day that at any rate they make enough of themselves. But it is very interesting to hear him go on about the French, and it is so much gain to me, so long as that is what I came for. I talk to him as much as I dare about Boston, but I do feel as if this were right down wrong – a stolen pleasure.

I can get all the Boston culture I want when I go back, if I carry out my plan, my happy vision, of going there to reside. I ought to direct all my efforts to European culture now, and keep

Boston to finish off. But it seems as if I couldn't help taking a peep now and then, in advance – with a Bostonian. I don't know when I may meet one again; but if there are many others like Mr Leverett there, I shall be certain not to want when I carry out my dream. He is just as full of culture as he can live. But it seems strange how many different sorts there are.

There are two of the English who I suppose are very culti-vated too; but it doesn't seem as if I could enter into theirs so easily, though I try all I can. I do love their way of speaking, and sometimes I feel almost as if it would be right to give up trying to learn French, and just try to learn to speak our own tongue as these English speak it. It isn't the things they say so much, though these are often rather curious, but it is in the way they pronounce, and the sweetness of their voice. It seems as if they must *try* a good deal to talk like that; but these English that are here don't seem to try at all, either to speak or do anything else. They are a young lady and her brother. I believe they belong to some noble family. I have had a good deal of intercourse with them, because I have felt more free to talk to them than to the Americans – on account of the language. It seems as if in talking with them I was almost learning a new one.

I never supposed, when I left Bangor, that I was coming to Europe to learn *English*! If I do learn it, I don't think you will understand me when I get back, and I don't think you'll like it much. I should be a good deal criticized if I spoke like that at Bangor. However, I verily believe Bangor is the most critical place on earth; I have seen nothing like it over here. Tell them all I have come to the conclusion that they are *a great deal too fastidious*. But I was speaking about this English young lady and her brother. I wish I could put them before you. She is lovely to look at; she seems so modest and retiring. In spite of this, however, she dresses in a way that attracts great attention, as I couldn't help noticing when one day I went out to walk with her. She was ever so much looked at; but she didn't seem to notice it, until at last I couldn't help calling attention to it. Mr Leverett thinks everything of it; he calls it the 'costume of the future'. I should call it rather the costume of the past – you know the English have such an attachment to the past. I said this the other day to Madame de Maisonrouge – that Miss Vane dressed in the costume of the past. *De l'an passé, vous voulez dire?* said Madame, with her little French laugh (you can get William Platt to translate this, he used to tell me he knew so much French).

You know I told you, in writing some time ago, that I had tried to get some insight into the position of woman in England, and, being here with Miss Vane, it has seemed to me to be a good opportunity to get a little more. I have asked her a great deal about it; but she doesn't seem able to give me much information. The first time I asked her she told me the position of a lady depended upon the rank of her father, her eldest brother, her husband, etc. She told me her own position was very good, because her father was some relation – I forget what – to a lord. She thinks everything of this; and that proves to me that the position of woman in her country cannot be satisfactory;

because, if it were, it wouldn't depend upon that of your relations, even your nearest. I don't know much about lords, and it does try my patience (though she is just as sweet as she can live) to hear her talk as if it were a matter of course that I should.

I feel as if it were right to ask her as often as I can if she doesn't consider everyone equal; but she always says she doesn't, and she confesses that she doesn't think she is equal to 'Lady Something-or-other', who is the wife of that relation of her father. I try and persuade her all I can that she is; but it seems as if she didn't want to be persuaded; and when I ask her if Lady So-and-so is of the same opinion (that Miss Vane isn't her equal), she looks so soft and pretty with her eyes, and says, 'Of course she is!' When I tell her that this is right down bad for Lady So-and-so, it seems as if she wouldn't believe me, and the only answer she will make is that Lady So-and-so is 'extremely nice'. I don't believe she is nice at all; if she were nice, she wouldn't have such ideas as that. I tell Miss Vane that at Bangor we think such ideas vulgar; but then she looks as though she had never heard of Bangor. I often want to shake her, though she *is* so sweet. If she isn't angry with the people who make her feel that way, I am angry for her. I am angry with her brother, too, for she is evidently very much afraid of him, and this gives me some further insight into the subject. She thinks everything of her brother, and thinks it natural that she should be afraid of him, not only physically (for this *is* natural as he is enormously tall and strong, and has very big fists), but morally and intellectually. She seems unable, however, to take in any argument, and she makes me realize what I have often heard – that if you are timid nothing will reason you out of it.

Mr Vane, also (the brother), seems to have the same prejudices, and when I tell him, as I often think it right to do, that his sister is not his subordinate, even if she does think so, but his equal, and, perhaps in some respects his superior, and that if my brother, in Bangor, were to treat me as he treats this poor young girl, who has not spirit enough to see the question in its true light, there would be an indignation-meeting of the citizens, to protest against such an outrage to the sanctity of womanhood – when I tell him all this, at breakfast or dinner, he bursts out laughing so loud that all the plates clatter on the table.

But at such a time as this there is always one person who seems interested in what I say – a German gentleman, a professor, who sits next to me at dinner, and whom I must tell you more about another time. He is very learned, and has a great desire for information; he appreciates a great many of my remarks, and, after dinner, in the salon, he often comes to me to ask me questions about them. I have to think a little, sometimes, to know what I did say, or what I do think. He takes you right up where you left off, and he is almost as fond of discussing things as William Platt is. He is splendidly educated, in the German style, and he told me the other day that he was an 'intellectual broom'. Well, if he is, he sweeps clean; I told him that. After he has been talking to me I feel as if I hadn't got a speck of dust left in my mind anywhere. It's a most delightful feeling. He says he's an observer; and I am sure there is plenty over here to observe. But I have told you enough for today. I don't know how much longer I shall stay here; I am getting on so fast that it sometimes seems as if I shouldn't need all the time I have laid out. I suppose your cold weather has promptly begun, as usual; it sometimes makes me envy you. The fall weather here is very dull and damp, and I feel very much as if I should like to be braced up.

VI

From Miss Evelyn Vane, *in Paris,*
to the Lady Augusta Fleming, *at Brighton*

Paris, September 30th

Dear Lady Augusta

I am afraid I shall not be able to come to you on January 7th, as you kindly proposed at Homburg. I am so very, very sorry; it is a great disappointment to me. But I have just heard that it has been settled that mamma and the children are coming abroad for a part of the winter, and mamma wishes me to go with them to Hyères, where Georgina has been ordered for her lungs. She has not been at all well these three months, and now that the damp weather has begun she is very poorly indeed; so that last week papa decided to have a consultation, and he and mamma went with her up to town and saw some three or four doctors.

They all of them ordered the south of France, but they didn't agree about the place; so that mamma herself decided for Hyères, because it is the most economical. I believe it is very dull, but I hope it will do Georgina good. I am afraid, however, that nothing will do her good until she consents to take more care of herself; I am afraid she is very wild and wilful, and mamma tells me that all this month it has taken papa's positive orders to make her stop in-doors. She is very cross (mamma writes me) about coming abroad, and doesn't seem at all to mind the expense that papa has been put to — talks very ill-naturedly about losing the hunting, etc. She expected to begin to hunt in December, and wants to know whether anybody keeps hounds at Hyères. Fancy a girl wanting to follow the hounds when her lungs are so bad! But I daresay that when she gets there she will be glad enough to keep quiet, as they say that the heat is intense. It may cure Georgina, but I am sure it will make the rest of us very ill.

Mamma, however, is only going to bring Mary and Gus and Fred and Adelaide abroad with her; the others will remain at Kingscote until February (about the 3rd), when they will go to Eastbourne for a month with Miss Turnover, the new govern-ess, who has turned out such a very nice person. She is going to take Miss Travers, who has been with us so long, but who is only qualified for the younger children, to Hyères, and I believe some of the Kingscote servants. She has perfect confidence in Miss T.; it is only a pity she has such an odd name. Mamma thought of asking her if she would mind taking another when she came; but papa thought she might object. Lady Battledown makes all her governesses take the same name; she gives £5 more a year for the purpose. I forget what it is she calls them; I think it's Johnson (which to me always suggests a lady's maid). Governesses shouldn't have too pretty a name; they shouldn't have a nicer name than the family.

I suppose you heard from the Desmonds that I did not go back to England with them. When it began to be talked about that Georgina should be taken abroad, mamma wrote to me that I had better stop in Paris for a month with Harold, so that she could pick me up on their way to Hyères. It saves the expense of my journey to Kingscote and back, and gives me the opportunity to 'finish' a little, in French.

You know Harold came here six weeks ago, to get up his French for those dreadful examinations that he has to pass so soon. He came to live with some French people that take in young men (and others) for this purpose; it's a kind of coaching place, only kept by women. Mamma had heard it was very nice; so she wrote to me that I was to come and stop here with Harold. The Desmonds brought me and made the arrangement, or the bargain, or whatever you call it. Poor Harold was naturally not at all pleased; but he has been very kind, and has treated me like an angel. He is getting on beautifully with his French; for though I don't think the place is so good as papa supposed, yet Harold is so immensely clever that he can scarcely help learning. I am afraid I learn much less, but, fortunately, I have not to pass an examination — except if mamma takes it into her head to examine me. But she will have so much to think of with Georgina that I hope this won't occur to her. If it does, I shall be, as Harold says, in a dreadful funk.

This is not such a nice place for a girl as for a young man, and the Desmonds thought it *exceedingly odd* that mamma should wish me to come here. As Mrs Desmond said, it is because she is so very unconventional. But you know Paris is so very amusing, and if only Harold remains good-natured about it, I shall be content to wait for the caravan (that's what he calls mamma and the children). The person who keeps the establishment, or whatever they call it, is rather odd, and *exceedingly foreign*; but she is wonderfully civil, and is perpetually sending to my door to see if I want anything. The servants are not at all like English servants, and come bursting in, the footman (they have only one) and the maids alike, at all sorts of hours, in the *most sudden way*. Then when one rings, it is half an hour before they come. All this is very uncomfortable, and I daresay it will be worse at Hyères. There, however, fortunately, we shall have our own people.

There are some very odd Americans here, who keep throwing Harold into fits of laughter. One is a dreadful little man who is always sitting over the fire, and talking about the colour of the sky. I don't believe he ever saw the sky except through the window-pane. The other day he took hold of my frock (that green one you thought so nice at Homburg) and told me that it reminded him of the texture of the Devonshire turf. And then he talked for half an hour about the Devonshire turf, which I thought such a very extraordinary subject. Harold says he is mad. It is very strange to be living in this way, with people one doesn't know. I mean that one doesn't know as one knows them in England.

The other Americans (beside the madman) are two girls, about my own age, one of whom is rather nice. She has a mother; but the mother is always sitting in her bedroom, which seems so very odd. I should like mamma to ask them to Kingscote, but I am afraid mamma wouldn't like the mother, who is rather vulgar. The other girl is rather vulgar too, and is travelling about quite alone. I think she is a kind of schoolmistress; but the other girl (I mean the nicer one, with the mother) tells me she is more respectable than she seems. She has, however, the most extraordinary opinions – wishes to do away with the aristocracy, thinks it wrong that Arthur should have Kingscote when papa dies, etc. I don't see what it signifies to her that poor Arthur should come into the property, which will be so delightful – except for papa dying. But Harold says she is mad. He chaffs her tremendously about her radicalism, and he is so immensely clever that she can't answer him, though she is rather clever, too.

There is also a Frenchman, a nephew, or cousin, or something, of the person of the house, who is extremely nasty; and a German professor, or doctor, who eats with his knife and is a great bore. I am so very sorry about giving up my visit. I am afraid you will never ask me again.

VII

From Léon Verdier, *in Paris, to* Prosper Gobain, *at Lille*

September 28th

My dear Prosper

It is a long time since I have given you of my news, and I don't
know what puts it into my head tonight to recall myself to your
affectionate memory. I suppose it is that when we are happy the
mind reverts instinctively to those with whom formerly we
shared our exaltations and depressions, and *je t'en ai trop dit,
dans le bon temps, mon gros Prosper*, and you always listened to
me too imperturbably, with your pipe in your mouth, your
waistcoat unbuttoned, for me not to feel that I can count upon
your sympathy today. *Nous en sommes nous flanquées, des confi-
dences* — in those happy days when my first thought in seeing an
adventure *poindre à l'horizon* was of the pleasure I should have in
relating it to the great Prosper. As I tell thee, I am happy; decidedly, I am happy, and from this affirmation I fancy you can
construct the rest. Shall I help thee a little? Take three adorable
girls . . . three, my good Prosper — the mystic number — neither
more nor less. Take them and place thy insatiable little Léon in
the midst of them! Is the situation sufficiently indicated, and do
you apprehend the motives of my felicity?

You expected, perhaps, I was going to tell you that I had
made my fortune, or that the Uncle Blondeau had at last

decided to return into the breast of nature, after having consti-
tuted me his universal legatee. But I needn't remind you that
women are always for something in the happiness of him who
writes to thee – for something in his happiness, and for a good
deal more in his misery. But don't let me talk of misery now;
time enough when it comes; *ces demoiselles* have gone to join
the serried ranks of their amiable predecessors. Excuse me – I
comprehend your impatience. I will tell you of whom *ces
demoiselles* consist.

You have heard me speak of my *cousine* de Maisonrouge, that
grande belle femme, who, after having married, *en secondes noces*
– there had been, to tell the truth, some irregularity about her
first union – a venerable relic of the old *noblesse* of Poitou, was
left, by the death of her husband, complicated by the indulgence
of expensive tastes on an income of 17,000 francs, on the pavement of Paris, with two little demons of daughters to bring up in
the path of virtue. She managed to bring them up; my little
cousins are rigidly virtuous. If you ask me how she managed it,
I can't tell you; it's no business of mine, and, *a fortiori*, none of
yours. She is now fifty years old (she confesses to thirty-seven),
and her daughters, whom she has never been able to marry, are
respectively twenty-seven and twenty-three (they confess to
twenty and to seventeen). Three years ago she had the thrice-
blessed idea of opening a sort of *pension* for the entertainment
and instruction of the blundering barbarians who come to Paris
in the hope of picking up a few stray particles of the language of
Voltaire – or of Zola. The idea *lui a porté bonheur*; the shop does

a very good business. Until within a few months ago it was carried on by my cousins alone; but lately the need of a few extensions and embellishments has caused itself to be felt. My cousin has undertaken them, regardless of expense; she has asked me to come and stay with her – board and lodging gratis – and keep an eye on the grammatical eccentricities of her *pensionnaires*. I am the extension, my good Prosper; I am the embellishment! I live for nothing, and I straighten up the accent of the prettiest English lips. The English lips are not all pretty, Heaven knows, but enough of them are so to make it a gaining bargain for me.

Just now, as I told you, I am in daily conversation with three separate pairs. The owner of one of them has private lessons; she pays extra. My cousin doesn't give me a sou of the money; but I make bold, nevertheless, to say that my trouble is remunerated. But I am well, very well, with the proprietors of the two other pairs. One of them is a little Anglaise, of about twenty – a little *figure de keepsake*; the most adorable miss that you ever, or at least that I ever, beheld. She is decorated all over with beads and bracelets and embroidered dandelions; but her principal decoration consists of the softest little grey eyes in the world, which rest upon you with a profundity of confidence – a confidence that I really feel some compunction in betraying. She has a tint as white as this sheet of paper, except just in the middle of each cheek, where it passes into the purest and most transparent, most liquid, carmine. Occasionally this rosy fluid overflows into the rest of her face – by which I mean that she blushes — as softly as the mark of your breath on the window-pane.

Like every Anglaise, she is rather pinched and prim in public; but it is very easy to see that when no one is looking *elle ne demande qu'à se laisser aller!* Whenever she wants it I am always there, and I have given her to understand that she can count upon me. I have every reason to believe that she appreciates the assurance, though I am bound in honesty to confess that with her the situation is a little less advanced than with the others. *Que voulez-vous?* The English are heavy, and the Anglaises move slowly, that's all. The movement, however, is perceptible, and once this fact is established I can let the pottage simmer. I can give her time to arrive, for I am over-well occupied with her *concurrentes. Celles-ci* don't keep me waiting, *par exemple!*

These young ladies are Americans, and you know that it is the national character to move fast. 'All right — go ahead!' (I am learning a great deal of English, or, rather, a great deal of American.) They go ahead at a rate that sometimes makes it difficult for me to keep up. One of them is prettier than the other; but this latter (the one that takes the private lessons) is really *une fille prodigieuse. Ah, par exemple, elle brûle ses vaisseux celle-la!* She threw herself into my arms the very first day, and I almost owed her a grudge for having deprived me of that pleasure of gradation, of carrying the defences, one by one, which is almost as great as that of entering the place.

Would you believe that at the end of exactly twelve minutes she gave me a rendezvous? It is true it was in the Galerie

d'Apollon, at the Louvre; but that was respectable for a beginning, and since then we have had them by the dozen; I have
ceased to keep the account. *Non, c'est une fille qui me dépasse.*

The little one (she has a mother somewhere, out of sight,
shut up in a closet or a trunk) is a good deal prettier, and,
perhaps, on that account *elle y met plus de façons.* She doesn't
knock about Paris with me by the hour; she contents herself
with long interviews in the *petit salon*, with the curtains half
drawn, beginning at about three o'clock, when everyone is *à la
promenade.* She is admirable, this little one; a little too thin, the
bones rather accentuated, but the detail, on the whole, most
satisfactory. And you can say anything to her. She takes the
trouble to appear not to understand, but her conduct, half an
hour afterwards, reassures you completely – oh, completely!

However, it is the tall one, the one of the private lessons, that
is the most remarkable. These private lessons, my good Prosper,
are the most brilliant invention of the age, and a real stroke of
genius on the part of Miss Miranda! They also take place in the
petit salon, but with the doors tightly closed, and with explicit
directions to everyone in the house that we are not to be
disturbed. And we are not, my good Prosper; we are not! Not a
sound, not a shadow, interrupts our felicity. My *cousine* is really
admirable; the shop deserves to succeed. Miss Miranda is tall
and rather flat; she is too pale; she hasn't the adorable *rougeurs*
of the little Anglaise. But she has bright, keen, inquisitive eyes,
superb teeth, a nose modelled by a sculptor, and a way of holding up her head and looking everyone in the face, which is the

most finished piece of impertinence I ever beheld. She is making the *tour du monde*, entirely alone, without even a soubrette to carry the ensign, for the purpose of seeing for herself *à quoi s'en tenir sur les hommes et les choses* – on *les hommes* particularly. *Dis donc*, Prosper, it must be a *drôle de pays* over there, where young persons animated by this ardent curiosity are manufactured! If we should turn the tables, some day, thou and I, and go over and see it for ourselves. It is as well that we should go and find them *chez elles*, as that they should come out here after us. *Dis donc, mon gros Prosper* . . .

VIII

From Dr Rudolf Staub, *in Paris, to*
Dr Julius Hirsch, *at Göttingen*

My dear Brother in Science

I resume my hasty notes, of which I sent you the first instalment some weeks ago. I mentioned then that I intended to leave my hotel, not finding it sufficiently local and national. It was kept by a Pomeranian, and the waiters, without exception, were from the Fatherland. I fancied myself at Berlin, Unter den Linden, and I reflected that, having taken the serious step of visiting the headquarters of the Gallic genius, I should try and project myself, as much as possible, into the circumstances which are in part the consequence and in part the cause of its irrepressible activity. It seemed to me that there could be no well-grounded knowledge without this preliminary operation of placing myself in relations, as slightly as possible modified by elements proceeding from a different combination of causes, with the spontaneous home-life of the country.

I accordingly engaged a room in the house of a lady of pure French extraction and education, who supplements the shortcomings of an income insufficient to the ever-growing demands of the Parisian system of sense-gratification, by providing food and lodging for a limited number of distinguished strangers. I should have preferred to have my room alone in the house, and to take my meals in a brewery, of very good appearance, which I speedily discovered in the same street; but this arrangement, though very lucidly proposed by myself, was not acceptable to the mistress of the establishment (a woman with a mathematical head), and I have consoled myself for the extra expense by fixing my thoughts upon the opportunity that conformity to the customs of the house gives me of studying the table-manners of my companions, and of observing the French nature at a peculiarly physiological moment, the moment when the satisfaction of the *taste*, which is the governing quality in its composition, produces a kind of exhalation, an intellectual transpiration, which, though light and perhaps invisible to a superficial spectator, is nevertheless appreciable by a properly adjusted instrument.

I have adjusted my instrument very satisfactorily (I mean the one I carry in my good, square German head), and I am not afraid of losing a single drop of this valuable fluid, as it condenses itself upon the plate of my observation. A prepared surface is what I need, and I have prepared my surface.

Unfortunately here, also, I find the individual native in the minority. There are only four French persons in the house – the individuals concerned in its management, three of whom are women, and one a man. This preponderance of the feminine element is, however, in itself characteristic, as I need not remind you what an abnormally developed part this sex has played in French history. The remaining figure is apparently that of a man, but I hesitate to classify him so superficially. He appears to me less human than simian, and whenever I hear him talk I seem to myself to have paused in the street to listen to the shrill clatter of a hand-organ, to which the gambols of a hairy *homunculus* form an accompaniment.

I mentioned to you before that my expectation of rough usage, in consequence of my German nationality, had proved completely unfounded. No one seems to know or to care what my nationality is, and I am treated, on the contrary, with the civility which is the portion of every traveller who pays the bill without scanning the items too narrowly. This, I confess, has been something of a surprise to me, and I have not yet made up my mind as to the fundamental cause of the anomaly. My determination to take up my abode in a French interior was largely dictated by the supposition that I should be substantially disagreeable to its inmates. I wished to observe the different forms taken by the irritation that I should naturally produce; for it is under the influence of irritation that the French character most completely expresses itself. My presence, however, does not appear to operate as a stimulus, and in this respect I am materially disappointed. They treat me as they treat everyone else; whereas, in order to be treated differently, I was resigned in advance to be treated worse. I have not, as I say, fully explained to myself this logical contradiction; but this is the explanation to which I tend. The French are so exclusively occupied with the idea of themselves, that in spite of the very definite image the German personality presented to them by the war of 1870, they have at present no distinct apprehension of its existence. They are not very sure that there are any Germans; they have already forgotten the convincing proofs of the fact that were presented to them nine years ago. A German was something disagreeable, which they determined to keep out of their conception of things. I therefore think that we are wrong to govern ourselves upon the hypothesis of the *revanche*; the French nature is too shallow for that large and powerful plant to bloom in it.

The English-speaking specimens, too, I have not been willing to neglect the opportunity to examine; and among these I have paid special attention to the American varieties, of which I find here several singular examples. The two most remarkable are a young man who presents all the characteristics of a period of national decadence; reminding me strongly of some diminutive Hellenized Roman of the third century. He is an illustration of the period of culture in which the faculty of appreciation has obtained such a preponderance over that of production that the latter sinks into a kind of rank sterility, and the mental condition becomes analogous to that of a malarious bog. I learn from him that there is an immense number of Americans exactly resembling him, and that the city of Boston, indeed, is almost exclusively composed of them. (He communicated this fact very proudly, as if it were greatly to the credit of his native country; little perceiving the truly sinister impression it made upon me.)

What strikes one in it is that it is a phenomenon to the best of my knowledge – and you know what my knowledge is – unprecedented and unique in the history of mankind; the arrival of a nation at an ultimate stage of evolution without having passed through the mediate one; the passage of the fruit, in other words, from crudity to rottenness, without the interposition of a period of useful (and ornamental) ripeness. With the Americans, indeed, the crudity and the rottenness are identical and simultaneous; it is impossible to say, as in the conversation of this deplorable young man, which is one and which is the other; they are inextricably mingled. I prefer the talk of the French *homunculus*; it is at least more amusing.

It is interesting in this manner to perceive, so largely developed, the germs of extinction in the so-called powerful Anglo-Saxon family. I find them in almost as recognizable a form in a young woman from the State of Maine, in the province of New England, with whom I have had a good deal of conversation. She differs somewhat from the young man I just mentioned, in that the faculty of production, of action, is, in her, less inanimate; she has more of the freshness and vigour that we suppose to belong to a young civilization. But unfortunately she produces nothing but evil, and her tastes and habits are similarly those of a Roman lady of the lower Empire. She makes no secret of them, and has, in fact, elaborated a complete system of licentious behaviour. As the opportunities she finds in her own country do not satisfy her, she has come to Europe 'to try', as she says, 'for herself'. It is the doctrine of universal experience professed with a cynicism that is really most extraordinary, and which, presenting itself in a young woman of considerable education, appears to me to be the judgement of a society.

Another observation which pushes me to the same induction – that of the premature vitiation of the American population – is the attitude of the Americans whom I have before me with regard to each other. There is another young lady here, who is less abnormally developed than the one I have just described, but who yet bears the stamp of this peculiar combination of incompleteness and effeteness. These three persons look with the greatest mistrust and aversion upon each other; and each has repeatedly taken me apart and assured me, secretly, that he or she only is the real, the genuine, the typical American. A type that has lost itself before it has been fixed – what can you look for from this?

Add to this that there are two young Englanders in the house, who hate all the Americans in a lump, making between them none of the distinctions and favourable comparisons which they insist upon, and you will, I think, hold me warranted in believing that, between precipitate decay and internecine enmities, the

English-speaking family is destined to consume itself, and that with its decline the prospect of general pervasiveness, to which I alluded above, will brighten for the deep-lunged children of the Fatherland!

IX

Miranda Hope *to her* Mother

October 22nd

Dear Mother

I am off in a day or two to visit some new country; I haven't yet decided which. I have satisfied myself with regard to France, and obtained a good knowledge of the language. I have enjoyed my visit to Madame de Maisonrouge deeply, and feel as if I were leaving a circle of real friends. Everything has gone on beautifully up to the end, and everyone has been as kind and attentive as if I were their own sister, especially Mr Verdier, the French gentleman, from whom I have gained more than I ever expected (in six weeks), and with whom I have promised to *correspond*. So you can imagine me dashing off the most correct French letters; and, if you don't believe it, I will keep the rough draft to show you when I go back.

The German gentleman is also more interesting, the more you know him; it seems sometimes as if I could fairly drink in his ideas. I have found out why the young lady from New York doesn't like me! It is because I said one day at dinner that I *admired* to go to the Louvre. Well, when I first came, it seemed as if I *did* admire everything!

Tell William Platt his letter has come. I knew he would have to write, and I was bound I would make him! I haven't decided what country I will visit yet; it seems as if there were so many to choose from. But I shall take care to pick out a good one, and to meet plenty of fresh experiences.

Dearest mother, my money holds out, and it is most interesting!

A Note on the Texts

The texts of the tales in this selection are taken from their original magazine publications (or in the case of 'The Romance of Certain Old Clothes' its publication in James's 1885 collection *Stories Revived*), and not from the amended versions James prepared for the New York edition of his works:

'A Tragedy of Error', *Continental Monthly* (February 1864); 'A Landscape-Painter', *Atlantic Monthly* (February 1866); 'A Day of Days', *Galaxy* (June 1866); 'My Friend Bingham', *Atlantic Monthly* (March 1867); 'The Story of a Masterpiece', *Galaxy* (January–February 1868); 'De Grey: A Romance', *Atlantic Monthly* (1868); 'The Romance of Certain Old Clothes', *Stories Revived* (1885); 'A Light Man', *Galaxy* (July, 1869); 'The Madonna of the Future', *Atlantic Monthly* (March 1873); 'The Last of the Valerii', *Atlantic Monthly* (January 1874); 'Madame de Mauves', *Galaxy* (February–March 1874); 'The Ghostly Rental', *Scribner's Monthly* (September 1876); 'The Pension Beaurepas', *Atlantic Monthly* (April 1879); 'A Bundle of Letters', *Parisian* (December 1879).